LAUNCH CODE

Michael Ridpath spent eight
years working for a bank in the
City before giving up his job
to write full-time. He lives in
London. Visit his website at
www.michaelridpath.com.

Also by Michael Ridpath

The Magnus Iceland Mysteries

Where the Shadows Lie
66° North
Meltwater
Sea of Stone
The Wanderer

Other novels

Amnesia
Traitor's Gate
Shadows of War
Free To Trade
Trading Reality
The Marketmaker
Final Venture
The Predator
Fatal Error
On The Edge
See No Evil

MICHAEL RIDPATH
LAUNCH CODE

CORVUS

Published in trade paperback in Great Britain in 2019 by Corvus,
an imprint of Atlantic Books Ltd.

10 9 8 7 6 5 4 3 2 1

A CIP catalogue record for this book is available
from the British Library.

Trade paperback ISBN: 978 1 78649 699 7
E-book ISBN: 978 1 78649 700 0

Printed in Great Britain by Bell and Bain Ltd, Glasgow

Corvus
An imprint of Atlantic Books Ltd
Ormond House
26–27 Boswell Street
London
WC1N 3JZ

www.corvus-books.co.uk

for Betsy and Jim

'Never, perhaps, in the post-war decades was the situation in the world as explosive and hence more difficult and unfavourable as in the first half of the 1980s.'

Mikhail Gorbachev, leader of the Soviet Union, 1986

'We may have been at the brink of nuclear war and not even known it.'

Robert Gates, Deputy Director of CIA
and later Secretary of Defense

PROLOGUE

November 1983, Norwegian Sea

The end of the world looks like this.

Man creates the means to obliterate the planet: sixteen Poseidon missiles, each with their own ten independent warheads, enough to provoke a massive retaliation from the country at which they are fired. Machines transmit the order. Humans obey.

The doctrine of Mutually Assured Destruction, the doctrine which preserves peace in a nuclear world, demands that humans will obey, and that the enemy knows that they will obey.

Humans like Lieutenant William M. Guth (USN), assistant weapons officer on the USS *Alexander Hamilton*, loitering one hundred and twenty miles north-east of the Faroe Islands, deep in the cold embrace of the Norwegian Sea.

The *Hamilton* was Bill Guth's first nuclear submarine. In the two years since he had joined the crew at the end of 1981, the Cold War had been steadily warming up. The rhetoric from the American president Reagan and the Soviet leader Andropov had become more heated, the Americans and the Russians were deploying intermediate-range nuclear missiles in Europe and in September a Korean airliner had been shot down having strayed into Soviet airspace over Eastern Siberia.

Yet Bill had become more confident in his own abilities and in the abilities of the crew members around him. They were never idle as they puttered along at three knots a few hundred feet beneath

1

the surface. Ever more inventive training exercises simulated all manner of disasters from fires on board, to leaks, to shutting down the submarine's nuclear reactor, to evading torpedo attacks.

And yes, to launching the *Alexander Hamilton*'s nuclear weapons.

As assistant weapons officer, Bill had an important role in the complicated launch sequence, along with the twenty or so 'missile techs' who worked alongside him, and his immediate boss, the weapons officer.

He was making his way up the ladder to the upper level of the missile compartment when the announcement echoed through the submarine.

'Alert One, Alert One!'

He scrambled to the top of the ladder, grabbed the bar over the hatch into the operations compartment and swung his six-foot frame feet first through the hole. He hurried the short distance to op-conn, the tiny room between the radio shack and the control room, where the printout of an Emergency Action Message waited for him. A few seconds later he was joined by his friend and fellow lieutenant, Lars da Silva.

Lars seemed tense, but calm. Beside them, the radio chief extracted code manuals from his safe and dropped them on the tiny desk with a thud.

'Let's do this,' said Lars.

Bill didn't feel calm; Bill felt scared.

This was their fifth patrol together. During that time Bill and Lars had decoded dozens of EAMs, real and simulated, many garbled in ingenious ways. Over the last two days a sequence of four EAMs had been received, each more concerning than the one preceding it. The most recent, received at 0512 that morning, had raised the level of readiness for nuclear war to DEFCON 2, which was only one step from launching missiles.

The whole crew had been waiting for the next message. Dreading it. And here it was.

Bill pushed the fear to one side and started decoding the string of four-letter groups.

This message wasn't garbled. This message was very clear.

Lars glanced up at Bill. 'Holy shit.'

Bill closed his eyes and nodded.

Bill had no time to think about the decoded message in his hand. He had trained for this. He knew what to do.

Followed by Lars, Bill carried the EAM through to the control room. The blood was thudding in his ears, and he was holding the scrap of paper so tightly it was shaking slightly, but he was careful to freeze the muscles in his face.

Maybe he looked as calm as the rest of the crew. Maybe they were as scared as he was.

He handed the message to the captain, who was waiting for him, a briefcase of top-secret launch manuals at his feet.

'Captain,' Bill began, uttering words he had used in training many times before. His voice sounded flat and surprisingly calm, at least to his own ears. 'We have received a properly formatted message from the National Command Authority for strategic missile launch.'

'I concur,' said Lars next to him.

Commander Driscoll was a short man with wavy iron-grey hair and round glasses. He exuded quiet authority. His voice, tinged with a slight Texan twang, was always measured and calm. He commanded with his eyes. They were blue, and by turns could be reassuring, inspiring, angry or urgent. Now they were alert, expectant, ready for the message that he knew was coming.

He reached out for it, reading it with the tall figure of Lieutenant Commander Robinson, the boat's executive officer, at his shoulder.

EMERGENCY ACTION MESSAGE
....

FROM: NATIONAL MILITARY COMMAND CENTER

TO: USS ALEXANDER HAMILTON (SSBN-617)

SUBJECT: NUCLEAR MISSILE LAUNCH -
   SINGLE INTEGRATED OPERATIONAL PLAN
   (SIOP) EXECUTION

REMARKS:
1. SET DEFCON ONE
2. RETARGET AND STRIKE
3. IMMEDIATE LAUNCH THREE (3) POSEIDON
    MISSILE SORTIES
4. TARGET PACKAGE SLBM 36155/4
5. AUTHENTICATION: ECHO TANGO TANGO
    ROMEO ZULU ALPHA HOTEL

'I concur,' said the XO.

'Captain, request permission to authenticate,' Bill asked.

'Permission granted.'

Each stage of the process, from the initial receipt of the EAM to the eventual launch, was carefully scripted with procedures that were spelled out in checklists and orange folders marked 'Top Secret', procedures that had been refined over the years to ensure that there were always at least two officers involved at each stage or, in the case of the launch order itself, four.

The crew knew each stage intimately, but part of the procedure was that the checklists had to be followed to the letter. Nothing could be assumed. Nothing could be skipped.

The next stage of the process required an authentication code on the message to be compared to a code printed on a card locked deep inside two safes on the submarine. This was to ensure that the message had really come from National Military Command Center, and not some maniac with a desire to start a nuclear war.

The safes were back in op-conn. Lars opened the outer safe, and Bill opened the inner one. He pulled out the small package, ripped off the silver wrapping, and took the card back to the captain. Bill read out the authentication code on the card to Lars.

It matched the code on the EAM.

'The message is authentic, sir,' Bill said.

'I concur,' said Lars.

The XO glanced at the card and the message. 'I concur.'

The captain reached for the 1-MC shipwide microphone. 'Man Battle Stations Missile for Strategic Launch. Set Condition 1 SQ. Spin up missiles one, two and nine. The release of nuclear weapons has been authorized. This is not a drill. This is the captain speaking.'

Although he had heard the words many times before in training – with the exception of 'this is not a drill' – they came as a shock to Bill. Once again he could feel fear gnawing at the edges of his consciousness, once again he banished it.

Focus. Concentrate. Do your job.

Just like everyone else.

The captain handed the mic to Robinson who repeated the message word for word. The crew would only follow launch orders if they had been given by both the captain and the XO, his second-in-command.

Immediately a loud *bong, bong, bong* reverberated through the boat. The general alarm. The submarine became alive with quiet, controlled movement, as more sailors squeezed into the already crowded control room.

This was the nerve centre of the boat. The captain stood on a raised metal platform beside the ship's two periscopes, the 'conn'. In front of him stood the diving officer overseeing a large ballast control panel and two young sailors gripping control columns with which they adjusted the submarine's attitude and direction. To the left and right of the room were panels of lamps, switches, buttons and monitors, and a small navigation plotting station with stools and a chart stand. The overhead was a mess of pipes, tubes, wires, microphones and intercom handsets. To the men quietly busying themselves, each wire, each lamp, each switch was familiar, as was its role in the smooth operation of the submarine. Everyone was wearing blue 'poopy-suit' coveralls: khaki belts for officers and chiefs, blue for sailors.

'Can you believe this, Bill?' Lars muttered quietly.

'No.' Part of him couldn't believe it, couldn't believe what the order meant. But what *did* it mean?

'Did you catch that target package?' Lars whispered. 'That was East Berlin. Moscow, Leningrad and East Berlin. That doesn't make any sense. Why East Berlin? That's gonna flatten West Berlin too.'

'Yeah, I saw that.'

'Well? Why? What's going on?'

'I don't know,' said Bill. Part of him was trying not to think about it. To follow protocols precisely. To do what he was supposed to do.

'It's the exact same target package we were given in that drill three weeks ago.'

'Yeah, I recognized it,' said Guth.

Bill and Lars were more than shipmates, they were friends. They had graduated in the same class from the Naval Academy at Annapolis, and had both joined the Blue Crew of the *Alexander Hamilton* on the same day.

They had talked about this, about the order to launch nuclear weapons, many times.

Lars stepped forward. 'Captain?' Lars was the same height as his commanding officer, but slighter. Usually the captain appeared calm and relaxed in the most stressful of situations, but now the tension showed in his clenched jaw and hunched shoulders.

His sharp eyes darted to the junior officer. 'Yes, Lieutenant da Silva?'

Lars swallowed. 'The target package makes no sense, sir. Moscow, Leningrad, East Berlin. It will destroy West Berlin. All those US troops stationed there. The civilian population.'

Bill was shocked at what Lars had said. It wasn't up to a junior officer to question launch orders. That was not part of the protocol.

The captain's eyes narrowed. Bill could feel the tension rising in the control room.

The captain paused. Paused rather than hesitated. He was taking Lars's comment seriously.

'The target package may not make sense to us, Lieutenant da Silva. But it is a properly formatted order. Our duty is to obey it, not to discuss it.'

Lars persevered. 'And it's the same target package we received three weeks ago.'

'It is,' said Driscoll.

'Isn't it possible that this could be a repeat of that exercise EAM sent in error?'

If this had been an exercise, Driscoll would have dismissed Lars from the control room with a crushing reprimand. And Bill knew that's what the rule book said he should do.

But this wasn't an exercise. Commander Driscoll was listening. And thinking. Double-checking his own assumptions.

The whole control room was listening too.

'The exercise target package may have been selected because the NMCC knew it was likely to be used. And now they want us to use it.'

'But why?' said Da Silva. 'Why East Berlin?'

'We don't know. But we're not supposed to know. XO?'

He turned to Lieutenant Commander Robinson. Unlike Bill or Lars, the XO had to agree with the launch orders, or nothing would happen.

Robinson was taller than his captain, balding, with intense dark eyes under thick eyebrows. This was his first patrol on the *Alexander Hamilton*, but already the junior officers and the crew respected him. As did Commander Driscoll.

'It is a properly formatted order, sir. And, as I explained before, in my opinion the likelihood of a Soviet first strike in the current situation is high.'

Robinson had come straight from a desk job at the Pentagon, where he had seen things that had troubled him. Things that he had passed on to the captain and the other officers in the wardroom the night before.

'Very well. I have listened to your concern, Lieutenant da Silva, but we have a valid order, which we will execute.' The captain grabbed a mic. 'Weapons, conn. Shift target package to SLBM three-six-one-five-five-slash-four. This is the captain.'

Driscoll handed the mic to Robinson. 'Shift target package to SLBM three-six-one-five-five-slash-four. This is the XO.'

'But, sir.' Lars moved closer to the captain. 'We should go to periscope depth and check the EAM. What if it is an error, sir?'

The captain's eyes focused on the junior officer, burning with authority through the lenses of his spectacles. 'Lieutenant da Silva, you know that's against all operating procedures. And for very good reason. Now get back to your post.'

There were Soviet fast-attack submarines in the Norwegian Sea, constantly on the lookout for American and British boomers. It was a fruitless task, because the only real way the Soviet submarines could find the Americans was by listening for them, and since vessels like the *Alexander Hamilton* glided slowly and silently hundreds of feet below the surface, the Russians never heard anything.

While submerged at patrol depth, the *Hamilton* could only receive radio communications, not transmit. To request confirmation of the Emergency Action Message, the *Hamilton* would have to rise to periscope depth and announce to Soviet listening stations exactly where she was. If indeed a nuclear war was breaking out, then any nearby Soviet attack submarine would swoop on the *Hamilton* and torpedo her before she had a chance to launch her birds. Which was why operating procedures forbade the course of action Lars was suggesting.

Lars stood his ground, struggling to control his agitation. 'Captain. We *must* check that message. If the message is an error and we launch those three missiles, the Soviets will retaliate and there will be a full-blown nuclear war. Our country will be obliterated. The *world* will be obliterated.'

Driscoll's response was rapid and firm. 'Lieutenant da Silva. You will not question my orders. Either you go back to your post right now, or I will have you relieved. Do I make myself clear?'

Lars blinked. 'Aye, aye, sir.' He turned away.

Bill, too, turned, to make his way down to his post in the missile control centre. The captain called after him. 'Lieutenant Guth!'

Bill stopped at the compartment exit, and Driscoll moved over to him, speaking in a low tone. 'Lieutenant Guth, unlock the small-arms locker and fetch me a sidearm. I have a feeling I may need it.'

'Aye, aye, sir.'

As assistant weapons officer, Bill was one of two men who had keys to the small-arms locker. The other was the chief of the boat, the master chief petty officer who was at that moment the diving officer, directing the submarine's manoeuvres.

Bill's brain was tumbling as he made his way aft to the locker. Lars had a point.

Should Bill have stood up for him? But then the captain had listened to Lars's point, had considered it, and made his decision. And the crew had to follow the captain's orders without question.

Even when nuclear missiles were about be launched. *Especially* when nuclear missiles were about to be launched.

Three missiles, each with ten warheads, thirty thermonuclear explosions. Millions dead in Moscow, Leningrad and Berlin.

A Russian response was inevitable. Soon thousands of warheads would be criss-crossing the globe. Minutes later, Washington would be obliterated. New York. Chicago. The small town on the banks of the Susquehanna where Bill had grown up. His house. His childhood bedroom. His mom and dad.

Donna.

The whole damned human race.

You could train for this, you could study for it, you could utter the commands and responses as many times as you liked, but nothing could prepare you for thermonuclear war.

A dark wave of dread broke over Bill, but he kept moving, doing what he had been ordered to do.

The captain had successfully established his authority. Lars had backed down. Bill wasn't sure it was a smart idea on the captain's part to arm himself. He needed to carry the ship's crew by his personality, by his authority, not by the barrel of a pistol. If the crew thought the captain believed he needed a gun to make his orders stand, wouldn't that suggest weakness rather than strength?

But the captain had given the order, and Bill would obey it.

The locker contained an arsenal of weapons: automatic rifles, shotguns and pistols, usually issued to the watch on deck to protect the ship in dock, although since the *Hamilton* spent most of its surface life tied up to a tender in the middle of a Scottish loch, they were seldom used. Very occasionally they were broken out during exercises simulating crews, or even the captain, going crazy.

Never for forcing an officer to obey an order.

Bill selected a Colt 1911 pistol and a holster and made his way back to the control room, receiving curious, anxious glances from sailors he passed. Bill proceeded at a rapid walk. He would be needed down in the missile centre where the three missiles were being 'spun up'. The fire control computer was feeding launch and targeting instructions to the missiles, a process that would take about fifteen minutes, at which point they would be ready to be fired, one by one.

He reached the control room, where he pushed past a petty officer examining a clipboard. Everyone had clipboards and checklists.

'XO, take the conn,' said the captain. 'I'm going to my stateroom to fetch my CIP key and the launch keys. The XO has the conn.'

The Captain's Indicator Panel key had to be inserted into the missile control panel in the control room to activate the weapon system. That, and the sixteen launch keys, one for each missile, were kept secured in a safe in the captain's stateroom, a safe to which only he knew the combination.

The captain stepped down from the raised platform next to the two periscopes and moved toward Bill.

He had only taken one step when a figure launched itself towards him. An arm was raised, holding something metal, and in an instant it descended towards the back of the captain's skull.

'Sir!' Bill shouted.

Driscoll ducked and twisted, and let out a cry as the wrench, for that's what it was, hit his shoulder with a crack.

Lars, legs apart to keep his balance, drew back his arm for another blow, but it was caught by a chief petty officer grabbing his wrist.

Driscoll's face was contorted with pain as he ducked and tried to get out of the way of his attacker.

'Guth!' he cried.

Bill grabbed the Colt from the holster and pointed it at Lars.

'Freeze!' he shouted. 'Put the wrench down or I'll shoot.'

Lars froze, as did the chief holding him.

'Shoot him, Bill,' Lars said, his eyes desperate, pleading. 'Shoot the captain. Now. Before he gets the keys.'

Bill knew what Lars was thinking. If Bill killed the captain, the combination to the safe in his stateroom would die with him: no one would be able to open it. And if they couldn't open the safe, they couldn't get access to the launch keys. And if they didn't have the launch keys, they couldn't launch the missiles.

'Shoot him,' Lars urged. 'You can stop a nuclear war if you shoot him. In the head.'

In the head. So he died before he could utter the combination to his safe.

Oh, Christ.

Everyone stood still. The captain was wincing in pain, grasping his shoulder, but he straightened and looked directly at Bill, his blue eyes commanding. 'Don't do it, son. Do what you have been ordered to do. You owe it to your country.'

Owe it to your country? What country? A nuclear wasteland?

Bill shifted the barrel of the pistol from Lars to the captain.

Oh, Christ.

Bill Guth made his decision.

Thursday 28 November 2019, Thanksgiving, Heathrow Airport

Toby Rosser grabbed the two large corrugated paper cups of coffee and returned to the scrum around the arrivals exit. He needed the caffeine. He was still recovering from the ridiculously early rise that morning. He and Alice had had to drive from their flat near King's Cross to Heathrow to meet an 0620 flight, and there was a two-and-a-half hour drive ahead of them, for which he had to be alert.

'Here you go.' He handed one cup to his wife. Toby knew he looked like he felt – crap – but Alice looked amazing. Even though she had gone to bed an hour after him because she had some work to finish, even though she was not working that day having taken the whole long weekend off, she looked amazing. Blonde hair cut down to her slim neck, blue sweater and jeans, both casual, both bought for a large sum the week before, cool grey eyes and the bright smile with which she bestowed her thanks. All amazing.

'Ten after seven,' said Alice. 'She should be through by now.'

'Maybe she checked a bag?'

'She's only coming for the weekend. And, believe me, Megan won't have much stuff.'

A bleary-eyed woman with a thin face, long pointed nose, curly dark hair and glasses emerged through the security doors shepherding two large roller suitcases on either side of her. Although Toby hadn't met Megan, he had seen pictures. But he wasn't sure this was her, especially given the suitcases. But then Toby noticed her chin; the Guth chin, a long, thin jaw that came to a square end with a little notch in it. All four Guth sisters sported it.

He glanced at his wife who was absorbed with her phone.

'Alice?' He nodded to the woman.

'Megan!'

The woman spotted her, the suitcases trundled up to full speed, and then the two sisters gave each other a tight hug.

'Megan, this is Toby.'

Megan looked up at Toby, blinked, and then launched herself at him. 'Hi, Toby.'

'Careful, Megan,' said Alice. 'Toby's English. You might confuse him.'

'Confused or not, I'm always happy to have American women throwing themselves at me,' said Toby. 'Especially before breakfast.'

'He's cute,' said Megan, examining Toby.

'No he's not,' said Alice. 'He looks disgusting. He hasn't even combed his hair, let alone taken a shower.' But she glanced at Toby with a suppressed smile of sisterly triumph.

Megan twitched her long nose. 'Hmm.' It was a friendly twitch.

Toby led the two women towards the car park.

'What's with the suitcases?' said Alice. 'That's a lot for one Thanksgiving weekend.'

'These are all my possessions,' said Megan. 'I'm quitting Tor Pharma and leaving Dallas.'

'And moving to Norfolk?'

'Temporarily. Suzy, my friend from college, has a place in New York, but her roommate is moving out in the new year. So I just need somewhere to stay until January.'

'Does Dad know about this?'

'No. It will be a nice surprise for him.'

'Do you have a job? In New York?'

Alice was known in her family for being pleasingly direct.

'Oh, yeah. Suzy says I can work with her.'

'That's good. What does she do?'

'She's an actor. But the job is waiting tables. The Belgian Beer Café is the name of it. Suzy told her boss I spent two years living in Brussels, so the job's mine.'

'You were twelve!'

'Hey. I speak French. And I can even do the Belgian accent if they want me to.'

'But what about that master's in mathematics? You're wasting yourself, Megan.'

'So I can count the waffles. In French. The job's mine.'

The two enormous suitcases barely fitted into the back of Toby and Alice's new Golf, but eventually they were crawling along the M25 in everyone else's rush hour.

Megan stared out of the window from the back seat. 'Guess they don't have Thanksgiving in this country, huh?'

Megan knew they didn't celebrate Thanksgiving in Britain. Alice's family had lived all over the world. Although Alice had been born in Virginia, she had attended various American schools in Surrey, Brussels, Mannheim and Saudi Arabia, from what Toby could work out, before their father had settled down in London. The three eldest sisters – Alice, Brooke and Megan – had American accents, although the youngest, Maya, sounded English: her formative years had been spent at a private girls' school near Regent's Park. Their father still lived in a flat in Kensington, but he and his wife had bought a house on the North Norfolk coast, and it was there that the Guth family celebrated en masse.

'You been to a Thanksgiving celebration before, Toby?' Megan asked.

'Yeah. Last year, with your dad in Kensington. I like it. Lots of food. Lots of wine. Family.'

'Sorry I couldn't make that,' said Megan.

'You're here now,' said Alice.

'Yeah. And sorry I didn't make your wedding either. I got this flu bug at the last minute. Who knew they got the flu in Texas? You'd think with all that sunshine . . .'

'You'd think,' said Alice, clearly unimpressed with Megan's excuse. Toby remembered her fury well. 'I'm afraid I gave your bridesmaid's dress to Oxfam.'

'That's a good cause.'

'Brooke called. She and Justin flew in from Chicago yesterday,' Alice said. 'They stayed in London last night and they're driving up to Norfolk in a rental car today. Maya's flight doesn't get in till midday, but she swears she'll still make it. So that's everyone.'

'Not quite everyone,' said Megan.

'No,' said Alice.

In the silence that followed, Toby knew they were both thinking about their mother. She would be in the minds of the sisters and their father as they sat around the dinner table.

'Did Dad bring randoms last year?' Megan asked.

'Dad brought randoms,' said Alice. Indeed he had invited a couple of American strays in London – a neighbour and some guy he had worked with twenty years before, and Alice had brought one of her own from work. That was something else Toby liked about Thanksgiving. And his father-in-law's generosity.

'Any randoms this year?'

'Just Uncle Lars,' said Alice.

'Uncle Lars! Isn't he in jail in Trinidad?'

'They must have let him out and I think it's Guadeloupe.'

'What!' said Toby.

'I've told you about him,' said Alice. 'He's a loser. But Dad likes him. They served in the Navy together.'

'Didn't Alice mention he was a drug-runner?' said Megan.

'No,' said Toby. 'Sounds like an unlikely friend for your dad.'

'Dad's loyal, you know that,' said Alice. 'And Uncle Lars was a long way down the food chain. He owned a sailboat in the Caribbean. Took tourists out on cruises. Or at least that's what he said he did. Then one day Dad gets a call and Lars says he needs a good lawyer in Guadeloupe. Dad found him one somehow. Lars said he was framed, but Dad didn't believe him. Neither did the judge.'

'I suppose that explains why you haven't seen him for a while?' said Toby.

'Not even a Christmas card.'

Megan hadn't slept on the plane, and they had no sooner hit the M25 than she was slumped on the back seat with her eyes closed. Alice pulled out her iPad to read a document. She was a lawyer at an American firm in the City and they made her work hard. Very hard.

It rained steadily on the journey, thick dark clouds pressing down, so low that they scraped the tower of Ely Cathedral, squatting on its little island in the fens.

The phone in Toby's pocket emitted a subdued double chirp. A text message.

Alice looked up. 'Shall I check it for you?'

'It'll only be Piet.'

'It might be important?'

'It won't be,' said Toby. Piet was Toby's partner at Beachwallet, a lanky Dutchman with whom Toby had worked for a couple of years at a consultancy. They had come up with the idea for Beachwallet together, in the Red Lion in Hoxton Street one evening. Piet was enthusiastic but headstrong, and sometimes just a little impatient. 'It's Thanksgiving. He can wait.'

'I wish you could tell my client that,' said Alice, nodding towards her iPad.

'It's good to get out of London.'

'It is, isn't it?' said Alice.

He took his eyes off the road ahead for an instant to see that she was giving him one of those smiles that he loved so much. Alice had a brisk professional smile, she had a friendly social smile, she had a warm smile for her friends, and then she had *that* smile. Just for him.

'Thank you for letting me into your family,' he said.

'Thank you for joining us.'

He wrenched his gaze back to the road.

They skirted King's Lynn, rotating around the sequence of giant roundabouts that protected the town, and crossed low ridges of ploughed fields and lonely farms, heading towards a wide band of blue sky nudging up against the grey blanket of cloud. They topped a hill and the North Sea stretched out in front of them, glittering in unlikely sunshine. Far out in the distance a copse of wind turbines fluttered in the strong breeze.

Toby felt his heart lift after the crowded grey streets of London and the heavy grey moisture above the fens. The sky, beyond the curtain of cloud, seemed to stretch for ever ahead, above and to either side.

They drove down to the coast road, and then along it for a few miles until they came to the village of Barnholt: a flint church with a stubby round tower, a pub, a farm shop, an ancient cross in a tiny green and a ribbon of houses running along the coast road and off a couple of lanes reaching towards the sea. Above the village, a windmill perched proudly on the low coastal ridge, its arms stretching wide in the November sun.

The house, Pear Tree Cottage, was at the end of one of the back lanes, which ran parallel to the coast road, with a view of a marsh and then a double rank of sand dunes. The building was long and low, constructed of chips of flint, its doors and windows framed in worn red brick. Originally two cottages, they had been knocked together to create a decent-sized house. Local legend had it that in the early part of the nineteenth century one of the cottages had been the operational base of a particularly successful local smuggler of Dutch gin and French brandy. A low flint wall sheltered the garden from the north wind and the pear tree, recently relieved of most of its leaves, shivered in the damp. In summer the house opened out in a riot of roses and hollyhocks. In November, it looked inwards, curled up in its flint shell, a ribbon of sweet-smelling wood smoke from its chimney promising warmth and cosiness inside.

They unfolded themselves from the car and stretched. The air cut into Toby's face, cold and bracing after the fug of the car, tinged with salt, a faint smell of marsh and the smoke from the fire inside. He opened the boot.

'Do you mind if we leave my bags in the trunk for now?' said Megan. 'Until I've had a chance to talk with Dad.'

Bill Guth met them as they approached the front door with a broad grin. He hugged his two daughters and then Toby. Although in his sixties, he was still trim, a little over six feet, with thick grey hair and kind, shrewd brown eyes.

A high-speed yelping bundle hurled itself past his legs and leaped up at Alice first, then Toby.

'Hi, Rickover!' said Alice, grabbing the fox terrier's ears. 'How are you, Ricky boy?'

Toby reached down too, and Rickover greeted him eagerly, licking his fingers. Toby and Rickover had a deal, but the dog would have to wait for a more private moment.

'Sorry you had to come up so early,' Alice's father said. 'I've gotten the turkey out of the refrigerator, Alice, but the rest is up to you.' He had a deep, pleasant voice, with a rich American accent he had preserved during his decades away.

'Did you have trouble finding one?' Alice asked.

'Some. You'd think it would be easy, this county is crawling with them, but it's the old story, they're all being grown for Christmas. I called the butcher in Burnham Market two weeks ago and he promised me one.'

'OK,' said Alice. 'I'll get to work.' Bill was actually a pretty good cook, but a major Thanksgiving dinner was beyond him, and Alice was happy to do it. 'You can help me, Dad. Do you mind if Toby takes a shower? He kinda needs one.'

Bill raised his eyebrows in mild disapproval – Toby thought more of his daughter than his son-in-law.

'Or a bath?' said Toby hopefully. Their flat in London only had a shower, and he remembered from previous visits a lovely big cast-iron bathtub in the main bathroom upstairs.

'Sure,' said Bill. 'You know the way. Have you got any more bags in the car? I can go get them.'

Alice turned to her sister and raised her eyebrows.

'Dad?' said Megan. 'I've got a little favour to ask you.'

2

The bath was great. Toby could extend his six-foot-long body, the water was hot, the taps were big and silver and powerful and it was placed right under a window with a view of the pale-blue Norfolk sky, framed by the dead leaves of a climbing rose knocking gently on the glass pane in the breeze.

He was going to enjoy the weekend.

Toby was an only child. His mother was a nurse in a GP's surgery in North London. Toby hadn't seen his own father for six years; he was a failed property developer who now lived in the Algarve with a third wife from Leicester who was only five years older than Toby himself. Toby was close to his mother, and saw her regularly, but since his grandparents had died the two of them didn't really seem like a family, more a partnership.

Whereas the Guth family was a real family. And a family that was happy to include him.

It was one of the many reasons he was glad to have married Alice.

'You took your time,' she said when Toby eventually appeared in the kitchen. Bill was sitting at the table with a mug of coffee. Megan was nowhere to be seen.

It occurred to Toby, not for the first time, that Alice was replacing her mother at the centre of the family, and that Bill was content to let her do it. 'Replacing' wasn't exactly the right word. And it certainly wasn't 'displacing'. It was more that Alice was taking on her mother's tasks, her obligations, in memory of her. Honouring her. Toby had

23

the impression that Alice and her father had developed an unspoken ritual, which Alice was happy to follow.

'How's it going?' Toby asked her, kissing the top of her head as she bent over a mixing bowl.

'Just making the stuffing. The turkey should go in in about twenty minutes.'

'I was just telling Alice,' Bill said. 'There's a guy coming to see me from Newcastle at four this afternoon. A historian. Wants to talk to me about the Navy in the 1980s.'

Toby knew that Bill had served on nuclear submarines before he and Alice's mother had married.

'Is that stuff still secret?' Toby asked.

'Most of it. I've told him there's a limit to what I can say, but he still wants to meet me. Would you like to sit in on it?'

'You should,' said Alice. She had a small smile of pleasure on her face. 'Dad can't talk about it, but the historian probably can. I think you'll find it interesting. I'd like to be there myself, but this turkey needs my attention.'

Toby felt like he was being cut into a family secret. He liked that. 'All right, thanks.'

'You can report back,' said Alice. 'Tell me all about it.'

'What about me?' said a voice at the door. It was Megan. 'Can I be there too?'

Toby felt a slight pause from both Alice and Bill. An unsaid shared pause of disapproval.

Megan stared at her father and smiled. A smile of defiance. A what-are-you-going-to-do-about-it? smile.

'Sure,' said Bill slowly. 'That would be great.'

Megan's smile gained a note of triumph and she left the kitchen.

3

The historian's name was Sam Bowen. He was small, round and soft, with short spiky black hair, intelligent eyes behind black-framed glasses, and a Brummie accent. He was about Toby's age, maybe a couple of years older.

Toby took an instant liking to him, as did Bill, although Toby could sense a wariness on the part of his father-in-law, and he wasn't exactly sure why.

Bill had made a cafetière of coffee and he, Sam, Toby and Megan all sat in the living room. It was a bright, pretty room, even in the late afternoon gloom, its yellow walls adorned with pictures of a combination of the Norfolk coast and various mismatched paintings Bill and his wife had picked up over the years. A thick oak beam bisected the ceiling, an inch above head height, pockmarked with age, probably supporting the cast-iron bath above. Two logs glowed in the fireplace. Family photos were scattered about the room: the Guth chin on display on daughters at various ages and sizes, as it was on Alice's mother, smiling benignly on them all. That's where they had got it; not a Guth chin originally after all.

Outside, the marsh brooded, settling itself for the evening.

'Well, thank you for seeing me, Lieutenant Guth—' the historian began, pulling a notebook out of the backpack he had laid beside his armchair.

'Bill. Call me Bill.' Bill's deep voice was welcoming.

'Bill.' Sam smiled. 'As I told you on the phone, I published a book last year on the Cuban missile crisis.'

'Yeah, I read a review of it,' said Bill. '*No Cigar*. Nice title.'

'Thank you. I'm following it up with a book about the near nuclear-missile launches during the Cold War. All those times when the system would have started a nuclear war if humans hadn't overridden it.'

'All those times? How many were there?' Bill asked.

'About a dozen that we know of. And there will have been many more that are still secret.'

Bill nodded.

'So that's why I want to ask you about your last patrol aboard the USS *Alexander Hamilton* in 1983.'

Toby's interest quickened. He could see where this was going.

'And that's why I can't tell you very much about it,' said Bill, apologetically. 'Operations were top secret then, and they are still top secret now. I checked yesterday after you called me.'

There was a look of mild disappointment on Sam's face, but he had clearly expected Bill's response.

'OK. I understand. Can you tell me a little about the patrol that isn't top secret?'

'That's not very much,' said Bill. 'The *Hamilton* was operating out of Holy Loch in Scotland at the time. We were flown in and out back to Groton in Connecticut when we were off-crew. I guess it was my first tour on submarines. My fifth patrol.'

'And your last?'

Bill nodded. 'Yes. My last.'

'And why was that? You were due to go out on another patrol before your tour ended.'

'I'm impressed by your research. The official reason was that I requested to leave so I could go to graduate school.'

'And the real reason?'

'As I told you, I can only discuss the official reason,' Bill replied calmly. He seemed unperturbed rather than confrontational.

'OK,' said Sam carefully. He made a note. 'Let me tell you what I think happened on board the USS *Alexander Hamilton* on 9 November 1983.'

'Go ahead.'

'You were on patrol somewhere in the North Atlantic. For the previous couple of days you had received a series of messages from the National Military Command Center in Washington raising your readiness for nuclear war to DEFCON 2. Then you received an order to launch three missiles targeted at Moscow, St Petersburg and East Berlin.'

'Leningrad,' corrected Bill.

'Are you confirming that Leningrad was one of the targets?' said Sam, a hint of excitement in his voice.

'No. I'm merely saying that St Petersburg was known as Leningrad in 1983,' said Bill with a small smile.

Sam Bowen hesitated, examining Bill closely to see what the smile meant. Was it confirmation of Sam's suggestion? Or was Bill winding the historian up? Toby wasn't sure.

'I'm sorry,' said Bill. 'I don't mean to tease you.' The smile went. It was confirmation.

There was silence as Sam processed this. Toby could sense that Megan was following this as closely as he was. He wondered how much she already knew about it, how much Alice knew. His wife's smile at Bill asking Toby to join him made sense now.

This was the family secret.

'Commander Driscoll was the commanding officer of the *Alexander Hamilton*,' Sam continued. 'He and the executive officer acknowledged the order as valid. And then a junior officer intervened.'

'Go on,' said Bill.

'The junior officer questioned the order. He pointed out that the target package didn't make sense and, furthermore, that it was identical to the package included in a drill a couple of weeks before. The drill had been designed to test the readiness of the crew to retarget unexpected coordinates.'

Sam hesitated, waiting for a response from Bill. He didn't receive one.

'There was a discussion in the control room, but the junior officer persuaded the captain and the executive officer to change their minds and not launch the missiles.'

Bill raised his eyebrows.

'That junior officer was you.'

Toby realized he had gasped. Sam glanced at him and then returned his gaze to Bill, who was motionless.

'What can I say?' said Bill. 'I've told you I can't respond.'

'All right,' said Sam. 'If I am correct, perhaps you could just scratch your right ear lobe. Off the record. I can assure you scratching can be off the record.'

Bill laughed at that, but stayed motionless.

Sam frowned. He couldn't be sure whether Bill was indicating that his version of events was incorrect, or that he just wasn't playing along. Toby felt sorry for the historian, but admired the way he kept his cool. This probably wasn't the first stone wall he had bumped into.

Sam put down his pen. 'Bill. We all know why this had to be top secret during the Cold War. It would have given the Soviets information about the US Navy's launch procedures, and it would have highlighted shortcomings in those procedures. But the Soviet Union doesn't exist anymore.'

'We still have nuclear submarines,' Bill said. 'And they still go out on strategic patrol. They could still be ordered to launch nuclear missiles.'

'Precisely,' said Sam. 'What my book will show is that there have been many times when governments' controls on the launch of nuclear missiles have failed. When the world nearly came to an end. And that we are still relying on many of those same controls. You, of all people, should be able to see how important it is to demonstrate that?'

Bill was very serious now. All trace of a smile gone.

Sam continued. 'You know that the reason the details of this patrol are still secret is to keep what really happened from the public, right, not the enemy? To stop the American people from knowing how close they or their parents came to being blown to kingdom come. It's a cover-up. They are making you cover up a mistake that was so serious in its consequences it almost finished the world.'

Sam stared at Bill intently through his glasses. 'And it wasn't your mistake. In fact, you are the one who fixed it.'

Bill winced and ran his fingers through his thick hair. 'It seems completely understandable to me that details of nuclear launch procedure are still top secret thirty-five years later,' he replied. 'You may be right that the powers-that-be want to cover up something that may or may not have happened then. But I am still bound by my obligation to respect that secrecy. Apart from anything else, the law is very clear. But it's also my duty to my country as a former naval officer. As I said, I checked yesterday, and what happened on that patrol is still Classified.'

Sam was getting close. He had a mild manner and a gentle voice, but one that suggested sincerity, and a certain power.

'Admiral Robinson?' he asked.

Bill nodded. 'The XO at the time. He stayed in the Navy and he's done very well. We've kept in touch.'

'I bet you have,' said Sam, a sharp note tingeing his words for the first time.

Bill noticed it, and Sam looked down at his notes, seeming to regret his lapse.

'Have *you* spoken with the admiral?' Bill asked.

'Yes. And a few others on the submarine. I couldn't speak to Commander Driscoll, of course.'

'No. But Lars da Silva said he had spoken with you.'

'That's right,' said Sam.

'And none of them have told you anything?'

'No one on the *Alexander Hamilton*,' said Sam. 'But you can imagine the incident made waves in the Pentagon. Top-secret waves, but waves nonetheless. I have two sources so far in Washington who were tasked with figuring out how to change things afterwards.'

'I see,' said Bill.

There was silence.

'Can I ask something?' Toby said.

Bill nodded.

'Did these "sources" tell you what the problem was?' Toby asked Sam. 'Presumably this message was indeed a false one?'

'It was,' said Sam. 'There had been a software upgrade, and the Emergency Action Messages were supposed to be operating on a ring-fenced part of the system to test it. But they were upgrading at the same time as NATO was running a command-and-control exercise to practice giving orders to launch nuclear strikes.'

'Able Archer 83,' said Bill.

'That's right,' said Sam. 'Of course those messages had to be ring-fenced from the operational system too. It was all too much for the new software, and no one noticed the glitch for forty-eight hours.'

'How could they let that happen?' said Toby.

'That is a very good question. You could almost use it as the subtitle of my book. It was a cock-up, of course. And the company involved was big and reputable. But something very similar had happened four years earlier when they were upgrading the NORAD nuclear warning system. Someone ran a training cassette on the live operational network that simulated two thousand two hundred Soviet missiles heading towards the United States. For six minutes the Pentagon thought nuclear war had started. They woke up Zbigniew Brzezinski, the National Security Adviser. Fortunately, just as Brzezinski was about to call President Carter and suggest full-scale retaliation, the Pentagon called back having checked with their radar units directly. None of them had actually picked up any incoming missiles.'

Sam looked directly at Bill. 'That was what was so scary about your incident. The *Alexander Hamilton* couldn't transmit to confirm the orders for fear of giving her position away to Soviet attack submarines. And the protocols forbade it. The protocols said that the captain should follow a properly formatted order to the letter without questioning it, and should launch his nuclear missiles. So it was impossible to do a reality check.'

'That is scary,' said Toby.

'The Fail Safe Commission changed the protocols in the 1990s, partly as a result of this incident. After that, if the captain didn't understand the reason for the order or suspected it might be an error, he was supposed to delay launching until he had had an opportunity to confirm.'

'That was very sensible,' said Bill.

'Did they consult you about that?' Sam asked.

'No. I had left the Navy by then. But I am sure they spoke to Glenn Robinson.'

'So I'm on the right track, then?' said Sam. 'I've just got one or two details wrong?'

Bill shrugged.

'Can I ask you about Lieutenant Naylor?' the historian said. 'I believe he was a fellow officer on the patrol. I understand he died?'

31

'Craig?' said Megan in surprise. Everyone turned to her and she looked embarrassed. 'Oops.'

'Yes, Craig,' said Bill. 'He was a good friend of mine,' Bill explained to Sam. 'We still speak about him in the family.'

'Oh, I see. Was his death anything to do with the launch orders?'

'Oh no. That was an accident. He somehow fell down a ladder and hit his head. He died a few days after the . . .'

Bill realized he had come close to admitting there *had* been a launch order. 'He died a few days after November ninth. His date of death will be on file.'

'It is,' said Sam. 'The eleventh of November.'

'Well then.'

The historian glanced at his notes, hesitating. 'One last thing. Did you know a woman named Pat Greenwald? A peace activist?'

'No. But I think my wife knew her. Back in the eighties.'

'You never spoke to her yourself?'

Bill shook his head.

The historian sighed. 'All right, thank you,' he said, packing up his notebook. 'But I *will* find out what happened that day on the submarine. I'm very persistent and I will give this project as long as it needs. There were a hundred and forty crew members on the *Hamilton*. Most of them will still be alive. Some of them will talk. And I have filed Freedom of Information requests with the US Navy and the Department of Defense.'

'I'm sorry I couldn't be more help,' said Bill. 'Genuinely.'

Sam smiled half-heartedly.

'There is one thing I can say,' said Bill.

'Yes?'

'Good luck.'

He seemed to mean it.

Sam didn't answer. If his patience had been stretched by Bill's stonewalling, he wasn't showing it, but it seemed to Toby he had come a long way for not very much.

'Hey, Sam,' Bill said. 'Are you driving back to Newcastle tonight?'

'No. I'm staying at the pub in the village. I'm going on to Cambridge tomorrow morning, and then I'm flying back to America for some more research.'

'Well, how about joining us for dinner?' said Bill. 'It's Thanksgiving.'

'Er . . .'

'Have you ever experienced a genuine American Thanksgiving?'

The historian hesitated, but then responded to Bill's warm, generous smile. 'All right. That would be nice. Thank you.'

Toby wondered whether this was just Bill's natural hospitality which was at its peak at Thanksgiving, or if he felt guilty about being so unhelpful. Or both. Probably both.

'Great. Be back here at about five-thirty. Lars da Silva will be here. But don't mention anything about Lieutenant Naylor. Craig's son will be here also, and it's a difficult subject with him.'

As Bill ushered Sam Bowen out of the front door, Toby went back to the kitchen where Alice's sister Brooke was helping her with vegetables. The two sisters were talking over one another in their excitement to see each other.

'Hey, Toby!' said Brooke, flashing her broad white smile. She put down her knife and gave him a hug. This was only the third time they had met, but she had always been very welcoming. Of the three sisters, Brooke was probably the one Alice was closest to. She was smaller than Alice, at twenty-nine a year younger, and her blonde hair was longer and curlier. She was a dentist in a suburb of Chicago: whether that was a cause or effect of her brilliant white teeth, Toby wasn't sure.

'Did you just get here?' he asked.

'About a half hour ago. We're staying in the Cottage. With Uncle Lars. Justin's there now.'

The Cottage was the nearest of a row of four small dwellings a few yards further back along the lane, with its own tiny garden. Bill had bought it to provide enough space for his large family when they were all together. The idea was to rent it out as a holiday cottage during the summer whenever it wasn't being used.

'Well?' said Alice. 'Did the historian tell you about how Dad's submarine nearly blew up the world?'

'He did! And about how your dad stopped them. It's an incredible story! Is it true?'

'I guess so. Dad will never confirm it, but Mom told us about it before she died. It's all Classified. I bet Dad didn't say anything to the historian, did he?'

'No.' Toby smiled. 'But he didn't deny it either. Why didn't you tell me about it?'

'Dad's very serious about none of us talking. Which is why I was pleased he asked you to join him. It's his way of telling you.'

'It makes him quite a hero.'

Alice smiled with pride. 'It does, doesn't it?'

'One thing I don't understand. Sam Bowen talked about an officer who died on the boat. Lieutenant Naylor. He said his son was going to be at dinner.'

Alice glanced at her sister, who was boiling some water in a pan.

Brooke looked up. Her married name was Opizzi, not Naylor. 'Yeah. That's Justin.'

She attacked a sweet potato with her vegetable knife.

'Craig Naylor was his father,' she went on. 'Dad, Uncle Lars and Craig were buddies on the sub. Justin wasn't born until after the patrol. After Craig died, Dad kept in touch with Justin and his mother – in fact, Justin used to come on vacation with us sometimes when we were kids.'

'So that's how you met?'

'You could say so. Although I didn't see him after the age of fourteen. Until I went to dental school in Chicago and he got in touch. He was working there.' Brooke moved the sweet potato slices to one side and reached for another. 'Best not to mention Craig, though, to Justin. He still gets upset about it.'

'OK,' said Toby. 'You didn't tell me any of this, Alice?'

'No,' said Alice, opening a can of mushroom soup. 'It never came up.' She frowned. 'Did this guy say he had found something out about Craig?'

'Not really. He had checked the date of his death, wanted to make sure it had nothing to do with the launch. Or near-launch. I got the impression it was something he was going to research. He's very thorough. He also mentioned a woman named Pat Greenberg? Something like that. Your dad said he didn't know her.'

Before Alice or Brooke could respond, Toby's phone chirped. It was Piet.

Toby answered. Piet wanted to schedule interviews with Toby for the following Monday. Beachwallet was hiring as fast as they could.

'How's Beachwallet doing?' asked Brooke when he had hung up.

'Good,' said Toby with a grin. 'It's been a struggle, but we're getting there. It looks like we've got a venture capitalist on board for a couple of million. We'll see.'

Piet and Toby had set up Beachwallet a year before, with some advice from Bill. The company was developing an app for young travellers to budget their holidays abroad, and to make payments in the necessary foreign currencies.

'Is Dad investing?' Brooke asked.

'Toby won't let him,' said Alice. 'He'd rather take money from evil venture capitalists instead.'

'Why's that, Toby?' said Brooke, pausing her chopping. She seemed genuinely interested.

'I suppose I'm just wary of mixing family and business.'

'Dad would love to do it,' said Alice.

Toby had been reluctant to take money from his new father-in-law only a few months into his marriage. He owed him enough already: although Toby and Alice split the mortgage payments equally on their one-bedroom flat in King's Cross, it had been bought with a deposit from Bill. Accepting that had pained Toby, but it had seemed pig-headed to refuse.

From the beginning of their relationship, Toby had vowed that he wouldn't become dependent on Alice's wealth, on Alice's father. It was a vow Alice had understood and respected. Between them, they had created a marriage of equals, something Toby was proud of, and he thought Alice was too. They both had serious jobs, they split the mortgage, they shared domestic chores, Toby intended to do his share when children came along.

It wasn't that he didn't trust his father-in-law's business acumen. After working all over the world for a US multinational, Bill had settled in London and invested in and managed a series of smallish defence communications companies in Britain and the rest of Europe. He had made good money out of it, many millions, exactly how many millions neither Alice nor Toby knew. And he had also learned how to keep small companies afloat.

But Toby was hesitant about binding his wife's family into his own precarious business affairs. It wasn't just pride in avoiding hand-outs. It seemed risky for a reason he couldn't quite pin down, something to do with a screw-up in one relationship leading to a screw-up in the other.

'I can see why you might want to be careful,' said Brooke.

Toby gave her a grateful smile.

Bill popped his head around the door. 'Can you manage another one for dinner, Alice? I know you can. There's no way you haven't made enough food.'

Alice grinned sheepishly, surveying the piles of food scattered around the kitchen. 'What do you think, Brooke?'

'I think we'll be OK.'

5

There was plenty of food. Despite the fact that there was turkey involved, it was slightly different to an English Christmas. No sausages, no bacon, mashed potato not roast. The stuffing seemed to have much more bread in it than its English equivalent, and there were Pennsylvanian vegetables: creamed dried sweetcorn, sweet potato and green beans in a mushroom sauce, which is where the Campbell's soup had come in. The cranberry sauce had been smuggled into the country by Brooke. It had all sounded a little weird when Alice had first described it, but it was delicious, in Toby's opinion. And there were unlimited quantities of a classy Puligny-Montrachet to wash it down.

They were crammed around the table in a dining room that wasn't quite big enough for the nine chairs. Guth family silver glimmered in the cosy yellow glow of dim wall lights, and the same thick beam ran across the ceiling from the living room next door. Outside, the marsh lurked in the darkness, and the wind from the sea rattled the windows intermittently. Everyone was there, apart from Maya. No one was worried about this; Maya was always late. It would have been more concerning if she had shown up on time.

The conversation flowed like a warm stream around the family, washing over the newer members, like Toby and Justin, and non-family like Sam Bowen and Lars da Silva, drawing them in. Alice and Brooke teased Megan about her future career as a waitress in the Belgian cafe, Megan and Bill teased Alice about how she had almost worked over the Thanksgiving weekend, and all three sisters teased their father about everything.

The dog was involved, of course. He planted himself beneath Sam's chair, his ears pricked as if listening to the conversation.

'Rickover seems to like you,' said Brooke.

'He's a nice dog,' said Sam, fondling the animal behind its ears. 'Named after the admiral?' He glanced at Bill, who nodded.

'I didn't realize Rickover was an admiral?' Toby said.

'He set up the nuclear submarine programme,' said Bill. 'He insisted on interviewing every midshipman himself. Scariest half hour of my life.'

'Then why did you name the dog after him?' Sam asked.

'Because Dad just likes telling admirals to sit,' said Alice.

'He was a fine man,' said Bill.

'And Rickover is a fine dog,' said Brooke. 'He definitely likes you, Sam.'

'And I like him,' said Sam.

'Are you sneaking him turkey?' Alice asked in her most inquisitorial voice.

Sam's chubby cheeks coloured red. 'Maybe.'

'I hope your admiral was less easily biddable,' Alice said.

'I never tried feeding *him* turkey,' said Bill with a laugh.

'Is there a Mrs Bowen?' Brooke asked Sam.

'My mum?' Sam said.

'You know what I mean!'

Sam grinned. 'Not yet. But soon.'

'Soon?' said Alice. 'Are you engaged?'

'Since last weekend. There's an old Roman fort way up in the Pennines we both really like: she's a historian too. We went for a walk up there on Sunday. That's where I asked her.'

'And she said yes?' said Brooke, her eyes wide.

'Of course she said yes, dummy,' said Megan. 'Otherwise they wouldn't be getting married.'

Brooke ignored her. 'What's her name?'

'Jasmine. Jazz.'

'Nice name. Not as nice as Rickover, of course. Have you fixed a date yet?'

'Not sure,' said Sam, grinning. 'We can't decide whether to have it before or after the baby is due.'

This prompted a slew of highly personal questions from the three Guth sisters, all of which Sam answered with good humour. Toby could see the tough truth-seeking historian wilting under the Guth charm offensive.

Toby was sitting next to the mysterious Uncle Lars. Although he must have been Bill's age, he appeared ten years older. Short steel-grey hair bristled over the brown dome of his skull, and two deep lines cut downwards one on either side of a full sandy moustache. He was thin and wiry, and looked like he had had a hard life. Jail did that to you, Toby supposed.

'Are you here on holiday?' Toby asked.

'Yeah,' said Lars. 'Primarily to see Bill, but I'm planning on going to London and maybe Bath or York. We served together on submarines, back in the day.'

'I know. I was there when Sam was talking to Bill this afternoon.'

'Oh, really?' Lars looked surprised. 'Did Bill tell him anything?' he asked quietly. Sam was at the other end of the table, safely out of earshot.

'No,' said Toby. 'A brick wall.'

'That's probably a good thing,' said Lars. 'Sam came all the way out to Wisconsin to speak with me a couple of weeks ago, and I didn't tell him anything either. A wasted trip if ever there was one. I don't understand why Bill invited him to dinner.'

'You know Bill better than I do,' said Toby. 'He's very hospitable.'

Lars grunted as he stabbed some turkey with a fork and pushed it into his mouth. 'He is that.'

41

'So you live in Wisconsin?' Toby asked. 'Is that where the Lars comes from?' Toby was dimly aware that Wisconsin had been settled by Scandinavians.

'That's right. My mother's family were Swedes from way back, but my dad came from Brazil. He's passed, but my mother's still alive. Barely. She's in a home now, but I figure she needs someone to come see her. So I decided to move back.' Lars looked straight at Toby with troubled green eyes. 'After they let me out of jail.'

Toby thought of saying 'that's nice' but realized that, although the sentiment was true, it sounded trite. He knew he was looking confused; an Englishman trying to be polite and not quite managing it.

'They did tell you that, didn't they? I spent eight years in prison in Guadeloupe?'

'Yes they did. That can't have been much fun.'

Dumb comment.

'No, it wasn't. Then again, prisons in the States are even worse. It wasn't the best period of my life.' He changed the subject. 'So you're the guy who married Alice?'

'I am.'

'She was a beautiful girl,' said Lars. 'She's a beautiful woman now. You're a lucky man.'

'I am,' Toby repeated. And he was. He really was.

He looked over to his wife, who was seated next to Sam, and seemed to be involved in an earnest conversation with him. Her earlier merriment had gone and she was frowning.

They were interrupted by the sound of the front door opening in the hallway, and the youngest Guth sister appeared. Maya was also the tallest, with unfeasibly long legs and long blonde hair that she wore like a club over one shoulder. She was still wearing her airline uniform, having arrived straight from Heathrow. There was a general hubbub of welcome as she greeted everyone and took her place at the table. She was soon plied with turkey and wine.

Bill introduced her to Sam.

'Are you finally going to tell us what Dad and Lars did on that submarine?' Maya asked in her English middle-class drawl.

'That's my plan,' said Sam. 'Once I've worked it out myself.'

'Hey, Sam?' said Megan, who was at the other end of the table from him. 'This afternoon, when you were trying to talk to Dad about his submarine, you mentioned that there had been a bunch of near-launches. Is that true?'

Bill frowned at his daughter. But the rest of the table were curious to hear Sam's answer. Including Lars.

'There were several that we know of,' he said. 'And probably lots that we don't.'

'Such as?'

'Well. In the Cuban missile crisis back in 1962, a Russian submarine was surrounded by US destroyers. The captain and the political officer wanted to launch a nuclear torpedo, but the officer in charge of the flotilla was also on board and he talked the captain out of it.' He glanced at Bill as he said this. 'Which is kind of like what might have happened on the *Alexander Hamilton*.'

If he was hoping for a response from Bill, he wasn't going to get one. Toby felt Lars shifting in his seat beside him.

'Also in '62, a US tactical missile squadron on Okinawa were ordered to fire their nuclear-tipped Mace missiles. The targets didn't make sense to the captain in charge of the squadron – they included places outside Russia. He asked for confirmation of the order and he got it. But he still didn't obey the command, and he sent two men armed with pistols to stop the lieutenant at a neighbouring bunker launching his own missiles.'

That might also sound familiar, Toby thought. Both Bill and Lars were listening intently.

'There was a bear that ran into the perimeter wire at an airfield in Duluth and set off an alarm. Someone got the alarms confused, thought war had started, and scrambled a squadron of nuclear-armed warplanes from a nearby base. There were the false readings at NORAD I told you about. That happened twice, in 1979 and again in 1980.

'Then, in 1983, the Soviet early-warning centre south-east of Moscow showed that the US had launched a nuclear attack. Fortunately, the officer on the watch had been involved in upgrading the computer system and he didn't trust it. So he did what we all do when the computer doesn't work. He turned it off and turned it on again.'

The table laughed nervously.

'And?' said Maya.

'And it still showed the missiles were coming.'

'So what did he do then?' Justin asked.

'Tried it again. Turned the system off and on again. Missiles were still there, but by that stage radar stations in the north of the Russia should have spotted the contacts and hadn't.'

'Jesus,' said Megan. 'So he could have reported the attack?'

'Not only could he have, he should have,' said Sam. 'No one in the west realized it at the time, but we were really close to nuclear war in 1983. The Soviet leadership were convinced that NATO was about to launch a surprise first strike. They would have launched their own missiles right away.'

There was silence, a rare occurrence with all four Guth sisters present.

Toby looked around the table. The sisters, he, Justin and Sam had all been born after 1983. They wouldn't have existed. Which would mean they wouldn't have experienced the firestorms, the global radiation, the death of billions of people, of every living thing on the planet. Or almost every living thing.

Megan raised her eyebrows at Toby. 'Do you have cockroaches in England?'

6

Toby had learned the year before that Thanksgiving wasn't just about giving thanks, or even about turkey, it was about football. American football.

Bill's super-smart TV could pick up any US sporting event. Neither of Bill's favourite teams were playing that day, neither Navy nor the Philadelphia Eagles, but the Washington Redskins were taking on the Dallas Cowboys, and Bill had spent a lot of time in Washington. Despite her professed hatred of Dallas, Megan was happy to root for the Cowboys, continuing what appeared to be a family tradition of supporting everyone else's enemy.

Alice had seen Sam out, before returning to the kitchen to supervise washing up. Although she seemed calm and business-like, Toby detected a hint of tension in her shoulders, a slight tightening of her lips.

'Are you OK?' he asked.

'Of course I am,' she said with a bright smile. 'Now go and watch the game. We've got this.'

The four women were doing the washing up, and the men were doing the TV watching. Toby considered arguing.

'Don't argue,' said his wife, and pushed him out of the room.

Bill, Lars and even Justin vied with each other to explain to Toby what was going on. Toby knew the rules, but not the strategy and tactics, a subject upon which Bill and Lars politely disagreed. Justin was less well informed than the older men, and less sure of his own opinions.

Toby hadn't spent much time with Justin. Brooke had travelled to England to see her father and elder sister a couple of times without him, and you don't speak to people much at your own wedding; Toby had attended Justin and Brooke's in Chicago, and they had both been to his and Alice's in Holland Park.

Justin was at least five years older than Toby, but he seemed a friendly enough ally. He was tall, with thinning red hair cut short, and brown eyes looking out of a round chubby face with an air of preoccupation, as if he was constantly harassed. The soft face contrasted with the taut, hard torso that nestled beneath his shirt, the neatly constructed muscles of an office worker who spends a lot of time in the gym. Toby suspected, and Alice had confirmed, that it wasn't Brooke who harassed Justin, but his work. He was employed by an old media company in Chicago that was under attack from new media, and Justin gave the impression of not quite being able to handle it. The gym helped, apparently, just not enough.

But Alice believed he was a good thing for Brooke, who was earning decent money as a dentist, and he treated her well.

Toby was surprised that no one had mentioned that Justin had known the Guth family from his childhood. On the one hand, why should they? On the other, he knew Alice well enough to know that the omission had been intentional.

Another Guth secret.

The women joined them in the living room. During the interminable commercial breaks, Bill reached for a tapestry and began stitching. It was one he had designed himself, a view of Barnholt from the sea, really just swathes of blue and green and grey and the windmill. Toby had been surprised when he had seen Bill working away with needle and yarn on his first trip up to Norfolk.

Alice had explained that it had started when Bill had finished off some needlepoint that her mother had been working on when she died, with Alice showing him how to do it. He found it had helped, and he worked on another that his wife had already bought. Then he began to design his own – all of Norfolk coastal scenes – which became increasingly less precise and more impressionistic. He never did them in London, only in Norfolk. Toby thought they were rather good.

Justin asked Toby a question.

'Did Sam say anything about my father this afternoon? Craig Naylor?'

Toby was sure that there was a reason that Justin had asked him and not Bill. But Bill answered.

'Just briefly,' he said. 'I told him what had happened.'

Justin glanced at Toby, who nodded.

'Did he talk about what my father did when the submarine got the orders to launch? What his reaction was?' Justin was once again asking Toby. Toby wasn't clear how much Justin knew about the near-launch, but it was obvious he had known more than Toby. Toby felt a flash of jealousy as he realized Brooke must have told her husband more than Alice had told him. Maybe Brooke trusted Justin more than Alice trusted Toby?

'No, he didn't,' said Toby.

'Craig was in a different part of the submarine,' said Bill. 'He was weapons officer, which meant he was down in the missile control centre. The discussion about the launch orders took place in the control room.'

Justin nodded, and the play started again. The Redskins were third down and five at the eleven-yard line.

The Redskins scored twice, then the Cowboys got a field goal. At half time, Alice announced that she had forgotten some of the food she needed for the following day, and she would pop out to Tesco in Hunstanton to pick it up. Toby offered to come too, as did Brooke, but Alice insisted on going alone, and so he turned his attention back to the half-time analysis.

7

Alice drove fast to Hunstanton. It wasn't far, and although it was dark, the roads were empty. The supermarket was just the other side of town and was open twenty-four hours a day.

Alice parked by the entrance and swiftly filled a basket with staples that they might need more of over the next couple of days: milk, bread, coffee, the kind of yoghurt that Maya liked. She swept her purchases through the self-service checkout, and then drove back to Barnholt.

She clenched the steering wheel tightly. She thought she had built a good rapport with Sam. He seemed to like her, indeed he seemed to enjoy the company of all the Guth family. She liked him.

But he was dangerous.

How dangerous, she didn't yet know.

Once she reached Barnholt, she turned off the main road, but rather than going on along the back lane to the house, she parked by the green, just opposite the King William. The lights were on and there were a number of cars in the parking lot: it wasn't quite closing time.

Alice took a deep breath, opened the car door, and stepped out into the night.

It was well after eleven by the time Alice got back to Pear Tree Cottage. She noticed that there were still lights on in the living room, and in her father's study upstairs.

She opened the front door and carried her two shopping bags through to the kitchen.

Toby joined her. 'The Redskins won,' he said.

'I bet Dad was pleased.'

He kissed the back of her neck. She didn't respond. 'You took your time,' he said. 'That's not much to show for an hour and a half in the supermarket. I was getting worried.'

'I had to go to King's Lynn to get everything I needed,' said Alice brusquely. 'Has everyone else gone to bed?'

'I think so. Shall I give you a hand?'

'No,' said Alice sharply. 'I'll put it all away; you won't know where it goes. You go upstairs and I'll be with you soon.'

But once she had put the groceries away, she crept upstairs to her father's study. By the time she slipped into bed next to her husband, he was fast asleep.

8

August 1983, Groton, Connecticut

I loved the Navy. I loved serving in submarines.

I loved the *Alexander Hamilton*.

She was a Lafayette-class submarine, built in 1962. For three years she had operated out of Holy Loch on the west coast of Scotland. An alternating series of Blue and Gold crews had flown back and forth from the submarine base at Groton in Connecticut to take her out into the depths of the North Atlantic Ocean and wait for the order to blow up the world.

You have to be kind of weird to enjoy working on submarines, especially on ballistic missile submarines which are designed, essentially, to do nothing for long periods of time. For ever, really. Ideally, boomers should never do anything at all.

Patrols last about seventy days. Seventy days of never seeing the sun, never seeing a cloud, never feeling a breath of wind on your face. Seventy days of being crammed in a fat metal tube with a hundred and thirty-nine other men, with no privacy, a bunk that is little more than a coffin, occasional showers that last seconds, food that has been stored for weeks and reheated in minutes. Seventy days where the days of the week and the hours of the day become disjointed and blurred and where the crew toil to keep the sub puttering quietly along at three knots, with its missile hatches firmly shut, slaves to the giant machine.

So why did I love it?

The physics fascinated me, still do. The power of nuclear fission has held me in awe since high school. The idea that all that energy could be contained in a reactor core the size of a small car and manoeuvred around the world's oceans amazed me. I wanted to be one of the guys taming that power, controlling it, manipulating it, directing it, its master not its slave.

The power of the dozens of nuclear warheads inspired awe in me also, but in an entirely different way. My father had been in the Navy in the Pacific, and had done his bit to make the world safe for democracy. I believed that the Cold War was a real struggle for the future of the world. I couldn't deny there was a chance that humanity might blow itself up, but I wanted to be one of those people capable of taking the responsibility to ensure nuclear weapons preserved peace, not destroyed everything. My country needed sensible, rational, reliable men to steward its nuclear arsenal, and I was proud to be one of those men.

The Navy encouraged the sense of an elite that went with serving on ballistic submarines, and I responded well to that. They were the great capital ships of the late-twentieth century, and I was glad to serve on them. I was proud of the insignia pinned to my chest: the golden pair of dolphins, the silver submarine with a gold star for each deterrence patrol. As befitted an elite service, discipline was a little more relaxed under the sea than above. And the crew were much smarter.

A submarine was stuffed full of physics and engineering nerds. Sonarmen who could rewire a recording studio, missile techs who were actual rocket scientists, engineers who could design a nuclear reactor. There were probably more men who could solve a differential equation on one submarine than on a fleet of surface ships or, for that matter, in the whole Marine Corps.

That might not have been strictly true, but I believed it was.

The crew of a submarine was a family, who worked together, slept together, kidded together, quarrelled together, and kept the world safe. Together.

My father owned and edited the newspaper in a small town in southern Pennsylvania. I knew he wanted me to take over from him eventually, but it became clear to both of us as I grew up that I was more interested in science than journalism. When I told him I wanted to go to the US Naval Academy at Annapolis, he hadn't argued. The Vietnam War was just coming to an end, joining the military was a far from fashionable thing for an eighteen year old to do, but he understood that I believed I was serving my country against a real enemy. He believed I was too.

I had graduated from the Academy, majoring in Physics rather than the more common Engineering, spent six months at the nuclear propulsion school in Florida, six months training on the prototype reactor in Idaho and then three months on the Submarine Officers Basic Course at Groton. After all that, I had joined the *Alexander Hamilton* as an ensign. I got my nuclear qualifications, had been promoted to lieutenant and completed my fourth patrol on the boat.

I had made friends, good friends. One of these was Lars da Silva, who had graduated in the same class as me from the Academy, and had also joined the *Hamilton* as an ensign. His olive skin, green eyes and thick blonde moustache testified to his heritage: his mother came from Midwestern Swedish stock and his father was Brazilian. We shared a stateroom with a third junior officer, Matt Curtis: it was known as the 'JO Jungle'.

Another was Craig Naylor. Craig was a couple of years older than Lars and me. Broad-chested with a round face and winning smile, he was serving his second tour on patrol, his first having been on a fast-attack submarine in the Pacific. He was one of the four 'department heads' on the boat. In his case he was weapons officer, which meant he was in charge of the missile command centre, and of actually launching the submarine's nuclear weapons.

Craig was married. Kind of. Two weeks after he had returned to his married quarters in Groton from his last patrol, his wife Maria had announced she was leaving him. She said it wasn't for anyone else; it was just that to be a submariner's spouse was to be a wife for only half the year, a half wife. It was no way for a woman to live her life, no way for a couple to coexist, no way to bring up children. She was going to end it before it drove her any crazier than she already was.

Craig was bewildered. Such separations were a common enough event in the submarine service; Maria did have logic on her side. But she had never mentioned any of this before. There had been no 'me or the Navy' ultimatum.

Then it had all become clear. There was a guy called Tony Opizzi; an insurance salesman based in nearby New London.

Craig had needed company, fast, and Lars and I were happy to provide it. No one could deny that Craig was an all-round good guy. He was a straightforward, upbeat man who just made you feel good about yourself. He was great to be with on a submarine. He was great to be with in a bar.

Lars and I were not the only people who felt sorry for Craig. His younger sister, Vicky, who had just started working for a bank on Wall Street, invited Craig and a couple of his friends to stay with her in the city over the Labor Day weekend.

Would Lars and I like to come?

You bet we would.

9

Vicky Naylor took us to a bar on the Upper West Side, four blocks from her apartment, where the three of us were crashing on her floor. There she introduced us to Kathleen and Donna, two friends from college.

The bar was jumping on a Friday night, even on a Labor Day weekend. I was a small-town guy, as was Lars. I loved the buzz of the city, the feeling of exhilaration on a big night out. Lars and I had travelled down to New York a few times on weekends over the previous couple of years. It was a great place to have a few beers, but we always felt out of place. Relations with civilians had gotten a little better since the seventies and Vietnam. On submarines we wore our hair a little bit longer, while everyone else now wore their hair a little bit shorter. But we were not yuppie bankers or lawyers, blowing our pay cheques on booze and cocaine. We weren't hip New York graduate students getting by in the big city on little money at the cool hang-outs.

We were in the military, and New York was not a military kind of town.

They could tell, the guys at the bar, their girlfriends, they could tell we were not one of them.

At least Kathleen and Donna knew who we were.

Vicky wasn't subtle. She was a large woman, red-haired like her brother, and like her brother good-hearted. She had a plan for Craig, and that plan involved Kathleen. Donna was the back-up.

I could see why the plan had seemed a good one. Kathleen was cute. Small, blonde, pert, upturned nose, white teeth, winning smile. Smart, although her voice had an irritating high pitch. She was a paralegal at a major commercial law firm, which partly explained why she had no boyfriend. The firm never let her out of the office; she was only able to join us that evening because of the Labor Day holiday. And Craig was good-looking with an easy charm. It should be a good match.

The plan should have worked, but what Vicky had failed to understand was that Craig had no interest in meeting a new woman. He wanted the one he already loved back, please.

Of course Lars and I had no such qualms, Lars especially. Kathleen was just his type. And I could see that Vicky had taken a shine to Lars. So the evening started off with a kind of circular balance. Kathleen was trying to impress Craig, whether of her own accord or just following her friend's instructions wasn't clear. Craig wanted to talk to his sister about his soon-to-be ex-wife. And Vicky really wanted to get to know Lars better.

Which left me with the back-up.

Donna.

Her honey-blonde hair was unfashionably long, she was wearing tight jeans and a white cotton top that showed off one pale shoulder – that was fashionable that year. A lop-sided smile hovered, never totally disappearing from her face, as if life left her mildly amused.

'I'm guessing you're not a banker,' I said.

'I might be,' said Donna. 'I work in an office. It has filing cabinets and paperclips and staplers.'

'Staplers? Wow.'

'Do you have staplers on your submarine?'

'Way too dangerous. Staplers flying around a confined space could kill someone.'

'Of course. You have to be highly skilled to use them. I am highly skilled and I have had lots of practice. I could show you some day.'

'That would be great,' I said. 'No one has ever offered to do that with me before.'

Donna frowned slightly.

'I'm sorry. That's very forward of me,' I said. 'We've just met, and we're already talking staples.'

The edge of Donna's lips twitched upwards, and her blue eyes crinkled. She took a sip of her beer.

I offered her a cigarette. She shook her head. 'I'm trying to quit.'

'Do you mind if I do?' I asked. She glanced at Lars and Vicky, who were both smoking, and shook her head again. I lit up. 'Where do you do your stapling?'

'For the United Nations. Their development program. Basically I'm a low-paid filing clerk. An idealistic low-paid filing clerk, making the world better one staple at a time.'

'That's very noble.'

'So you don't think I look like a banker, huh?' The corner of her lip twitched.

'Do I look like a sailor?'

'I have no idea what a sailor looks like. Do you have tattoos? Do you eat spinach?'

'Seriously? You don't know anyone in the Navy?'

Donna shook her head. 'Apart from Mr Hosier who lives next door to my parents back home. I think he was in the Navy in the Korean War.'

'What about the army?'

Donna shook her head again.

'No one from college?'

'We all went to Swarthmore. They're not big on the military at Swarthmore.' Swarthmore was a small liberal arts college in

Pennsylvania, not too far from where I grew up; it was founded by Quakers, famous for their pacifism. She shrugged. 'Sorry.'

The Vietnam War had finished the year before I went to the Academy, and probably three or four years before Donna had gone to college, but it certainly wasn't forgotten, especially by my generation. A lot of people – an awful lot of women – my age seemed to think that you had to be either a moron or a traitor to join the military. A traitor, not to your country, but to the nobler cause of world peace.

I realized that Donna was probably one of those women. It was only then that I noticed the yellow and black 'No Nukes' button on the denim jacket draped on the back of her chair.

Donna was definitely one of those women.

Oh well.

'Hey, Vicky, Bill doesn't think I look like a banker!' Donna said.

'Don't be fooled,' said Vicky. 'Donna was always much smarter at economics than I was. And math. You wouldn't believe how many bankers I work with who couldn't figure out a square root if you paid them.'

'Really?' said Craig.

'Oh yeah. You'd run rings round all of them. But they have the gift of the bullshit. They know how to make other people do their square roots for them.'

'Is it that bad?' said Craig.

'No,' said Vicky. 'I like it, actually. And I'm pretty good at it.'

'So what's it like sailing on a submarine, Craig?' said Kathleen.

'I bet it smells,' said Vicky. 'All those men. They don't take proper showers.'

'Actually, it does smell pretty bad,' said Craig. 'At least at first. But you get used to it after a few hours, and then you don't notice it.'

'How long do you go underwater for?' asked Kathleen.

'Two months, usually,' said Craig. 'Sometimes three. The only limit is the amount of food the boat can carry.'

'And our sanity,' said Lars. 'Folks get a bit ratty toward the end of patrol. There's something called "hate week", happens a couple of weeks before the end of the patrol when we just all want to go home, see the sky. You get quarrels, the odd fight, guys jumping down each other's throats.'

'And does your submarine have nuclear missiles?' asked Kathleen.

'It does,' said Vicky. 'And they put Craig in charge of them. He's the guy who presses the button, God help us.'

'Wow,' said Kathleen uncertainly.

I glanced at Donna. The mild amusement had left her face. She saw me looking at her and I averted my eyes.

'There are a bunch of controls,' I said. 'Procedures to stop Craig from launching any missiles just because he's had a bad day and he feels like it.'

'Well, I'm sure glad to hear that,' said Vicky.

Everyone around the table laughed. Nearly everyone.

'Doesn't it trouble you?' said Donna. 'That you might bring humanity to an end?'

Here we go, I thought.

'What troubles me is that I come back from two months away at work to find my wife has run off with an insurance salesman,' said Craig, bitterly.

'I never liked that woman,' said Vicky.

'I did,' said Craig, downing his beer. 'I still do. *That* is the trouble.'

More beer. It was Molson, Canadian, fairly strong. The women were drinking it at the same pace as the men and were getting drunker faster. Craig, Lars and I had had lots of practice, despite the enforced two-month stretches of abstinence underwater.

'No, seriously,' said Donna. 'Doesn't it worry you? That you might be the ones who blow up the world?'

Craig replied, politely. 'No. I believe that what we are doing on our submarine is stopping the Russians from winning. We're in a war against the Soviets. It may be a Cold War, but it's still a war. And the moment we give up, they win. The world will become communist. Starts with Asia. Then Europe. And then New York City.'

'You don't really think that, do you?' said Donna.

'I do.'

'And what about you?' she asked Lars.

Lars took a long drag on his cigarette. 'Uh-huh,' he said.

'And you?' She turned to me. I thought I saw a flash of hope in her eyes, maybe hope that I would agree with her.

'Craig's right.'

'So it's better dead than red, is it?' Donna said. 'If we ever got rid of all our nuclear weapons, we could use some of the money to help out all those starving people in Africa and Asia, instead of trashing their countries to make sure the Russians don't get them. We could stop a nuclear holocaust from happening. We have the power to do it.'

'I disagree,' said Craig. I admired his patience.

'What do you think, Vicky?' Donna asked. 'Do you think your brother should be riding around in a lethal weapon for months on end waiting to blow up the world?'

'Donna, I think my brother is serving my country, and I'm proud of him,' said Vicky. She said it quietly and firmly.

'Yeah, OK,' said Donna, realizing she had gone a bit too far. 'I'm sorry, Craig. I'm sorry, you guys. I know you think . . .' She corrected herself. 'I know you *are* serving your country, and I know that's a noble thing to do, and that our fathers' generation saved us from the Nazis and the Japanese. I get that, and I respect that.'

'Doesn't sound like it,' said Lars.

Donna ignored him. 'But don't you see that you are just doing what *they* want you to? You are being brainwashed.'

'And who are "they"?' said Lars. 'The "military–industrial complex"? What even is that?'

'Yes, the military. The big corporations, especially the defence companies. President Reagan. Casper Weinberger. It was Eisenhower who came up with the term "military–industrial complex". He was a general, he should know. They want to make the world safe for American capital and they don't care who gets hurt on the way. Some of them even think you can win a nuclear war. How can you win a nuclear war?'

'You can't win a nuclear war,' I said. I could feel the impatience in my voice. 'You have to stop one from starting.'

'And you really think riding around in a nuclear submarine helps do that?'

'Yes. It's called deterrence.'

Donna snorted. 'Oh yeah. MAD. Why don't they just call it crazy?'

She was referring to the doctrine of mutually assured destruction.

'You may call it crazy, but it's working,' I said. 'Have you ever wondered why we haven't had World War Three yet? When we have the two most powerful nations in the world at loggerheads? When there have been all those flashpoints around the world: Korea, Vietnam, Berlin, Hungary, Czechoslovakia? That Korean Airlines flight that was just shot down? Do you really think if nuclear weapons hadn't existed we wouldn't have had a conventional war by now? A bigger and nastier war even than the last one?'

'Everyone assumes the Russians want to attack us,' Donna said. 'We have no proof of that. Just what the CIA and the military tells us.'

'Hey,' said Craig. 'They shot down an unarmed civilian airliner a couple of days ago. Looks to me like they are attacking us.' A Korean Airlines 747, which had strayed into Russian airspace, had been destroyed two days before. It was still unclear why, or what the United States would do about it. The Soviets were denying they had anything to do with it, but no one believed them.

'They probably thought it was a spy plane,' said Donna.

'The Russians don't want to attack us, because they know we will attack them,' I said. 'And everyone will lose. And that only works if they believe that we will definitely respond. Which we will. Which Craig and Lars and I will. That's why they don't attack us. And actually, that's why *we* don't attack them.'

'But why do you need so many missiles?' Donna said. 'What do you call it, "overkill"? Isn't one enough? One bomb dropped on Moscow to wipe them all out?'

'It's because of what you said earlier,' I said. 'We all need to make sure that no one can win a nuclear war. That's what our submarines are for. If the Russians launched a surprise attack on us, took out Washington and our land-based missiles, and our bombers, the *Hamilton* would still be there, hidden in the Atlantic, ready to take out their biggest cities.'

'And then we all die?'

'No. None of us dies! That's the whole point. The Cold War has been going on thirty-five years, and we haven't blown up the world yet.'

Donna's blue eyes flashed at me. There was a touch of colour in her pale cheeks. But she was listening to me, I could tell she was listening. The rest of the group was watching us.

She took a swig from her beer bottle. 'There has to be a better way,' she said.

'I hope they find one,' I said. 'I really do.'

There was silence around the table for a moment. Then Vicky broke it. 'Why don't we go eat? There's a good Mexican place a couple of blocks away.'

The restaurant was indeed good and not too expensive. I noticed that Donna was careful not to sit next to me; I was at one corner of the table for six, and she was at the corner diagonally opposite. Everyone else soon forgot our conversation and even Craig seemed to forget his wife.

As the crowd laughed, I smiled almost politely. I couldn't help glancing surreptitiously at Donna, as she teased Vicky, laughed at something Craig said or expressed horror at one of Kathleen's stories. She was so warm, so engaged, so *alive*.

And so beautiful. She was really beautiful.

I felt depressed about our argument. Not about the substance: I knew many people thought the way Donna did, and I was as confident as I could be that she was wrong. I didn't for one moment doubt the worth of what Lars and Craig and I and all the other Blue Crew on the *Alexander Hamilton* were doing.

It was more that I felt cut off from the rest of society, or certainly from my own generation. It wasn't just that millions of Americans didn't appreciate what we were doing spending four months of the year underwater protecting them from World War Three, it was that they didn't even understand it. They thought *we* were the enemy.

On the submarine, everyone understood. It was like going back to your family: they might not always like you, but they understood you and they accepted you.

That didn't seem healthy. If the only place you could be accepted was three hundred feet beneath the Atlantic, that didn't seem healthy at all.

Donna spotted me looking at her, hesitated just for a second and then we both looked away.

Eventually, we all spilled out of the restaurant on to Broadway. The temperature had cooled a little, and a breeze threaded its way from the Hudson through the tall buildings toward us, bringing the sweet smell of New York garbage with it. The taxis roared by in waves, let loose by the synchronized traffic lights.

We walked back toward Vicky's apartment, via the 86th Street Subway stop for Donna to take the subway home downtown to St Mark's Place. Kathleen had already grabbed a taxi across the park to the East Side.

I was trailing a few feet behind the other four, when Donna slipped back to join me.

'Can I have one of those cigarettes after all?' she asked.

'Sure.' I gave her one and lit up myself.

She took a deep drag. 'That tastes so good,' she said. 'I think I might have had a little too much to drink.'

'Are you sure you shouldn't get a cab?' It was dark, and I knew there were no-go areas in New York. I just didn't know exactly where they were.

'I'll be OK,' Donna said. 'I also know I've spent too much money already tonight. Are you all right? You seemed a little preoccupied?'

'Oh, I'm fine,' I said. 'It was a good evening.'

'Hey, I'm sorry I beat up on you so much back there,' she said. 'It was tacky. And I know you really believe what you were telling me.'

'I do,' I said.

'I should know better. I've had non-violence training, you know. They teach you to engage respectfully with the other side. I don't think I was very respectful.'

'They?'

'The people who organize the protests.'

'Oh. I can confirm you weren't violent.'

'Yeah. Well, I hope you have a good mission, or whatever you call it. You know, it all goes well.'

What? You mean I don't blow up the world? I felt like saying, but didn't.

We walked on in silence for a block. I saw the subway sign over the other side of the street.

I had an idea. It was probably a dumb idea, but I had no time to think it through.

'I'm going to see my parents in Pennsylvania for a few days tomorrow.'

'Oh yeah? Where do they live?'

'Lancaster County.' The green railings of the subway station were getting closer. I didn't have time to discuss Pennsylvania geography.

I stopped. She stopped. 'Look. I can drop by New York on my way back to Groton. Do you want to come out for dinner with me next week? Thursday evening?'

She looked at me as if I was crazy. 'You're asking me for a date? After how mean I was to you?'

'I seem to be,' I said, making a brave face of it.

She blinked. She raised one side of her lip. She clearly found that pretty funny.

'OK.'

'OK?' I hadn't expected that.

The others had stopped and turned to look for us.

'Where?' she asked reasonably.

'I have no idea,' I said. 'It never really occurred to me you would say yes.'

She laughed. 'All right. How about da Gennaro's in Little Italy? Seven o'clock.'

10

I had a knot in my stomach when I woke up the next morning on the sofa in Vicky's living room. Her roommate, also a banker, had left the city for the weekend, leaving space for the three of us. Barely.

We took Vicky out for an early brunch, drank Bloody Marys and mimosas and ate steak because we could. The knot was still there. I didn't tell the others that I had asked Donna out later that week.

Vicky's plan with Kathleen and her brother hadn't worked out, but Craig was in a much better frame of mind, despite a mild hangover, and so Vicky thought she had achieved something. Craig and Lars were returning to Groton that afternoon and I was getting the bus to Philadelphia from the Port Authority.

In Philadelphia, I caught another bus on to the small town near Lancaster where my parents lived. The knot was still there the whole time. It was definitely Donna-related. Was it nerves? Was it excitement? I wasn't sure.

My mom and dad were pleased to see me. They were good like that: they were always pleased to see me. I realized I had been wrong in thinking that the entire world outside the Navy was against me, against the crew of the *Hamilton*. They were on my side. They were proud of me.

Of course they could never really understand what life on a submarine was like, but they were genuinely interested. My father had chased Japanese submarines in a destroyer during the war, and he was curious what it was like beneath the waves.

They showed just as much interest in my sister's job as a research chemist working for a drug company in Philadelphia. If my father still felt any disappointment that neither of us had shown any interest in the family newspaper, he certainly didn't show it.

I left for New York on Thursday morning and got into the city about three o'clock. I pushed myself through the Port Authority bus station crowd of spaced-out crazies, panhandlers and dazed and frightened out-of-towners, and walked the few blocks to Penn Station, to check the time of the last train to New London that night.

Then I had three and a half hours to kill.

I continued south, not caring where those New York no-go areas were, having just battled my way through one of them. It was hot and humid and noisy, exhaust fumes from the endless traffic mixing with the aroma of soft pretzels from the carts on street corners. I sweated steadily.

Eventually I reached Wall Street itself, a narrow dark canyon running downhill between sheer cliffs of stone and glass towers. Men my age in suits and women in National Football League shoulder pads powered along the sidewalks, driven with an urgency that reminded me of a fire emergency drill on the *Hamilton*. Vicky had said she worked for a firm called Bloomfield Weiss somewhere on an adjoining street; presumably at that very moment she was learning how to ask people to calculate square roots for her.

An urgent beat emanated from a knot of suits on the sidewalk; something had distracted them. I took a look. A young black kid, no more than twelve, was breakdancing on a mat in their midst, writhing to the bass of the boom-box beside him. The kid was doing well – his upturned baseball cap was half full of coins and dollar bills.

I walked down the street and found a bench in Battery Park next to an old guy muttering to himself and sipping something out of a brown paper bag. On closer inspection, he wasn't that old. Forty, maybe even thirty-five. A Vietnam vet. Someone who had lost his life for his country, even though he could still breathe. And drink.

'How are you doin', man?' I said.

He turned, looked at me as if I was crazy, and then carried on with his monologue. I pulled out a ten from my wallet and offered it to him.

'Keep your goddamn money,' he snarled.

So I kept it. A wave of shame washed over me. Shame that I had offered him the money. Shame that I hadn't insisted that he take it. But most of all, shame that I claimed I was serving my country, when all I was doing was eating, sleeping and working in the safety of a metal tube hundreds of feet beneath the sea.

This guy had served his country.

I stared out at the orange Staten Island ferries scurrying across the harbour under the gaze of the Statue of Liberty.

My stomach flipped.

What was this? It was true I had only ever had one long-term girlfriend before, Christina, whom I had met senior year in high school. We had made it through three of the four years of college. In the years since then there had been several other women, but none of them had lasted. It wasn't just that the punishing schedule of months on patrol messed things up. They just weren't special enough to make the effort, and it took some effort to maintain a relationship in the Navy.

None of them had knotted my stomach like this.

I headed back into the heat and bustle of the city. I stopped at an air-conditioned bar on Broadway and had a beer to cool down after all the walking, and to calm my nerves. Thirty minutes to wait. This was stupid. Donna thought I was a mass murderer. She had only agreed to have dinner with me because she felt guilty about being rude. And because she was drunk. She was drunk, wasn't she? Would she even remember?

This was going to be a disaster. Possibly a humiliating disaster if we argued again. A change of plan was required. Just buy her a drink and then if things looked as bad as I was pretty sure they would, make my excuses and leave.

I had planned to get to the restaurant, an old pink building on the corner of Mulberry Street, five minutes early, but I mistimed it and was three minutes late. A bad start: we naval officers are precise about time.

I walked past the window of the restaurant, and saw she was already there, waiting, alone at a table a few feet away from the window.

She was looking away from me, toward an old reproduction poster of Ravenna, her lips in that half-smile.

She was indeed beautiful.

I saw her begin to turn. My instinct was to pull back, to make sure she didn't see me staring, but something made me keep still.

I held her gaze.

The half-smile became a full smile.

I never did catch that last train to New London.

11

Friday 29 November 2019, Day after Thanksgiving, Norfolk, England

'Oh, shit.'

Toby opened his eyes and rolled over. His wife was sitting up in bed scowling at her iPad.

'What is it?' he asked her.

'You know that acquisition I'm working on? In France?'

'Yes.' Alice was always working on some acquisition or other, and they were often in France, since she spoke good French. She was good about never being too specific, at least until deals had been announced. Confidentiality.

'They want to make an announcement to the market Monday morning.'

'Uh-huh.'

'Don wants me to come in later today and Saturday to work on it.'

Toby sat up, rubbing his eyes. 'Have you told him you can't? He of all people should understand it's Thanksgiving.' Don was American. Alice worked for an American law firm.

'That's the problem. He's in the States, so he can't do anything. The problem is the stupid client doesn't realize it's Thanksgiving.'

'And what country does the stupid client come from?'

'Britain.'

'What are you going to do?'

Alice sighed. 'I'm going to have to go in.'

'Wait a minute,' said Toby. 'Did Don ask you or tell you?'

'He asked me.'

'Well then?'

'Don't guilt-trip me on this!' Alice said. 'I know we should stay here. But unless I go back today, there's a good chance the client will lose the deal.'

And that would be Alice's fault. Or she would believe it was her fault. And a deal falling through because it was her fault was not something Alice could countenance.

'OK,' said Toby. 'I won't guilt-trip you. I promise.'

Alice's glare softened. She reached out for Toby's hand under the covers and squeezed it. 'I'm sorry, Toby. I know you're worried about me. I just don't have any choice.'

'I know,' Toby said. He knew she really didn't want to let her family down. That was why she was upset: because, forced to choose between client and family, she was going to choose client and she hated herself for it. 'You wouldn't leave now unless you had to. And your dad and sisters will know that too. Shall we go after breakfast?'

Alice leaned over and kissed Toby on the lips. 'Thank you.'

Alice made pancakes for breakfast. American pancakes, small and round and thick, topped with thin rashers of bacon and maple syrup – real maple syrup from Vermont, brought over on the plane the day before by Brooke.

Alice's strategy was to pick off her family members one by one as they dribbled in to the kitchen. Toby could see them all question her decision, but none of them spoke their doubts out loud. They knew they couldn't argue with Alice on this one.

A look nearing pain crossed Bill's face when she told him. She said she was sorry and gave him a hug.

Not for the first time Toby resolved that when Beachwallet became a proper company with lots of staff he wouldn't make them work over Thanksgiving. Or Bastille Day. Or Yom Kippur or Eid. Hell, he would give them St George's Day off.

The front door banged and Justin appeared, followed by his wife. 'Jeez. This town is crawling with cops,' he said.

'Well, we saw two of them,' said Brooke.

'Two is crawling for Barnholt,' said Bill.

'Must be investigating Alice's pancakes,' said Maya, who was wearing disconcertingly skimpy nightwear.

'Oh and, Dad,' said Brooke. 'There's a leak in the faucet in the bathroom in the Cottage. It's nothing big, but I thought I ought to tell you.'

'Thanks, Brooke. I'll take a look.' He grinned at Toby. 'One thing about living on a submarine. You learn how to take care of leaks.'

The doorbell rang, and Rickover started barking.

'Sounds like you were right, Maya,' said Bill. 'Quiet, Ricky!' He went out to the hall and they heard the murmur of a man's voice asking if he could come in.

Bill led two men into the kitchen, Rickover inspecting their heels, and explained that it was Thanksgiving and his family were staying with him. One was a couple of years younger than Toby. He was slim and fair-haired; he wore a suit and tie, and he spoke with a slight northern accent. His accomplice was old enough to be his father and was in uniform, the paraphernalia of the modern policeman hanging off his large frame on a belt and stab-proof vest.

They introduced themselves as DC Atkinson and PC Easter.

'Can I offer you guys a pancake?' said Alice.

'They are good,' said Maya.

The younger policeman glanced at the pancakes and at Maya and seemed to like what he saw on both counts, but he shook his head.

'I'm afraid we have some bad news,' he said. 'I believe you know a gentleman by the name of Sam Bowen?' He directed the question to Bill.

'Yes,' said Bill. 'Or at least we met him for the first time yesterday. He spent Thanksgiving with us. Why? Has he had an accident?'

That must be it, thought Toby. A head-on collision on one of those treacherous bends on Norfolk roads, some idiot overtaking when they shouldn't. Maybe Sam was the idiot? That didn't seem likely.

'No, not an accident,' said the young detective. 'He was killed last night at the King William. Stabbed. We believe it was murder.'

12

Toby was stunned. They were all stunned, and showed it in different ways. Alice's face was stricken with horror. Brooke looked as if she was about to cry. Megan's jaw was open. Maya appeared confused. Only Bill seemed to take it coolly.

Sam seemed such an unlikely victim to Toby. Young, inoffensive. Toby remembered Sam talking about his girlfriend in Newcastle, his parents in Birmingham. Why would anyone want to kill him?

An answer sprang immediately to Toby's mind: it couldn't have been the conversation the day before, could it? Those questions about Bill and the *Alexander Hamilton*? No. There would be a simpler reason, and the police would find it.

'That's awful, said Bill. 'What can we tell you?'

'Do you mind if we sit down?' asked the detective.

'Sure.'

He pulled out his notebook, and looked up as Lars walked in the front door.

'What's with the cops? They're everywhere.' He stopped short as he entered the kitchen. 'What's happened?'

'The historian who came around yesterday has been murdered,' said Bill.

It seemed to take a moment for the words to register, but they did eventually. 'No shit,' said Lars.

Bill told the policemen the bare bones of how Sam had come to see him for an hour or so the afternoon before, and how he had returned for dinner. The detective jotted it all down, and then went off to report to his superiors, requesting that nobody leave, and promising that he and his colleagues would be back to ask more detailed questions.

And they were, about an hour later. The police officer in charge was a detective inspector named Creswell, a round-faced woman with pink cheeks but shadowed eyes. She and a detective sergeant interviewed Bill in the living room. The rest of them were split up between two detective constables, DC Atkinson and an older man, from his accent a local, who set themselves up in the dining room and Bill's study upstairs.

Alice was badly shaken. She fired off an email to her work saying it was unlikely she would be able to get there until that evening. Toby tried to draw her out on speculating what had happened to Sam and why, but she was having none of it. All she seemed to be worried about was getting back to London and her legal drafts.

After Bill emerged from the living room, Alice was called in.

Toby was sitting next to Justin at the kitchen table. He looked preoccupied, which was hardly surprising.

'Man, this is the kind of thing you'd expect in Chicago, not in England,' he said. 'Or at least not in a tiny village.'

'Have you been involved in a murder investigation before?' Toby asked. He thought Chicago was supposed to be a violent town, but he didn't really know what that meant.

'No,' said Justin. 'To be fair, it all depends where you live in Chicago. Our neighbourhood is pretty safe.'

'You would think Barnholt would be pretty safe.'

'Brooke is not taking this well.' She was currently being interviewed in the dining room. 'She really liked that guy Sam. And his girlfriend was pregnant!'

'Yeah,' said Toby. 'Poor guy. Poor her.' He thought of how he would feel if Alice had been murdered just before they were married. It was too horrible to contemplate. And there was the pregnancy. Was that a good thing, that part of Sam would live on? Or a bad thing? Once again, too horrible to contemplate.

But it had happened.

'I'm glad Alice is around,' Justin said. 'Brooke really looks up to her.'

'They all do,' said Toby.

'She's a strong woman,' said Justin.

'Yes,' said Toby. 'You must have known their mother?'

'I did,' said Justin. 'I spent a lot of time with the Guth family when I was a kid. After Craig died, Bill acted like a kind of godfather to me. I told you Craig was my real father?'

Toby nodded.

'They were both good to me, Bill and Donna. I discovered they helped pay for my college education, although they never admitted it. I never got on with my dad, or step-dad as he turned out to be. It wasn't really his fault – we are just different. But Bill and Donna were always there for me. She was a strong woman too.'

'I wish I had known her,' said Toby. Apart from anything else, knowing her would have helped him to understand the Guth family. To understand his wife. 'Was she anything like Alice?'

'A bit. A lot less corporate. She was sort of a middle-aged hippie. Really kind, though. Like Bill.'

'Alice misses her,' said Toby.

'So does Brooke. They all do.'

Brooke appeared, looking pale, her eyes red, and told Justin to take her place in the dining room with DC Atkinson.

Alice was still ensconced in the living room, when Toby was sent in after Justin.

DC Atkinson seemed keyed up, as well he might be. Toby imagined murder investigations were not a common occurrence in

North Norfolk. But the police officer was calm and professional and meticulous in his questioning.

He started by asking Toby about the meeting with Sam Bowen. The detective was more concerned with the way Sam and Bill had behaved than the substance of the discussion; Toby said no more than that the historian was asking about an erroneous order to launch nuclear missiles from an American submarine on a patrol during the Cold War. Toby recounted that neither Bill nor Sam seemed nervous or antagonistic, although Bill refused to be specific about events which he considered still to be secret. Sam seemed to have expected that.

Then followed minute questioning about who had been where when during the day. Toby described the comings and goings at Thanksgiving dinner and during the football game on TV afterwards, finishing with how he stayed up late for his wife returning with the shopping from King's Lynn. Here the questioning became very detailed, with Toby asked to account for Alice's arrival to the minute, which he couldn't quite do. 'About half past eleven' was the best he could manage.

Then DC Atkinson put down his pen and looked Toby straight in the eye.

'Did your wife tell you she had just been to see Sam Bowen?'

Toby hesitated. His instinct was to say 'what?', but he held back, overwhelmed by a competing instinct to protect Alice.

From what?

Atkinson was watching him. Toby realized his hesitation and obvious surprise had given the policeman his answer anyway.

'No, she didn't,' he admitted.

'Do you know why she might have wanted to see him?'

'Er. No,' said Toby. 'Perhaps she was trying to find out more about the events on the submarine?'

'Did she indicate she had more questions for Sam?'

'No,' said Toby.

'So that's just a guess?'

'Yes,' said Toby, deciding to do no more guessing. 'How do you know she met him?'

'She was seen by the landlord's wife at the pub,' said the policeman. 'And Alice confirmed it to us herself just now.'

'Oh.'

'But she didn't tell you?'

'No.'

'Why not?'

I have no bloody idea, thought Toby. 'I don't know.'

His instinct was to cover for his wife. Rationality told him there was nothing to cover for. There must be a perfectly good reason. It wasn't just that Alice was his wife; she just didn't do bad things.

'One last question. Had Alice ever mentioned Sam Bowen before today?'

'No,' said Toby, more forcefully. 'Never.'

Alice was in the kitchen, with everyone else. She looked tense.

DC Atkinson followed Toby and asked for Megan.

'Is she the last?' said Maya.

'I think so,' said Bill. 'Are you two still leaving today?' he asked Alice.

Alice didn't answer. She was staring out of the window at the bare dripping branches of the pear tree in the garden and the soggy marsh beyond. A mist was retreating across the reeds back towards the sea from where it had come.

'Alice?'

'What? Oh, yeah. We have to go this evening.'

'Alice? Can I have a word with you for a second?' Toby asked. He meant it to sound casual, but Alice's glare told him it didn't sound casual to her.

'What about?'

'You know what about.'

The others were listening and pretending not to.

She shrugged. 'OK. Let's go upstairs.'

They went up to their bedroom. Alice sat on the bed and stared at an old print on the far wall: logs floating down a broad American river. She avoided Toby's eye.

'The police said you saw Sam last night.'

'The police are correct.'

'Why didn't you tell me?'

'I don't have to tell you where I'm going.'

Toby sat on the bed next to her. 'Oh come on, Alice. You told me you were going to Tesco's. You went to see a guy who got himself murdered last night. You were hiding it from me.'

Alice was still staring at the print.

'Why?'

Alice shrugged.

'What did you talk to him about? I saw you speaking to Sam at dinner; you looked worried. Did your dad know you were seeing him? Was Sam OK when you met him?'

'Please don't ask me these questions, Toby,' Alice muttered.

'Hey, look, these are fair questions!' Toby said. 'Are you in some kind of trouble?'

Alice looked up at Toby. A tear was running down her cheek. Alice rarely cried.

'No, Toby. I'm begging you. *Please* don't ask any more questions. I've had enough of that from the police. And I'm going to have to talk to Dad. But not you. Please, not you.'

She looked miserable. A sob escaped from her chest, and then another. Toby put his arm around her and pulled her to him. 'Toby just . . . please just . . . just stick with me, OK? Don't ask questions, just be on my side.'

'All right,' Toby said, stroking her hair. 'It's all OK, Alice.'

But Toby was pretty sure it was not OK.

Toby needed to get out of the house. The police had gone. Alice was cooped up in their bedroom, trying to control her deal from afar via her iPad. Although neither of them said it, they both knew it was unlikely the police would let her go back to London that evening.

He took Rickover with him, breaking out a Polo mint for him as soon as he had shut the front door. On a previous visit Alice had told Toby Rickover loved Polos, although the vet had said they were bad for him and had banned them. Toby liked to sneak him one every now and then in a shameless bid to win the dog's affections. Which frankly wasn't that difficult.

'Hey, Toby! Mind if I join you?'

It was Lars. He looked haggard, the two creases slicing his cheeks had deepened and his yellowish moustache pointed downwards. But he managed a smile.

'Sure.'

Lars took out a cigarette and lit up. 'Where are you headed?'

'I was thinking of going down to the sea.' There was a raised path along a dyke that ran half a mile through the marsh to the dunes and the beach beyond.

'Want to check out the pub?'

'All right.'

The King William was set back from the coast road on a small green, in the middle of which stood a grey stone obelisk bearing worn ancient carvings. Pre-Christian, apparently. The pub didn't look much from the outside, a rectangular red-brick building, but inside the wood fire, the thick beams and the array of old fishing trinkets dangling from the wall created a pocket of warmth against the wind and damp of the Norfolk coast outside. Toby had been to Barnholt with Alice to visit his father-in-law a few times, and usually managed to sneak out to the pub by himself for a quick pint of Wherry. The food was pretty good too: they would all go there for a meal occasionally when no one wanted to cook.

But half the tiny green was now cordoned off with police tape. Two officers in uniform were guarding the crime scene from a TV crew who were packing equipment into a van having taken their shots of the pub, and a couple of local women who were chatting and pointing. More uniformed police officers and crime-scene technicians in forensics overalls streamed in and out of the building from an assortment of police vehicles parked by the green.

'Do you know anything more about how he was killed?' Toby asked Lars.

'I asked the detective who interviewed me. All he said was he was found dead in his room this morning. Someone had stabbed him.'

'And they have no idea who?'

'I asked that too. They said it was too early to say.'

Rickover darted out under the tape, but Toby successfully called him back, helped with the bribe of another Polo.

One of the police officers moved his gaze from the women to Toby and Lars and the dog. It made Toby feel guilty, which was ridiculous. Lars, too, seemed uncomfortable. 'Let's go down to the sea,' Toby said.

So they turned back down the lane and followed the raised path towards the sea. Moist green fields bordered by ditches and wire fences lay on one side of the dyke, while on the other a wide stretch of brown and orange saltmarsh was bisected by a winding creek of mud and grey tidal water. Ahead stretched a wall of grass-covered humps of sand. The fields were empty of animals at this time of year, save for a powerful red bull and his black-and-white consort, chewing cud amicably side by side.

Lars seemed tense and uncommunicative, but he also appeared glad of Toby's company.

'Do you think the murder had anything to do with what Sam was working on?' Toby asked.

'You mean the *Hamilton*? No,' said Lars. 'Definitely not.'

It struck Toby that that was wishful thinking. 'Are you sure? It seems a bit of a coincidence. He comes here asking questions about something that's been hushed up for thirty-five years and then he is killed?'

'That's just what it is,' said Lars. 'A coincidence. Maybe it was a jealous husband? Or his girlfriend? He mentioned a girlfriend. Maybe she just discovered something.'

'They'd just got engaged!' said Toby. 'That would be a strange time to kill your boyfriend. Plus, she's pregnant, the poor woman.' Toby winced as he thought of Sam's girlfriend – Jazz was her name, he remembered. Her life together with Sam shattered. A baby to bring up by herself, without the man who had helped make it.

'OK.' Lars realized he had gone too far with the girlfriend, but he wasn't going to give up entirely. 'Perhaps it was a serial killer. You have those in England, right?'

'I haven't read of any other murders like that around here.'

'They've got to start somewhere.'

Lars was floundering, which made Toby even more convinced that Sam's murder was related to the submarine. And then there was Alice. 'Did the police mention Alice?'

'You mean her seeing Sam last night? Yes, they did. I didn't know anything about it; I thought she had gone to the grocery store.'

'Yeah, that's what I thought,' said Toby.

'So you don't know what she spoke to Sam about?' Lars said. 'Did she tell you?'

'No. But my guess is it's about what happened on that submarine.'

'Weird she won't tell you?' Lars said. Toby thought it was weird, but he didn't like Lars's question, and so he didn't answer it.

It was quiet on the dyke. Back inland, a volley of distant shotguns popped. Down on the mud flats a curlew cried, and a stand of tall brown bulrushes whispered in the breeze as they bowed and curtsied to the ditch running along the side of the path. A squadron of twenty or so geese honked gently as they patrolled overhead in an elegant V formation.

A lonely figure marched towards them on the raised path, carrying a tripod on his shoulder: a moustachioed birdwatcher, who exchanged nods and grunts with them as they eventually passed each other.

'Why did you come over to England, Lars?' Toby asked.

'To see my old friend, Bill. I told you.'

'But why now? Did it have something to do with Sam Bowen? You said he had visited you in America?'

Lars looked for a moment that he was about to claim it was another coincidence, but he thought better of it. 'It's true I did want to see Bill again. But it's also true that Sam's questions made me think of our time in the Navy together.'

'Is what he said accurate?' Toby asked. 'About the order to launch your missiles?'

'Hey. You heard Bill. It's Classified.'

'But is he on the right track?'

'Yeah. He's on the right track.'

Toby ran through the conversation with Sam in his mind. 'Sam said something about how it was impossible for him to talk to the captain of the submarine. It sounded like the captain was dead.'

'He is,' said Lars.

'Was that related to the near launch?'

Lars hesitated before replying. 'In a manner of speaking.'

'Because I wondered if that was how Bill "persuaded" the captain to change his mind. By killing him. I don't know how nuclear submarines work, but presumably the captain has to authorize a launch, and if he's dead . . .'

'You're just guessing,' said Lars, avoiding Toby's eye.

'I am, but am I right?'

'Toby. You're fishing and I'm not going to bite. I'm just not going to. You got that?'

'All right,' said Toby. 'I've got it.' He *was* just guessing, but he was pretty sure he was guessing correctly.

They walked on.

'Do you mind if I ask you what it was like?' Toby asked. 'To know you had come so close to blowing up the world?'

'No, that's OK,' said Lars. 'It kind of screws you up, is the truth. It screwed up all of us. All of us on the submarine. Especially those of us who were involved in the argument whether to launch: me, Bill, the XO. I mean, if it had gone the other way . . .'

'But it didn't.'

'No, it didn't. And that's a good thing, and you would think that would be enough. You'd think we could just forget it and get on with our lives. But . . .' Lars took a deep breath. 'We can't.'

Toby waited to see whether Lars would volunteer more, but he had fallen silent.

They had reached the sand dunes, and cut through them on a twisting path of wooden boards to the narrow beach. The tide was high, and they could only see fifty yards or so out to sea, before the grey water merged into white fog. The air was damp and salty.

The beach was empty, save for a green fibreglass boat, little more than a tub, that was hauled up to the edge of the sand against the dunes a few hundred yards away.

Out here, they were quite alone, out of sight of the village or even the marsh. Just sand and sea merging into the milky sky.

'There must be more to it than Bill let on,' said Toby. 'You wouldn't have come all this way if there wasn't more.'

Lars glanced at Toby and then stared out into the fog.

'Oh yeah,' he said. 'There's more to it. A lot more.'

13

Alice was glad that when she was finally let out of the interview with the detective inspector, Toby was nowhere to be seen. She needed some time by herself. She needed to think.

She hurried upstairs to their bedroom and shut the door firmly behind her. She picked up her iPad, stared at one of the half dozen draft documents she was supposed to be working on, and then tossed it on to the bed. Who was she kidding?

She looked around the room, her room. It was old: the floor was uneven, sloping upwards on one side, toward the window. She had been a student when her parents had bought the place, and scraps of her childhood had survived in that room: in the small bookshelf, her complete set of Harry Potter supported Virginia Woolf on one side and *The Master and Margarita* on the other. A poster from a 2010 Taylor Swift concert faced the old photograph of the loggers on the Susquehanna that had followed her from bedroom to bedroom all over the world.

She moved over to the window and gazed out at the marsh. Two figures and a dog were making their way along the dyke and had nearly reached the dunes. That must be Toby, Rickover and someone else: it looked like Uncle Lars.

She hoped Toby would be away for a while. She felt badly about snapping at him earlier when he had asked her about seeing Sam. It had been a fair question. It was going to be hard to face him, but she would have to. She needed to rely on him, to trust him to stick with her even though she had lied to him.

She had as good as lied to the police as well; she certainly hadn't told them the whole truth.

What the hell should she do now?

She couldn't ask her dad.

She wished her mother was still around. She would know. Her mother was the wisest person Alice had met. Alice liked to think that a lot of that wisdom had rubbed off on her, her daughter.

They had been very close. Mom had been close to all the daughters, but in different ways. Alice was the oldest, and the one that their mother had relied on most, especially in those final months. It didn't seem so at the time, but in fact it had been fortunate that Mom had been diagnosed just as Alice was in her final months at law school. She had still managed to pass her exams, and the timing meant she could fly over to England right afterwards to spend the last months of her mother's life with her while she studied for the New York bar. There were only three of these: the cancer had been advanced when it was diagnosed.

Alice had helped her father look after her mother and had supported him in his dark moments. She had comforted her sisters: Brooke was at graduate school in Chicago, Megan was a sophomore at college and Maya still at her private girls' school in London. She had spent a lot of time with her mother, most of it up here in Barnholt, walking with her while she could still walk, reading to her. And talking to her.

Mom had more or less explicitly laid the burden of looking after Bill and the other girls on Alice, knowing all the time that it was a burden Alice would be happy to shoulder.

And she had told Alice other things.

One morning, towards the end, when her mother was barely strong enough to get in the car, Alice had driven her along the coast to a spot where it was possible to park on a hard concrete apron right by a creek. The place was popular with boaters of all kinds: kayaks, dinghies, sailing boats, fishing boats and skiffs bobbed on the incoming tide, ready to be taken the half mile through the marshes to the sea.

Alice had parked high up on the concrete, near the sea wall, but there were three cars parked close to the creek, one of which was an expensive electric-blue Jaguar. She and her mother spent a couple of hours just sitting in the car together, watching the boats being lifted from the muddy banks of the creek by the incoming tide, and the sea creep over the concrete towards the wheels of the parked cars. The two old bangers were quickly moved, but the Jaguar seemed to have been abandoned as the water lapped at its tyres.

Alice had a desire to do something to save the vehicle – what, she wasn't sure – but her mother was watching transfixed, a wicked half-smile on her face. So Alice did nothing. And in their mutual helplessness against the relentless tide, she felt a kind of mutual strength. She knew her mother felt it too.

The water had just about reached the underside of the chassis, when they heard loud, deep shouts, and a large figure in dark red trousers splashed through the water to his Jag, cursing. The vehicle started, and he reversed off the concrete in a thick spray of seawater.

Donna smiled at her daughter. 'Oh well,' she said, with a chuckle.

'We had better move soon,' said Alice. The water was still a dozen or so yards away from their car, but it was getting closer.

'Wait a moment, sweetie,' her mother had said. 'There are some things I ought to explain. About Dad and me. Things somebody should know, and I'm sure Dad will never tell you.'

*

Two weeks later, the end had come. Her mother's ashes were now resting in St Peter's churchyard beneath an ancient yew tree, barely a hundred yards away from Pear Tree Cottage.

Alice had been ready. It had felt good to help her father to sort through her mother's stuff, to help him administer the estate, to comfort her sisters, to make sure that the Guth family remained strong together.

She had passed the bar exam and joined a New York law firm. As soon as she could, she had secured a transfer to their London office so she could be near her father. And there she had met Toby. Tall, dark, with warm brown eyes that seemed to understand her immediately, she had fallen for him. Hard.

Alice was good under pressure, she thrived under pressure. The challenge of being a good lawyer, a good wife, a good daughter and a good sister all at the same time stretched her, but she liked it that way. And one day, perhaps one day quite soon, she would be a good mother as well.

But this? This was stretching even her to breaking point.

Did she have a breaking point? Everyone had a breaking point. So where was hers?

She didn't know, and she was determined not to find out.

'OK, Mom,' she said out loud, to the marsh. 'I can do this.'

14

Brooke, Megan and Justin were hanging out in the kitchen when Toby and Lars returned.

'Want some coffee?' Megan asked.

'Thanks,' said Toby, accepting a cup. 'Where's Alice?'

'Upstairs,' said Megan. 'Working on her big deal, I guess. I don't know how she can think about that with all this going on.'

'Alice can focus,' said Toby. Although he agreed with Megan.

'Hey, Lars,' said Justin. There was an ominous tone to his voice that Toby hadn't heard before; Justin was usually a model of politeness. He was sitting upright at the kitchen table, arms crossed, his shirt pulled tight over his bulging chest. 'I just talked to Vicky on the phone.'

'Who's Vicky?' said Lars.

'You know who Vicky is,' said Justin coolly. 'Craig's sister. My aunt.'

'Oh yeah, yeah. Vicky,' said Lars. 'I know.' He sat down at the kitchen table opposite Justin. Brooke was seated next to her husband looking hunched and miserable, gnawing at her thumb.

'Can I have some of that coffee, Megan?' Lars asked.

'Sure,' said Megan, pouring him a cup.

'I called Mom first,' said Justin. 'To tell her what had happened to Sam Bowen. She said Sam had come to visit her in New London but she hadn't told him anything. Apart from to speak to Craig's sister Vicky. So I called Vicky in New Jersey. She was really upset that Sam had been murdered.'

'Of course she was,' said Lars.

'She told me what she had told him.'

'Told him?'

'Yes. About that last patrol. And Craig.' Justin was staring directly at Lars as he spoke.

'Oh.' Lars shifted uncomfortably in his chair.

'You told Vicky right after the patrol that my father's death wasn't an accident. You said he was killed.'

'What? Poor Vicky must be confused. I never said that.'

'She says you did.' Justin's voice had become quieter, but they could all feel the anger. 'She says you told her exactly that: "Craig was killed."'

Lars's discomfort increased. 'Like I told you, she got confused. It was late one night. We had both been drinking, we were both upset about Craig. "Craig was killed" doesn't mean someone killed him. She just got it wrong, is all.'

'She said you wouldn't tell her what really happened.'

Lars sighed. 'I did tell her what really happened. It was an emergency drill and Craig was sliding down one of those metal ladders on submarines. They're steep, you hold on to the railings on either side, and slip down. People do it all the time, they never fall. Never. But Craig must have caught his foot in a step or something, because he tumbled and hit his head. He was out cold for an hour at least. We were worried, but then he came round. And a couple of days later he got a headache, lay down and just died.' Lars took a deep breath. 'Right there. Just died.'

Lars stared at Justin. 'They said afterward it was bleeding in the brain caused by the fall. But I told Vicky all that.'

'And she didn't believe you?'

Lars rubbed his moustache. 'She thought I'd said it wasn't an accident. Wait! She told Sam Bowen that, didn't she?'

'Yes, she did,' said Justin. 'And he had told her about the false launch order. She thinks the two are related.'

Lars snorted. 'So that's why Sam asked about Craig's accident? Bill explained it all to him. They can't have been related. The argument about whether to launch the missiles took place in the control room. Craig was in the missile control centre. It's a whole different department. It's on a different level.'

'Were you there?' Justin asked. 'In the control room? When the order came in?'

'Yes, I was,' said Lars. 'I decoded it. With Bill.'

'What happened?' said Justin.

Lars hesitated. 'I can't tell you, Justin. I'm sorry but I really can't tell you. All I can say is your father wasn't involved.'

'What is this?' said Justin, his voice rising for the first time. 'You left the Navy decades ago. The Cold War is finished. Which enemies of ours are going to care about what happened on that submarine? Arab terrorists? The Taliban? Just tell me! Tell me what happened to my father!'

Brooke moved her hand to clasp her husband's but he flicked it away. He looked angry and he looked determined.

'What about you, Toby? Did you hear Sam Bowen say anything about my father's death?'

'No, Justin. Only what Lars just told you.'

Justin seemed on the brink of accusing Toby of being part of whatever cover-up he imagined was going on, but he thought better of it.

'Why does nobody ever tell me the truth?' he said, his voice quiet again. 'It took me thirteen years to discover that Craig was my real father. And now you are hiding from me how he died.' He glared at Lars as he said this, but also at Megan and Brooke as representatives of the Guth family. Toby suspected his real anger was directed at Bill.

'I'm out of here.' Shaking his head, he got up and left the room. A moment later the front door banged and they saw him head out to the cottage next door. With a look of contempt at Lars, Brooke hurried after him.

'Well this is a fun Thanksgiving, huh?' said Megan, now left alone with Toby in the kitchen.

Toby grinned. 'The turkey was good.'

'That's true. My sister is a good cook.'

'Your sister is a very good cook.'

Toby sat with Megan in companionable silence, staring at his coffee. His phone chirped and he checked it. He looked up and saw her watching him, a long dark curl hanging over her glasses. She looked very little like her sisters. She was shorter than them, darker, less leggy. Her eyes were almost black, compared to Alice's grey, or Maya and Brooke's clear blue. But she had the Guth sisters' chin, of course.

'Do you know what happened on that submarine?' he asked.

'Not really,' said Megan. 'No more than you do. Mom told us all before she died, which was, like, seven years ago now. She spoke with us one by one. She had cancer, the treatment hadn't worked and we knew it was terminal. She said Dad would never tell us himself, but she wanted us to know that he had stopped his captain blowing up the world. She just said that the submarine had received orders to launch their missiles, that the captain of the ship was about to obey them and Dad stopped him.'

'She didn't say how?' Toby asked. 'Because I was wondering whether your father . . . ' He hesitated. 'Whether your father might have stopped him permanently.'

'What, you mean killed him?' said Megan.

Toby nodded. 'It's just a guess. But if the captain was dead, presumably he couldn't order the missile launch. And Sam did imply that the captain was no longer around.'

Megan raised her eyebrows. 'You realize that's my dad you're accusing of killing someone? Your father-in-law?' She seemed surprised rather than offended.

'Yeah, I'm sorry. I have no proof. It's just a guess. Did your mother say anything about it?'

'A wild guess,' said Megan. 'And one I wouldn't share with Alice if I were you. No. Mom gave me no details. But she did say we weren't to tell anyone, and we weren't to let on to Dad that we knew. She told us we could tell our own children eventually. Obviously we talked about it among ourselves. We were amazed and really proud, which is of course why Mom told us.'

'But now Bill knows you know?'

'Yeah. That was my fault. Naturally. He and I were having a fight. I think it was about me dropping out of college to be with my boyfriend – what a bad idea *that* was – and I said something dumb like: "Just because you stopped us all from getting blown up, doesn't mean you get to decide what we do with our lives." Oops.'

'He wasn't pleased?'

'No. You've seen how seriously he takes that Classified crap – as if it still mattered. But to Dad it does. He signed up to serve his country when he was eighteen and, as far as he's concerned, he's never going to stop doing it, however dumb it may be.'

She winced at the memory. 'The worst bit was he thought Mom had betrayed him. But after a while I think he realized it was a good thing. It was like a bond between us: our own family secret. And we did a pretty good job of keeping it. I haven't told anyone. Neither has Maya, I don't think. And Alice didn't tell you, did she?'

'No. But she seemed pleased when Bill asked me to join him with Sam.'

Megan smiled. 'That was his way of cutting you in, without him or Alice having to tell you directly. That's so typical. Of both of them.'

'Brooke told Justin, though, didn't she?'

'Yes. Brooke tells Justin everything.'

'That has something to be said for it,' said Toby.

'Maybe. It pissed the rest of us off. But we figured Brooke felt bad about Craig being Justin's father and no one telling him. You heard Justin just now, didn't you?'

'Yes. What was that all about?'

'Justin's mom Maria was married to Craig. Then, soon after Craig died, she married a guy called Tony Opizzi. Justin was born, and everyone assumed he was Tony's son. Justin's older than us, but we used to see him a lot when we were kids. Dad's his godfather, and he used to come to stay with us when we were living in Europe; he even went on vacation with us a couple of times. We all thought he was great: the big brother we never had.

'Anyway, as Justin got a little older he started looking a lot like Craig. I mean, a *lot* like him. Mom and Dad noticed. Justin's mom noticed and Tony noticed; but they probably knew right from the beginning. Obviously they didn't tell us kids. Or Justin. Then Alice and Justin were looking at that photo of Dad and Uncle Lars and Craig in the living room. We were living in England at the time, in Cobham; Justin was about sixteen and Alice must have been ten. And Alice was like: "Hey, Justin, this guy Craig looks just like you." And Justin figured it out.'

Toby winced.

'Yeah. Justin lost it. And you know what? He was right: they should have told him. After that, he stopped coming to visit us. We didn't see him until a few years ago when Brooke went to grad school in Chicago and hooked up with him there. I think she always had a thing for him. She's seven years younger, but that matters a lot less when you're twenty-four than when you're nine. We all worshipped him, even Maya who was only little. He played with her all the time and she loved it.'

'All of you? Even Alice?'

Megan's dark eyes flashed and she smiled. 'Especially Alice.'

Toby opened the bedroom door with some trepidation. Alice was sitting on the bed, her arms wrapped around her bunched-up knees. Her face was flushed but there were no tears. 'Oh, Toby,' she said.

Toby closed the door and hopped on to the bed next to her.

'Toby, you're not going to ask me any questions, are you?'

'No, Alice. No I'm not.'

Alice gave everyone, even her family – especially her family – the impression of extreme competence, of absolute self-confidence, of an ability to deal with any crisis. But Toby knew that underneath she was just as vulnerable and insecure as anyone else. More so. She had spent her girlhood, her adolescence, her adulthood working to hide this from everyone. But Toby knew. It was their secret.

'Come here.' Toby pulled her towards him. After a minute or so, she looked up and kissed him, softly at first and then with more urgency. Toby's groin knew what was coming next before his brain did, and within a minute they were naked and entwined on the bed, moving against each other with just enough restraint not to be heard downstairs. But then the bed creaked and Alice let out a little cry.

Afterwards, he lay on top of her, spent, resting his weight on his elbows, protecting her.

She smiled up at him.

'What's that?' she said.

Toby raised his head. A gentle murmuring seeped into the bedroom from the marshes outside.

'I don't know.'

'I think it's the geese.'

The murmur became a clamour. They both climbed out of bed and went to the window. The sun had just set, and the sky above the marshes to the west was on fire, as red and gold burnished the underbelly of dark clouds. Beneath these, a swirl of hundreds of long black shapes with sweeping wings beat their way northwards towards the sea. They were coming in waves of V formations, which elegantly shifted shape as if in response to a set of complex commands or a mysterious pre-arranged routine.

Geese. Hundreds of them. No, thousands. Making a hell of a racket.

'They've come from the fields inland and they're headed back out to the mudflats to roost,' said Alice.

'They're magnificent.'

'Aren't they?'

Still they kept coming. Alice and Toby watched as the fire in the western sky slowly burnt itself out and darkness took over. The last V had just passed overhead when two pairs of headlights approached the house along the lane outside. Two cars pulled up, one with police markings and the other a silver Ford Fiesta, presumably belonging to a detective.

'Oh, shit,' said Alice as she drew back from the window and picked up her clothes.

'They may not want to speak to you,' Toby said.

'I think they probably will,' said Alice, as she wriggled into her jeans.

Toby pulled on his own clothes and followed his wife downstairs. DC Atkinson and two other police officers were waiting for them in the hall, with Bill. Megan was watching from the kitchen door.

The detective took a step towards the staircase, his expression grave.

'Alice Rosser. You are under arrest on suspicion of the murder of Sam Bowen.'

15

September 1983, Groton, Connecticut

Craig, Lars and I met Vicky, Kathleen and Donna at the New London Union Station in my old 1975 Mustang.

I had phoned Donna the evening after our date in Little Italy and the conversation had gone well. We had spoken several times and then I received a wonderful letter from her: warm, witty, frank. I had thought I was not much of a letter writer, but my reply had gone better than I had expected. I told her about life on the base, and about Craig's mood swings between despair over Maria and a determination to get very drunk. She told me about the woman at the desk next to hers who had taken the day off because she was too embarrassed to show up for work with a giant spot on her nose, and the old guy who liked to declaim filthy Restoration poetry to her on the steps of her apartment building. It had taken her some time to identify the poems, but now she was sure they were by the Earl of Rochester.

Then she wrote me a six-page letter about her brother. She had just received a letter from him; the first for three years. He was living in the woods somewhere in the Upper Peninsula of Michigan. He said he was 'getting his shit together' and had gotten a job at a hotel as a bartender for the summer. I wrote her about my dad's newspaper, how proud I was of it, and how I thought maybe the real reason I hadn't taken up journalism was that I couldn't do it justice. I asked her for more about her brother.

She said he had been really smart in high school. His teachers encouraged him to apply to an Ivy League college, but he had decided not to defer his Vietnam draft. He had gone; he had come back; he had changed for ever. He had refused to speak about it to her or to anyone else, except for once, when he was drunk and in tears. He had told her it wasn't what he had suffered in Vietnam, or even what he had seen that screwed him up, it was what he had done. He wouldn't say what that was and Donna wouldn't ask him.

She didn't have to say that that was what had made her a pacifist, but I knew she wanted to explain it to me, that she wanted me to understand. I took that to mean she cared about my opinion of her, and that pleased me. But I couldn't help thinking about the guy in Battery Park I had tried to give ten dollars to.

The phone calls were brief and light; it was always good to hear her voice. The letters were the real communication between us.

I went down to New York to stay for the weekend with Donna in her tiny studio apartment in the East Village. I don't know whether it was the letters, or what it was, but it seemed like we knew each other really well, even though this was only the third time we had met. I knew her and yet there was so much I wanted to find out. We talked and talked. I had a lot I wanted to tell, a lot I wanted to hear.

We avoided discussing nuclear weapons directly, or nuclear power in general, but it was obvious she had been an active protester in college, and still was. She was upset about South Africa too, and apartheid; she wanted the big multinational firms to divest from the country. I hadn't really given the subject much thought before, but she persuaded me.

Of course, we didn't just talk. We fooled around. A lot.

She announced that she, Kathleen and Vicky had decided to come up to Groton for the following weekend. Being married, Craig had his own small house off base, and their idea was that the women would stay there with him. There must be plenty of room now Maria had moved out.

I wasn't so sure. I came up with a plan.

Donna smiled when she saw me at the train station and she kissed me, but unlike the week before in New York, I sensed she didn't quite share my excitement. It worried me for an instant, then I decided to ignore it. At least she had left the little anti-nuclear buttons off her denim jacket for her visit to a naval base.

The New London Submarine Base wasn't in New London at all, but over the bridge on the opposite side of the Thames River from that port, a couple of miles north of the town of Groton. Craig's house was in a large development of small cookie-cutter cream-and-light blue dwellings plopped down on to acres of sun-browned mown grass just a half mile away. It might have seemed bland and suburban, but actually the place had a warm, friendly, secure feel to it. There were kids and signs of kids everywhere: swings, bikes, small trampolines. It was a little patch of suburban America that the men who lived half their lives there were serving to protect when they were away at sea: the loyal wives waiting to greet their husbands after their tour, the toddlers running to Dad.

Maria had left Craig a single man among happy families, and he hated it. But his house was a good place for Lars, him and me to bring a case of beer and drink it.

Lars joined us. It was a warm September day, in the seventies, and Craig poured the girls iced tea, and a beer for himself. Lars and I stuck to the iced tea.

'This is a great place!' said Kathleen with credible politeness.

'It's a little small,' said Vicky.

'Yeah. It's probably too small for the three of you,' said Craig. 'But Bill has a solution.'

Donna looked at me, eyebrows raised, half-smile poised.

'Have you ever been to Mystic, Donna?' Mystic was the next town up the coast, an old port and shipbuilding centre.

'No,' she said.

'I've booked us a night at an inn there. Right in the middle of town. You know, to make space here for the others.'

Vicky laughed. 'Can't you take me as well?'

For a second, Donna's half-smile froze. Then she grinned. 'That sounds great.'

We had lunch at Craig's house, tuna-melt sandwiches – his specialty – and then Donna and I set off for Mystic, which was only ten miles away.

'Are you OK with this?' I asked as we hit the highway just outside the development. 'It's just I wanted to spend some time alone with you. And it's a nice inn.'

Donna smiled warmly. 'Of course I'm OK with this,' she said, and she leaned over to kiss my cheek. 'I said it's a great idea.' She put her hand on my leg. She had sensed my apprehension. 'I meant that.'

Donna was as charmed by Mystic as I hoped she would be. The inn I had booked was right by the river in the centre of the small town, next to an old iron drawbridge that was periodically raised in a grand salute to let a yacht pass through on its way out into Long Island Sound.

We found a place for dinner with a terrace overlooking the water.

In the nineteenth century, the port had been a thriving centre of New England industry, and many of the old buildings and ships still survived. On one side of the river they were preserved in a museum, exactly as they would have looked over a century before. On the other, they gleamed in white clapboard, with immaculate lawns and picket fences beneath a green wooded ridge.

One house in particular caught my eye. It was slightly bigger than the others, stuck out on a point in the river. I wondered who owned it. A current captain of industry, probably, or finance. Maybe it was inherited. I wondered if I would ever own a house like that. I couldn't quite see how, unless I became an admiral. I had no idea how much admirals earned or houses like that cost, but it seemed like a suitable house for an admiral.

'What are you looking at?' Donna asked.

'I was looking at that house,' I said, pointing to it. 'And wondering whether I could ever own one like it.'

'Dream on,' said Donna. 'Where would you get that kind of money? Unless you became a pirate? You know, a kind of modern-day John Paul Jones, sneaking up on galleons in your submarine.'

'He wasn't a pirate,' I said. 'He was a hero of the US Navy. I could become an admiral one day, I guess. An admiral should be able to live in a house like that.'

Donna's eyes widened. 'An admiral? That's ambitious.'

I shrugged. I was tempted to apply modesty, and I normally would have done, but with Donna I felt an urge to be honest. Honest with myself as much as with her.

'I guess I am. Secretly. I really like the Navy. And I'm a pretty good naval officer. Our commanding officer is a guy called Ray Driscoll. He has this air of calm about him that makes you trust him, makes you want to please him. Makes you want to do the right thing for him and for your crew. I admire him. And I think I could do what he does just as well as him.'

For a moment, I thought Donna was going to tease me, but she smiled. 'I can see that. You'd be good at it.'

'Of course, being an admiral is different to commanding a submarine. Administration. Politics. But I like to think I can do that too. So I guess I *am* ambitious. What about you?'

'Me? God, I don't know.' Donna sipped her wine. 'I'd like to make the world just a little bit better, but that turns out to be really hard. You'd think the UN Development Program would be able to do that. All those people. All that money. The big shiny offices. All those staplers.' She smiled. 'But sometimes I wonder how much it achieves. Whether its purpose isn't just to make people like me feel good about themselves.'

'They must achieve something, surely?'

'Oh they do, I guess. But I have this friend who was at Swarthmore with me. He wanted to do the same thing as me, make the world a better place. He's doing a master's in Agriculture. He says it's all about digging one well at a time. He's right.'

A couple of sculls glided along the calm evening water, their oars flowing in an easy rhythm. It was almost dark. The restaurant was full now, conversation a relaxed murmur as the diners enjoyed the dusk.

Donna grinned and reached across to take my hand. 'Hey. This is a lovely place. I'm glad you brought me here.'

'So am I.'

'Did you ever do that?' Donna asked. 'Row? It looks fun. Especially on an evening like tonight.'

'I did it for a couple of years when I was a kid. It's hard work. There was a river that flowed right by our house.'

'Which one was that?'

'The Susquehanna.'

'Wait. Lancaster County. Isn't that near Three Mile Island?'

'About fifteen miles away. Next county down the river.'

'So that's why you give off that faint glow in the dark. And I thought it was the submarine.'

'OK, OK,' I said. 'That was not the nuclear industry's greatest moment.' I braced myself for a broadside. After that first night, we had successfully managed to avoid quarrelling about things nuclear, but Three Mile Island was the site of the worst nuclear accident in US history, and it had only happened three years before.

'I've been there, you know?' Donna said. 'Three Mile Island.'

'Driving a uranium delivery truck?'

'Chaining myself to a fence. And I've been to Groton before. A couple of years ago.'

'Two years ago? The launch of the *Corpus Christi*?'

A pack of demonstrators had tried to disrupt the launch of a nuclear submarine from the General Dynamics boatyard in Groton itself, a few miles downriver from the sub base.

'That's the one.'

'Were you arrested?'

'Not that time.'

I was tempted to ask what time Donna *had* been arrested, but decided against it.

She was looking at me, quizzically.

'What is it?' I said.

'I know we've been careful to avoid the subject of your job…'

'But?'

'But. I've been thinking about it. I get that you genuinely believe in nuclear deterrence. I know you've thought a lot about it, and I respect that. But if you were ordered to press the button or whatever you do on a submarine, would you really do it?'

'Absolutely,' I said. 'Unless everyone knows that people like me will do what they are ordered to do, then the deterrence won't work. War will become *more* likely not less.'

'OK. I get that. Or I get that you believe that. But by that stage, a major nuclear war will have started and the planet will be over. And you would want to play a part in that?'

'You're right, I have thought about it,' I said. 'The truth is, on the submarine we would never know for sure that there was a full nuclear exchange going on. It's possible that there is a limited nuclear war. Just a few missiles. Or the United States is firing first.'

105

'And that's OK? It sounds worse, if anything.'

'No. No, it's not OK at all. But it's not my job to think about that. Other people have that job, in particular the president, who is elected by the people. It's my job to follow orders. Nothing will work as it should unless people like me follow orders.'

Donna didn't look convinced. But I got the impression she was trying to understand me as much as convert me.

'What about an accident? An accidental launch?'

'That couldn't happen. There are so many measures in place to make sure that couldn't happen.'

'They said that about Three Mile Island, didn't they? They thought they had safety procedures in place for every eventuality. But then a combination of things went wrong: a filter got blocked, a valve got stuck, an operator missed a warning light and manually overrode the automatic emergency cooling system. They hadn't prepared for that particular combination. And the darn thing nearly went into meltdown.'

She had a point about Three Mile Island, and she had clearly taken the trouble to study the details, as had I. That accident had shaken me, and some of the others. Especially Lars. He hadn't liked the thought that so many smart people could be so stupid.

'The Navy is much more thorough,' I said. But even as I said it I wasn't entirely sure I believed it.

'So what if the captain goes crazy and decides to take out Russia by himself and orders the launch of his missiles?'

'We have procedures to deal with that,' I said.

'What are they?'

'I can't tell you but, believe me, a captain couldn't launch missiles on his own authority.'

'Are you sure about that?'

'Certain.' Unless everyone heard the XO repeat the captain's instructions, the crew wouldn't obey his orders. And then the weapons officer had to extract the firing trigger from a safe to which only he knew the combination, so the captain and XO together couldn't order a launch. A rogue captain was something the Navy had prepared for and indeed something the crew trained for.

'What if the order comes from some Dr Strangelove wireless operator pretending he got it from the president?'

'They've thought of that too.' Authentication codes would ensure any launch order was properly authorized.

'OK. So they've thought of the obvious stuff. But what about the stuff they haven't thought about? The non-obvious stuff? Or the combinations of the obvious stuff? Combinations like Three Mile Island.'

'Donna. There are so many checks and counter-checks, an accidental launch just couldn't happen. Believe me, it just couldn't.'

Donna paused, thinking it through. Her logical thought process was unnerving me more than emotional idealism would have done. 'All right. But let's say your submarine receives an order to launch its missiles, and you personally are not sure about it. You think there might be something wrong. What do you do then? Do you follow orders? Do you press the button? Or do you use your common sense and refuse?'

'That wouldn't happen,' I said.

Donna raised her eyebrows.

'That wouldn't happen.' And then I repeated it again to myself.

16

Late the next morning, we took a walk along the river through the old buildings and the schooners. We had swiftly recovered from the 'following orders' conversation, and it had been a great evening. A great night.

'You know we're flying out to Scotland at the end of the week?' I said. 'I usually look forward to the patrols, it's what it's all about after all, but I'm not so sure this time.'

I glanced at Donna. Maybe I was looking for some agreement from her. No, I was definitely looking for some agreement from her. But she didn't say anything.

'You're a great letter writer, you know that?' I said.

Donna murmured her assent, head down.

'Well, they have this thing called a familygram,' I said. 'Obviously it's impossible to receive mail when we are out at sea, but they do let us have these familygrams. They are like telegrams: you can send eight per patrol, you are only allowed forty words, and they get censored. So they are not private. But the crew all love getting them.'

Nothing from Donna.

'Would you send me some?'

I had been looking forward to asking Donna, had been looking forward to her joking about what she would put in them, and then agreeing. All the single guys on the submarines were jealous of those with wives or girlfriends. A familygram from your mom was nice to get, but not quite the same.

Suddenly, I wasn't sure what she would say.

'Donna?'

She stopped. We were right by the water, a few feet from one of the old vessels that had been built in a Mystic shipyard, a dignified three-masted bark.

She looked at me. 'I've been thinking.'

Oh, no, I thought. Not that. Shit. Shit, shit, shit! Don't think! I wanted to shout.

But she had been thinking.

'You saw what happened to Craig. And there was that other officer on your ship, you told me about, the one who tried to kill himself because his girlfriend left him?'

That was the previous executive officer. His wife had walked out on him a year before and he hadn't handled it well.

'Yes, but he had other problems. Drugs.' He had been taken off the boat and replaced with a new XO, Lieutenant Commander Robinson. The crew had felt sorry for him but, in truth, nobody had liked him; Robinson seemed a whole lot better.

'You have to admit, submarines are not great for relationships, are they? Am I wrong?'

I took a deep breath. 'No, you're not wrong. But this relationship has just started. We have to give it a chance.' I felt everything crashing down around me.

I reached for her hand. 'I meant to tell you this last night. I think I love you. No, I *do* love you. I'm sure of it.'

There were tears in Donna's eyes. 'And I can feel myself falling in love with you. That's the problem. That's the whole problem. If this was just a casual relationship, just sex and a few laughs, it would be great. But it's more than that.'

'Is it the nuclear thing? Is it that you can't fall in love with a guy who's serving his country?'

'Partly. Maybe. But it's mostly I don't want to fall in love with a guy who spends half his life away from me.'

Did she want me to give up the Navy? Was that what she was asking me to do? Would I do it? The Navy meant everything to me. But so did Donna.

'And no, I'm not asking you to give up submarines for me. We haven't got to that stage yet. And we should never get to that stage.'

I just looked at her. I didn't know what to say. 'When did you decide this?'

'A couple of days ago. I thought I should tell you face to face rather than writing a letter. I was going to spit it out immediately and get the next train back to New York. But then you said you had booked the inn, and you looked so excited about it, and I couldn't bear to let you down and I wanted to be with you really badly.' A tear was running down her cheek. 'I should have told you yesterday.'

'No you shouldn't,' I said. 'If we are only ever going to have a few days together, I wouldn't want to have missed one of them. Especially this one.'

My brain was racing. What could I say to stop her? What could I do? Demonstrating how much she meant to me wouldn't do it. That was the whole problem.

The worst thing was, I knew what she was saying. I almost agreed with her. She was right. You had to be an idiot to go out with a submariner.

And whatever else she was, Donna was not an idiot. Neither was she one to change her mind.

I looked at her beautiful, tear-stained face.

'OK.'

What else could I have said?

17

Friday 29 November 2019, Norfolk

The police didn't just take Alice; they took Bill and Lars as well. But not Toby. They refused to take Toby.

Bill and Lars were not under arrest; the police wanted to ask them some more questions and they wanted to do it at the station.

Serious questions then.

And they had a warrant to search Alice's belongings and to take away her laptop, iPad and phone.

Toby was angry the police wouldn't take him too. He was angry they had arrested Alice. He was angry that they were stupid enough to think Alice had killed anyone. And he was angry with Bill for letting them arrest her. He was sure there were things that Bill could tell them that would get Alice off the hook.

But he held it all in, at least until they were all out of the house. He had watched as two officers went through Alice's clothes and her briefcase, and didn't object when they rummaged through his own underwear mixed with hers. Being angry wouldn't help; the police wouldn't release a murder suspect just because her husband was angry.

At last they were gone. He, Maya and Megan stared out of the kitchen window at their departing car.

'What a bunch of bloody idiots!' Toby said. 'How can they think Alice killed anyone?'

'They are,' said Maya. 'They'll realize their mistake, don't worry, Toby.' She put a hand on his arm. She seemed to have recovered her habitual air of detachment. 'I'm going up to my room. Let me know if there is any news.'

Megan followed her out of the kitchen.

Toby was left alone with Rickover, who seemed as unhappy as the rest of them. He broke out a Polo for the dog.

It was all going to be all right, he told himself. Bill would hire a good lawyer who would find ways to show that Alice couldn't possibly have killed Sam, despite having been seen visiting him at the time of his death. And that there was a perfectly good reason why she should lie to her husband about where she was.

Why did she do that? Didn't she trust him? Why couldn't she have trusted him with whatever it was that she was thinking? With whatever she was talking to Sam about?

Rickover whined. Toby bent down to scratch him behind the ears. 'You and me both,' he said.

Megan returned, carrying a bottle of wine. She reached up for two glasses from a kitchen cupboard, found a corkscrew and went to work.

'Here,' she said.

Toby took his glass gratefully.

'To freedom,' said Megan and knocked back half her glass in a gulp. Then the other half, and she refilled it.

'To Alice's freedom,' said Toby. He drained his own glass and thrust it out. Then he slipped the dog another mint.

'Does Alice know you do that?'

'No.'

Megan cocked her head. 'Bet she does.'

'Probably,' said Toby.

They drank again, more slowly this time. The wine was very good. Toby checked the bottle: a 2006 Margaux.

'Don't worry,' said Megan. 'There are six of them.'

'I can't believe they've arrested her,' said Toby.

'Maya's right. They'll realize their mistake soon enough.'

'I think your father might be able to help her,' said Toby. 'I'm sure there are things he knows that he's not saying that would explain what's going on.'

'Oh yeah,' said Megan.

'Do you have any idea what those things might be?'

Megan shook her head. 'No more than you. Alice might know. There's stuff Dad would tell Alice that he wouldn't tell the rest of us.'

'I can believe that,' said Toby. He drained his glass. He was feeling slightly better: the alcohol and the company.

Rickover whined.

'Do you reckon it's his suppertime?' Toby said.

'Could be.'

'There must be dog food in this house somewhere.' The two of them searched the kitchen, and found a stash. They poured some into Rickover's bowl; he seemed to appreciate it.

The wine was fast disappearing.

'You really love her, don't you?' Megan said.

'Of course I do.'

'Don't you think she is a bit uptight?'

'Yeah, she's uptight. But that's part of why I love her.'

'Oh, I'm not knocking it. I just don't know how you can stand it. Miss Perfect.'

Toby felt a flash of anger. 'Hey! Miss Perfect is in jail on a murder charge.'

For a moment Megan looked as if she was about to argue, then she slumped back in her chair. 'Sorry. You are right, of course. I always want to argue with Alice, even when she's not here. And Dad. We need another bottle. They're in the basement.'

Toby went down to the dusty cellar and found the five bottles of Margaux. He hesitated; did they really need such an expensive wine? They did. He grabbed two and returned to the kitchen.

'It's Alice who keeps our family together,' said Megan. 'It looks like it's Dad, but it's Alice who keeps *him* together. Maybe that's why I give her a hard time. Maybe I'm jealous that it's not me everyone relies on.' She attempted a grin. 'Although they'd all be in real trouble if they did that. I'm the flaky one.'

Toby opened one of the bottles and poured two more glasses. He wasn't going to contradict her.

'I'm scared, Toby,' Megan said. 'We need Alice. Alice is the one to spring *me* from jail, not the other way around.'

'Bill will sort it,' said Toby, with more confidence than he felt. He frowned. 'You don't think your dad believes she actually did it, do you?'

'No. No way,' said Megan. 'If there was a problem, Alice would find a solution, and a lot better one than murder. Dad knows that. Alice would never kill anyone. Alice wouldn't drive at thirty-one through the village; you know her.'

'I do.'

'Well then?'

Toby didn't answer.

'Hey, Toby.' Megan put her hand on his. 'Don't doubt her. You can't doubt her. She needs you.' Her brown eyes stared intensely at him through her glasses.

'I'm not doubting her,' Toby protested, but he knew that was exactly what he was doing. He didn't really believe that Alice was capable of murder. But he could believe that she wouldn't shrink from a difficult course of action if she decided it was the right one. 'Something's going on that she's not telling me, clearly. And it's probably something pretty bad.'

Megan withdrew her hand and drank her wine. 'Maybe we should figure out what exactly that is.'

18

They were getting close to the bottom of the second bottle but no closer to figuring anything out, when Rickover leapt up from beneath the table and started barking. A moment later they heard a car pull up outside.

Bill and Lars appeared. But no Alice.

Bill glanced at the three bottles on the table. 'Is that the Margaux?' he said.

'Yeah,' said Megan. 'Want some?'

Bill looked about to protest. Then he grabbed a couple of glasses from the cupboard and pulled up a chair next to Toby. His face, usually so strong, had become haggard. 'Yes.'

Megan filled the glasses. Lars and Bill drank from theirs.

'So, they didn't release Alice?' Toby said.

'No,' Bill replied. 'They're keeping her in overnight. The good news is they haven't charged her.'

'That's good news?' said Megan. 'How long can they lock her up for?'

'Thirty-six hours, apparently. I made a couple of calls and I've gotten hold of a good criminal solicitor from London. She's driving up here now.'

'That's something,' said Toby. 'Good. Thank you.'

Bill raised his eyebrows in a 'she's my daughter' gesture. 'She's going to be OK. The lawyer has told her not to say anything until tomorrow morning.'

'What about us?' said Toby. 'Presumably we have to answer the police's questions.'

'Yes,' said Bill. 'But we don't have to tell them too much.'

Toby felt a flash of anger in his chest, not helped by the three-quarters of a bottle of Bordeaux he had drunk. 'Why shouldn't we tell them everything?' he said. 'It's the truth that's going to free Alice.'

Bill gave him a tired smile. 'That's correct. Probably. But it's best to let the lawyer decide the strategy. She was very firm on that.'

'What did they ask you, Lars?' It was Megan. Interesting she asked Lars and not her father, Toby thought. Smart.

'Same as before,' said Lars with a glance at Bill. 'What happened on the submarine. What Sam spoke to us about. His visit with me in Wisconsin a couple of weeks ago. Where everyone was last night.'

'And what did you tell them?' Megan said.

'The truth,' said Bill.

'Did you tell them what happened on the submarine?' said Toby.

'No,' said Bill. 'We can't. It's Classified. And it has nothing to do with Sam Bowen's death.'

'How do we know that?'

'I know,' said Bill, his deep voice at its most authoritative. 'And you shouldn't tell them the details of what Sam spoke about either.'

'Why not?' Toby asked. 'If it will get Alice out of jail.'

'Because it won't get Alice out of jail.'

'How can you be so sure?'

For a second, Bill looked irritated. But then he controlled himself. 'I can be sure because I *know* it has no relevance. Look, Toby. And Megan. I shouldn't have invited you in to that meeting with Sam. I only did it because it seemed like a safe way for you to hear what. . .' Here he paused. 'What *may* have happened on the *Alexander*

Hamilton. But I would never have done it if I knew the police would be asking questions about it the next day. So I would like you both to promise me you won't tell the police the details.'

Megan nodded. 'OK, Dad.'

Bill glanced at Toby.

'I don't know,' Toby said. 'I mean, it's a murder inquiry. If they ask me questions, aren't I obliged to answer them?'

Bill looked at his son-in-law levelly. 'Do what you can, OK?'

Toby nodded. 'All right.' But he didn't think it was all right.

Outside, somewhere over the dark marshes, an owl hooted.

The wine was having its effect. After having deadened the initial worry, Toby now felt his emotions churning. He was worried about Alice. While he was pleased that Bill had got her a hot-shot London solicitor, his instinct was to tell the police as much rather than as little as possible. If Alice was innocent, the only thing preventing the police from letting her go was that they didn't know the truth, so anything Toby or Bill or any of the rest of the family could do to help reveal the truth must help.

If Alice was innocent.

Toby knew she was innocent. But did Bill think that? Did the solicitor?

Toby glanced at Megan, who was looking right at him. He could tell she was thinking the same thing.

Trust in the solicitor? Or trust in telling the truth? Toby's brain was fuzzy. Things would be clearer in the morning. He poured himself another drink, realizing as he did so that he would probably have one hell of a headache in the morning. Maybe things wouldn't necessarily be clearer; at that moment he didn't care.

Then they heard the sound of footsteps outside and the front door opened. Justin came in, followed by Brooke. His brown eyes were hard, as were the muscles under his sweatshirt. The habitual friendliness of his expression had disappeared. Toby was only just now beginning to realize what a big guy Justin was.

'Well?' he said to Bill. It was more of a demand than a question.

Bill turned to his other son-in-law and gave him a patient smile. 'Have a seat, Justin. Do you want some wine? Brooke?'

'No, thank you,' said Justin. He remained standing. But Megan got to her feet and fetched a full glass for her sister, who took it without acknowledgement.

'Did you tell them about my father?' Justin demanded.

'What do you mean?'

'I mean, I was at the police station this afternoon. I put them in touch with Vicky in New Jersey, and I know they're going to talk to her about what happened to her brother on the sub. Sam Bowen's girlfriend is in Norfolk and has been speaking with them. She says that Sam thought the death of one of the officers on the submarine might be suspicious. That's got to be my father's.'

Bill glanced at Brooke, who was looking down at her wine. 'Justin,' Bill said. His voice was tight, he cleared his throat and tried again. 'Justin.'

It was clear to Toby Bill was having trouble keeping calm. It was also clear that Bill and Lars hadn't told Megan and him everything about what the police had asked them at the station.

'I understand that you are upset by Craig's death,' Bill continued, looking up at his son-in-law. 'But I was there. It was an accident, I know that and you should believe it. And it doesn't have anything to do with Sam Bowen's death.'

'So you say,' said Justin, coldly.

Bill slammed his fist down on the table. Toby's wine glass toppled, spilling a dribble, and Rickover yelped. 'Yes, Justin, I do say so! It turned out that Craig was your father, but you never knew him. I did. He was a good friend of mine, and it was a tragedy that he died.

That's why I looked after you and your mother, even though she had just run off with someone else. And now my daughter is in jail. So, yes, I do say I don't want you feeding the police bullshit that you know nothing about and don't understand.'

Brooke reached for her husband's sleeve, but he batted her hand away.

Toby had never seen Bill this angry before. But Bill's voice carried authority as well as rage, and for a moment Justin hesitated. But only for a moment.

'You can't shut down the truth like that,' said Justin. 'Your submarine refuses an order to launch nuclear missiles. My father dies in a so-called accident. The guy who puts those things together is murdered. There's something there, Bill, there's something there. And you getting so upset about it just makes me more sure. You feel guilty. You *are* guilty.'

'Are you saying I killed Sam Bowen?' Bill's tone was menacing.

'Not Sam Bowen.'

Bill hesitated, letting the implication sink in. 'That's ridiculous,' he said. 'I am telling you, Justin. Don't go there. This is stuff you don't understand. Craig was in the missile control centre when the order came in. Lars and I decoded it, and we discussed it with the captain and the executive officer in the control room. Craig died several days later.'

'So you say.'

'Yes! So I say. And it's *my* daughter who is in jail. If you screw this thing up so she goes down on a murder charge, I swear I'll . . .'

'You'll what?' said Justin.

There was silence around the table as Bill glared at his son-in-law.

Then Lars coughed. 'I killed him,' he said, quietly. 'Craig, I mean. I killed Craig. On the submarine.'

'What?' Justin stared at him. They all did.

'It was an accident. We had a fight. Craig fell and hit his head. He died a couple days later.'

The anger on Justin's face was replaced by confusion.

Lars turned towards him, his eyes full of sadness. 'I'm sorry, man. I killed your father.'

Justin sat heavily on one of the chairs around the kitchen table. 'Why?' he said softly.

'Why what?' said Lars.

'Why did you kill him?'

Lars glanced at Bill. 'It was an accident,' he said. 'We got into a fight. It wasn't even a real fight – I just pushed him. But he lost his balance and fell. Hit his head against a bulkhead. Then he lost consciousness. He came around, but a couple of days later he collapsed and died, just as Bill said. Bleeding in the brain.'

The family were all looking at Justin, waiting for him to take the lead with the questions.

'OK,' he said. 'So why did you have the fight?'

'It was an argument.'

'An argument? About what?'

'A girl.'

'What girl?'

'I don't know,' said Lars. 'I don't remember. It doesn't matter – it's not important.'

'Was it my mother?'

'No. Absolutely not. It wasn't your mother.'

'So you killed him?'

Lars paused and then nodded. 'Yeah. Yeah, I did. And I'm sorry.'

'And what happened? Were you arrested? Court martialled, maybe? Sent to jail?'

Lars shook his head. 'No. With the near launch the Navy decided not to prosecute me. It *was* an accident.'

'You mean the Navy covered it up?'

Lars didn't answer.

'Right. They covered it up. No wonder Vicky was angry.' Justin sat back, his face pale. 'Why didn't you tell me? Why didn't any of you tell me?'

'We didn't know,' said Brooke.

'You knew,' said Justin to Bill.

Bill hesitated, glanced at Lars, and nodded.

'You make me sick,' said Justin, pulling himself to his feet. 'All of you.' He glared down at Lars. 'You sit there like you're apologizing for – I don't know – spilling the wine or something, when what you did was murder my father.'

Justin's muscles tensed. Lars was over sixty and in poor shape. Justin was in his thirties and in top physical form. It looked like he was about to beat the shit out of Lars.

Toby got to his feet. Unsteadily. He had drunk a lot, but he would intervene if he had to.

Brooke put her hand on Justin's arm. Justin looked at his wife, at Toby and then back at Lars. 'An apology doesn't cut it, Lars.' And he stalked from the room.

Brooke turned to her family. 'Couldn't you have told us about this, Dad? Told me? Justin has a right to know what happened to his father. It had nothing to do with those stupid missiles after all, so you could have told us. Dad, you should have trusted me!'

'It was my fault,' said Lars. 'I made him promise to keep quiet.'

Brooke looked at her father for a response, but he seemed helpless. 'Sorry,' he said, eventually.

A tear leaked from Brooke's eye, and then another. 'Justin is right. "Sorry" doesn't cut it. I'm going to the Cottage now. He needs me. Good night.'

And with that she left the house.

19

October 1983, Holy Loch

I glanced back at the heather-clad mountain that rose above the ancient village of Kilmun on the north shore of the loch. It was 0800 and the sun was just rising to the east, a red glow wriggling beneath the grey cloud to paint the heather a glorious brown and purple.

Craig, Lars and I had used a brief afternoon of freedom to climb the mountain a few days before. We liked to do that whenever we could during the ten-day turnover when we were relieving the Gold Crew. The view from the summit was spectacular: Loch Long in one direction, the island of Arran in another, and to the south the River Clyde reaching up towards the metropolis of Glasgow. The other officers chose to use what spare time they had to travel into Greenock, or even Glasgow itself, but we preferred the sense of space, of clear Scottish air that the mountain afforded.

It set us up for the seventy days underwater.

I wouldn't have long to enjoy the view. The first couple of miles of the journey out to sea were the quietest, especially in winter when the pleasure boats were either safely moored or out of the water. The submarine tender USS *Hunley* squatted in the middle of the loch, usually with one or two submarines snuggled up to it. At that moment there was only one tied up there: the *Will Rogers*, another Lafayette-class nuclear submarine, which had arrived back from patrol two days before.

The US nuclear submarines of SUBRON 14 operated out of a forward base in Scotland because from there they could quickly take up a patrol within missile range of the Soviet Union. But rather than keeping both crews for each submarine stationed in Britain, the Navy shuttled them back and forth by plane from Connecticut. I would rather have spent more time in Scotland, among the brooding hills we glimpsed only too briefly.

The loch was deep and silent. Centuries before it had been revered as a holy place after a ship returning from the Crusades sank there, filled with earth from the Holy Land. Now monsters of destruction lurked at its centre.

The submarine's bridge was perched at the top of the 'sail', a structure that rose up from the hull, towards the bow, like a giant fin. There were six of us up there, crammed into a very small space. I was the officer of the deck. Then there was the captain, Commander Driscoll; Ensign Marber, the most junior officer on the boat; the quartermaster; a lookout and a Scottish pilot, a dour tub of a man with a ruby-red face who would guide us through the sea lane once we reached the Clyde. Beneath us, in the control room, the XO oversaw the navigators and the helmsman and planesman who would manoeuvre the *Alexander Hamilton* out to sea.

Driscoll grinned at me as he lit up a stogie and waved it to the east. 'That's the first time I've seen the dawn on the way out this tour, Bill,' he said. 'The problem with Holy Loch is you don't often get to see the sun. I like to see the sun before we dive. Always saw the sun leaving Guam.'

The *Hamilton* was my first submarine, but the captain had been XO on a boomer out of Guam. The difference between Guam and Holy Loch was only apparent on the first and last days of a patrol. The rest of the time the Pacific was pretty much the same as the North Atlantic, at least when you were a couple of hundred feet beneath it.

I was interrupted by the phone. 'Bridge, navigator. Five hundred yards to the turn, counting down the turn.'

'Navigator, bridge, aye,' I answered, looking ahead to a buoy at the entrance to the loch. The *Alexander Hamilton* was sleek and graceful underwater, but on the surface she was a four-hundred-foot clumsy lump of metal, desperately slow to respond to her rudder. The navigators, the captain and I always had to be thinking two waypoints ahead, getting the lines of approach just right.

Time to concentrate.

Several hours later, we had threaded our way through the crowded shipping lanes of the Firth of Clyde into the Irish Sea. There was quite a chop out there, and the big submarine was rolling as it ploughed through the water, its bow-wave kicking up a surging spray. The sun had long disappeared, as had the pilot back to shore and the captain down below. Above was the dark grey of low cloud, all around the lighter grey of the sea. Out there somewhere was the Scottish mainland, hidden beneath the heavy cloak of moisture.

There were still two vessels visible, a local fishing boat ahead and a Russian 'trawler' three miles to starboard. These 'trawlers' were crammed full of electronic equipment and lurked outside the submarine bases tracking who came in and out.

The radar display showed another contact twelve miles to the north-west, out of sight in the grey murk. It was HMS *Minerva*, a British frigate. She had made brief contact with an Alfa-class Soviet attack submarine in the area. Once again, not a surprise.

The Alfa would try to track the *Hamilton* once she was underwater, taking advantage of the bottleneck we would have to pass through – the North Channel between Antrim and the Mull of Kintyre. It would be a fruitless task. We would shake her and, once we had, the *Hamilton* could run so quietly that the Soviet sub would never pick us up.

'Rig the bridge for dive and lay below.' It was Robinson, the new XO, from the control room.

'Rig the bridge for dive and lay below, aye,' I replied. We were answering ahead one-third at a speed of about five knots. I ordered the quartermaster to disconnect the 'suitcase', a portable silver case full of communications and navigation equipment used while the submarine was on the surface.

'Clear the bridge.' The quartermaster was first down, with the communications suitcase, followed by the lookout and Ensign Marber.

I took one last look at the wet grey world, savouring the cold mixture of air and moisture on my cheek, and dropped down the ladder myself, shutting and dogging the watertight hatch. 'Last man down. Hatch secured. Bridge is rigged for dive.'

'Submerge the ship,' the XO ordered. 'Make your depth sixty feet.'

Immediately the diving klaxon sounded twice, a distinctive *ah-oo-gah* blare. 'Dive! Dive!'

The helmsman rang up to two-thirds ahead, and the planesman set the vessel to five-degrees-down bubble. The chief of the watch opened the ballast tank vents.

The nose of the *Alexander Hamilton* dipped forward, and I could hear the Irish Sea slurping over the deck above.

We were going down, and staying down. For more than two months.

20

November 1983, Norwegian Sea

'How about *Barbarella*?'

Craig glanced at the other officers seated around the wardroom table. We were four weeks into the patrol, coming up to the halfway point, and we were discussing important matters: what movie to watch that evening.

'We saw *Barbarella* two weeks ago,' said Lars.

'Yeah, but a movie like that you only appreciate properly the second time you see it, you know?'

'Weps, you've got to have seen *Barbarella* half a dozen times,' Lars said. On the submarine, Craig, like every weapons officer before him, was always known as 'Weps'. Craig had a thing for Jane Fonda, and since Maria had walked out on him it was getting out of control. There was even a poster of her on the wall of his rack. 'What about *Blade Runner*?'

'I hate sci-fi.'

'What do you think *Barbarella* is? A war movie?'

Commander Driscoll stirred at the head of the table. 'How about *The Magnificent Seven*, gentlemen?'

Craig knew when he was defeated. 'I think *The Magnificent Seven* is an excellent choice, sir. I've always been a great fan of Mr Brynner.' He managed to inject just the right amount of humour into his obedience.

There were eight of the ship's fourteen officers present at the table, the rest were on watch or asleep. The wardroom was the most luxurious space on the submarine. It was dominated by a rectangular table with a blue cloth, white china and the ship's silver. Fake wood lined the bulkhead, upon which was mounted a mishmash of instruments, framed photographs, typed instructions, exhortations such as 'transients kill' and 'think quiet', and a TV screen with a VHS recorder. Behind the captain was a portrait of Alexander Hamilton himself, General Washington's chief of staff, one of the Founding Fathers and the first secretary of the Treasury. His pointed nose and long chin had become so familiar to us over the previous year and a half, he felt like one of the crew.

The captain sat at the head of the table, with the XO on his right. A steward served us food that was surprisingly good. It was the same fare as the crew, but the submarine service claimed they provided the best food in the Navy. We had just finished ice cream sundaes, and were waiting for coffee.

There was no alcohol served on the vessel. Which was probably wise when things were getting tense.

And things *were* getting tense. That was why the captain, who usually let his officers squabble over the choice of movie, had exercised his authority. When things got tough, he liked to watch *The Magnificent Seven*. He had chosen it after the reactor scram the previous January, and when we had successfully evaded two Soviet attack submarines in the Greenland Sea during our last patrol.

Soon after I had joined the Navy in 1975, the Cold War had begun to thaw amid Strategic Arms Limitation Talks and détente. But, since Ronald Reagan had become president, all that had changed. Now the messages emanating from the White House were all about increasing, not decreasing, nuclear weapons, cruise missiles were being deployed in Europe and there were plans to develop anti-ballistic missile systems in space. And then in September the Russians had shot down the Korean airliner.

The *Alexander Hamilton* had received two Emergency Action Messages that day. The first, which I had decoded with Lars, was for information only. It announced the start of a major NATO exercise known as Able Archer, which was designed to test the NATO command structure's response to a conventional attack by the Soviet Union that went nuclear. That in itself wasn't concerning. We had been briefed at the start of the patrol to expect the exercise.

The second EAM of the day was much more worrying. It had raised the state of nuclear readiness to DEFCON 3, with no explanation. There were five levels of readiness, ranging from DEFCON 5, which applied nearly all the time, down to DEFCON 1 which meant launch of nuclear missiles was imminent.

The technical definition of DEFCON 3 was not particularly alarming: 'increase in force readiness above that required for normal readiness'. But during the whole Cold War, DEFCON 3 had only been set three times: in the Cuban Missile Crisis in 1962 – when it had eventually reached DEFCON 2, during the Yom Kippur war between Israel and the Arabs in 1974, and in 1976 after a flare-up on the Korean peninsula.

So DEFCON 3 was a big deal.

Of course, the crew of the *Alexander Hamilton* had reacted to the change in status with calm professionalism, and Commander Driscoll had briefed the officers and senior chiefs two hours earlier, as much to steady nerves as anything else. Which was why we were still watching a movie that evening.

In theory, officers were not supposed to 'talk shop' in the wardroom. In practice, on the *Hamilton* it was allowed at the end of the meal.

I had a question.

'Sir? Do you think the DEFCON 3 status has anything to do with Able Archer?'

Every officer in the room looked at the captain, who took a moment to puff on his cigar. He seemed to come to a decision and turned to his right. 'XO? Can you tell these gentlemen what you told me earlier?'

Lieutenant Commander Robinson seemed surprised by this request. He raised his eyebrows, but Driscoll nodded, confirming his instruction.

'Aye, captain.' He leaned forward and looked at the rest of us around the table. 'What I am about to say is Classified. Secret. And some of it is speculation.'

'But it is directly relevant to the situation we find ourselves in,' said the captain. 'I think you need to know the answer to your question, Bill.'

'As most of you know, I was transferred to the *Hamilton* directly from the Pentagon,' Robinson began. 'I worked on planning the Able Archer 83 exercise for six months. We do Able Archer exercises every year, but this year it's a bit different. This time the scenario is that the Warsaw Pact invades West Germany, reaches the Rhine and SACEUR decides to respond by nuclear signalling.'

SACEUR stood for the Supreme Allied Commander Europe. 'What kind of nuclear signalling?' I asked.

'Limited nuclear attacks on some Eastern European cities.'

I nodded. But 'nuclear signalling' struck me as a seriously bad idea.

'From there, the situation escalates further, and two days later NATO will order a full-scale nuclear attack.'

This was roughly what had been described to us at our briefing.

'Now unlike previous years, this exercise involves signals between SACEUR in Brussels, the various NATO governments and strategic commands. A new encryption system has been instituted for the exercise. These signals won't be sent to individual SSBNs. So the DEFCON 3 instruction we received is not part of the exercise.'

That was bad news. That meant it was for real. 'So there is no link with Able Archer?' I said.

'I believe there might be,' the XO said. His thick black eyebrows were furrowed over his dark eyes.

'In the Pentagon, I was working closely with a CIA officer who was an expert on Soviet nuclear doctrine. His view was that the Russians fear we are about to launch a first strike.'

'*We* are about to launch a first strike? That's absurd,' said Craig. 'Surely they are the ones who are going to launch the strike if anyone is?'

'That is what NATO has always believed. And that's what they still believe. But my CIA colleague, and a number of others including agents on the ground, think otherwise. And if the Soviets think we are going to launch a first strike, they will expect us to do it under the cover of a military exercise.'

'Like Able Archer?' I said.

'Like Able Archer. Especially if, unlike previous years, it involves signals traffic to air, sea and missile headquarters around Europe. And especially if this traffic uses new encryption. The Soviets will ask themselves why the new codes? And they will decide it's because we are planning to do something we don't want them to anticipate. Like a pre-emptive strike.'

I glanced at Driscoll. He looked grim.

'Then why did NATO go ahead with the exercise?' I asked.

'Because it was assessed that the Russians don't really believe that we would launch a first strike.'

'That makes sense to me,' said Craig. 'Why would we? That's not the kind of thing the United States would do. They should know that, they've got their own spies.'

'It's the spies who are the most wary. Now that Andropov is in charge, the Kremlin is run by the KGB. According to the CIA, he believes that President Reagan is setting up the US to be able to launch a decapitation strike on Moscow. He thinks that's why we are deploying Pershing missiles in Europe. They can reach Moscow in six minutes, before the Soviets have time to respond and order a counter strike.'

'I still don't see why we would do that,' Craig said.

'We know we wouldn't do that, but the Soviets don't. They are paranoid. Or at least some people in our intelligence community believe they are. So when they see Able Archer 83 going into action, they will put their own forces on alert.'

The XO hesitated, glancing at his captain. Driscoll gave another discreet nod.

'They may even decide to get their own strike in first.'

'Is that's what's happening here?' I asked.

Robinson shrugged.

Driscoll interrupted. 'We don't know, Bill,' he said. 'All we can know is that it *might* be happening. We need to be ready.'

Ready for what? was the question we all wanted to ask, but we didn't because we all knew the answer.

Ready for nuclear war.

'Thank you, XO,' Driscoll said. 'Very well, gentlemen. I'm just going up to the conn.' He glanced at the clock on the bulkhead. 'We start the movie at 2015.'

The captain left, followed by the XO and the other three officers, leaving Craig, Lars and me.

'Jesus,' I said.

'I don't believe it,' said Craig. 'The Russians wouldn't be that stupid. That's the whole point of us, isn't it? They launch a first strike, we finish them off. They know that.'

'Yeah, but . . .' I hesitated. 'Wars sometimes start with people being stupid. Misunderstandings.'

'Not nuclear wars,' said Craig.

'If there's going to be a nuclear war, that's how it would start. One side misunderstanding what the other side plans to do.'

'But there's not going to be a nuclear war.'

'What about the First World War?' I asked. It had always worried me, the First World War. The major powers of Europe had blundered into a war by accident and millions had died. If they had done it once they could do it again.

'My point,' said Craig. 'It wasn't a nuclear war. Then nobody in charge knew how bad a modern war could be. Now they all do.'

'That's true,' I admitted.

But I wasn't convinced. And Craig could tell I wasn't convinced.

'Has Donna been getting to you?' he said.

'No,' I replied.

'You mean she never spoke to you about this shit?'

'Not much,' I said. 'We avoided the subject. We respected each other's points of view.'

'Remember the FBI came around to ask us about her?' said Craig. 'Her and some woman named Pat Greenwald. They said Donna was a serious peacenik. Maybe more than that.'

It was true: two FBI agents had arrived at the base just before we flew out to Scotland to ask the three of us about Donna. I had told them we had broken up, and I would probably never see her again. And I had had no idea who Pat Greenwald was.

'I heard her getting worked up in that bar in New York,' said Lars.

'Well, maybe we did discuss it once,' I admitted, remembering our conversation in Mystic. 'She asked me if I would go ahead with a nuclear launch if I was ordered to. I said I would.'

'I hope so,' said Craig. 'Because I'm the weps on this boat and you're the assistant weps and I need for you to obey my orders.'

'Hey, of course I will,' I said, realizing I was straying on to difficult territory. 'And I told her that. Even if I think the order is an error, I said I would obey it.'

'Good,' said Craig. He seemed comforted.

'Even if you think it's an error?' Lars asked.

'Yes,' I said. 'We have to, don't we? We have no way of confirming.'

'Won't happen,' said Craig. 'There are too many checks in the system.'

'But what about Three Mile Island?' I said. 'There were a load of checks there. They failed.'

'That was a bunch of badly trained civilians making sloppy decisions and cutting corners,' said Craig. 'That could never happen in the Navy. Right?'

He was glaring at me. Both as a friend and, much more importantly, as my senior officer. There was really only one answer I could give him if I wanted to stay in the Navy.

'Right.'

We watched *The Magnificent Seven*. Yul Brynner and his crew saved the Mexican village and saw off the bandits, and the captain was happy.

Later, Lars and I were in our racks in the JO Jungle; Matt Curtis, our roommate, was on duty in manoeuvring. I had been trying to get to sleep for an hour, and failing. This was bad. If things got hairy it would be important to be well rested.

'Bill?'

It was Lars from the middle rack just beneath mine, a coffin six-foot six-inches long and two-foot six-inches high, in which he was wedged during his sleeping hours. Mine wasn't any bigger; the enlisted men's quarters were even smaller.

'Yeah?'

'I think the XO is wrong. Even if they do think we might launch a first strike, it wouldn't make sense for them to launch theirs first. We would still obliterate them and they know that.'

'I hope so,' I said. 'But people screw up.'

'Yeah,' said Lars. 'People screw up. Man, I'm more worried about someone giving us a launch order by mistake. Donna was right about that. I know we have all those checks, but they had those at Three Mile Island. I think if there is going to be a nuclear war, *that's* how it will start. Someone giving the wrong order to someone else who presses the button.'

I got a grip. 'Donna was wrong. If we all keep our heads and do our jobs there's not going be a war. There can't be. It's madness.'

Lars didn't answer.

21

Saturday 30 November 2019, Norfolk

By the time Toby got down to breakfast it was half past eight and most of the family were already there; only Brooke and her husband were absent.

'How did you sleep?' said Bill, mixing politeness with genuine interest.

'Not well.'

'And how's your head?' said Megan, with a chirpy glee that was not at all polite.

'Not good,' Toby said, exercising his right to British understatement.

He was getting old. Not only were the hangovers getting worse, but he was also finding it harder to sleep, especially after too much red wine. It wasn't true what they said about expensive wine causing less damage the morning after.

His wife being locked up in a police station hadn't helped.

When he had first got to bed, he had shared Justin's anger with the Guth family and their secrets. The Guth family including Alice.

There was stuff she knew that she wasn't telling him, and he was quite sure she wasn't telling the police. Stuff about the submarine. Stuff about Craig. Other stuff, no doubt. He found himself blaming her pig-headedness for getting herself in jail.

Was Justin right that Craig's death back in 1983 had something to do with Sam's? If so, why would Alice care? Although he could see why Justin might.

But as Toby had lain in bed and stewed, the anger had shifted shape into concern. He had no idea what a police cell was like. Was it like one of those American drunk tanks you saw on TV? Was Alice alone? Was she asleep? What was she thinking? What was she thinking about him? Was she OK? Obviously she wasn't OK. Could she handle it? Although her family, her friends and her colleagues thought Alice could handle anything, Toby knew there were limits, and he feared Alice was near hers.

He knew he should have confidence in Alice's ability to get herself out of jail: in her ingenuity, in her father's influence and effectiveness, in her *innocence*. But in the small hours of the morning, he was afraid that somehow she would remain ensnared in the justice system. That she would be tried and found guilty for murder. That she would spend the rest of her life in jail. Away from him.

He couldn't let that happen.

And then he thought of Sam, and of his pregnant girlfriend. It was so much worse for her – worse than for Alice, worse than for the rest of the Guth family. Sam had struck him as a really nice guy and he was far too young to die.

Who the hell had killed him? Was it someone currently asleep in that very house? Or in the Cottage next door? Or was it, after all, Alice, in her police cell?

Eventually, sleep had pulled Toby under and freed him from his increasingly muddled speculation.

He glanced at the row of wine bottles by the kitchen window, and poured himself some coffee. Without Alice around to organize it, breakfast was just toast and blueberry jam, which for some reason the Guths kept in the fridge. No marmalade.

'Are you going to see the lawyer this morning?' he asked Bill.

'Yes. A bit later. I'm meeting someone here first.'

'Can I come?' Toby asked.

'No, don't worry. I'll handle the lawyer. And the police won't let either of us see Alice.'

'I'd like to try,' Toby said. 'And I'd like to talk to this lawyer. I'm sure she's good, and I'm sure you can handle her, but Alice is my wife, and I'd like to be involved.'

'OK,' Bill said. 'I'll take you.'

'Who are you meeting here?' Megan asked her father.

Bill hesitated, but then decided to reply. 'Admiral Robinson. He was the executive officer on the *Alexander Hamilton*. He retired a few months ago.'

'Interesting,' said Megan. 'So he flew over from the States?'

'Yeah,' said Bill, looking uncomfortable. 'I contacted him when I heard about Sam Bowen. I guess he jumped on a plane.'

'Why?' said Megan.

Bill looked at his daughter, the blunt questions clearly riling him. 'I guess he'll tell me when I see him.'

Toby wanted to ask more, as did Megan, such as if Sam's murder had nothing to do with the *Alexander Hamilton* why was an admiral flying all the way here from America? But they could both tell from her father's face there was no point.

Toby slotted some bread in the toaster, and Brooke appeared in the kitchen.

She looked nervous, but then she had looked nervous ever since Sam had been killed.

'Brooke! Have some breakfast,' Bill said. 'Where's Justin?'

'He's taking the bags out of the Cottage to our car,' said Brooke. 'We're leaving.'

'Back to Chicago?' said Bill.

'No. We've got a room in Hunstanton. Justin wants to stay around in case the police need him.'

Bill's lips pursed. He clearly didn't like that response. 'Can't you stay? I know Justin is angry, but we need you here.'

Megan nodded vigorously in agreement, although Toby noticed Maya just looked on, her expression blank.

'Justin feels . . .' Brooke searched for the word. 'Betrayed. And I kind of understand that. I'm sorry, Dad.'

She hesitated and then rushed over to give him a quick kiss on the forehead. Megan got to her feet to give her a hug, as did Maya. With a wave to Lars and Toby, she was gone.

'She should have stayed without him,' Bill said.

'You make her choose between us and her husband, she's going to choose her husband,' Megan said. 'And you can see Justin's point.'

'I cannot see Justin's point,' Bill growled. 'I thought that guy had more sense. He used to.'

Maya was still standing from her hug with her sister. 'Daddy?'

'Yes?' Bill's expression was wary.

'I'm really sorry, but I'm going to have to fly out of Heathrow this afternoon. To New York. The airline has been in touch. I'm really, really sorry.'

'What! Didn't you tell them there was a family emergency?'

'I'd cashed in some chips to spend Thanksgiving here. They wanted me to do a New York sector and I couldn't say no. Airlines are tough on their employees these days.'

'Didn't you tell them about Alice?'

'I didn't tell them my sister had been accused of murder. Hopefully, they won't find out. I'm sorry I've got to leave, Daddy. It's not like I can do anything useful here.'

Bill shook his head and looked down at his coffee. 'When are you going?'

Maya glanced at the clock on the wall. 'In about an hour.'

'OK,' said Bill, defeated. 'Do what you have to do.' He got to his feet. 'I'll be in my study.'

'I'd better go and pack,' said Maya after he'd left the room.

'You've got a boyfriend there,' said Megan.

'What?'

Megan just raised her eyebrows. Maya coloured and repeated herself. 'I've got to go and pack.'

'She always does that,' said Megan, after Maya had left the room. 'If there's any family trouble, she runs.'

'How did you know there was a boyfriend?'

'I could tell. There are lots of boyfriends with Maya. There's always a boyfriend. But I can't believe she is walking out on us now.'

Megan grinned sheepishly at Toby. 'I'm the only sister left. That doesn't bode well for Alice.'

'Your dad will do what's necessary,' said Lars.

'I hope so,' said Megan, doubt in her voice.

Toby buttered his toast.

'I'm going for a walk,' said Lars.

'Can you hang on a couple of minutes until I've finished this?' said Toby. 'And we had better take Rickover.'

22

Bill kept his house a little on the warm side, in Toby's opinion, and so it was a relief to get out into the fresh Norfolk air.

It was a clear late-autumn day, with only a few white puffs of cloud skipping through the sky. There was a stiff breeze, and it was cold on Toby's cheeks, invigorating.

Lars headed out across the dyke towards the sea, and Toby was happy to follow him. The marsh was alive with the gurgle of water and the fluster of small unseen birds. The tide was low in the creek, and a pair of curlews picked their way carefully over the mud towards a beached red fishing boat, tied uselessly to its orange mooring. Behind them, the village of grey flint and red brick curled up safe and cosy between the marsh and the low ridge behind it, watched over by the windmill. Rickover was happy sniffing the morning news: the dyke was a favourite of dog walkers.

They didn't speak for several minutes. Toby was wary of Lars. He was a criminal, he had been in jail. He had just admitted to killing someone thirty-five years before. Yet something drew Toby to him. Maybe it was Lars's vulnerability – life had given him a rough ride. But Toby also sensed integrity in Lars. Loyalty. Honour. Despite himself, he almost trusted him.

Almost.

Toby hunched up in his coat and scarf. 'This has got to seem cold to you.'

'Are you kidding?' said Lars. 'This is nothing compared to Wisconsin. And it's good to be outside.'

'Yes, sorry,' Toby said. 'I was thinking of the Caribbean.'

'I try not to,' said Lars.

They were at the dunes, and followed the board path through the sand, temporarily sheltered from the wind. A cloud of small brown birds erupted from a black thorn bush next to them, chattered and settled down twenty yards away.

'I should probably tell the police about that,' he said. 'The jail time.'

'Don't they know?'

'Not yet,' said Lars. 'I'm kind of hoping they don't find out. They may check with the States, but I haven't gotten a criminal record there. Maybe they'll never figure it out?'

'I have no idea,' Toby replied. 'But this is a murder investigation; they are going to be thorough.'

'At least I've got a good alibi. Brooke, Justin and me went back to the Cottage after the game. We'd all flown here from the States – we all had jet-lag. Brooke and Justin stayed up late in the Cottage living room; they would have seen me leave.'

'Justin will probably tell them you killed Craig.' Part of Toby was glad of that; it might distract attention from Alice. Even if Lars was innocent it would be good to muddy the investigation.

Maybe he wasn't innocent, despite his alibi.

'I guess he will,' said Lars. 'But that was investigated. The Navy didn't even convict me of manslaughter, just assault. After what had happened on the submarine, everyone was happy to keep things quiet.'

'Why did you tell him?' Toby said. 'It's obvious he's going to tell the police.'

'Bill's in a lot of trouble right now, with Alice being a suspect and everything. And I get why Justin is so upset about Craig. *I'm* still upset about Craig; he was a good friend of mine. I just couldn't sit and watch Bill's family being torn apart in front of my eyes.' He sighed. 'Justin's right. We should have told him the truth long ago.'

'And it really was an accident?'

Lars didn't reply. They emerged from the dunes on to the beach. The tide was most of the way out, and the sea was barely visible – just a line of breakers in the distance, whispering to them over the sand.

They stopped to take in the view. Now, in clear sunlight rather than the gloom of the day before, the vastness of sand, sea and sky opened out before them. London, even the coast road and the sleepy village of Barnholt, was far behind them, well out of sight behind the dunes. Rickover scampered off.

'Not really, no. I meant to hit him. I meant to hurt him, not kill him. And when he fell and hit his head, it didn't seem too serious. But he died. The Navy should have court martialled me for manslaughter.'

'Is that when you left?' Toby asked.

'Yes. They gave me an honourable discharge. I was out of there as soon as possible.'

'Because of Craig?'

'Yeah. And because we had nearly blown up the world. I didn't want to be part of it any more. I hated the Navy. I hated America.'

Lars started off across the sand towards the distant waves. 'I went to Brazil. My dad's folks still lived in Rio – they were schoolteachers like my dad. I thought I could learn Portuguese, become a Brazilian, sail. I used to enjoy sailing on Lake Michigan with my dad and I thought I could be a proper sailor, not a mass murderer skulking under the waves, hugging nuclear missiles. That's why I originally joined the Navy, you know? To go out to sea. Turned out I ended up going *under* the sea.'

'Brazil sounds idyllic.'

'It didn't work out. Brazil's economy was in a bad way after the debt crisis. The locals were friendly, but they treated me as a Yankee. A Yankee without money is a Yankee without a point as far as they were concerned. But I met this American guy who had friends in Tortola, friends who could get us a job, and so I decided to tag along with him up there.'

Lars glanced at Toby. 'The friends weren't exactly legit. At first I earned a little money by looking the other way. Then I scraped enough together to buy my own boat, with a loan from the friends. I did some charters for tourists. But I did other work too. And one day I was caught. In Guadeloupe.'

'And ended up in jail?'

'That's right. And I'd still be there if Bill hadn't gotten me a hot-shot lawyer. Bill has always been there for me. He understands. He's always understood.'

'He left the Navy too, didn't he?'

Lars nodded. 'Yes. A lot of people thought that was a shame. Bill could have gone far, maybe all the way like Robinson.'

'What about the captain? If he had lived, would he have become an admiral?'

Lars sighed. 'I don't know. Yeah, probably.'

Once again, Toby wondered how Commander Driscoll had died.

They strode across the reddish sand, skirting a wide, shallow pool of seawater left by the retreating tide. A band of washed-up razor-clam shells crunched underfoot. The beach was empty with the exception of three figures walking a bounding dog along the base of the dunes.

'I'm sorry about Alice,' Lars said. 'But I'm sure Bill will get her out. I told you how he got me off the worst charges in Guadeloupe.'

'You know Alice isn't guilty, don't you?' Toby said.

'Uh-huh,' said Lars in agreement. But unenthusiastic agreement. Lars didn't really know whether Alice was guilty or not.

'Can you help me?' Toby said. 'I need to get the police to release her.'

'Help you how?'

'By telling me what happened on the submarine.'

Lars shook his head. 'I'm sorry, Toby. That's Bill's call. He's right; it's still Classified. And he's also right that it has no relevance.'

'It must have some relevance! Or at least the police must think it has. If it truly isn't important, we need to explain to them why.'

'Leave it to Bill, Toby. Leave it to Bill.'

They walked all the way to the waves, dodging grey strips of shallow seawater lurking in the sand. It took less time than Toby had expected: the waves turned out to be no more than six inches high, tickling the beach.

Lars realized what was happening first.

'That tide's coming in fast!'

They reversed direction and headed back towards the dunes, the water lapping on their heels. Toby scanned the beach ahead of them: the tide was swooping around them in a flanking movement. They ended up running to a point where the beach inclined slightly upwards, slowing the incoming sea.

Lars turned to watch the water close over the patch of sand on which they had been walking only a few minutes before. 'Now that doesn't happen on Lake Michigan.'

23

Alice didn't really like Lisa Beckwith. Worse, she didn't trust her. As a corporate lawyer, she was ignorant of her criminal brethren. Corporate law, at least as Alice's firm practised it, involved big deals, big brains and big fees. In particular it involved large piles of paper, virtual paper leafed through in electronic form on tablets or computers. She assumed most of the time criminal law involved lesser cases, lesser brains, lesser fees. Many corporate lawyers assumed that a criminal lawyer's job was to guide guilty felons through a chaotic and overstretched legal process. Difficult, frustrating, but small time.

But Alice also knew that murder trials were big deals in themselves, that not everyone accused of a crime was guilty of it, and in certain cases considerable ingenuity and knowledge of the law was required to get an innocent accused off the hook. Or a guilty one for that matter.

Lisa Beckwith was small and dark and had the worn face of a woman who had seen it all before. But her eyes were intelligent and alive and Alice could tell at once she was engaged. She wanted this case, and she wanted to get Alice off.

Which was all to the good.

Despite the lack of trust, which Alice was pretty sure was reflected by Lisa, the two lawyers had quickly developed something of a rapport, or at least a modus operandi. Overnight Alice had worried about how she could withhold information from her solicitor without actually lying to her, or undermining her innocence. But

151

Lisa made it easy. She knew exactly what questions to ask and, more importantly what questions *not* to ask. Her goal was not to prove Alice's innocence, but to thwart the police's attempts to prove her guilt. And she was optimistic.

It wasn't surprising that the police had arrested Alice. She was the last person to see Sam alive and she had hidden the fact she had gone to meet him at the pub from her family.

But Lisa believed the police would need more than that to charge her. Forensics were not helping them. Alice's fingerprints were present in Sam's bedroom. But the police hadn't found a murder weapon. And, most significantly, they hadn't found any of Sam's blood on the clothes Alice was wearing that night. There was quite a lot of blood on Sam and on the floor of his bedroom. Lisa would argue that there should be quite a lot of blood on Sam's murderer. Who therefore could not be Alice.

The police were also struggling with motive. They had no real idea why Alice might have killed Sam. They had guesses but, according to Lisa, the less they knew, the less they could guess. One such theory was that Alice and Sam knew each other already, which was ridiculous. Another was that there was something suspicious about Craig Naylor's death on the submarine. If the police were on the wrong track, Lisa urged Alice to leave them there, wasting time.

The implication was that if they were on the right track, Alice should leave them there too.

Lisa insisted that Alice tell the police the bare minimum, a strategy that Alice was happy to follow. It made the interviews with the police easier, once she had got over the awkwardness of refusing to answer their perfectly reasonable questions. It meant she didn't have to worry about keeping her story straight, about avoiding lies.

She could do this.

But after hours of questioning both by the police and by her own solicitor, she was tired and it was a relief to be allowed back into her police cell. And to have time alone to think.

She thought of Toby. He would be worried about her, she knew that. He would be figuring out ways to help her.

But would he believe in her innocence?

Of course, he would deny that he suspected her. He would claim that he didn't believe a word of the police's suspicions, that he was certain it was all some terrible mistake.

But would he doubt her? And if he did doubt her, would he abandon her?

If Toby abandoned her, it would all be over. She would crumble inside. And outside.

She couldn't believe Toby would abandon her. She couldn't *allow* herself to believe that.

She thought about her mother and her father and how she always seemed to be looking after them both. Even though her mother was dead seven years. Even though her father seemed competent and solidly reliable. More than that: businessmen paid Bill Guth good money to fix things, and he fixed them.

Alice remembered the night about a month after her mother's death and a week before she was due to return to the States to take her bar exam. Her father had been devastated, but he seemed to be handling it well; with help from Alice.

Bill had spent the day in Paris on business. Maya was seventeen, still at school and living at home at the Kensington flat. She had asked Alice to join her at a party, as long as Alice promised to leave early. Which she had done: having a procession of young English eighteen-year-olds hitting on her was just embarrassing. She was old enough to be their elder sister, for God's sakes!

Maya was having fun, though, when Alice left.

Alice had arrived home at about ten to find her father in the living room working his way through a bottle of Templeton rye whiskey, and listening to the Eurythmics. Alice knew the bottle had been nearly full that morning; now it was two-thirds empty.

'How are you, Alice?' Bill asked from his slumped position on the sofa. He was careful not to slur his words. *Very* careful.

Alice told him briefly about the party that Maya had invited her to, and he nodded in slightly the wrong places.

Alice had seen her dad slightly drunk once or twice. But never like this.

But if his seventeen-year-old daughter was allowed to get drunk, why shouldn't he?

She was about to withdraw and put herself to bed, when she hesitated. This was wrong.

'What happened in Paris, Dad?'

'Oh, nothing,' Bill said. 'My meeting only took an hour, so I had most of the afternoon to kill. I wandered around. Sat in a cafe with a glass of wine. Caught the flight home.'

'What happened, Dad?' said Alice, sitting next to him.

Bill put down his glass of whiskey and closed his eyes. Then he opened them and looked straight at Alice. 'I thought I saw her,' he said. 'In the Jardin du Luxembourg. There was this woman with long honey-coloured hair talking to an older lady. I couldn't see her face, but from the back she looked just like Donna. Not Donna now, but Donna when we were young. When we listened to this,' he waved vaguely towards the speaker.

'I called out to her – "Donna!". I knew when I was doing it it was stupid, but I couldn't help it. Just in case. It wasn't her, of course. But it stabbed me. Right here.' He jabbed his chest. 'I hadn't thought of her all day; it must have been the first day since she died I haven't thought of her. And then I did. And I couldn't stop thinking about her, how I would never see her again.' A tear ran down his cheek, then another. For a few seconds he fought it, and then he began to sob. 'Sorry, Alice. I'm sorry. It must be the whiskey.'

'It's OK, Dad. It's OK. Really. We all cry all the time. Why shouldn't you?'

Alice reached out and squeezed his hand. She hadn't yet gone a day without thinking about her mother. She couldn't imagine ever doing that.

'It's just as bad for you, isn't it, honey?' said Bill.

'It's just bad, Dad. It's just bad. For all of us.'

'Yeah.' Her father took another swig of whiskey.

'But what's with the booze? I get that you are sad. But I haven't seen you drinking up till now?'

'That's because I haven't. I've been trying to hold it all together. But, you know, sometimes, I just don't care. I want to feel numb. I want to feel wasted. I even want to feel wrecked tomorrow morning.'

'I see,' said Alice.

She left him to the whiskey and went up to bed.

But early the next evening, when her father produced another bottle, Scotch this time, Alice talked to him. Quietly. Gently. A bit like the way she knew her mother would have talked to him. Sure he had the right to get himself wasted every night, and in fact a lot of people would completely understand if he did. Alice wasn't going to stop him. But was he sure that was what he really wanted to do?

And was he sure that was what Donna wanted him to do?

He drank no more than a couple of glasses that night, and just a couple of beers or glasses of wine each evening until Alice left. Once she got back to New York, she spoke to him every day, and she was pretty sure he hadn't relapsed, or at least if he had it was only once or twice.

Bill Guth had held together. Thanks to Alice.

24

As Toby and Lars got back to Pear Tree Cottage, Maya was just shutting the boot of her small rental car. She was wearing her flight attendant's uniform.

'I'm glad I saw you before I left,' she said, giving Toby a hug. 'Don't worry. They'll let Alice go. Daddy's got some honcho with him now. Bye, Lars. See you soon.'

And she was gone.

Toby and Lars went into the kitchen where Megan was waiting for them. She pointed to the living room and made a face.

'The admiral?' Toby asked.

She nodded. 'And another one. A Brit. I think he's a spook.'

They heard footsteps in the hallway, and then Bill appeared followed by two men.

'You're back!' he said. 'Toby. Let me introduce Admiral Robinson and Dominic Prestwitch, who works for the British government.'

Admiral Robinson extended a hand. Although he must have been a few years older than Bill, he didn't look it. What remained of his hair was still dark, and there was vigour in his handshake. His dark eyes were quick and intelligent. He looked like a man who got things done, who was used to giving crisp orders which were crisply obeyed. 'Good to meet you, Toby. And great to see you, Lars. How are you doing?'

'I'm doing good,' said Lars, shaking his hand. The admiral clapped him on the shoulder but, despite the admiral's bonhomie, Lars seemed wary.

Dominic Prestwitch was much younger than his colleague. Early thirties, thick brown hair greased into a fashionable quiff, glasses, a grey suit and a lime green tie. A pair of buck teeth threatened to escape his upper lip, but were successfully contained.

'Toby. Can we have a word? In the living room?'

Bill led Toby through with the two other men following. They all sat down.

Bill looked to his former shipmate. 'Glenn?'

The admiral leaned forward, asserting his authority. And he had authority.

'Bill told me about the death of the poor historian as soon as it happened,' the admiral started. 'And I came right away. I'm sorry to hear that your wife has been arrested. I'm sure it's a misunderstanding.'

'So am I,' Toby said.

'Bill mentioned that you heard what the historian thought happened on the USS *Alexander Hamilton* in 1983?'

'I did, although Bill didn't confirm it.' Toby thought there was no harm in letting the admiral know Bill had done what he was supposed to do.

'I'm sure he didn't. As he has explained to you, that information is Classified.'

'He has,' Toby said. 'But I know no more than Sam Bowen. Both Bill and Lars da Silva have been discreet.'

'We're here to make sure you don't tell anyone anything you know or find out about the *Alexander Hamilton*,' the admiral said.

'But presumably those are US secrets. I'm a British citizen.'

'Precisely,' said the admiral. 'This is where Dominic comes in.'

Prestwitch reached into his pocket and produced a warrant card. Toby examined it. 'MI5? Isn't it supposed to be secret? I mean, are you allowed to admit that you work there?'

'I can these days,' Prestwitch said. 'Things have changed.' He bent down and reached into his briefcase, pulling out a one-page form.

'What's this?' Toby asked. But one glance told him. 'The Official Secrets Act?' His name was printed in a box near the top. The signature space was blank.

'That's right,' said Prestwitch. 'As you know, both the UK and the US still operate a fleet of ballistic missile submarines to deter foreign aggressors. And we assess that what happened on the USS *Alexander Hamilton* in 1983 is still a threat to security. So it's just as important to our government as to the Americans' that you don't talk about it.'

'But I explained, I know nothing.'

'You know something,' said the admiral. 'And Bill says you are a smart guy. You might end up knowing more.'

'So this silences me?' Toby said, picking up the sheet of paper.

'It does,' said Prestwitch.

'But why should I sign it? My wife is in a police station suspected of murder. It seems to me likely that the knowledge of whatever happened on the submarine might help set her free.'

'It won't,' said Bill.

'You say that, but I don't know it!' Toby protested.

'You should sign it because you are a British citizen, and because it is important to your country,' said Prestwitch.

'And my wife?' A thought occurred to Toby. 'Can you get the police to release my wife?'

Prestwitch replied carefully. 'If your wife did murder Sam Bowen, and if the police have solid evidence that she did, then we can't help her.'

'Of course she didn't murder him!' Toby protested.

'In which case we may be able to help. I will certainly be speaking to the police and, without being specific, I can provide them with guidance.'

'So, if Alice is innocent, which she is, you can get her off?'

159

'I can help,' said Prestwitch. 'I can't guarantee they'll let her go.'

Toby flung the form on to the coffee table. 'Then why should I sign?'

'There is another way of looking at it,' Prestwitch said. 'If you don't sign, we certainly won't help Alice.'

'Is that a threat?'

'Damn it, Toby!' Bill interrupted. 'Stop playing games. You should sign this because your country asks you to, and because it might help Alice. Aren't those good enough reasons? And if they are not, sign it because *I* am asking you.'

Alice's father had never spoken to Toby like that before. But there had never been so much at stake before.

Toby was reluctant. But then he asked himself would signing the document make it more or less likely that Alice would be released?

Having MI5 on your side must be a good thing. Bill clearly thought so.

Toby picked up the form, took Prestwitch's pen and signed.

25

November 1983, Norwegian Sea

'Don't do it, son. Do what you have been ordered to do. You owe it to your country.'

Commander Driscoll's eyes were steady as they looked down the barrel of the Colt 1911, his left hand clutching the shoulder that had been smashed by Lars's wrench.

My aim was remarkably firm as I focused on Driscoll's forehead. The control room was crammed full of men, and they were all staring at me in silence.

'You gotta shoot him, Bill,' Lars said. He was standing barely a foot away from the captain, the wrench still in his hand. Williamson, a large navigation petty officer, was poised just behind Lars, ready if Lars took another swing at the captain.

I ignored them all.

Driscoll was right, of course. My duty as a naval officer was to put down the gun and let him go ahead with the launch. My duty as a naval officer was to play my part in sending three nuclear missiles – thirty warheads – to Moscow, Leningrad and East Berlin. Warheads that would flatten cities and kill millions. Warheads that would probably provoke massive nuclear retaliation from the Warsaw Pact.

Certainly provoke it, if what the XO had said the night before about the Soviets' nervousness was true.

Unless the Soviets had already launched their missiles, getting their own pre-emption in first before NATO could initiate the first strike the Russians were convinced was on its way under cover of Able Archer 83.

In that case, we were the second strike. Our job, our duty, was to launch our missiles.

All of them. Not three of them. Why three? And why the same three targets that we had been given in a training exercise two weeks before? And why East Berlin?

The standard orders for a nuclear submarine launch, the ones that occurred most often in their drills, were a response to an all-out Soviet nuclear strike. That was, after all, the principal reason for the existence of the American ballistic missile submarines. Dotted around the world's oceans, gliding quietly at three knots several hundred feet down, they were impossible for the Soviets to find and destroy. So if the Russians ever launched a nuclear attack on the United States, even a surprise one, the submarines would be there to retaliate. Between them they had the firepower to destroy every major Russian city, to kill tens of millions of Russian citizens.

Which was why the Russians would have to be insane to launch a nuclear attack on the United States.

But drill EAMs usually contained a section giving background, declaring that the Russians had launched their missiles, or were on the brink of launching their missiles. This one didn't. In fact, neither had any of the EAMs we had received over the previous twenty-four hours.

No explanation at all. Odd.

Moscow and Leningrad made sense as targets, but East Berlin? That was seriously strange. East Berlin was never included in the *Hamilton*'s targets and for a very good reason. Nuclear warheads detonating there would destroy West Berlin too, massacring not just a couple of million of the citizens of one of the United States' closest allies, West Germany, but also thousands of NATO servicemen. Including Americans.

Never included? East Berlin had been featured in that one drill EAM we had received three weeks before. At the time, we had assumed that was an exercise in retargeting to unfamiliar co-ordinates. Could it be, as the captain had suggested, that it was preparation for the target package that the National Military Command Center always expected the *Hamilton* to use in a war?

Maybe. But I thought it unlikely. It seemed more likely to me that the same message had simply been resent in error.

If there were already thousands of missiles criss-crossing the skies above the waves, then three more wouldn't make any difference. But if there were none as yet, if the Soviets did indeed have their own fingers hovering above the nuclear button, then the *Alexander Hamilton*'s three missiles would set all the others on their way.

The world would be finished.

So I should shoot the man in front of me. Commander Driscoll, a man whom I liked and admired. A man whom I was pleased to call my commanding officer. A man with an ex-wife and two kids.

Despite being in the Navy for eight years, I had never killed anyone before. I had never been asked to kill anyone before.

Did I have the courage to do it?

To save the human race?

Yes, I did.

What would God want? Would God want me to take another man's life? I wasn't an avid Christian, I never went to the small services on the submarine led by Chief Kunkel, but I had been to Sunday school as a kid and I did still occasionally attend church with my parents. I believed in God.

Would God expect me to kill one man to save mankind? Yes. But was God trying to end the world? Was this some biblically inspired Armageddon?

I'd need a theology degree to sort that one out. I had no idea what God wanted, and no time to figure it out.

What would Donna say?

Shoot him. Shoot him now.

But Donna was wrong about this stuff. Wasn't she?

If I didn't shoot him, Donna would die. But perhaps there was a missile heading for New York right now. Perhaps Donna would die anyway.

'Do your duty, son.' Driscoll's voice was calm. Almost friendly. His blue eyes, as always, commanded.

These thoughts flashed through my brain in seconds. A very few seconds. But I had to make a decision.

The Navy had anticipated this. Some of the brightest minds in the country had spent years thinking about moments like this. It wasn't up to me, a lowly lieutenant, to make this decision. How could it be? How could someone like me possibly be relied upon to make a decision this difficult this quickly and under this pressure?

The Navy had it figured out. There were other people who decided. In particular, the President of the United States. Then there were others further down the line. On the *Hamilton*, there were at most two men who could decide not to follow orders, the captain and the executive officer, and in a case like this it was clear they should do what they were commanded to do.

And so should I.

'COB?' I said.

Piatnik, the chief of the boat, or 'COB', who was standing not six feet away from me responded. 'Sir?'

I lowered the pistol and handed it to him, along with the holster.

The relief in the control room was palpable. Petty Officer Williamson immediately grabbed Lars, and hurled him to the floor.

Another crewman snatched the wrench. It only took Driscoll a second to reassert his authority.

'COB, give me the weapon. Arrest Lieutenant da Silva and lock him up with an armed guard.'

He strapped on the holster, and approached me, stopping right in front of me, his face not six inches from mine. 'Lieutenant Guth. You did your duty. We are going to need you in the next few minutes. Are you willing to continue doing your duty?'

There was only one answer now. I stood to attention. 'Aye aye, captain.'

Driscoll stared at me for a moment. Given what I had just done, he was taking quite a leap of faith to trust me. Almost done. What I had actually done was save his life. 'Very good,' he said. 'Now, I'm going to my stateroom for the keys.'

There was silence as the captain left the control room. The crew were still transfixed by what had happened.

'Back to work, gentlemen,' said Robinson from the conn. 'COB. Take Lieutenant da Silva to my stateroom and lock him in there.' The submarine was too small to carry its own brig. The XO's stateroom was as good a place as any to hold a prisoner.

I waited for the captain to return. He was quick.

'Captain in the control room,' announced a petty officer. Driscoll appeared with four keys on dull green lanyards around his neck: the CIP key and three missile launch keys.

The captain took off the lanyard holding the purple CIP key and inserted it into the captain's indicator panel, turning it and flipping up the Permission to Fire toggle switch. The panel lit up with green and red lights indicating the status of the sixteen missiles.

Driscoll took off the three lanyards for the launch keys, and handed them to me. I hurried at a rapid walk aft to the missile compartment and slid down the ladder to the missile control centre, where I passed the keys on to a missile tech to insert in the gas generators attached to missiles one, two and nine. This would arm them, generating the steam that would propel the missiles out of the submarine and above the ocean's surface, where their solid-fuel rockets would then ignite and take them up and away through the earth's atmosphere.

It took about twenty minutes to 'spin up' the missiles. 'Spinning up' referred to the tiny beryllium balls spinning at thousands of revolutions per second within each missile's inertial navigation system. During that time a host of other operations were initiated for each of the three missiles. The three-stage solid-fuel propulsion system was activated, and target coordinates and the coordinates of the submarine were fed into the fire control computer, which downloaded the results to each missile. Diagnostic tests were run on everything.

Once the missiles were spun up, the captain would grant the weapons officer permission to launch. The weapons officer would open a small safe in the missile control centre with a combination only he knew. Inside was a grey removable handle on which nuzzled a simple red pistol trigger. The weapons officer would insert the lead from the handle into the launch control console, give the order to prepare the first missile and, once the missile hatch was open to the outside sea, squeeze the trigger. The missile would fly. It would take about a minute to prepare the second missile and then the third.

Launching missiles made a lot of noise. Every Soviet attack submarine in the area would know exactly where we were. So the tactical systems officer would be devising a torpedo evasion plan to go deep, go quiet and hide the instant the birds were away. Except the tactical systems officer was Lars, who was now locked up in the XO's stateroom; one of the other junior officers would have to do it.

The most dangerous part of the whole process for the crew of the *Alexander Hamilton* was in the couple of hours after launch.

Unless you counted the inevitable day when we would be forced to surface and face a world poisoned by radioactivity in the depths of a nuclear winter. And you probably should count that.

The time waiting for the missiles to spin up was tense, even in an exercise. It was even tenser now in the missile control centre.

I took my seat in front of the launch control console. The missile control centre was cooler than the rest of the ship, in an attempt to counteract the heat generated by the rows of computers down there.

'What was the delay?' Craig asked me.

'They were discussing the order.'

'The targeting? East Berlin?'

I nodded.

'That seemed weird to me,' said Craig. 'But they decided to go ahead?'

There were two missile techs near us, who could easily hear what we were saying. I lowered my voice to just above a whisper. 'Lars objected.'

'He did?'

'Yes. He said he thought the order might be an error. They had given us no context. East Berlin didn't make sense. Only three missiles didn't make sense. The fact it was the same target package as the exercise they gave us a couple of weeks ago didn't make sense.'

'I get what he's saying,' said Craig. 'What did the captain say?'

'He thought about it. Said we go ahead.'

'And the XO?'

'Concurred.'

Craig frowned. He didn't look as if he agreed with that conclusion. 'OK,' he said with a sigh.

He paused as an instruction came through the intercom from the conn. 'The firing order will be one, nine, two,' he announced to his team over the missile control centre circuit.

'Lars took a swing at the captain,' I said. 'With a wrench. Could have killed him. He was *trying* to kill him.'

'What!'

The missile tech in the seat next to Craig, a petty officer named Morgan, glanced up at me, shocked. But everyone on the boat would know what had just happened in the control room soon enough.

'He was stopped,' I said. '*I* stopped him. Now he's under arrest.'

'I bet he is. So he cracked?'

I nodded. But as I did so, I wasn't sure that Lars had cracked. And I knew I hadn't explained my own role to Craig entirely accurately.

The minutes ticked by. The missile department was a good team. We worked well together. We had practiced this countless times.

This was going to happen.

The missile control centre lurched and tilted as the submarine rose toward launch depth of one hundred and fifty feet.

As I leafed through the checklists in the launch manuals and played my part in the dozens of procedures required to ready the missiles, to check and double check the targeting, my mind was divided in two. One half was concentrating on what I was doing, what I had been trained to do.

The other half was thinking about what the consequences were.

And I knew I wasn't alone. The team appeared to be entirely focused on their job. But I could tell from the tension in the shoulders of those missile techs hunched over their instruments and in the sneaked glances between one crew member and another, especially those whom I knew were close buddies, that they were all thinking of what was about to happen, what might be happening at that very moment.

The New London Submarine Base would be on the Soviet target list. It was unlikely that families would be evacuated in time. So every crew member with a wife would probably lose her that day, lose their children.

Maybe they would be the lucky ones, dying instantly in a thermonuclear explosion, rather than slowly from radiation poisoning.

The world had finally gone mad.

Or had it? There was a chance, a slim chance perhaps, that Lars was right. That despite the Soviet leadership's paranoia, the doctrine of Mutual Assured Deterrence was holding. That the EAM we had received was just an enormous screw-up.

Suddenly it was clear to me. If the launch order was genuine, we were already involved in a nuclear war or soon would be. A war no one would win. The *Alexander Hamilton*'s participation would make no difference one way or another.

But if the launch message was an error? Then what we did would make a very great deal of difference.

This was a problem with only one correct answer. And Lars had found it.

I heard Craig talking into his headset next to me. 'Conn, weapons. Three minutes to 1SQ.'

I glanced over to the fire control console. There were sixteen columns, one for each missile, but only three were lit up. The bottom four lights were labelled 1SQ, DENOTE, PREPARE and AWAY. All four buttons shone red. Soon, one by one, they would turn to green. The DENOTE and PREPARE launch phases took less than sixty seconds, during which the outer hatch of each missile was opened to the sea one by one. When the AWAY button turned green the missiles would be in the air.

A digital readout above the panel counted down to an estimate of when all three missiles would be spun up. Two minutes and fifty seconds.

Driscoll's voice came over the 1-MC, echoing throughout the submarine. 'This is the captain. Estimated time to 1SQ three minutes. Prepare for missile launch.'

'Craig?' I stood close to him, my voice low. I addressed him as 'Craig', not 'Weps'.

'Yes?'

'That target package makes no sense, right?'

Craig turned to me. 'Someone in NMCC must think it makes sense.'

'There is a chance it's an error, don't you think?'

'Hey, Bill. We only have ninety seconds to 1SQ. You said the captain and the XO discussed this. You and I have to obey orders.'

I glanced at the safe, positioned right above Craig between the fire control and the launch control consoles. 'You don't have to open that.'

Craig's eyes darted to the combination lock and then back to me. He was hesitating.

'If you don't open it, and you refuse to tell anyone else the combination, then the birds won't fly.'

Craig closed his eyes. Then he opened them. Doubt was replaced by determination. 'Lieutenant Guth. We have our orders. You will follow them, as will I.'

'Craig?' I pleaded.

'Back to your station, Lieutenant Guth.' Craig grabbed the intercom.

I went back to my post. I glanced at the panel. The missiles would be spun up in less than a minute.

Then the captain would give Craig permission to fire and he would open the safe.

Lars's words came back to me. *You can stop a nuclear war if you shoot him. In the head.* Because the captain's head was where the combination to the safe in his stateroom was stored.

It was too late to stop the captain fetching his launch keys from the safe in his stateroom. The only way now to prevent the launch of the missiles was to stop Craig from opening the missile control centre safe and extracting the trigger. He was the only one who knew the combination. So he had to be stopped in such a way that he couldn't tell a fellow officer those numbers.

He had to be killed.

My friend, one of my best friends, had to be killed. By me. In the next few seconds.

I didn't have a gun. But Lars had chosen a good weapon. There were wrenches stowed all over the submarine in positions that were easy to grab in the event of a leak. In peacetime submarines didn't leak, but in wartime when under attack from enemy torpedoes or depth charges, it could easily happen.

The nearest wrench was hanging in a pouch just behind me, maybe three feet from Craig.

Missile number nine spun up first, swiftly followed by number two.

Then the last 1SQ button turned from red to green.

'Conn, weapons. The weapons system is at 1SQ.' Craig was speaking into the intercom. He listened to an instruction and repeated it. 'Permission to fire, aye.'

Do it!

I slowly got to my feet and moved nonchalantly towards the wrench as Craig stood and reached up to the safe, his fingers touching the tumbler.

Out of the corner of my eye I saw Petty Officer Morgan watching me: he was the missile tech who had overheard what Lars had tried to do in the control room.

In one swift movement I whipped the wrench out of its pouch and lifted it. But Morgan was quick. He threw himself at me. I leapt backwards, crashing into an instrument panel, as Morgan clutched my free arm, the arm not holding the wrench.

I brought the tool down hard on his shoulder. He released his grip and fell to the floor screaming.

The other missile techs were slower than Morgan. They were still at their positions, staring at me and at their colleague writhing in agony on the floor. They hadn't trained for this; it took them a second or two to tear themselves away from the procedures on which they were so totally focused.

Craig's fingers were on the combination as he glanced swiftly back at me.

If he had turned to face me, he could almost certainly have protected himself from my blows for the couple of seconds necessary for the rest of the crew to overpower me. He would then have had plenty of time to open the safe.

But he didn't make that choice. He turned his back on me and spun the dial five times to the left, stopping on the first number of the combination, and then spun it to the right to the next number.

Perhaps he thought the other missile techs' reactions were as quick as Morgan's. Perhaps he thought he had time to set the final number on the dial and return it to zero before I got to him.

He had misjudged.

Just as he was setting the third number, and the missile chief was finally rushing me, I brought the wrench crashing down on the back of Craig's head.

26

Saturday 30 November 2019, Norfolk

Toby went with Bill to the police station in King's Lynn, an imposing 1920s building just off the main road through town, with four brick pillars and a large blue light over the entrance. They waited half an hour for Robinson and Prestwitch to get there first, in the hope they might pave the way for Alice's release. Toby felt the tension in Bill. He wanted to lash out at his father-in-law, blame him for getting Alice locked up, but he knew it was fruitless, so he held back.

He sensed a similar grudging self-control on Bill's part.

If Prestwitch had spoken to the police, it hadn't yet secured Alice's release. And, as expected, the police wouldn't let Toby speak to his wife. But he did get five minutes with Lisa Beckwith, Alice's new solicitor from London, who took him to a coffee shop round the corner from the station, while Bill was being interviewed again.

She was very small, very thin with hard brown eyes and an air of suppressed aggression that Toby found comforting in the circumstances. Her advice to Toby was to say as little as possible to the police; she was gratified to hear that he had signed the Official Secrets Act. He should stick to the story he had given them about Alice's whereabouts, and resist the urge to expand on it or embellish it.

She said she was confident that Alice would be released, but Toby didn't believe her. She also told him she had advised Alice to say nothing.

'Why do you do that?' Toby asked. 'It's not as if she's guilty or has anything to hide. We *want* the police to figure out the truth, so why don't we help them do it?'

'That's not exactly what we want the police to do,' said Lisa firmly. 'We don't need to prove she's innocent. We don't need to show the police who did kill Sam Bowen. All we need to do is prevent the police from gathering enough evidence to convict Alice.'

'But—'

'Toby. I know what I'm doing. Please help us. Keep quiet.' It was more of an order than a request.

Back at the station, DC Atkinson wanted to speak to Toby again. He looked on edge. Excited. Impatient. He led Toby through to a featureless interview room and switched on the recording equipment.

No small talk.

'Did Sam Bowen ask Bill Guth about the death of Lieutenant Craig Naylor on the submarine?'

'As I believe you know, I have now signed the Official Secrets Act,' Toby replied.

'What Sam Bowen asked Mr Guth is not an official secret.'

Wasn't it? Toby didn't know. So he answered the question. 'Yes, Sam did ask Bill about Craig's death.'

'Good. And what was Mr Guth's reply?'

Toby wanted to answer. He wanted to help. But he had signed the act, as Bill had said, for his country and for his father-in-law. And although he disagreed with Lisa Beckwith's strategy, there was no doubt that she knew more about keeping suspects out of jail than he did.

'That is secret,' said Toby. 'It relates to what happened on the submarine.'

DC Atkinson couldn't hide his irritation. He leaned forward. Tried a smile. 'Look, Toby. You have to help us here. We're just trying to find out what really happened. If your wife is innocent, she has nothing to fear from that, right?'

Toby didn't answer.

'We now believe that the reason Sam Bowen was murdered is that he knew something, or suspected something about the death of Lieutenant Naylor on the USS *Alexander Hamilton*. Justin Opizzi told us that Naylor was his biological father, and that Naylor's sister Vicky Wenzel was always suspicious about the death. Sam's girlfriend said Sam was suspicious about it too, and although the murderer took his computer and his notebook, and seems to have hacked into his Cloud back-up and deleted his files, there is one note on his desk back at home which suggests he was following that line of inquiry.'

'What was that?' Toby asked, curious.

'Craig Naylor's name circled with an exclamation mark next to it on a pad of paper.'

'That doesn't sound conclusive,' Toby said.

'It isn't. Which is why I need you to tell me what you know about Lieutenant Naylor's death.'

What did Toby know? That Bill had claimed it was an accident. That Justin had suspected Bill of killing Naylor. That Lars had admitted to killing Naylor himself.

It was useful stuff. None of it seemed to him to point to Alice killing Sam. But, on the other hand, he didn't know why she had met the historian that evening.

Best just to trust Alice's solicitor.

'I'm sorry,' said Toby. 'I can't tell you.'

Frustrated, Atkinson terminated the interview and kicked Toby out of the interview room.

*

175

Bill was waiting for him at the entrance to the police station. But as he was leaving, Toby held the door for a small woman also on her way out. Her long hair was dyed blue, and her freckled cheeks were drawn firmly downwards on either side of her mouth. She was very thin, but Toby noticed there was a slight bump at her waist.

She hurried out of the police station and down the steps to the pavement.

'Hang on, Bill,' said Toby, and he rushed after her. 'Excuse me,' he said in as friendly a voice as he could muster.

The woman didn't look at him.

'Are you Jasmine, by any chance?'

The woman stopped to face him, a glimmer of curiosity in her dead eyes. 'Maybe.'

'I just wanted to say how sorry I am about Sam.'

'Sam? Who are you? How do you know about Sam?'

'Oh, he came to Thanksgiving at our house on Thursday. It was the first time I had met him, but I liked him.' Toby hesitated. Nothing he could say would be satisfactory, but he couldn't just say nothing. 'I am really sorry for you. And his parents,' he added.

'So you are from the family of the woman who killed him?'

'Yes. She's my wife. And she didn't kill him, I'm sure of it.'

'Then why isn't she talking to the police? Why isn't she helping them like any decent citizen would do?'

A good question. 'I don't know,' said Toby. 'But I do know she can't have killed him.'

The woman's shoulders slumped. 'Whoever she is, she's innocent until proved guilty, I get that. And she's your wife, so you think she's innocent. I get that too. But I don't care. If the police find she's guilty I hope they lock her up and throw away the key. If she's innocent, then they can let her go. I won't want to see her then, and I don't want to see you now. Do you understand me?'

Toby nodded. 'I understand.'

'Good. Now let me get back to my shitty life. Goodbye.'

She turned and left Toby watching her forlornly.

'Was that Sam's girlfriend?' Bill asked at Toby's shoulder.

'Uh-huh.'

'I suspected it might be. I thought it best to leave her alone.'

'Good call,' said Toby.

'Did they ask you about Craig's death?' said Bill as he drove Toby back to Barnholt.

'Yes.'

'Did you tell them anything?'

'No.'

'Good man,' said Bill.

Toby's phone buzzed. It was Piet. Toby ignored it.

Toby stared out of the window at the industrial buildings guarding the northern outskirts of King's Lynn, dismal beneath a layer of grey clouds that was gathering from the south.

He thought of his disastrous conversation with Sam Bowen's girlfriend. He had just been thinking of himself, how he wanted to express his own sorrow and sympathy for her. He hadn't been thinking of her. She clearly had no interest in him or his sympathy, and why should she?

She had a point about Alice. Lisa Beckwith's strategy was all very well, but if Alice was innocent, surely the easiest way to get her off the hook was to prove it to the police? Or give them enough information so they could figure it out for themselves.

It was true that Alice knew what had happened on the submarine, she knew that was secret and she took that seriously. But if Sam had told the world that her father had saved it back in 1983, would that be such a bad thing? Would it be worth Alice killing Sam for?

The answer was clearly no.

Maybe defence solicitors had learned through experience that being helpful didn't work as well as keeping quiet and being obstructive. That was probably because most of their clients were guilty.

Then it dawned on Toby.

He turned to Bill. 'Does Alice's solicitor think she killed Sam Bowen?'

Bill focused on the road ahead. 'I don't know. Maybe.'

Then an even more troubling thought occurred to Toby. 'Do *you* think Alice killed him?'

'Of course not,' said Bill.

But he didn't take his eyes off the road; he didn't look at Toby.

Toby wasn't sure he believed him.

When they returned to Barnholt, Toby went up to his bedroom and Bill scurried off to his study.

Toby had just flopped on to the bed, when there was a knock at the door. It was Megan. 'Want to grab some lunch?'

'Sure. There's got to be some cold turkey left.'

'I was thinking of going out. To the King Willie. I need to get away from this house.'

'Won't it still be cordoned off?'

'It might be. If it is, we can go to Thurstead. There's a good pub there, I think.'

'All right.' Toby pulled himself off the bed. 'Shall we ask your dad?'

'Let's not ask my dad. With everything that's going on, I bet he's doing his needlepoint in his study. We wouldn't want to disturb that.'

It had just started to rain, but the walk was only five minutes. The King William was now open, although there was a police car stationed at the entrance to the car park, an officer sheltering inside. Toby nodded to him as they entered the pub.

The pub was virtually empty, just two couples in their sixties eating lunch, and a man in painters' overalls refreshing himself with a quick pint. A fire crackled in a large brick fireplace, its sweet smell tempering the sour odour of stale beer.

Toby ordered two pints of Wherry, a ploughman's for him and a scampi and chips for Megan, from a middle-aged woman with bright-yellow hair in a ponytail. A disconcertingly large wart drooped from a sagging cheek.

'When did the police let you open?' Megan asked.

'Just half an hour ago,' said the woman. She glanced around the empty bar. 'We should have more people here on a Saturday lunchtime.'

'Do you think the murder will put them off?' Megan asked.

'I don't know.' The woman looked guilty. 'But it's not the kind of thing I should worry about, at least not yet. That poor man!'

'It's awful, isn't it?' said Megan. 'He was visiting us. He stayed for Thanksgiving dinner, just before he died.'

'And I saw him when he got back here,' said the woman. 'He was full of good cheer. He told me he enjoyed your dinner.'

Her warm smile turned into a frown. She fingered the wart on her cheek.

'Yes,' said Megan. 'It's my sister who they've arrested. But they've got the wrong person. Alice didn't kill him.'

The landlady took a moment to decide how to respond. 'Oh, I do hope not,' she said. 'She looked like such a nice young lady. She came to visit Mr Bowen that evening. It was almost closing time – they had a quick drink and then they both went up to his room.'

'How long was she with him?' Megan asked.

'Oh I don't know. I didn't see her come down. Or him, as a matter of fact. I found him in the morning when I brought him his coffee. He was collapsed by the side of the bed, still wearing his clothes. At first I thought he'd had a heart attack or something, although he seemed a bit young for that. Then I saw the blood.' She shuddered. 'Dreadful. Was your sister his girlfriend? The police didn't say.'

'She wasn't,' Megan said. 'This is Alice's husband.'

Toby smiled at the landlady stiffly.

'Oh, I didn't mean to imply—'

'Of course not,' Toby said. 'Thursday was the first time they had met.'

'That will be twenty-two forty,' said the woman, shutting down the conversation.

Megan chose a table with a view of the green. An old red telephone box stood a respectful distance from the much older cross. It no longer housed a payphone, but a defibrillator. A nice idea but, as the landlady had discovered, there were some sudden attacks for which it was no help.

'It kind of feels like the family is falling apart,' Megan said. 'Alice locked up. Brooke and Maya running away. Mom's gone. And Dad seems so fricking evasive. It feels like me and you are the only ones who still care. Which, given my track record, is downright weird.'

'Your track record?'

Megan shrugged. 'I was always the naughty one of the four of us. And I lost it when Mom died. Made some poor life choices. Dropped out of college and ran off with a guy who made a living spreading malware on the Internet. I wound up my dad at every opportunity, and Alice – like the time I skipped your wedding at the last minute. And probably the reason I'm quitting my job and doing this waitress thing in New York is to piss them off. I'm surprised they put up with me. Alice must have told you?'

'She did say you were difficult,' Toby admitted. 'Although I'm not sure that's the way you seem to me.'

Megan flashed him a quick smile. 'Oh, I am. She was right. I used to take all the stuff she did for us all for granted. But now . . . I don't know. We need to get her out of jail.'

'We do.'

'What did you think of her lawyer?'

'She's a tough nut and she's clearly competent. But I'm worried she thinks Alice killed Sam.'

'Really? Isn't it her job to think Alice is innocent?'

Toby shrugged. 'As long as she puts forward a good case, it probably doesn't much matter.'

'Alice's law firm will be wondering where she is over the weekend. Too bad.'

'I sent them an email to tell them she couldn't make it.'

'Did you say why?'

'No. I lied.'

'Toby!' But Megan's horror was feigned. There were a lot of lies flying around at the moment, small ones and big ones. 'That woman works too hard.'

'Oh, I don't know,' said Toby.

'Oh, give me a break! She works twelve-hour days seven days a week. Doesn't she?'

'Longer hours than that sometimes, but not *every* day.'

'Can't you tell her to stop?'

'She likes it,' said Toby.

'Doesn't it piss you off?'

'Sometimes. But it's kind of who she is. The woman I married.'

'She'll be going crazy in jail. Nothing to do.'

'But a lot to think about.'

The food came, delivered by a girl careful not to make eye contact with them, under the stern gaze of the woman at the bar. It looked like Alice's family were already at village pariah status.

'Justin was pretty upset when he accused Bill of killing Craig,' Toby said.

'Wasn't he? I never realized he was such a gorilla. He usually comes across as civilized to me. But he kind of worships Craig.'

'I was going to say, he didn't even know him. And presumably there is a Mr Opizzi who acted like his father?'

'Yeah. Justin's rough on him – has been ever since he figured out what happened. Because of course it means his mom was having an affair with Tony Opizzi while Justin's hero naval-officer dad was still alive. Justin treats his dad, or step-dad, as a loser deadbeat. Brooke finds it all very awkward.'

'Doesn't sound much fun for Mr Opizzi.'

'It isn't. Brooke says he's kinda nice. But then he did steal Craig's wife.'

Toby spread some sweet pickle on his cheese, and popped it in his mouth. 'Do you think there really is something suspicious about Craig's death? Now Lars claims he killed Craig by accident. In a fight over a girl. Do you think that's all it is?'

Megan shrugged. 'Who knows?'

'Does that make Lars a murderer? Because if he is a murderer, the police should know.'

'He says the Navy didn't prosecute him.'

'Yeah,' said Toby. 'But they were in full cover-up mode.'

'Do you think he killed Sam? Maybe Lars is the one who should be in custody, not Alice?'

'Maybe. But the landlady just told us that Sam was still wearing his clothes. That kind of implies it wasn't too late in the night – he hadn't gone to bed yet. And Lars told me the police were happy with his alibi. Justin and Brooke stayed up in the Cottage after the game, and they would have noticed Lars leaving.'

The idea that Lars had killed Sam Bowen did not appeal to Toby. Toby liked Lars. Felt sorry for him. Admired the way he had volunteered the truth about Craig to Justin. 'Any idea who the girl might be? The one Lars and Craig were arguing over when they had that fight?'

'I'm not sure there was a girl,' Megan said.

'What do you mean?'

Megan didn't answer, but toyed with her scampi.

'Megan? What is it?'

'*Somebody* has to care who killed that poor historian,' she said.

'The police do.'

'Do they? It seems to me they are trying to pin it on Alice. And all that lawyer is trying to do is stop them. I'm sure Dad and Lars know stuff they are not saying. Aren't you?'

Toby nodded.

'If we are going to get Alice off, we need to show who did kill Sam Bowen.'

'You said that before. But how can we do that?'

Megan put down her fork and stared at her beer. She was thinking. Toby waited.

'Toby?'

'Yes?'

'I haven't been entirely straight with you.'

'Oh?' Toby was curious, but also disappointed. He had come to assume that Megan was the one member of the Guth family who *was* entirely straight with him.

'Finish your lunch. There's something I should show you.'

28

When they got back to Pear Tree Cottage there was no sign of Bill. He was probably in his study upstairs, working on his tapestry.

The study was at the other end of the landing from his bedroom. Megan whispered that Toby should go into his own room for a minute and then join her in Bill's bedroom. She would warn him if the coast wasn't clear.

Toby was uneasy, but he did what he was asked. Megan was waiting for him in Bill's bedroom. A four-poster bed dominated the room, with a view over the marsh to the dunes. Delicate, elegant English antiques surrounded the bed: two bedside tables, a small chest of drawers and a chair covered with a tapestry of daffodils. There was a feminine feel to the room – something about the pattern of the curtains and the bedspread; and the tapestry on the chair wasn't one of Bill's.

It had been Bill's wife's room.

'Here,' Megan whispered. She beckoned Toby to a built-in wardrobe that took up most of one wall.

'Lift me up,' she said.

Toby bent down, grabbed her legs, and raised her up so she could reach into the darkness at the back of a shelf that ran above the wardrobe. She pulled out a small wicker basket.

Toby lowered her. She squatted on the floor next to the basket. It was full of letters, still in their envelopes, softened and crinkled, about thirty of them, addressed to Donna Threadgold at 8 St Mark's Place Apt 19, New York City. Megan riffled through them, checking the postmarks.

'This is it,' she said, extracting one. The postmark was January 20 1984.

With a glance at the open door, she pulled out three sheets of paper covered in handwriting, and passed them to Toby. 'Read that.'

He read it. 'Jesus!' he whispered. Then he read it again.

'I know, right?' said Megan.

'But this means Lars just lied to Justin? About Craig.'

'Yep. I'm sorry I didn't tell you before.'

'And you didn't tell the police?'

'They didn't ask me, or at least they haven't yet. And I don't think I will tell them. I came across the letters a couple of months after Mom died and I was going through her clothes. They were right up there, behind some shoe boxes. I shouldn't have read them, but I just wanted to find out more about her. So I did. And this is what I found.'

They heard a door open down the landing and the floorboards creak.

They both stood up and listened. It was Bill. The most likely thing was for him to turn off the landing and head down the stairs.

But the footsteps came closer.

'Shit!' Megan said. 'He's coming! Give that to me!'

'No,' Toby said. 'We need to discuss this with him.'

'No we don't! Jesus Christ, Toby! Stick it back in the basket. Quick!'

Toby turned towards the door.

Which opened.

Bill jerked upright in surprise when he saw Megan and Toby in his bedroom. He took in the basket. The letter in Toby's hands.

'What the hell?'

Megan looked scared. 'Sorry, Dad.'

'Is that a letter? Is that one of my letters to your mother?'

'Yeah. I found them when I was looking through her stuff.'

'And you showed them to Toby? What are you thinking? Those are private!'

'Yes, I know. But—'

'But what?'

'This one mentions what happened to Craig,' Toby said quietly. 'On the submarine.'

'Give it to me!' Bill held out his hand.

'No.'

'What do you mean "no"? Give it to me right now.' Bill took a step towards Toby.

Toby faced him. 'No.'

'I've had enough of this. I want you out of my house now!' Bill was shouting. 'And you, Megan. Right now! And give me that damn letter.'

He reached out to grab it, but Toby held on to the sheets with both hands. Bill tugged gently, but it was clear that he couldn't get it away from Toby without ripping it. Bill didn't want to rip it.

'Let it go!'

'No,' said Toby. For a moment he thought Bill was going to slug him, but he stood his ground. 'Not until you explain it. You need to tell me what is going on here. What happened to Craig and what it has to do with Alice.'

'I have to do no such thing. That's my private correspondence.'

'Yes, you do,' said Toby, his eyes fixed on Bill's. 'Alice is in police custody. Unless someone does something she will be charged with murder. She may go to jail for the rest of her life. You need to explain this.'

Bill stiffened. Then he released the letter and walked over to the window. It had stopped raining; the marsh gleamed grey-green in the low November sunlight.

Toby and Megan watched his broad back. He took a deep breath and turned to them.

'OK,' he said. 'Sit down. There's a lot to tell you.'

November 1983, Norwegian Sea

A petty officer, flanked by two sailors, flung open the door to the XO's stateroom and shoved me inside.

The missile chief had grabbed me as Craig crumpled to the floor, next to Morgan who was groaning in pain. I dropped the wrench. We all stared at the blood seeping through Craig's hair. I didn't know if he was dead. He looked it.

Within a minute the XO was in the missile compartment, taking control. A minute later, I was in his stateroom. With Lars.

Lars was pacing the tiny room. He stopped and stared at me. He grinned, but his eyes were wild. 'I heard the announcement terminating missile launch,' he said. 'Did you do it?'

'Do what?' I said, although I knew what he meant.

'Kill Driscoll?'

I shook my head and lowered it.

'Weps?'

I nodded.

'Thank God,' Lars said.

I looked at him. Part of me thought he was crazy. Part of me thought he was the only sane one on board.

'Actually, I'm not sure he's dead,' I said.

'What do you mean?'

'I hit him hard over the head. With a wrench, like you tried to do.'

'And you don't think you killed him?'

'He's out cold, that's for sure.' I felt my throat constrict and my eyes water. It took me by surprise; I never cried.

Lars threw his arm around me. 'Well done!' he said. 'Well done, Bill.'

I pushed him away and slumped on to the XO's bed. 'I probably killed him, Lars.'

'And stopped a war.'

'We don't know that!'

Lars bent down and grabbed my shoulders. 'Look! If there's a war, we're all dead. But if there isn't, it's just Craig.'

'Just Craig? But he was my friend. *Our* friend.'

'Yes he was,' said Justin. 'But you did the right thing.'

'I don't know. But I've done it now.'

I sat and Lars paced. I looked around the XO's stateroom. It was freakishly neat. With so many people crammed into a submarine, everything on board had to be tidy. But the XO's desk was completely clear, with the exception of a black-and-white photograph of a woman set at a forty-five degree angle; the books on his shelf were perfectly vertical. It was as if he had used a protractor to adjust the placement of his things.

I stared at Mrs Robinson, if that's who she was. She was beautiful. An open face, wide clear eyes, a smile that made your heart leap.

How long did she have to live? Was she dead already?

I sat on the bed, hoping. But I wasn't sure what to hope for. That the launch order was an error, obviously. But that meant that I had to hope that Craig was dead, so that he couldn't pass on the combination to his safe to anyone.

I didn't want to hope for that.

But what difference did it make what I hoped for? I had done what I had done. If I was lucky I would live with the consequences.

The door was flung open and the XO entered.

I leaped to attention. Lars glanced at me and did the same.

Lieutenant Commander Robinson's dark eyes flashed with anger. 'You are both under arrest. You will be court martialled when we return to port. For murder. For attempted murder. For mutiny. And probably for a whole lot of other crimes.'

'Aye aye, sir,' I said.

Robinson glared at us; the anger verged on hatred. 'The rest of the crew were willing to do our duty, what we have trained for years to do, but you two have let us all down. The entire crew of the submarine. The Navy. Your country.'

Neither Lars nor I said anything. Maybe he was right? It was done now.

'If it was up to me, I would have had you both shot. Now.'

'Is Weps alive, XO?' I asked.

'Yes,' said the XO. He gave me a tight smile. 'He's unconscious, but alive.'

'Will he come around?'

'We don't know. But if he does we will launch those missiles, I can assure you.'

We waited.

The submarine was still operating under 'operational security condition alpha', which was the quietest operational mode. Non-essential machines such as washing machines, fans and the trash compactor were turned off, and the crew were particularly vigilant to avoid accidental bumps and clangs known as 'transients' which might alert Soviet attack submarines in the area.

A wrench dropped on the floor definitely counted as a transient.

So the submarine was quiet. In the XO's stateroom we should still be able to hear announcements over the 1-MC shipwide broadcasts, but not the more specific orders. Changes in depth might give us a clue as to what was going on – the submarine would tilt either up or down.

Lars's pacing was irritating me. It was difficult enough sitting still when you had a specific role as part of the crew, you knew what was going on and you had been trained for it.

But sitting on a bunk in a tiny stateroom with no clue what was happening in the outside world? That was difficult.

The speaker in the stateroom kicked into life. 'Secure from battle stations missile.' It was the captain's voice.

A few seconds later the floor tilted downwards from the right of the stateroom, the direction of the bow. The crew was standing down from battle stations missile and we were descending.

'What do you think that means?' said Lars.

'I guess it must mean that Craig hasn't come around,' I said. 'They were probably waiting for him to wake up and tell them the combination. But he hasn't, so they have given up on launching the missiles and descended again.'

'Thank God for that!' Lars said. 'I mean that we haven't started a war. Not about Craig.'

'Maybe he's dead?' The relief I felt was only partial, and Lars's face, his whole being, was still tight with tension. 'Maybe a war had already started.'

'I wish they'd tell us what's going on!'

Lars banged on the door, which was opened by a petty officer armed with a rifle. Another stood back, watching.

'Can you tell us what's happening?'

'No, sir,' said the petty officer. His name was Calhoun, and when he was on watch, he was a throttleman in manoeuvring.

'I want to speak to the XO. We need to know what's happening!'

The petty officer hesitated. 'Please step back into the stateroom, sir, and I will pass on your message.'

Five minutes later, the door opened. It was Calhoun again. 'The XO says he is too busy to speak with you, sir.'

'Screw him!' said Lars as the guard closed the door. 'We've got to know what's going on out there!'

I agreed, but I wasn't at all surprised that the XO hadn't come down to enlighten us.

'We don't even know if war has broken out,' Lars said.

I shook my head.

'Do you think the captain knows?'

'How could he? We would have heard the Alert One alarm if there had been another EAM.'

'I'm sure that message was an error,' said Lars.

'I'm not,' I said. 'It might have been. I know we were right to do what we did. But it's just as likely that there are missiles flying around out there.'

We were both quiet.

'They would have struck by now, wouldn't they?' said Lars.

'Some,' I said. It would depend when they were launched and where they were launched from, but if Russia and NATO were flinging thousands of warheads at each other, some would have landed. A lot would have landed.

I tried to imagine it. It was clear what would happen to the direct targets like New York and indeed the New London Submarine Base. Flattened. Massive explosions and temperatures at thousands of degrees. Anyone close to a thermonuclear explosion would die instantly. Millions would be dead in the world's great cities. Washington. Moscow. London. Paris.

New York.

Donna.

It wouldn't have hurt. There would have been a brief warning, enough to provoke panic in the powerless civilians who heard it, but actually many New Yorkers would take a while to figure out what the Civil Defense sirens meant.

Then almost instant death.

And what about my parents, on the banks of the Susquehanna? They might still be alive. How long before the fallout would kill them? A day, maybe two at most, given the amounts of radiation in the atmosphere around the eastern United States. I remembered the symptoms from my radiation sickness training: vomiting, diarrhoea, headaches, fever and then death.

'So if there is a war, what happens to us?' said Lars.

'I guess they will let us out of this stateroom. And then we all stay submerged for as long as we can.' A Lafayette-class submarine could stay under water for at least fifteen years. But humans couldn't.

'How long do you figure we've got before we run out of food?'

'We're a month into the patrol. Three months maybe, with aggressive rationing, perhaps four?'

'And then what?'

'We surface somewhere. New Zealand? And hope there are still people alive.' This was something we had never discussed, or only in jest. I remembered a conversation over a few beers with Craig about giant mutant bunnies. I also remembered laughing at the time.

'Did you ever see *On The Beach*?' Lars asked.

'I read the book.' It was a novel by Nevile Shute set in Australia a year after a nuclear war had wiped out life in the northern hemisphere. The population waited as the radiation cloud drifted slowly southwards. In the end, everyone died.

Everyone.

'But that was in the fifties,' I said. 'There's going to be much more radiation now. There will be nowhere to go.'

Lars propelled himself at the door and banged. 'Tell us what the fuck is going on out there!' he yelled.

194

The door remained shut.

I tapped Lars on the sleeve. 'Hey, man. Calm down. There's nothing we can do here except wait. All will become clear in time.'

Lars pushed himself away from the door and resumed pacing.

I sat back down on the XO's bunk, my mind a jumble of my parents and Donna. And trees and streams and meadows. Birdsong.

I had thought long and hard about a nuclear war since I had joined the Navy at eighteen; I was sure we all had. But it had always been in the abstract. Now, because it was so real, it was difficult to process.

The 1-MC burst into life. 'Man battle stations torpedo!' Usually this would have been followed by the loud bong-bong-bong of the general alarm, but the captain must have ordered silence to avoid alerting any nearby Soviet attack subs.

'What's that about?' said Lars. 'Are we under attack?'

The floor of the stateroom tilted up and to the right. The *Hamilton* was ascending steadily. 'I don't think so,' I said. If we had been, the submarine's movement would have been much more extreme as it evaded a possible torpedo, the 'angles and dangles' we had practised ad nauseam.

We had no idea how deep the submarine was, but the ascent took a while. When the boat eventually levelled out, I could feel a slight movement from side to side signifying we were near the surface. 'I think we are at periscope depth.'

'That means he's going to transmit!' said Lars.

'It also means we're sitting ducks,' I said. 'If a war has started, the Soviets will hear us right away. They'll be after us.'

That was why the captain had ordered battle stations torpedo – in case the *Hamilton* got into a shooting battle with a Soviet fast-attack submarine. In addition to nuclear missiles, the *Hamilton* carried anti-submarine torpedoes. The Soviet submarines were faster and more agile; they would know exactly where we were, and we wouldn't locate them until they were upon us. The *Hamilton*'s significant advantage was its ability to hide silently, but by rising to surface depth and broadcasting to the world, we had thrown that advantage away.

If the Russians could get to us before we had finished transmitting and dived again, they would sink us.

We would have a minute or two's warning. When the sonar shack detected an incoming torpedo, the captain would instantly start throwing his big vessel about in an attempt to dodge it. That, Lars and I would feel.

But the huge submarine was steady, swaying a tiny amount in the chop above the surface, as the captain contacted the outside world – probably COMSUBLANT, the headquarters for the Atlantic submarine fleet in Norfolk, Virginia.

Lars stopped pacing. We both stared at the tiny speaker in the stateroom.

At last, it came to life.

'This is the captain. I have been advised by COMSUBLANT that the previous EAM we received authorizing the use of nuclear weapons was an error. The use of nuclear weapons has *not* been authorized. The change of readiness to DEFCON 3 was also an error. We remain at DEFCON 5. Stand down from battle stations torpedo.'

'Thank God!' I leaped to my feat. Lars punched the air. We embraced.

DEFCON 5 meant no war. No attack by a Soviet submarine. No nuclear holocaust.

Lars stood back. On the other side of the stateroom door we could hear a cheer ripple throughout the vessel.

'Jesus,' he said. 'That was close.'

'So close.'

I felt drained as the tension left my body. I could scarcely move my limbs.

I took a deep breath. 'I sure hope Craig lives.'

I rapped on the door again. Our two guards wouldn't let us out, even though they were both grinning.

After an hour, a sailor with a sidearm came to escort me to the captain's stateroom.

I knocked and entered.

Commander Driscoll was sitting at his desk. He seemed ten years older than the last time I saw him. His face, normally so calm under pressure, looked ravaged.

'Take a seat.' He indicated the bed.

I sat down.

'Bill. You did the right thing,' he said. 'As did da Silva. Even when he was trying to kill me, he did the right thing.'

'Thank you, sir.'

'And I didn't.' Driscoll ran his hands through his hair. 'If we had launched those missiles as I had ordered, the Soviets would definitely have retaliated, especially if the XO is right about them expecting a pre-emptive attack from us. Millions of people would have died, hundreds of millions. And it would have been my fault.'

He gave a hollow laugh. 'I might never have found out it was the *Hamilton* that had started it, if we had launched. But as it is, I know I would have begun a nuclear war if you hadn't stopped me. That's something I'm going to have to live with for the rest of my life.' He winced. 'That's going to be difficult.'

'You did what your orders told you to do,' I said. 'You followed procedure. That's what you are supposed to do in a crisis.' And I meant it. I understood what Driscoll had chosen to do; I had been through the same thought process myself.

But Driscoll shook his head. 'You and da Silva figured it out. The procedures were wrong. There was only one correct alternative. I should have chosen it.'

'How's Weps?'

'He's come around. We have the combination to his safe. Who knows? We may yet need it.'

I swallowed. 'Can I see him?'

It took a while. The captain kept Lars and me under armed guard in our stateroom, the JO Jungle. He explained he had to. We had breached Navy regulations in about as serious a way as was possible. And the submarine was still on patrol. She still might be ordered to launch her missiles, in which case the captain decided Lars and I should be kept away from where we could do further damage.

The wardroom steward brought us supper, and then there was a knock at the door. It was the XO, come to take me to the wardroom to speak to Craig.

Like the captain, the XO looked drained. I didn't know what to say to him.

'Bill,' he said, as we walked along the passageway, every passing sailor staring at us. 'I'm sorry for what I said back there. And I'm sorry for backing the captain to accept the launch order. I was wrong.' He sucked through his teeth. 'I was really worried that the Soviets were going to launch a nuclear strike in response to Able Archer. So when we received that EAM, I immediately assumed that's what had happened. I thought we couldn't afford to screw around worrying about erroneous messages. I was so wrong.'

What could I say? How could I absolve a man from nearly blowing up the world? I settled on 'thank you'. It takes some courage for a senior officer to apologize to a junior one.

Craig was in the wardroom, slumped in his usual chair, a thick bandage obscuring the top of his head. He looked rough.

He lifted his head as I came in, his eyes hostile.

'How is it?' I asked.

'It hurts like hell.'

I took a deep breath. 'Sorry.'

Craig just stared at me. 'You tried to kill me,' he said. 'I was doing my duty and you tried to kill me.'

I had feared that response. It was true, of course, but somehow I had hoped that Craig would forgive me.

'At least we are still alive.'

'You didn't know the launch order was an error,' Craig said. 'How could you?'

'You said yourself that East Berlin was weird.'

'Yes, but in a real war there will be orders that seem weird. And we will follow them.'

'Like I said, Craig. I'm sorry.'

Craig looked down at his fingernails. 'Get out.'

I never saw Craig again. Two days later the XO came into the JO Jungle where Lars and I were still in custody to tell us that Craig had just collapsed. They were watching a movie in the wardroom – not *Barbarella* – and he had just keeled over.

He died nine hours later. Bleeding in the brain from the initial blow with the wrench.

I had killed him after all.

30

Saturday 30 November 2019, Norfolk

'Wow,' said Megan. 'So you killed Craig on purpose? I knew Craig had died in an accident on board the submarine, so I assumed from the letter it was your fault somehow, and you had never admitted it to anyone but Mom.'

She took the letter from Toby and read the passage aloud: '*I still can't get over what I did to Craig. I'll never forgive myself. I just try not to think about it.*' She looked up at her father.

'Well, it wasn't an accident,' said Bill. 'But you can see why I struck him with that wrench?' Bill's expression mixed pain and pleading as he faced his daughter.

'Oh my God, yes,' said Megan. She got up and flung her arms around him. 'You had to do it. If you hadn't done it, we wouldn't be here. No one would be here.'

Bill's face broke into a smile over Megan's shoulder.

'Craig really was a good friend. He was also a good man. He was just wrong. Following orders right then was a very bad call.'

'I can see why the Navy wanted to keep it all a secret,' said Toby.

'So can I,' said Megan, breaking away from her father. 'Who would trust them with a nuclear submarine after that? I know I wouldn't.'

'Yes, they did keep it secret,' said Bill. 'But they also made changes to the launch protocols so it couldn't happen again. If a submarine gets a doubtful order now, the captain is required to go to periscope depth and check it.'

'What had gone wrong?'

'Same as what happened a couple of years before at NORAD when they thought the Soviets were attacking us. A systems upgrade test went wrong. Lars was right: the fact the target was exactly the same as the exercise and the lack of context in raising readiness to DEFCON 3 should have alerted us. But, on the other hand, launch protocol said Commander Driscoll had to obey the order, not question it.'

'And was the XO right about Able Archer?' Toby asked. 'Did the Soviets really think we were about to attack them?'

'Yes,' Bill nodded. 'Robinson was absolutely right, although the high-ups in the CIA overruled him and his colleague. But a secret report was written by the CIA in the 1990s that suggested that Andropov really *was* convinced the United States was planning a decapitation first strike. When they intercepted our signals during Able Archer, the Soviets put their nuclear forces on high alert.' Bill blew out through his cheeks. 'It was close. And if the *Alexander Hamilton had* launched its birds, there is no doubt the Soviets would have retaliated with everything they had.'

The three of them sat in silence as they thought about what Bill had just said, Megan and Toby on the bed, Bill on the delicate chair with the tapestry.

'Can I have my letter back now?' said Bill, holding out his hand.

'Oh, yes, sorry,' said Toby. He wasn't apologizing for reading the section where Bill was telling Donna about how bad he felt about killing Craig. But there was stuff in there about how much Bill loved her, and other stuff which Toby had no business reading. Somehow it seemed worse now she was dead. And now Bill had told Toby more about her.

He slipped the letter back in its envelope and handed it back to Bill.

'I wish I had known Donna,' he said. 'She sounded . . . unique. Special.'

'She was,' said Megan.

Bill grinned gratefully at his daughter.

'Why did Lars claim to have killed Craig?' Toby asked.

'That took me completely by surprise,' said Bill. 'I don't know. I haven't spoken to him yet about it. Loyalty, I guess. Despite his faults, Lars is a good friend. He could probably see how upset Justin was with me.'

'Are you going to tell Justin?' Megan said. 'That it was you who killed his father?'

'No,' said Bill. 'This stuff is genuinely top secret. I shouldn't have told you. Donna shouldn't have told you girls anything about it. And you shouldn't tell anyone else. Even the police.'

'But it's just a cover-up,' Toby said. 'What kind of state secret is that?'

'I know it's a cover-up,' said Bill. 'But it's still necessary. Nuclear deterrence only works if people trust it. People on your own side, and the enemy, whoever they turn out to be. This is the kind of story that could undermine that trust.'

Toby wasn't convinced. Bill noticed. 'You have signed the Official Secrets Act, Toby.'

He had. In a way he was grateful. That meant he didn't have to agonize over whether to tell the police; his duty was clear and spelled out. Or his duty to his country was.

'What about Alice?' he said.

'What about her?'

'You've been saying all along that what happened on the *Alexander Hamilton* had nothing to do with Sam Bowen's murder. But given what you have just told us, are you sure that's the case? It's a cover-up, isn't it? Did the US Navy kill him? The CIA? To keep him quiet.'

'No. No, absolutely not. The CIA has done some unpleasant stuff over the years, but they don't kill journalists or historians who are asking difficult questions.'

'Can you be certain?'

'Absolutely. If they did that, imagine the outcry? It would also be illegal.' Bill coughed. 'I did check with Admiral Robinson, and he confirmed it. He worked in the Office of Naval Intelligence after the *Hamilton* – he has good contacts.'

'So what was Alice doing talking to Sam? Was she asking him about Craig's death?'

Bill didn't answer. He was looking worried.

'What is it, Dad?' Megan asked.

Bill hesitated. 'Ever since Mom died, Alice has always been protective of me. She knew that it was me who killed Craig.'

'You *told* her,' Megan said.

'Not me. Your mother.'

'Wait. Did she tell Brooke and Maya too?' Sisterly outrage at being left out was rising in Megan's voice.

'No. Just Alice. She wanted to tell one of you.'

And she had chosen Alice, Toby thought. That figured. And Alice hadn't told Toby. That figured as well. And, actually, that was fair enough.

Megan grunted. She accepted it was fair enough too.

'OK,' said Toby. 'So you think that Alice was trying to persuade Sam to drop the questions about Craig's death?'

'Perhaps.' Bill looked uncomfortable. Exceedingly uncomfortable.

'My God!' Toby said. 'You do think Alice killed him.'

'No,' said Bill. 'No, I couldn't possibly believe she could do that. Not Alice.'

'Yes you do.'

Bill pursed his lips. 'Let's just say I don't think it would be good for Alice's case if the police came to the conclusion that that's what she was talking to him about.'

Part of Toby was outraged.

Part of him understood it.

They heard the front door bang downstairs. 'Hello!' It was Lars's voice. 'Anyone at home?'

'I'll talk to him,' Toby said, and he left Megan and her father in the bedroom.

Lars was in the kitchen, still in his rain jacket. 'Hey, Toby,' he said. 'How did it go at the police station?'

'They wouldn't let me see Alice. And she is still locked up.'

'Have they charged her yet?'

'Not yet. We don't know whether they will. They can hold her for thirty-six hours without charging her, so technically they could let her out really early tomorrow morning, but her lawyer says if they are going to release her, it will be later today.'

'Good luck.'

'Yeah.'

Given what he had just learned, Toby was hopeful that he could prise more information out of Lars about what had happened on the submarine. Confirm Bill's story, perhaps. Give him a clue why Sam Bowen was killed, a clue he could use to get Alice freed. But it would be difficult to talk to Lars in the house with Bill and Megan around.

'Hey, Lars. Now it's stopped raining, do you want to get out of the house? Go for another walk on the beach? With Rickover, of course.'

The dog was on his feet, looking expectantly up at the two men. His vote was clear.

'Sure,' said Lars. 'Let's go.'

They were donning their coats in the hallway when Bill came down the stairs and greeted Lars. 'I'm just going to King's Lynn to get a new faucet for the Cottage bathroom,' he said. 'I shouldn't be too long.'

'We're going for a walk down to the beach,' said Lars. 'If you like, I'll help you fix it when I get back.'

'Glorified plumbers,' said Megan from the stairs. 'That's all these submarine guys are, glorified plumbers. Give them a wrench and they're happy.'

Toby, Bill and Lars all stared at her. 'Have fun,' she said, reddening, and she turned and hurried back up the stairs.

'You know,' said Bill to Toby with a sigh. 'My daughter really should engage brain before mouth. But that's just an engineer talking.'

31

They went the same route they had chosen that morning, down to the sea and then right along the dunes. The North Sea was closer this time – the tide had come in and was on its way back out. They could hear the waves clearly, and the grass on the dunes rustling in the breeze.

There was always a breeze.

'I like it here,' said Lars. 'I love the sea. Just the sound of it, you know? It calms me down. But I think I prefer being on top of it than underneath it.'

'It makes a good change from London,' said Toby. 'Especially in a rainy November.'

'I can see why Bill comes up here so much.'

'Have you taken a look around outside Barnholt?'

'I went for a little drive along the coast in the rain this morning. Had lunch in a pub somewhere.'

'I've been talking to Bill,' Toby said.

'Oh yeah?'

'Yeah. He told me what happened on the *Alexander Hamilton*. About how it was you who first tried to incapacitate the captain. About how you were arrested and then Bill smashed Craig over the head with a wrench. And about how the captain then checked his orders and found the launch instruction was an error.'

'He told you all that? That surprises me.'

'Megan had found a letter from Bill to Donna that referred to it. Is that right? What Bill said?'

'Yeah, that sounds about right.'

'So why did you lie to Justin about killing Craig?'

They were walking on the firmer sand just below the high tide mark, next to the dunes. The wide expanse of beach was almost empty. A woman with a dog was way ahead of them, and a couple were hunched against the breeze down by the sea.

'Bill has been awfully good to me over the years. And to Justin. Bill wrote me when Justin figured out Craig was his real father; that really cut Bill up. And then he lost Donna, and his daughter was accused of murder. He didn't need Justin causing trouble. It just suddenly occurred to me that it would be better all around if Justin thought I killed Craig. After all, I had tried to kill Commander Driscoll. He didn't need Justin hating him. I couldn't give a shit if Justin hates me. Also . . .' he hesitated.

Toby waited.

'I meant to kill Commander Driscoll, I really did. But I'm kind of glad I didn't and it was Bill who ended up killing someone. And that someone was our friend. I've always felt guilty about that. So, I was happy to take on a little of the blame.'

'Weren't you afraid the police would find out what you had told Justin?'

'Not really. The Navy would never set them straight. Frankly, I'm more worried about the stretch in jail in Guadeloupe. It doesn't look like that has surfaced yet, but it probably will.'

'I'm amazed they managed to keep what happened on the *Hamilton* quiet for so long.'

'It's quite an achievement,' said Lars. 'There were a hundred forty men on that submarine. But we were all shaken by what happened. Bill and I left the Navy, and so did over half the crew. Most of them failed the Personal Reliability Program that's supposed to confirm you are psychologically prepared to press the button.

208

After you have been through what we went through, the answer has to be: not really.'

'Were you and Bill court martialled?'

'No. Commander Driscoll and the XO came up with a story. I'm not sure how much of the truth they told to their senior officers, but it was made real clear to the crew that no one should ever speak about what happened on the submarine. Bill was a hero. And so was I, kind of.'

'What happened to Commander Driscoll? You told me he was dead, and I assumed Bill had killed him to stop the launch.'

'He did die,' said Lars. 'A few months later.'

'How?' Toby asked. But he knew as he asked the question what the answer was going to be.

'Blew his brains out. He was a decent guy, but he couldn't handle knowing he had nearly destroyed humanity. Once he was sure the cover-up would stick, he checked out. It was sad.' Lars stared at his feet trudging through the sand. 'Made me wonder what I was still doing on this earth. Still does, sometimes.'

'And the XO? He stayed?'

'Yeah.' Lars hesitated. 'He had his own issues. But he's done well. Vice Admiral. With the captain gone, he's the one who holds us all together. Goes to the reunions. Keeps the crew in line.'

Toby thought how quick Bill had been to get in touch with Admiral Robinson after Sam's murder.

'And it's held?'

'It seems to have,' said Lars. 'When Sam Bowen came to see me in Wisconsin, he said the rumours about the *Hamilton* had started from guys who had worked in the Pentagon. I guess a number of people there must have known what happened; Bill told me they set up some commission afterwards to change the launch protocols.'

They walked on in silence. The beach was empty now, apart from the small green boat dragged up against the dunes. Far out to sea, distant windmills waved desultorily towards them.

Toby tried to imagine what it would have been like to have come that close to finishing the world. He couldn't.

Donna must have felt vindicated. That was probably why she and Bill had got back together again.

Then Toby remembered something.

'Bill said that the FBI came to see him at the submarine base. And you and Craig. About Donna. Is that right?'

Lars stiffened. 'I don't remember.'

Oh yes you do, thought Toby.

'Yeah. And there was a woman she had been talking to. Pat Greenberg, I think her name was?'

Lars shook his head.

Toby decided to confront him. 'Lars. You're holding back on me.'

Lars glanced out to sea before looking straight at Toby. 'Maybe I am. But don't go there, Toby. I mean it, don't go there. I'm really surprised Bill told you about that.'

'It was only in passing,' Toby said.

'He's losing it,' said Lars.

'Why were the FBI interested in Donna?'

Lars stopped. 'No, Toby. Do you hear me? No.'

They faced each other. Toby knew he was getting close to something. And he wasn't going to let Lars shut him down.

'Alice is under arrest; the police think she's a murderer. If you know something, you have to tell the police. Or at least tell me. We can figure out what to do together.'

Toby could see Lars was wavering.

'Did you kill Sam, Lars?'

'No,' Lars replied firmly, as if relieved to be able to give a straight answer.

'Then do you know who did?'

There was a loud crack, and a look of surprise flashed across Lars's face. A crimson hole appeared on his chest. Another crack, another hole.

As Lars's legs gave way and he slumped to the ground, Toby dived to his right.

There was a third crack, and sand erupted a foot in front of Toby's face.

The dunes were no more than ten yards away.

Toby pushed himself to his feet and sprinted for them, crouching low.

A fourth shot. Toby didn't know where it had landed; all he knew was it had missed him.

He flung himself into a shallow gap between the dunes and crawled as fast as he could.

He thought that fourth shot had come from the green boat: he believed he had seen a muzzle flash in his peripheral vision, but he wasn't really sure. He also wasn't sure what to do. Hide? Or run?

Toby glanced around him. To his left was the beach and the sea. Ahead was a shallow hollow of beach grass, with the dunes rising in a row beyond it. And beyond that was the marsh and the dyke.

He dashed across the hollow, Rickover on his heels, waiting for the crack of the rifle or the blow of a bullet in the centre of his back, but it never came. He sprinted up and over a dune, and slid down the other side. Here the dunes were bunched more closely together, which was good. He spotted two humps of grass-covered sand, each about ten feet high, and darted between them. Fear spurred him on, but fear sharpened his mind.

The marsh stretched ahead, or rather the fields next to the marsh, surrounded by wire fences, ditches and bulrushes. To the right, the path lay in a high straight line on top of the dyke back to the village.

Exposed. Very exposed.

Over to the left, at least half a mile away along the coast, the dunes rose into something more substantial, crowned with thick green pine trees.

That was a better bet. But how to get there without being seen?

Hide. The ditch would be good, except it ran in a dead straight line, and it would be easy for the shooter to get a good line of sight along it. Toby examined the bulrushes. He would have to cross the ditch and the fence; which should be possible, but would slow him down in the open. Once in the rushes he would be hard to spot.

Rickover was looking up at him, with a confused expression on his face, wondering what he would do next.

Shooing off the dog wouldn't work. Would he keep quiet with Toby in the bulrushes? Maybe, if Toby hugged him close.

No time to waste. He was just about to make a dash for it, when caution got the better of him, and he tentatively leaned out from behind his dune.

A figure holding a rifle was crouching low and making its way towards the base of the dyke, with its back to Toby. Toby couldn't see who it was, beyond that it was a man, he was above average height and he was wearing a green coat of some kind and a woolly hat.

Toby didn't hang around to stare.

Abandoning the bulrush idea, he doubled back through the dunes, across the sandy hollow, and out on to the beach, Rickover keeping pace.

He estimated the pine woods were half a mile away. Toby was reasonably fit, but the sand would slow him down: maybe three to four minutes at full speed. With luck, the shooter would still be creeping around the dyke on the other side of the dunes, out of sight.

Without luck? Better not think about that.

He glanced back at Lars's body, lying crumpled on the beach, not moving. If he wasn't dead already, there was nothing Toby could do to save him now. If Toby went back to check on him, he would most likely wind up sprawled on the sand next to Lars, a couple of bullets in his own body.

So he started running, slowing briefly as he passed the boat, which was little more than a fibreglass tub. There were indeed footprints behind it, and a couple of casings. He bent low, grabbed one and ran on. Every few seconds, he looked over his shoulder, but no sign of the shooter.

He was getting closer to the pine woods. His breath was short and his chest was pounding, but he kept his legs pumping. Rickover, now several yards behind him, began yapping with the excitement.

Toby looked over his shoulder to tell the dog to be quiet. Way behind, beyond the green boat, he saw a figure spill out of the dunes.

The figure stopped and raised his rifle.

Once again, Toby darted into the dunes, just as he heard the rifle crack. He had no idea where the bullet landed; all he knew was it hadn't been in him.

The sand was softer in the dunes and it was slower going. But he was out of sight of the shooter, and soon he reached a barbed-wire fence bordering the pine wood. He flung himself over it, rolled, and pulled himself to his feet. Through the trees he spotted a small car park.

Three vehicles stood close to each other: a white Range Rover and two smaller hatchbacks, one silver and one blue. A tall woman was loading a golden retriever into the back of the Range Rover.

Toby sprinted for the car, yelling and waving, but the woman had climbed inside and didn't hear him.

He listened out for the sound of another rifle shot, but all he could hear was Rickover yelping somewhere behind him.

He threw himself at the car door on the passenger side, yanked it open and jumped in. 'Drive!' he said.

The woman was about forty, with well-groomed blonde hair. She was wearing a Barbour. 'I beg your pardon?' she said, her voice cut glass. 'Will you please get out of my car?'

'There's a man with a gun,' Toby said. 'Just drive.'

'Get out of my car, or I will call the police.'

'I'll call the police,' said Toby. 'You drive, for God's sake! Didn't you hear the shots?'

The woman looked at him. Rickover was barking furiously outside the passenger door. The retriever licked Toby's ear.

'OK,' said the woman. 'Let your dog in.'

Toby opened his door and Rickover jumped up on to his lap. The woman put the Range Rover into reverse and the vehicle leaped backwards. She slammed the gear into first, and the car surged forward.

'Where to?' said the woman.

'Anywhere,' said Toby, reaching for his phone. 'Just drive fast.' He punched out 999, while the woman did as he had told her, the car reaching fifty over the bumpy track, flinging Toby and the two dogs off their seats.

The track from the car park led away from Barnholt through the pine trees. Within two minutes they had reached the main road.

'Which way?' the woman asked.

'King's Lynn,' said Toby to her, and 'Police,' to his phone.

32

Toby sat in the interview room sipping a cup of tea. It had sugar in it: at least three spoonfuls. He didn't take sugar, but it tasted good. Some cop technique for dealing with shock, maybe.

He and his volunteer getaway driver, whose name was Caroline, had remained remarkably cool as they had sped to King's Lynn. A series of police cars hurtled past them towards the coast, until one peeled off and escorted them to the police station.

The police had told Toby they wanted to interview him right away, but he had been waiting fifteen minutes, time to let the jumble of thoughts and emotions begin to settle.

His heart was still beating rapidly from adrenalin or shock or both. Toby had never seen a dead body before. Lars's surprised expression was seared into his brain, as were the two red holes opening up in his chest. Toby knew he would never forget them.

He wasn't just shocked, he was sorry. He'd realized that, despite Lars's dodgy background, he liked him. In fact, he admired him. It was Lars who had decided to risk everything to stop the launch. Lars had been willing to own up falsely to killing Craig, out of loyalty to Bill.

Shocked, sorry and scared. Someone had nearly killed him less than an hour before. The shot had hit the sand only inches away from his nose. He was lucky to be alive. And unless the police caught the shooter right away, he might have another go at Toby.

Toby wanted to help the police find the man, whoever he was. He strongly suspected the shooting had something to do with the near-launch on the *Hamilton*, although he had no idea what. He regretted signing the damned Official Secrets Act. Should he just ignore it?

And then there was Alice. She was off the hook now. Wasn't she?

He had to find a way to tell the police what he knew.

The door opened and DC Atkinson came in, together with his boss, DI Creswell. They both smiled at him as they took their seats on the other side of the interview table.

Atkinson started. 'How are you feeling, Toby? That must have been quite a shock.'

'It was. But I'm OK. Did you catch him?'

'Not yet,' said Creswell. 'But we're looking for him. We're fortunate: because we are so close to the royal residence at Sandringham we are well prepared for this kind of thing.'

'Anything you can tell us would be useful,' Atkinson said. 'While it's fresh in your mind.'

So Toby told them what had happened in as much detail as he could from when he and Lars had left the house. He described what little he had seen of the shooter, and gave them the casing he had found by the green boat. He mentioned the other two cars in the car park and the couple walking down by the sea. Atkinson told him one of the cars, the blue one, belonged to the couple, and they were unlikely suspects: retired, living in a nearby village, originally from Cheshire. Toby was unable to describe the silver hatchback in any detail.

'And what were you and Lars talking about on your walk?'

Here we go, thought Toby. 'The murder of Sam Bowen. And what happened on the *Alexander Hamilton* in 1983.'

'And what was that?' asked Atkinson.

'I can't tell you.'

Atkinson glanced at his boss, who leaned forward. 'Toby,' she said in a quiet, reasonable voice. 'A man has just been murdered. You were nearly shot as well. We need you to help us.'

'You are quite right,' said Toby. 'I really want to help you, but I did sign that piece of paper. I want to talk to that guy from MI5 who came up here yesterday – Prestwitch his name was. You probably spoke to him?'

'We did,' said Creswell.

'Well get him up here,' said Toby. 'I'll tell him what I know, and he should tell you. I certainly hope he will.'

'That'll be the day,' muttered Atkinson. Creswell looked at him sharply.

'OK. We will arrange that. Was there anything in your conversation that you think wasn't an official secret?'

Toby thought back to the discussion. It had pretty much all been related to the *Alexander Hamilton*. He told them what Lars had said about going for a drive along the coast earlier that day.

'I asked him directly whether he had killed Sam Bowen himself.'

'And what did Lars say?'

'He said he hadn't. And, for what it's worth, I believe him. Especially since he is dead now himself.'

'All right,' said Creswell. 'Can you tell me why you thought he might have killed Sam Bowen?'

'I had a strong feeling that there was something Lars wasn't telling me,' said Toby. 'I thought it was maybe that. But it wasn't. It must have been something else. So I asked him whether he knew who had killed Sam.'

'Did he?'

'That's when he was shot.'

Creswell stared at Toby hard, assessing whether to believe him. He genuinely wanted to help her.

He had an idea.

'There is one thing I can tell you,' he said. 'Lars told Justin that it was him who killed Craig on the submarine.'

Creswell raised her eyebrows. 'Really?'

'You're probably wondering why I can tell you that when I said I wouldn't divulge any secrets about what happened on the *Hamilton*?'

Creswell nodded slowly. 'But don't let us stop you.'

Toby considered his next statement carefully before he spoke. 'Lars's claim doesn't fall under that.'

'How can that be?' said Atkinson.

Inspector Creswell gave Toby a small smile of understanding. 'Because it didn't happen. Lars didn't actually kill Lieutenant Naylor, so it's not Classified information.'

Toby kept his face expressionless. She was on the right track.

'Sorry I can't say more,' he said. 'But I would like to help. Once I can talk to MI5.'

'OK,' said Creswell. She terminated the interview. 'We'll get you back to Barnholt now. We'll leave an armed police guard there overnight, but I hope we'll catch this guy before too long. I'm sure we will want to speak to you again tomorrow, and we will get Mr Prestwitch or one of his colleagues here as soon as possible.'

'Thank you,' said Toby. 'Have you released Alice?'

'Not yet,' said the inspector, friendliness replaced by caution.

'Why not? She can't possibly have shot Lars.'

'That doesn't mean she didn't murder Sam Bowen. We still have a few more hours to decide whether to charge her.'

'That's ridiculous!' Toby said, anger rising.

Something close to sympathy crept into the inspector's expression. 'Look at it from our point of view. She was the last person to see Sam Bowen alive, either just before or when he was killed. She has given us no explanation of what she discussed with him, or even where she was beyond her initial lie about going to the supermarket in Lynn. Neither she, nor you, nor Bill Guth have told us what it is about events on the *Alexander Hamilton* that might have caused her to meet Sam Bowen or possibly kill him. Alice has to be our top suspect. I know she's your wife, but you must see that.'

'But she didn't kill him!' Toby protested.

'We don't know that,' said Creswell kindly. 'You go back to Barnholt now, and leave it to us and Alice and her lawyer to sort out, eh? You've had a rough afternoon.'

Anger flared, but was soon doused by a wave of exhaustion. The inspector was right; Toby should leave it to Lisa Beckwith to look after Alice. Maybe when he spoke to MI5 things would be clearer. He was tired. He needed to get back to Pear Tree Cottage.

Bill was waiting for him at the police station, looking anxious, as well he might.

'How are you doing, Toby?'

'In the car,' said Toby between gritted teeth.

It was dark outside as they made their way to the nearby car park where Bill had left his Range Rover.

'Bill. What the hell is going on?' Toby said, once he was inside.

'I don't know any more than you,' said Bill. 'My friend has been killed and my daughter is a murder suspect.'

'Yeah,' said Toby. 'And some poor historian has been murdered as well. And don't try to pretend that it doesn't have something to do with that missile launch and Craig's death, because obviously it must do. Just tell me what.'

'Hey, I told you all I knew this afternoon,' said Bill, as he guided the Range Rover through the streets of King's Lynn. 'You didn't give any of that to the police, did you?'

'No,' said Toby. 'But why do you care? Isn't it more important that we get Alice out of jail and find the maniac who shot Lars? And, by the way, tried to shoot me and will probably shoot you.'

'I'm telling you, Toby, I have no idea why any of this is happening!'

'Well, I don't believe you.'

They drove back to Barnholt in silence, Toby letting his fury boil. He wasn't sure how much of his anger was justified and how much was a reaction to almost getting killed, but, frankly, he didn't care.

Megan was waiting for them, her eyes red behind her glasses. Toby was surprised, as was Bill, when she threw her arms around him as he walked in the door. She held him tight for a few seconds. Then she pulled away.

'Poor Lars,' she said.

Yes. Poor Lars.

'Are you going to tell his family?' Toby asked Bill.

'Yes. His mother has dementia and is in a home in Wisconsin, but I know he had a brother. I'd better see if I can track him down.'

'Glass of wine?' said Megan, once her father had left the kitchen.

'Go on,' said Toby. Sweet tea could only achieve so much.

Megan poured two glasses of red and they sat down at the kitchen table opposite each other.

'It was terrible to hear about Lars,' said Megan. She hesitated and looked Toby in the eye. 'But I was so scared that you had nearly been killed.'

She held out her hand. He gave her his and she squeezed it. She didn't let it go.

Toby found her touch comforting. There was something strangely solid and reliable about his scatty sister-in-law.

'Are they releasing Alice?' Megan asked.

'I don't know,' said Toby. 'They are going to decide whether to charge her tonight.'

'But how can they think she killed Sam Bowen after what happened to Lars this afternoon?'

Toby shrugged. 'I don't know. I told them to get MI5 up here so I can talk to them. About what your father told us.'

'Is that a good idea?' Megan said.

'I think so. It seemed to me like a way around the Official Secrets problem. MI5 can help the police.'

'Only if they want to,' said Megan.

'What do you mean?'

Megan sipped her wine thoughtfully. 'We know that the US Navy wanted to cover things up. We know that this Admiral Robinson guy has recruited MI5 to help them cover things up. And now Lars has been killed.'

'Are you suggesting MI5 did that?'

'Or the CIA. Or the FBI. I don't know. I *am* suggesting that they might not want the Norfolk police to discover what really happened.'

'I see what you mean,' said Toby. 'But I'm kind of committed now.'

'Just be careful,' said Megan. 'Please.'

'OK,' said Toby. 'But now I'm not sure what being careful means.'

They heard a car pulling up outside and blue lights danced over the kitchen wall. Toby looked out of the kitchen window and saw two cars parked on the lane beyond the garden wall: a police vehicle and DC Atkinson's silver Fiesta. He opened the front door to a pair of armed police officers, who instructed him to draw all the curtains in the house, and not to leave unless absolutely necessary, and then only after informing them. They would keep an eye on the house overnight.

Behind the uniformed policemen stood Atkinson and a fellow detective. While Megan showed them Lars's room in the next-door cottage, Toby went around the house drawing the curtains. They were already closed in Bill's tiny study: Bill was on the phone, looking sombre.

Back in the kitchen, Megan opened a couple of cartons of pea and ham soup for the three of them for supper, and warmed them up.

Toby laid the table, and poured them both some more wine.

'I'm glad the cops are here,' said Megan. 'Because whoever killed Lars is still out there. And you realize he might be after you?'

'I doubt it,' said Toby. 'Lars knew something and I don't. My guess is I was just shot at as an afterthought.' Yet he had been wondering whether he had been a target in addition to Lars, for some reason he had no way of knowing. He hoped that with the police after him, the shooter would either lie low or leave the county, but he couldn't be sure of that.

Lars's killer could be out there in the marshes at that very moment. Toby took a gulp of wine.

'Did you hear what Dad said about the FBI investigating Mom?' Megan said.

'Yes, I did.'

'I wonder what that was about?'

'He said they thought she was a peacenik.'

Megan smiled. 'She was certainly that. I used to wonder how someone who was so strongly anti-nuclear weapons married an officer on a nuclear submarine. Now I guess I know. They must have gotten back together afterward.'

'I asked Lars about that. About the FBI and that woman, Pat Greenberg?'

'Greenwald, I think.'

'All right. Greenwald.'

'And what did Lars say?'

'Nothing,' said Toby. 'I think I had just about persuaded him to talk, and then he was shot.'

Megan paused, thinking. 'Didn't Sam Bowen ask Dad about a Pat Greenwald?'

'That's right! Your dad said he had never spoken to her.'

'But she was a friend of Mom's. A peace activist.'

Megan ladled the soup into bowls and called out to her father upstairs.

He had managed to track down Lars's brother's number in Milwaukee and broken the news to him. The brother had promised to tell their mother, although he doubted she would remember it. And then he would have to tell her again. And again.

They sat in silence as they ate their soup. Bill looked strained, as well he might. Toby liked Lars and had witnessed his death close up. But Lars was an old friend of Bill's: they had been through a lot together.

'Who is Pat Greenwald?' Toby asked him.

'Who?'

'You know. The woman the FBI mentioned when they warned you about Donna. You told us this afternoon.'

'I did, didn't I?'

'And Sam Bowen asked you about her. You told him you never met her.'

Bill nodded.

'Well?'

Bill was silent.

'Dad?' It was Megan. 'You need to stop hiding stuff from us. You need to trust us.'

'It's not that simple, Megan.'

'No, it's not simple! That's the point. It's really complicated. And unless someone takes the initiative to figure out what's really going on here, Alice will go to jail and Toby will get shot and maybe you will too.'

Megan's eyes were alight and her cheeks flushed as she glared at her father.

'I can't do it, Megan. How many times do I have to tell you, this stuff is secret and it's secret for a reason? I've already told you way more than I should have.'

'But not enough,' said Megan. She eyed her father. 'I get that you and Toby can't tell the British police what you know, but there's no reason why I shouldn't.'

'Yes there is!' Bill protested. 'I trusted you, Megan.'

'No you didn't! You didn't trust me enough. Trust me now. Tell me about Pat Greenwald.'

'Are you threatening me?' Bill's voice was low, as he stared at his daughter.

'Yes.' Megan stared back. 'I *will* go to the police.'

Bill looked at his son-in-law and his daughter. And sighed.

'All right. Give me some of that wine.'

33

December 1983, North Atlantic

'Gentlemen. Would you mind leaving the XO and me with Bill and Lars?'

Supper was over, and coffee had been served in the wardroom. It was the first evening Lars and I had been allowed out of the JO Jungle. The *Alexander Hamilton* had come off strategic alert two weeks early and was heading back to Holy Loch. After some discussion, and some scrabbling around to rearrange schedules so that another SSBN would be in place to cover for her, COMSUBLANT had decided to bring the *Hamilton* home. There were things to discuss.

Now the *Hamilton* was off strategic alert and would not be ordered to launch her nuclear missiles, the captain had decided he could set us free. Lars and I had been nervous about mixing with our fellow officers after what had happened. Craig was not just my friend, he was popular with the other officers and with the crew. And I had killed him. And Lars had tried to kill the ship's commanding officer. If a submarine operates much of the time like a large family, then Commander Driscoll was the father. Patricide doesn't go down well with the siblings.

It was immediately clear that the half dozen other officers were equally wary about socializing with us. But the captain led by example, welcoming us both vigorously and treating us as if we had merely slipped away from the submarine for a week or so, perhaps on some brief training course, and had now returned. Soon the tension broke into nervous hilarity, almost as if we had all been knocking back a few cocktails before dinner.

I was grateful. I, too, felt part of the *Hamilton* family, and I felt vulnerable. I realized I craved acceptance from the rest of the crew.

'It's good to have you both back in the wardroom,' said Driscoll once the other officers had left. 'You will be back on watch from oh-six-hundred tomorrow morning.'

'It's good to be back here,' I said. While both the captain and the XO had visited us frequently in our stateroom over the previous week, this was different. This was normality.

'The XO and I have concocted a simple story to explain Weps's death. We outlined it to the officers and the chiefs this afternoon, and they say the crew will accept it. The whole ship feels grateful that the world hasn't been obliterated, and that is thanks to you gentlemen.'

'Are you using the accidental fall?' Lars said. The captain had discussed this with us over the previous couple of days. To move between different levels of the operations compartment, the crew had to climb metal ladders, or to slide down them, holding both railings as they did so. The story was that Craig had somehow caught his foot while doing this, and had knocked himself unconscious. He had come around, but then died several days later.

'Yes,' said Driscoll. 'The XO will brief you on the details in a moment.'

'But will the whole crew's stories match in an investigation?' I asked. I could imagine a determined investigator swiftly finding conflicting narratives.

'My hope is that no one will ask,' said Driscoll. 'I'll tell Commodore Jackman what actually happened, but I'm one hundred per cent sure the Navy will want to cover this up. If I give them a credible story that is already in place, they will go with it.'

Commodore Jackman was the commanding officer of SUBRON 14, the squadron of which the *Hamilton* was a part.

'Have you told them about us yet?' Lars asked.

'No. But I will do all I can to make sure that you don't suffer consequences for what you did. If they try to court martial you, well, I hold some cards.'

'We both do,' said Robinson with a smile.

'Obviously, I can't guarantee anything. But one thing I need to know is: do you want to stay in the Navy? I'm sure boomers are out of the question, probably for any of us, but you could maybe serve on fast attacks? I need to know what you want before I can push for it.'

He looked at both of us. Lars and I had discussed this over the previous few days together. I knew what Lars's response was.

'I want out,' said Lars. 'I'd like to think I have been a good officer in the past. But I'm damn sure I can't be again in the future.'

'I understand,' said the captain. 'Lieutenant Guth?'

'I'm sorry, sir, but I can't give you a straight answer to that yet,' I said. 'There's still some things I need to figure out.'

Driscoll frowned. 'All right. We all need to figure stuff out. But let me know as soon as you have. The XO will brief you on what we're saying happened to Weps.'

The captain left the wardroom.

The XO sipped his coffee, his dark eyes fixed on us.

'I admire you guys,' he said. 'That takes real courage, to do what you did.'

Lars and I were silent. It *had* taken courage. But.

'The courage to kill your friend,' I said.

'Yeah,' said the XO. 'But it's also the courage, the intelligence, to figure out that you owe your loyalty to the human race, more than just the US Navy. I'm not sure I could figure that out. In fact, I know

I couldn't.' He paused and stared at his cup. 'Truth is, I didn't.' He looked up. 'That's going to be difficult for me to live with.'

'I don't blame you,' I said. 'I wouldn't have done what I did if Lars hadn't shown me it was the right thing to do.'

'And now we are going to cover it up,' said the XO.

'That has to be right,' said Lars. 'From our point of view as well as the Navy's. If this got out it would undermine the whole nuclear deterrence regime.' That was something else that Lars and I had discussed at length.

'I'm not so sure,' said the XO. 'We assume that the Russians want to attack us, they want to destroy us with their nuclear weapons, and the only thing that's stopping them is our nuclear weapons. But that's not correct.'

'Isn't it?' said Lars. 'Because it seems to me that the communists are trying to take over the whole world and have been ever since the Russian revolution. "Workers of the world unite." That's the whole world.'

'Sure, that's how it started,' said the XO. 'But then Stalin changed the slogan to "Socialism in one country." Not the whole world.'

'He was happy to swallow up Eastern Europe. And what about Vietnam? And Syria? And Africa? What about Cuba?'

'We have been just as aggressive as the Soviets in all those places,' said the XO. 'More so, really. All those dictatorships we have propped up in South America. Fidel Castro didn't even know he was a communist until we told him he was.'

'That can't be right,' said Lars. 'Are you trying to tell me Castro isn't a communist?'

'He is now,' said Robinson. 'I'm just saying maybe we made him that way.'

'We are only protecting ourselves and the free world,' said Lars. 'Hell, that's one of the reasons I joined the damn Navy.'

'Yes,' said the XO. 'I get that. But I wonder if the Russians think we are an equal threat to their socialist world. In fact, now I believe they think we are a bigger threat. I think they are more scared of us than we are of them.'

'Is this your CIA friend at the Pentagon?' I said.

'Yeah. And he is convincing. Ronald Reagan is talking about the arms race as a race the US can win. And the Soviets are asking themselves the question, what does losing the arms race mean? What does losing the Cold War mean? Does it mean the US launches a nuclear decapitation strike?'

'I'm with Craig on this,' said Lars. 'That just doesn't sound right to me.' He leaned forward. 'That's not why I took a swing at Commander Driscoll. I wasn't thinking about the rights and wrongs of my country's nuclear strategy. I was just taking the only chance I could see to stop the world from blowing itself up.'

'Me too,' I said.

'Yes, yes, I'm really glad you did it,' said the XO. 'But the more I think about it, the more I think that deterrence only works when we and the Soviets understand what we are doing, and trust each other.'

'*Trust* each other?'

'Yeah. They trust us to be ready to press the button if they launch missiles, and we trust them to do the same thing. Result: nobody launches anything.'

'Except we nearly did,' I said.

'That's right,' said the XO. 'And one day there will be some Russian crew on a submarine or in a missile bunker who might nearly make the same mistake. All I'm saying is that it might be better for trust in each other if we told each other all about it.'

I understood what the XO was saying. I wasn't sure I agreed with him, but I understood him.

'That's why this Able Archer exercise was so screwed up,' the XO went on. 'All it did was make them think we had the capability to launch a pre-emptive strike. It may even have made them think that that's what we were actually doing. It brought nuclear war closer, not further away.'

'So what should the exercise have done?'

'Been more open. Not used new codes or such widespread radio messages. Showed them and us that NATO could defend Europe. That if the Soviets attacked, we would respond. But that we had neither the interest nor the capability to attack them first.'

I glanced at Lars. The XO had a point.

'So are you saying you are not going along with the cover story?' Lars asked.

The XO smiled. 'Oh, no. In the real world, that's the best option. And it's also the best way of making sure that you guys don't get court martialled.'

Lars nodded. 'Thank you,' he said.

'XO?' I asked.

'Yes?'

'Are *you* going to stay in the Navy?'

Lieutenant Commander Robinson smiled. 'I've been thinking about that too. And yes. If they'll allow me, I'll stay. Now. Let me tell you how Weps fell down that ladder.'

January 1984, New York City

New York looked spellbinding in the snow. The north-east of the United States had spent three days in a blizzard, but the storm had spun off into the Atlantic overnight, leaving the city glistening brilliant white.

My train down from New London had been delayed three hours, but had eventually pulled in to Penn Station. I wandered through the streets, passing rosy-cheeked New Yorkers gazing in dazed wonder at their city's new cloak. And the odd wad of cardboard and blankets in doorways, beneath which other New Yorkers, whose cheeks were grey and black, burrowed.

I made my way to St Mark's Place, and stood to one side as a woman bundled up in scarf and greatcoat emerged from Donna's building, her scalp pink in the cold beneath her green Mohawk. The East Village was the East Village, even at ten degrees below freezing.

I pressed Donna's buzzer.

'Hello?'

I swallowed. 'Hi. It's Bill. Can I come in?'

Silence.

'Donna?'

'Bill. You shouldn't be here. We agreed not to see each other anymore.'

'Well, I am here. And I have something to tell you.' More silence. 'And it's freezing.'

The door buzzed and I pushed my way into the building.

Donna's apartment was warm and she was wearing an old green Joni Mitchell T-shirt I recognized. Her honey-blonde hair had been cut shorter, but the little notch was still there in her chin. It was more than three months since I had seen her, and she looked more beautiful than I remembered. I just wanted to grab her and kiss her.

But I stood in the doorway. 'Hi,' I said, smiling. Hoping to coax out that familiar lop-sided hint of amusement.

I failed.

'You had better come in,' she said, looking away from me. 'Do you want coffee?'

'Please.'

She busied herself with the coffee maker. I took the opportunity to stare at her back while she couldn't see me. I wanted to wrap my arms around her so badly.

'How's the stapling going?' I said.

'It's OK,' she grunted.

'Just OK?'

'No,' she said, a hint of bitterness in her voice. 'I've decided it's a waste of time. I'm going to law school in the fall. Penn, if I can get in.'

'I'm surprised,' I said. 'I never thought of you as a lawyer.'

'Not *that* kind of lawyer,' Donna said. 'I've realized that if you want to actually help people, you need the law on your side. Protesting can only get you so far.'

'I see.'

She poured two cups of coffee and gave me one. No milk – she remembered that.

'I know about Craig,' she said. 'Vicky told me.' Her voice softened a touch. 'I'm sorry.'

'Thanks.'

'OK,' she said, sitting on her bed and pointing to the one armchair in her studio. 'Say what you've got to say and then go.'

'Can't I drink my coffee?'

'Say what you've got to say, drink your coffee and then go.'

I sipped from my mug. I had expected a small protest from Donna at my appearance. It's true she had insisted we shouldn't see each other again. But not this hostility. It was as if she hated me.

I wanted to ask why. But I decided to say what I had come there to say.

I had agonized over whether to come. The captain and the XO had concocted a story for what had or had not happened on the *Alexander Hamilton*, and how Craig had died. The other officers had bought into it, as had the crew – and the Navy. And we had all sworn not to tell anyone.

And here I was planning to speak with Donna.

But I couldn't help it. She was why Lars and then I had questioned orders and then disobeyed them. She was why the USS *Alexander Hamilton* had not launched those three missiles at Moscow, Leningrad and Berlin.

She was why there had not been a world war. She had to know.

'OK,' I said. 'We were about four weeks into the patrol . . .'

She listened closely, hunched over her mug of coffee, hanging on my every word.

When I was done she was silent for a moment. 'Wow,' she said.

And then a tear ran down her cheek.

I stood up, moved on to the bed beside her, and put my arms around her shoulders. At first she was stiff, but then she sobbed and squeezed herself into my arms.

'Why are you crying?' I said.

'I don't know.' Her face was buried so deeply in my chest I could barely hear her.

I waited. Eventually, she broke away. She sniffed and wiped her nose.

'I found it really hard when we broke up. I missed you. So I decided to hate you, hate what you stand for. Hate you for being willing to blow up the world. And then you get the order to do it, and you do this.'

'I killed Craig,' I said.

'I know. That must have been horrible. Despite what I've just said, he was a good guy. I don't know why I'm crying. It should be for him. Poor Vicky. I saw her just before Christmas and she said he had died on patrol in a freak accident. She was really upset. I thought maybe that's what you wanted to tell me.'

'I bet she was upset.' I took a deep breath. Would I have to face Vicky? Lie? I would rather not; in fact I would do anything in my power to avoid her.

'Don't tell her,' I said. 'Don't tell anyone. Everything I've told you is top secret. I shouldn't have told you.'

'I'm glad you did.'

'In particular, don't tell Pat Greenwald.'

'Did I tell you about Pat?'

'No. the FBI did. Who is she?'

'The FBI?'

'Yes. Two goons came to see me in September just before we headed out to Scotland. Said that you were a peace activist – which I told them I knew already – and that you knew Pat Greenwald who had some contact with the KGB.'

'The KGB? That's ridiculous. And you're telling me that the FBI has been spying on me?'

'Looks like it.'

'Jesus.'

'So does this woman have anything to do with the KGB?'

'No! Absolutely not. I met her at Seneca this summer. You know – the women's peace camp upstate? We bonded.'

'So she doesn't talk to any Russians?'

'She speaks to a couple of Soviet peace organizations,' Donna admitted.

'Controlled by the KGB?'

'We're not that stupid. We want peace, we don't want the Soviets to win the Cold War.'

'OK,' I said, 'but whoever she is, you won't tell her any of this, will you? Because I could get into serious trouble. Rest-of-my-life in prison type trouble.'

'No,' said Donna. 'I won't tell her. I won't tell anyone. I promise.'

'Good.' But I was nervous. Could I trust her? Should I have told her?

She sipped her coffee. 'I was right, wasn't I?'

'About the risk of an accidental launch order? Yes, you were absolutely right. And it was only because you and I had had that argument in Mystic that I told Lars about it. And that's why he tried to stop Commander Driscoll.'

'Is he in trouble? Are you in trouble?'

'Neither of us is. What we did is in breach of all kinds of Navy regulations, but, hey, the world didn't end.'

Donna smiled. Laughed. Wiped her eyes. 'I don't know why this makes me so emotional. It must be worse for you.'

'I can handle it,' I said. 'Lars is finding it difficult. He's been drinking heavily ever since we got back Stateside. Two nights ago he was high on the base. That was really dumb. They don't like sailors driving nuclear submarines high on drugs.'

'I get that. What are you going to do?' A cloud of wariness passed across her eyes. 'You are not going out on patrol again, are you?'

'I'm up before the Personal Reliability Program next week. They'll tell me they can't trust me to press the button next time, and they'll be right. They'll revoke my certification.'

'So will you leave the Navy?'

'I don't know. In theory I could serve on fast-attack submarines, and you would be surprised how many desks there are with submarine officers sitting behind them. But yeah, I might leave the Navy.' I looked into her clear blue eyes. 'It kinda depends on you.'

'Me?'

Her eyes softened as she understood. Very slowly she raised her face towards mine.

And then she kissed me.

35

May 1996, Cobham, England

Saturday mornings were crazy in the Guth household. Actually, I suspect that every morning was crazy, but I was at work Monday to Friday and on Sunday we shared kid duty.

Saturday, it was just me. Donna stayed in bed, or sometimes went outside for a walk. Alone.

There were four kids by that stage. Maya was nine months old and crawling, Megan two and terrible. Brooke was five and Alice was six and my loyal assistant. Maya was angelic, of course, and Alice did a great job entertaining her. Megan and Brooke were more work.

We had been in England a couple of years. I had been transferred by my employer, a US defence communications company based in Virginia, to their European headquarters which was near Reading. We had rented a small house in Cobham, because it was close to the American school. At that stage, only Alice was attending the elementary school, but the idea was everyone would go there in time.

Donna had given up her legal career, at least temporarily, after Megan was born. Four kids under seven is a lot to manage.

The doorbell rang. It was two clean-cut American men – one white, one black – dressed in white shirts, ties and suits. On a Saturday morning. I wasn't surprised when they showed me FBI ID.

I was surprised when they said they wanted to speak with Donna and me together.

That took a few minutes to sort out, but Donna got dressed and came downstairs, and the four girls were successfully installed in front of the Saturday morning cartoons in the living room.

'You're a bit far from home, aren't you?' I asked. I had had some dealings with American intelligence since moving to England, but that had been the CIA, not the FBI. The FBI classically dealt with domestic US crimes.

Like spying.

'We would like to ask both of you about a woman named Patricia Greenwald,' the black taller one began. He had introduced himself as Agent Watkins. The other one was Agent Macdonald.

Yes. Like spying.

Donna frowned. I knew she wouldn't like that subject. 'Aren't you done with all that? The Cold War is over, peace has broken out. Or haven't you heard?'

'Thankfully that's true. But the end of the Cold War has brought some interesting new facts to light. KGB and Stasi files in Moscow and East Berlin.'

'Hey. You spent the whole of the eighties claiming that the Russians were funding the peace movement and it was all bullshit. You knew it was all bullshit, and now we know. So why don't you give up? It's yesterday's news.'

Agent Watkins smiled politely. 'You are correct we got that wrong. The KGB and the GRU *were* trying to fund the peace movement, but the peace activists managed to avoid taking their money. Mostly.'

'Mostly? Are you saying that Pat Greenwald took Russian money?'

'We think that Pat Greenwald may have been an agent for the KGB.'

'That's absurd!' said Donna.

'It may be. But that's what we are investigating. And that's why we need to speak with you. Now, how did you know Pat Greenwald?'

Donna glanced at me in frustration.

'Tell them, Donna,' I said. 'If she was a spy, we need to help them. And if she wasn't, then maybe we can help them see that.'

Donna scowled. 'OK. Pat was an assistant professor at Hunter College. She was also one of the foremost peace activists in New York. She was an organizer of that big Freeze anti-nuclear rally in Central Park in 1982 where a million people showed up. And she was a member of WAND – that's Women's Action for Nuclear Disarmament. I met her at the peace camp outside the Seneca nuclear weapons depot in upstate New York, and I stayed in touch with her when I got back to the city.'

'Did she show any signs of communist sympathies? Or sympathies toward the Soviet Union?'

'No!' said Donna. 'You guys should get this by now. We were opposed to nuclear weapons whoever had them. We were not opposed to the United States. And we certainly didn't like Brezhnev – or Andropov I think it was then. I forget, they all died so quickly.'

'What about the Gorky Trust Group?' said Agent Watkins. 'Did she ever mention that?'

'Yes, she did,' said Donna. 'I remember her speaking about them. But they weren't communists. The whole point about them was they were dissidents. They were a bunch of scientists mostly from the city of Gorky. I think it was a closed city then, no westerners could go there. The point is that they were against nuclear weapons just like we were.'

'Did you ever meet them?'

'Pat dealt with them mostly. But a physicist came to speak to us all once. What was her name? Boyarova?'

'That's correct. Irena Boyarova,' Watkins said.

'OK. Yeah, she spoke to us. She was inspiring, actually.'

'She worked for the KGB,' the other, shorter agent said. Agent Macdonald.

Donna just snorted.

'We suspected it at the time,' said Macdonald. 'The KGB archive backs that up.'

'But you just heard that Donna only met her once, and that was as part of a crowd,' I protested.

Agent Watkins ignored my comment. 'That wasn't all the files said about Dr Greenwald. Mr Guth: did you ever meet Greenwald?'

'Me? No.'

'Or Irena Boyarova?'

'Of course not.'

'I see.' Watkins paused. 'Did you ever tell your wife about what happened aboard the USS *Alexander Hamilton* in November 1983?'

I hate lying. I might lie *for* my country; I had no desire to lie *to* my country. But I had no choice. I had known when I had decided to tell Donna everything that the day might come when a FBI agent might sit me down and ask me the kind of questions he was asking me now.

And I had decided then that if that happened, I would lie.

'No, I didn't. I mean, I told her that Lieutenant Naylor died in an accident. She knew Craig; she went to college with his sister. But I didn't tell her anything else.'

The agent turned to Donna. 'Mrs Guth. Did your husband tell you what happened on the submarine on that patrol?'

'Er. I thought he had. He said Craig fell down a ladder and hit his head, but he didn't die for several days. Was there something else?'

Donna glanced at me, with a look of puzzlement. Her face hardened. 'Was there a radiation leak?'

I had never realized that my wife was such a good liar.

'Not that kind of leak,' said Watkins. 'Everything that happened on board the USS *Alexander Hamilton* on that patrol is in the KGB's files. And it came via Irena Boyarova.'

'So where did she get it?' I asked.

'From an officer on the submarine. An officer who was there.'

'And it's not just the order to launch nuclear missiles,' said Agent MacDonald. 'There was other information too. About the organization of the submarine fleet in the North Atlantic. About targets. And technical details about the Poseidon missiles themselves.'

'Do the files say which officer?'

'No,' Watkins replied. 'But given Mrs Guth was then your girlfriend, and she knew Greenwald at the time, and Greenwald knew Boyarova, it seems natural for us to consider that it might be you.'

Donna looked at me in something close to panic.

I paused to think. 'OK,' I said. 'I see that. Let me start by saying it wasn't me. I never divulged what happened to anyone, let alone a Russian.'

'OK,' said Watkins. 'If you aren't responsible, do you know who is?'

I had no clue. No clue at all. I could see how I was the most likely spy. So likely, I was surprised they hadn't already arrested me and bundled me off to some cell in the FBI building in Washington.

I immediately wondered whether I should start by coming clean about what I had told Donna. That she knew about the near-launch. But would that get her into trouble?

For a second I thought that maybe *she* had given the information to the KGB after all, or maybe just to Pat Greenwald in an innocent discussion about nuclear accidents. *That* was the most likely explanation.

But even that would be enough to place us both in deep trouble.

I exchanged glances with Donna. She was a smart woman. And

by that stage we had been married for ten years. We knew each other very well. She knew what I was thinking.

And I knew there was something she wasn't telling me.

That scared me.

She leaned back in the armchair. The three of us, me and the two FBI agents, watched her.

She spoke. 'I told someone about Pat. About her contact with the Gorky Group. One of Bill's fellow officers.' She sighed. 'Through Bill, he knew my politics. He wanted me to put him in touch with a peace activist who had contacts with Russia. I thought he just wanted to join the cause. It never occurred to me he would want to give away secrets.'

'Who?' Agent Watkins asked.

'Commander Driscoll.'

36

Saturday 30 November 2019, Norfolk

'So that's who Pat Greenwald was,' said Bill. He took a last spoonful of soup, which was cold by now, and sat back in his chair.

'Wait,' said Megan. 'Wasn't Commander Driscoll the captain?'

'That's right,' said Bill. 'It's confusing. The captain of a nuclear submarine usually has the rank of commander.'

'Didn't he kill himself?' said Toby.

Bill breathed in deeply and nodded. 'Yes, he did. A few months after the near-launch incident. We all thought it was because he couldn't get over what happened then. But maybe it was because he told the Russians stuff he shouldn't have. Who knows? It's very sad.'

'Did the FBI investigate him?' said Megan.

'Probably,' said Bill. 'I don't know. I never heard any more about it. I didn't ask, and they didn't tell me. My guess is they dropped it. Nobody wanted to bring up the near-launch, even after the Cold War was over.'

'What about Pat Greenwald?' said Megan. 'Did the FBI investigate her?'

Bill shrugged. 'No idea.'

'Does Admiral Robinson know all this?' Toby asked.

'Yes he does. I told him at the time. He told me to forget it.'

'Part of the great cover-up?'

'What can I say?' said Bill.

'Does Prestwitch know?' said Toby.

243

'I'm not sure.' Bill frowned. 'Probably not. I doubt that US intelligence would like to share that kind of screw-up with their allies. Why do you ask?'

'Because I told the police I would tell Prestwitch everything I knew about Craig's death.'

'Why would you do that?' said Bill.

'To help them find who killed Sam Bowen,' Toby said. 'And now Lars. And to get Alice out of jail.'

'But I told you all about the *Hamilton*'s last patrol on condition you would keep it quiet.'

'You made me sign the Official Secrets Act. Which is why I told the police I would talk to MI5. Then they can decide what to tell them.'

'No, Toby. Don't do that. I'm warning you. I trusted you.'

'No, Bill. Someone's got to help the police. Someone's got to help Alice.'

'If all this becomes public, Donna will be accused of being a spy.'

'Mom's dead, Dad,' said Megan.

'Yes. And I want her to rest in peace.'

'Are you concerned that you might be prosecuted?' Megan said.

'Maybe,' said Bill.

'I don't understand why. You didn't know anything about it,' said Toby.

'If you are telling us the whole truth,' said Megan.

Bill's shoulders slumped and he poured himself another glass of wine.

'Don't either of you see the real reason why I don't want the cops to find out any of this?'

Megan and Toby were silent.

'Isn't it obvious?'

It wasn't to Toby and Megan.

'Because I think Alice killed Sam Bowen.'

37

Megan looked at Toby and then her father. 'You're crazy. Why would she do that?'

'To protect me.'

'From what?'

'From Sam Bowen publishing his book and accusing me and your mom of being spies. From me being charged with treason.'

'But that wasn't ever going to happen, was it?'

'I think Alice thought it might,' said Bill. 'It's the only thing that makes sense. I know Donna told her a lot before she died, a lot more than she told the rest of you girls. I saw her talking to Sam Bowen at the dinner table, and then she went to see him at the pub. She must have thought I was in danger of being unmasked.'

'And so she killed him?' said Megan. 'That's absurd. I can't believe Alice would kill anyone. Can you, Toby?'

'No, of course not,' Toby replied loyally. But actually he thought it was just possible that Alice *could* kill someone to protect her father. Not to protect herself, not to protect Toby, but to protect Bill? Maybe.

Bill could see Toby's doubt. 'You know I'm right,' he said. 'I've tried to hide from this myself. I don't *want* to think my daughter killed anyone. And I still hope to God I'm wrong. But whatever she's done, she's still my daughter. Your wife. Your sister. We still have to do all we can to protect her.'

'Have you spoken to her about it?' Toby said.

'No.'

'Why not?'

'At first I didn't want to believe it. And then when the police arrested her, I didn't have the chance. Besides, I don't know what I'd say to her.'

Toby snorted. But, actually, he sympathized with Bill. He didn't want to admit to himself that he suspected Alice of murder, let alone to her.

'Look, I only told you all this because I thought you both had a right to understand what happened,' Bill said. 'And because I wanted you to realize that you shouldn't talk about any of this to the cops.'

'And Prestwitch?'

'And Prestwitch. You can maybe tell him that it was actually me who killed Craig – the admiral probably told him that already – but nothing about Greenwald. You owe it to Alice.'

'No. I don't believe she killed anyone.'

Bill stared at Toby. 'All right. Even if you don't think she killed anyone, surely you can see that the police might suspect she did. And if you tell them about Pat Greenwald, they will think she had a motive. You can't take that risk.'

Toby drained his glass. 'What about Lars? We know Alice can't possibly have killed him. So who do you think shot him?'

'I don't know,' said Bill.

'Did he know about the FBI investigation?'

'Yes. They interviewed him after me. Went all the way to the Caribbean to do it.'

'Could that be why he was killed?'

'Who knows?' said Bill. 'I certainly don't. Doesn't make any sense to me. It's Alice I'm worried about.'

Megan cleared soup bowls from the kitchen table. Bill and Toby sat opposite each other, a quarter-full bottle of red wine between them. Toby didn't know what to believe. If Alice thought that her parents were at risk of being exposed as spies, she would take action to protect them. But she wouldn't go as far as killing anyone, surely?

And how come he had had no inkling of all of this?

That was easier to believe. This was exactly the kind of secret that Alice would want to keep from him.

He was damn sure Alice wouldn't kill anyone to protect him. It occurred to Toby that Alice loved her father more than him. It had always been obvious, but he had never admitted it to himself. And it made him feel kind of jealous. Which was really stupid.

He didn't know what to do. Should he just trust Bill and do as he asked? How would he feel if the police used information he had given them via Prestwitch to build a stronger case against Alice?

The front door opened and Brooke appeared. Her cheeks were pale and lined, and her hair hung lank about her face. She caught the atmosphere around the kitchen table immediately.

'Hello,' she said, tentatively.

'Hi, Brooke,' said Megan.

'Have you heard the news?' said Bill.

'Have they caught the murderer?'

'Uncle Lars has been shot,' said Megan. 'Killed.'

'Oh, God,' said Brooke. Her hand flew to her mouth and she dropped into one of the chairs around the table. 'What happened?'

'It was just this afternoon,' said Toby. 'I was walking with him out there on the beach and he was shot. Like by a sniper. He almost got me too.'

'Oh my God,' said Brooke. 'Do they know who it was?'

'No,' said Bill. 'Or not yet. The police are looking for him.'

'Did you see him?' Brooke asked Toby.

'Not really. I saw a figure from a distance, but I couldn't catch his face.'

'Well, I'm glad you're all right.'

'Do you want some wine?' Megan asked.

'I'd better not,' said Brooke. 'I'm driving. We're staying at a hotel in Hunstanton. Justin is back there now.'

'Thanks for coming,' Bill said to his daughter, summoning up a weak smile.

'Oh, I'm so sorry, Dad!' said Brooke. 'About earlier. But you know how important Craig is to Justin. He's become this mythical figure: his father, the hero who saved the world. With you. So when he heard Lars had killed Craig, he found it hard to take.'

'So I noticed.'

'He's been obsessing over it ever since,' said Brooke. 'He's gotten it into his head that Lars killed Craig on the submarine and then he killed the historian to stop him from telling anyone. He went right over to the police station today to say that, in fact, he is not sure what time he saw Lars in the Cottage on Thursday night. We both told the police we stayed up in the Cottage living room with jet lag that evening, and heard Lars going to the bathroom just before midnight. In other words, Justin is now saying that Lars might have had time to kill Sam Bowen.'

'What did the police say?' said Bill.

'I don't know,' said Brooke. 'Justin says they listened but he got the impression they weren't going to *do* anything. And, frankly, whatever Justin says, I know he and I were in that living room reading until at least one a.m., and we would have noticed if Lars left the Cottage. Have they released Alice yet?'

'Not yet,' said Bill. 'And we don't know whether they will.'

Brooke's gloomy face brightened a little. 'But Alice can't have killed Lars. So doesn't that mean she didn't kill Sam Bowen?'

Bill winced and scratched his head. 'I don't know what it means.'

'Were you with Justin this afternoon?' Megan asked.

'No. Right after we checked in to the hotel this morning, he went to the police in King's Lynn. He tried to make me change my story as well to implicate Lars, but I wouldn't do it. He had the rental car, so I've been cooped up in a tiny hotel room all day.'

'Did Justin go straight back to you from King's Lynn police station?' Megan asked.

'Oh my God! You think Justin killed Lars!'

'He knows how to use a gun, doesn't he?'

'He goes deer hunting sometimes with his cousin. That doesn't mean he shot Lars.'

'No, I know,' said Megan. 'I'm just saying.'

'Saying what?'

Megan shrugged.

Bill cleared his throat. 'Brooke. You should tell your husband that Lars lied when he said it was him who killed Craig Naylor. It wasn't him, it was me. Lars was just covering for me.'

'Dad! Why didn't you say anything?'

'I don't know. I should have.'

'Can I tell Justin why you killed Craig?'

Bill shook his head. 'I'm sorry. You can't.'

'Oh, because it's Classified. I'm getting bored with that excuse.'

'You're not the only one,' said Megan.

Tears flowed from Brooke's eyes. 'You know what this means? Justin will never forgive you.'

The rest she left unsaid. That it would become very difficult for Brooke to see her father in future, or any of the rest of the family.

'I hope one day he will,' Bill said.

'This must have something to do with that order to launch missiles,' said Brooke. 'It *must*.'

'That is why I can't tell you about it. Or Justin.'

'But what if . . .'

We let the unasked question hang there for a moment. Then Megan completed it. 'What if Justin shot Lars because he thought Lars had killed his father and in fact it wasn't Lars, it was Dad?'

'Oh, Megan! That's not what I was going to say at all.'

'Megan!' Bill barked. 'Have some compassion, will you?'

He stood up and moved around the kitchen table towards Brooke.

She pushed back her chair and leaped to her feet. 'No, Dad. You killed my husband's father and won't tell me why. And you, Megan, accuse him of being a murderer.' She bit back a sob. 'Justin is a good man and I love him.'

Bill hesitated.

'Goodbye.' Brooke turned away from them and hurried out of the kitchen. A moment later they heard her car set off down the lane.

38

'Why did I do that?'

Megan was staring morosely at her recently refilled glass of wine. Bill had disappeared upstairs to his study and his needlepoint.

'I mean – we told Brooke Lars had been killed and then I virtually accused her husband of killing him, all in one fell swoop.'

'It did seem a little abrupt,' said Toby.

'And then Dad goes and tells her *he* killed her husband's father. Like that's going to help anyone. He's kept all these damn secrets for so long, you'd think he could keep another one.'

'You'd think so,' said Toby. But, in reality, he thought it would be a very good thing if the Guth family kept a lot fewer secrets from each other.

'Poor Brooke! I wish Alice was here. She'd know what to do. She wouldn't start accusing various people in the family of killing other people. She'd get us to stick together. She'd get Dad to tell everyone what really happened on the submarine. And she would figure out who really killed Sam Bowen and Lars.'

'I think you are giving her too much credit,' said Toby. 'It seems to me she is as guilty as Bill about keeping secrets.'

'Maybe she has some plan? Now. Maybe Alice knows what's going on?'

'I think that's what Bill is afraid of,' said Toby. 'That Alice knows what's going on.'

'Dad can't be right that Alice killed Sam, can he?'

'Of course not,' said Toby. Firmly. His belief in his wife's innocence was unshakeable. He couldn't allow it to be shaken. 'No chance.'

'You're right,' said Megan. She stood up and put the bowls in the dishwasher. She began to wash up the small number of pots on the kitchen counter. Toby grabbed a dish towel and started drying.

Megan had the last pot in the washing up bowl, and she was staring down at the suds, shoulders hunched and lips pursed. She let out a sob.

'Come here,' said Toby.

He was a lot taller than Megan, who pressed her face closely into his chest. The sobs came faster, and he held her close.

His phone buzzed. He broke away from Megan and checked the screen. It was Alice. 'Hey! Are they letting you go?'

'Yes. Just now.'

'That's great! So they've admitted you've got nothing to do with it?'

'I don't think so. They had to let me go or charge me. And they haven't gotten enough evidence to charge me. Yet.'

'Oh well. It's great you're out.'

'Toby? Can you come and get me?'

Toby glanced at the two bottles of wine on the table and felt foolish. 'I can't. I've had too much to drink.'

'Oh, Toby!'

'I can get a taxi and come and fetch you.'

'Don't worry. I can get a cab from here myself.'

'I can ask your dad if he can go and get you. He hasn't had as much to drink as me.'

'Hey, it's fine, Toby. I'll see you soon.'

Megan went up to her room, and Toby waited for Alice alone in the kitchen, restricting himself to one more glass of wine.

He thought about the shooter. Megan was right: he could still be after Toby. He felt safe enough inside the house with two armed policemen watching, but that wouldn't last for ever. At some point soon Toby would return to London. Where he would be a sitting target.

The police, or someone, had to figure out who the shooter was and catch him.

He checked the window and saw the two policemen in their car parked on the other side of the lane. He boiled a kettle and made them both a mug of tea: surely even in these days of Starbucks and triple lattes all policemen still liked tea.

He took two mugs outside. The policemen were grateful, but ushered him back into the house with an admonition to stay put. He glanced back at the dark marsh, wondering whether anyone really was out there. An unseen owl hooted on its night patrol.

It would know.

Twenty minutes later, a taxi pulled up outside the house, and Toby opened the front door for his wife. She stood there, her skin wan in the porch light, her face taut. She looked exhausted but somehow composed, as if she had just pulled an all-nighter at her law firm on a big deal.

They both hesitated, both unsure of how she would behave towards him. Then she threw herself into his chest, and held him tight. She was the second Guth sister to do that to him that evening; he wrapped his arms around her and squeezed.

Alice looked up. 'Toby, they said that Lars has been shot and killed on the beach. And someone shot at you too!'

'That's right.'

'God, I'm so glad they missed! I mean missed you. Poor Uncle Lars.'

'Come in,' Toby said. 'Have a glass of wine.'

'Is there anything to eat? I'm starving. There must be some cold turkey left?'

'Yeah. Or I think there's some soup. I can warm that up for you?'

'That would be good. Thanks.'

She came into the kitchen and Toby emptied the remains of the carton of soup into a bowl and stuck it in the microwave.

'Tell me what happened. On the beach.'

Toby told her as he watched the bowl of soup circle in the microwave, but he was interrupted just as the machine pinged.

'Alice! You're out!' said Bill, appearing at the kitchen door.

'What did you expect?' said Alice. 'They couldn't keep me any longer without charging me.'

Bill held open his arms for her. Alice ignored him, and started eating her soup. Bill let his arms drop.

That was the second Guth sister to reject him that evening, Toby thought.

'I'm sorry about Uncle Lars, Dad. I know he was a good friend of yours.'

'Yes,' said Bill. 'Yes, he was. And he was a brave man. I've told Toby and Megan the real story of what happened on the submarine.'

'Really?' Alice glanced sharply at Toby, making him feel unaccountably guilty. 'It's a shame no one will know about what Lars did. His family.'

'Yes. I guess I am lucky Donna told you girls.'

'You're also lucky you're not dead.'

Bill raised his eyebrows, stunned.

'I mean, someone tried to kill Toby this afternoon, didn't they?'

'Yes, they did.'

'And no one knows why?'

'I'd like to speak to you about that.'

'Not tonight, Dad. Not tonight.'

Bill sat down opposite his daughter. 'There are things we must discuss.'

'And there's soup I've got to eat,' said Alice. 'Look, Dad. I've been questioned by the police all day. I'm exhausted. I just want to eat something and go to sleep. OK?'

'All right,' Bill nodded, controlling his impatience.

Toby joined them at the kitchen table, and there was a painful silence as Alice finished her soup. Toby wondered what Bill wanted to say to Alice and what Alice didn't want to say to Bill. He also marvelled at how Alice had somehow managed to take control of the situation within moments of returning.

She finished her soup, and got to her feet. 'Well, goodnight,' she said. She hesitated and then kissed her father on the top of his head, eliciting a brief smile.

'I'll be up in a moment,' said Toby.

'Do you think she knows you suspect her of killing Sam?' Toby said to his father-in-law after Alice had gone.

Bill shrugged. 'Who knows what Alice knows?'

Toby joined her in their bedroom twenty minutes later. The light was off and Alice was on her side facing away from the door.

'You OK?' Toby said as he undressed.

There was no reply for several seconds. Then Alice spoke. 'No. You?'

'No.'

Toby undressed and got into bed. It had been a truly dreadful day. He had seen a man get killed only two feet away from him. He had nearly been killed himself. And Alice? God knows what Alice thought. God knows what Alice had done.

Toby had always felt comfortable in the Guth family, secure in its warmth and its minor arguments. But now it was blowing up around him, and there was nothing he could do about it.

At least he had Alice.

Didn't he?

He turned, reached over and touched her back.

She tensed. He left his hand there. Then she rolled over and grabbed him by the shoulders tightly. 'God, Toby, I'm so glad you are still alive!'

'So am I,' he said. 'Believe me, so am I.'

She kissed him, gently for a few seconds, and then urgently, and then she was on top of him and he inside her.

39

Megan sat on her bed and stared at the four walls of her crappy little room. It was the smallest in the house; well maybe Maya's was smaller, but Maya's was cuter and had a view out over the marshes, whereas Megan's room looked out over a scruffy field to a row of back gardens in the village. It was true she could see the windmill on the hill above Barnholt, the real windmill with its broad wooden sails, not one of those giant propellers spinning out to sea.

There was no floor space. One large suitcase remained upright and unopened, the contents of the other covered the carpet. It was not as if there was anywhere to hang anything.

Megan wondered if this was where she would stay for the next few weeks in Norfolk. Surely, once everyone else had left and Dad had returned to London, she could take over Alice and Toby's room?

This was so not working out as she had planned. As in most big families, Megan assumed, each child had their role. Alice was the conscientious elder daughter, Maya was the youngest cutest one, Brooke was the anxious one, and Megan was the naughty one.

She had enjoyed this role as a child, getting into scrapes and rubbing her father and mother, both of whom she loved desperately, up the wrong way. She had run away from the house in Cobham when she was eight, and hidden herself away in nearby woods until two a.m.; she had got caught smoking when she was twelve at the International School in Brussels and she had been discovered by her Australian boyfriend's mother having sex with him when they were both aged fourteen in the garage in the expat compound in Riyadh. He wasn't even really a boyfriend, but he was a kindred spirit and he had his own issues which intrigued her.

Then their mother had died. Megan was nineteen and at college. All four girls had reacted in different ways. Maya's beauty had become soulful, and she had withdrawn from the family; Brooke's anxiety had increased to the point where their father sent her to a therapist; Alice had taken over from their mother in running the family and Megan became that bit more disruptive. She dropped out of college. She found a boyfriend who was a jerk and a criminal. She took stupid jobs that didn't suit her. She occasionally sought her father's advice, but, whenever she did so, she was careful not to follow it. She let her sisters down, especially Alice.

She didn't exactly do it on purpose. When she had accepted the invitation to Alice and Toby's wedding in London, she thought she was going to go. It was just, when the day arrived, she didn't. Why should she? They didn't really want her there. The family wouldn't notice her absence: they would probably be glad she wasn't around to embarrass them all. She was doing them a favour by not showing up.

And all that was fine, because she knew that her mom and dad loved her, and even when her mom died she knew that Dad together with Alice could cope. She was safe screwing up her life, because her family would always be there for her.

But now what was she doing? Behaving like a brat. Coming home with all her stuff like some freshman dropping out of college. Being rude to her father.

This time the family could not cope. The family was falling apart around her. Alice was in trouble. Dad was losing control. Brooke had run away scared, following her own husband who felt justifiably betrayed. Maya had slipped away without anyone noticing.

Which left Megan. And Toby.

She liked Toby. He was kind. He was concerned – not just for Alice, but for all of them, including her. He took her seriously.

It was no surprise that Alice had nabbed him; Alice was always going to marry a kind, supportive, good-looking husband.

Now Megan had a job to do. She had to pull her family back together again. None of her sisters could do it.

She was smart. At least as smart as Alice – no, she must stop comparing herself to her sister!

She couldn't believe her father's fear that Alice had killed Sam Bowen. Like Toby, she *wouldn't* believe it. The police couldn't figure out what was going on, so she must.

She opened her computer and began tapping out ideas. Things she knew. Things she suspected.

Then she looked for connections.

Assuming her father was telling the truth, there seemed to be two possible avenues to follow, both connected to the *Alexander Hamilton*: Craig Naylor's death on board the submarine and Commander Driscoll's approach to Pat Greenwald.

First Megan checked online for any traces of reporting on the *Hamilton*'s near-launch back in 1983. Unsurprisingly, there was nothing. There were articles and extracts from books on the other near misses that Sam Bowen had mentioned: the false readings of missile attacks at NORAD and at the Soviet early-warning centre in the early eighties.

Next, Lieutenant Naylor's death. There was very little about this either. In fact, all Megan could find was an obituary in the local paper of the town in New Jersey where he had grown up and where his parents lived. There was a photograph of someone who looked very much like Justin Opizzi. Craig had been a good-looking guy with a warm, open face and a military haircut. He had played for the high school baseball team, and left a grieving wife, Maria, a father who was a lawyer, and a mother, as well as a younger sister, Victoria. There was a memorial service at the local Presbyterian church.

Nothing about how he had died. And nothing about how he had separated from his wife.

Megan didn't know whether Craig's parents were still alive: it was possible. But his sister was, as was his ex-wife, Justin's mother; Justin had spoken to them both about Craig's death.

Megan had never met Vicky, nor had she heard any mention of her within her family, although she had heard quite a lot about Craig himself. Given what Justin had said about Vicky's suspicions of Craig's death, and her own father's reluctance to face her, it was quite probable that Bill and Vicky had avoided each other over the years.

Should Megan try to contact Vicky?

Maybe. From what Justin had reported, she sounded as if she was still angry about her brother's death. It was possible that Justin hadn't asked her the right questions, or hadn't been entirely honest about what she had told him.

Megan hesitated. Justin would not be at all happy if she contacted her, and neither would her father. But then Justin wasn't happy anyway, and pissing off her father was nothing new. She considered a phone call, but decided on an email. A little searching on the Internet yielded Vicky's email address, and she quickly tapped out a brief message:

Hi Vicky,

My name is Megan Guth: I am Bill Guth's daughter. I am with my father and the rest of my family in England. You may have heard that Sam Bowen, whom I understand you have met, was murdered a couple of days ago, and that Lars da Silva was shot earlier today.

I'm sure the British police have been in contact, but do you mind
if I ask you a few questions? This is tearing my family apart, and I
need some answers.

Regards,

Megan Guth

Megan hesitated before hitting *Send*. It was likely Vicky would
ignore the message. And if she didn't, she would ask Megan what
really happened on the submarine, and Megan wouldn't be able to
tell her.

What the hell? Megan had to do something. She clicked *Send*.

If Craig Naylor's death was indeed what had spurred Sam Bowen's
murder, the most likely reason seemed to be that someone was trying
to prevent that news from coming out. Who? Her father? Alice
protecting her father? The US Navy or the US intelligence services?

And what about Lars's death? Well, that could be an attempt to
shut him up as well. Or it could be Justin taking revenge on who he
believed had killed his natural father. But was there any reason that
Justin might have killed Sam Bowen?

None that Megan could think of.

Unless maybe Justin was concerned that the world would find
out that his father wasn't a hero after all, but had actually wanted
to start a nuclear war? That couldn't be right: it was clear Justin
had no idea what had happened on that submarine; that was what
was driving him so crazy.

She heard a car pull up outside and Alice enter the house, but
Megan ignored her sister.

OK, Commander Driscoll next, and then Pat Greenwald.

Once again, the only substantive mention of Commander Driscoll
was a brief obituary in a Wichita Falls newspaper from July 1984.
Nothing about the cause of death, just that it had been 'sudden'.

Blowing your brains out counted as 'sudden'. Megan jotted down the names of his brother and parents, and his ex-wife and their two children.

She was more hopeful in her search for Pat Greenwald, and indeed there was quite a lot about her involvement in the anti-nuclear movement in the 1980s and 1990s. There was even a short Wikipedia entry for her. Which stated that she was murdered in 1996.

What!

Megan's fingers flew over the keys as she did some more Googling. Greenwald had been killed only yards from her home in Brooklyn Heights in a mugging gone wrong. The perpetrators had never been caught, but there had been a number of murders in the area related to the crack cocaine epidemic.

She was survived by a husband, an academic at Columbia University named Ron Greenwald, and a son, Henry.

1996? That was when her father had said that the FBI had visited him and her mother in England to ask about Pat Greenwald. Could that be a coincidence? It could be. But then again, it might not be.

Naturally, there was no indication that Pat Greenwald had been suspected of being a Russian spy. Megan started Googling her husband, who was a professor of Earth and Environmental Sciences. He had written a number of books and articles about environmental issues, including nuclear energy. But there was virtually nothing about him joining his wife in the anti-nuclear movement in the eighties and nineties.

He, too, had died. Of cancer in 2012, the same year as Megan's mother. Now, that must be a coincidence.

There was one son, Henry. Megan Googled him. Nothing. Checked him out on Facebook and narrowed the few Henry Greenwalds down to one guy who was thirty-nine, a geriatrician living in Brooklyn, married with two kids. He wasn't an active user of the service. Not expecting much, Megan clicked on Henry's Facebook friends. There were not many of them. On the second page she saw a name she recognized.

Sam Bowen.

It was *the* Sam Bowen. Writer and historian at Newcastle University.

So Sam had stumbled upon Pat Greenwald after all. She was certainly someone many people would want to keep out of his book.

Megan considered a message on Facebook, or sending Henry an email directly.

But then she had a better idea.

40

January 1984, New York City

Donna and I spent the entire weekend in her apartment, with the exception of two quick forays by me into the snow to pick up Chinese takeout on Saturday night and bagels and the *New York Times* on Sunday morning.

I had to return to the base on Sunday evening, so I called to find out the schedule for the last train back to New London. When the time came, we put on our clothes, and Donna accompanied me on a walk through the snowy city to Penn Station.

It was dark, but the newly fallen snow glimmered in the street lights. Silhouettes drifted past us. As we skirted Washington Square, four separate men offered to sell us drugs.

After almost thirty-six hours of almost constant talking, we fell silent, happy to be in each other's company, walking hand in hand.

Things were changing, and I was excited.

Then I started to think.

We were on Broadway, not far from Penn Station. The area was getting distinctly sleazier, but somehow the snow made it feel safer.

'What's up?' said Donna.

'Nothing's up,' I said, summoning a smile.

'Oh, come on. Something's up? Are you worried about going back to base?'

'It's not that,' I said.

'Then what is it?'

I didn't want to tell her.

She squeezed my hand.

I knew what she meant by that gesture. I didn't have to tell her if I didn't want to. But she would like it if I did, if I trusted her with my thoughts.

OK.

'It's the cover-up,' I said.

'What, don't you think it will hold?'

'No. I think if the Navy wants to cover something up it will stay covered up. Especially if it's about nuclear weapons. It's just I'm not sure they should want to do that.'

'Now you're beginning to sound like me.'

'Is that what you've been thinking?'

'Yes, but I wasn't going to say it. And if they don't cover it up what would happen to you? You'd get court martialled, right?'

'Maybe,' I said. 'I don't know. But if they do cover it up and I tell anybody, then I definitely will be in trouble.'

'I get that,' said Donna.

I was grateful for her understanding. The reason I had been reluctant to tell her what I was thinking was that I had been afraid she would urge me to blow the whistle and I would have ended up in an argument with her, when what I really wanted to do was explain how I felt.

'I killed my best friend. I saw the world almost blow itself up. The Navy can't deny that happened. *I* can't deny that happened. We have to tell someone.'

'I can see why I might think you should,' said Donna carefully. 'But why do you say that?'

'It's just too big a deal. The world has to know about it so it can react. Take steps to deal with something similar occurring in future. If something like this happened on the *Hamilton* it can happen somewhere else. It *will* happen somewhere else. And we won't be prepared.'

'So who do you want to tell?'

'The American government – I bet the Navy won't inform Congress. The American people. Maybe even the Russians. After all, they are the guys who will be deciding whether to retaliate next time.'

'So why don't you do it?'

'Because I'm a coward. They would call it treason and I'd go to jail for the rest of my life. And – don't laugh at this – because I gave them my word.'

But Donna laughed. 'You are such a boy scout!' She squeezed my hand. 'But that's OK. I admire honesty; I like people you can trust.'

I smiled. We were at the entrance to the station. I actually felt better having shared my worry with Donna. It hadn't gone away; it would probably never go away. I was going to have to learn to live with it, and maybe she could help with that.

When we parted I promised to see her in two weekends' time. She smiled broadly when she heard this, a smile I held in my mind the entire train journey back to Connecticut.

41

February 1984, New York City

I shivered as I stood on the small rise overlooking the model boat pond in Central Park. Scraps of brown snow clung to tree trunks and the ankles of Hans Christian Andersen on the far side of the water. The temperature had wavered within a degree or two of freezing for the past week, and the thaw had been slow. What remained of the snow, which had been so pristine when I had visited the city two weeks before, was now grey, shot through with streaks of brown.

I watched as a black poodle lifted its leg a few yards away. And yellow.

'Got a cigarette?' said Donna, threading her arm through mine and huddling close, as much to make use of me as a windbreak as through a sudden burst of affection.

I lit one for her, shielding the flame from the cold breeze whipping through the streets of the Upper East Side into the park. 'She's late,' I said, checking my watch.

'She's always late,' said Donna.

'You didn't tell me that,' said Bill. 'And why didn't she pick a cafe? It's freezing out here.'

'She wants to make sure she's not being followed.'

'People follow her?'

Donna shrugged. 'Maybe. From what you said, people follow me.'

I didn't answer, but actually I was glad Pat Greenwald was taking precautions. I certainly didn't want anyone to know I was meeting her.

269

It had been Donna's idea. After that night together in her studio in St Mark's Place, things had moved fast. As expected, I had failed the Personal Reliability Program, which meant I could no longer work on nuclear missile submarines. I had told Commander Driscoll that I had decided I wanted to leave the Navy. And I had sent off for information from business schools, in particular Wharton, which was affiliated with Penn where Donna was applying to law school. A new life was opening up for me, a life with Donna, and I was excited.

So was she.

And then it had all nearly gotten screwed up.

I had arrived in New York on Friday evening, and Donna and I had gone straight to a little restaurant in the West Village for dinner. I had managed to extend the weekend to Monday – Donna had negotiated to take that day off – and I was looking forward to it.

But as soon as we had ordered our food, Donna said she had something to tell me, and she thought she had better tell me right away.

She had told Pat Greenwald that I had been on board a submarine that had been ordered to launch its nuclear missiles.

I was furious. We argued. I announced I would take the first train back to Groton the following morning. I felt she had betrayed my trust. She agreed she had, but she had only done it because I had told her I knew the events on the *Hamilton* were too important to bury. She said Pat had promised not to tell anyone else, and anyway Donna hadn't given her any details. It was entirely up to me what happened next.

What can I say? Donna won me over. I was falling heavily in love with her. The life that was suddenly appearing in front of me appealed so strongly, that I couldn't contemplate losing it. And she was right: after what I had witnessed on board the *Hamilton,* after what I had done, I could never be in favour of nuclear weapons, or even neutral towards them. She was helping me do what I wanted to do, but was too afraid to.

So I had agreed to meet with Pat Greenwald at lunch time on Monday.

'There she is,' Donna said, pointing to a tall woman walking rapidly toward us with long strides.

Pat Greenwald was younger than I had expected – about thirty. She was wearing jeans, a black coat plastered with buttons and a green-and-white woolly hat, similarly splattered. Despite the buttons' earnest exhortations, the effect was strangely childish, as though she had emerged from a kindergarten school yard.

'You must be Bill.' She held out her gloved hand, which I shook. 'I'm Pat.'

Shrewd blue eyes smiled out of a long face, and dark curly hair leaked out of the hat. Her voice was deep and husky. She had charm – charisma even.

'That's me.'

'Shall we walk?'

I couldn't help scanning the pond for potential watchers, although I suspected that if they were any good I wouldn't be able to spot them.

Pat noticed. 'Don't worry, I've been careful. No one followed me.' Then she grinned. 'Actually, it's good you are worried. Hold that attitude.'

She set off at a good pace. I walked next to her and Donna trailed a couple of feet behind us.

'You should understand, Bill, that I won't repeat anything you tell me without your permission.'

'How do I know I can trust you?' I asked.

'Fair question,' said Pat. 'I keep my word. And think about it: if I said that a sailor told me that a submarine had been ordered to launch its nuclear weapons, the Navy would deny it. You would deny it. No one would believe me. I would just lose all credibility.' She turned to me. 'I need my credibility. And we need for you to say it yourself.'

'I can't do that.'

'You must. Don't you see that we can never know the true danger of nuclear weapons, or nuclear energy for that matter, because every time something goes wrong the authorities hush it up? This may not be the first time a submarine has been ordered to launch nuclear weapons. How would we know? If it had happened before it would have been kept quiet. Not just from the public, but within the Navy. It would be kept quiet from people like you whose job it is to use these weapons. Right?'

'Right.'

She was undoubtedly correct. That was the trouble: that was the truth I wanted to hide from.

'So how can we help you make this public? What support would you need?'

I shook my head. 'I can't.'

'It would make a huge difference to the people's attitude toward nuclear weapons. We have been searching for a way to make the ordinary person in the street realize that we all have to do something about the bombs. This could be it. Don't you see?'

I saw. But. 'Sorry, Pat. I just can't do it.'

'The public will be overwhelmingly on your side,' Pat went on. 'You will be a hero; the man who saved the world. They won't be able to prosecute you – it would look really bad. We'll whip up support for you, not just here but all over the world. If you prefer, you can make the announcement from somewhere else. West Germany, for example. Or Switzerland.'

'So I would be a martyr? Or a fugitive? Those would be my choices?'

'You would be a brave man,' said Pat. 'Doing the right thing.'

'Donna really didn't tell you much about what happened, did she?' I said.

Pat shook her head.

'The thing is, I killed someone. A good friend. I had to – it was the only way to stop the process. Right at the end, an officer opens a safe containing the trigger for the missiles. Only he knows the combination. I killed that officer, just before he opened the safe.'

'Oh,' said Pat.

'So, you see, the Navy could court martial me for murder as well as mutiny and treason. But they have decided not to.'

'In return for you keeping quiet?'

'Yes,' I said. 'You just told me you keep your word. Well, I do too.'

She led us deeper into the park into a warren of narrow paths and steep little hills winding through trees. Here, in the cold shade, snow clung to the frozen earth.

'All right,' she said. 'I have another idea.'

I waited.

'You know that our movement is pushing for unilateral nuclear disarmament?'

'Yes.'

'Do you have a problem with that?'

'Yes, I do.' I was glad to have the opportunity to make the point. 'The only reason there hasn't been a nuclear war in the last thirty years is that both sides have nuclear weapons. Deterrence has worked. If one side reduces its nuclear arsenal then the other side might think they could win a war. And we'll have one.'

'And do you still think that? After what happened on your submarine?'

'I don't know,' I said. 'Maybe. But now I'm concerned there will be a nuclear war anyway. An accidental nuclear war.'

'OK. A few years ago I would have disagreed with you about deterrence. I thought all nuclear weapons were bad and to do anything other than scrap them immediately was insane. But now quite a few of us think that we need to encourage nuclear disarmament throughout the world. Here, but also in Britain and France and China. Maybe soon in Israel. And in Russia.'

'Russia? How are you going to do that?'

'We have been in contact with Russians who think like we do. In particular, physicists who understand the damage that nuclear war would do. I know that in the west we assume that the Soviets are itching to wipe America off the face of the earth, but actually they are as scared of nuclear war as we are. Remember the Cuban missile crisis? The Russians blinked. They didn't want a world war then; they don't want one now. And, more to the point, they can't afford more nuclear weapons.'

'So what are you suggesting? That I speak to the Russians?'

'Yes. Not to the government, but to the peace activists we know.'

I frowned. 'Are you sure they aren't just fronts for the Russian government?'

'Yes, quite sure. The Russians are not very subtle about the way they try to co-opt our peace movement. They finance the World Peace Council, everyone knows that. The Peace Council tries to give us money; we refuse. No, these people are different. In particular the person I'm thinking of. Donna has met her.'

I glanced back at Donna, who was listening. She nodded. 'It's the Gorky Trust Group. Remember I told you about them?'

'Gorky is a secure Soviet city,' Pat said. 'Our contact is a physicist there.'

'I know Gorky,' I said. 'It often turns up in our target packages.'

That shut Pat up for a moment. 'Don't you see?' she said. 'If the Russian peace activists know that the United States nearly launched nuclear weapons at them by mistake, then maybe they will let us know of similar incidents there. And then if we reduce our missiles, maybe they will reduce theirs. The only way we are going to stop this insane race is if Russia and the United States begin to trust each other. The Russians get that. There's a Moscow Trust Group and now this Gorky one.'

I shook my head. 'That's never going to work in the real world,' I said.

'It was working!' Pat said. 'That's what the SALT talks were all about. Until Reagan came in and started talking about winning the nuclear arms race just when we were about to wind it down. And you can help that.'

I didn't answer.

The trees opened up on a lake, surrounded by rocks. It was extraordinary to think that we were in the middle of one of the biggest cities on earth.

'Well?' Pat said.

'No,' I said.

'He'll think about it,' said Donna.

'No, Donna,' I protested, as Pat left us to walk back to Hunter College, and Donna and I headed south through the park.

'Just think about it,' Donna said.

'It would be treason. I would be betraying my country. That's not something I would be prepared to do.'

'But don't you see, you are betraying your country by saying nothing!' Donna said. 'And not just your country, every country in the world. The human race!'

I shook my head.

'Just think about it, please.'

We walked around the lake, together but apart. This worried me. I had hoped that my experience on the *Hamilton* would bring us closer together, bridge that divide of our views on nuclear weapons. But it looked as if, far from burying the question, it was raising it up between us.

Donna's fingers found mine. 'Bill. You can do what you want on this. I like you a lot, and I will still like you if you decide to keep quiet and not see Pat's contact. I'm not going to try to coerce you to do something you don't want to do. That's not how our relationship should work.'

I squeezed her hand: it was what I wanted to hear.

'Just think about it for a few days. That's all I ask. And then, if you want, I will tell Pat you don't want to see her or her Russian friend.'

'OK,' I said.

'Maybe speak to Lars about it? See what he thinks?'

While Lars and I were waiting for our discharges to come through, we remained at the base, but were removed from working with the rest of the *Alexander Hamilton*'s crew. We were given the kind of superfluous administrative jobs that the Navy excels at creating; mine was in the department responsible for linen supplies. My office was, literally, a linen closet. It felt a bit like life on a submarine: there wasn't even a window.

Lars had a top-secret filing assignment and was just as bored as me. We had found throwing ourselves around a squash court a good way of getting over our frustration. We were evenly matched: I was the more skilful, but Lars was very quick around the court, and able to reach even my subtlest of drop shots.

A couple of days after I got back to the base from New York we were alone in the locker room after a game when I told him about my conversation with Pat Greenwald and her suggestion that I might talk to the Russians.

He was shocked.

'Do you think I'm crazy?' I asked him.

'Why not just talk to the papers? Off the record,' said Lars. 'That way everyone would know, including the Russians. They'll have people who read our newspapers.'

'I thought of that,' I said. 'And, in fact, that's what Pat Greenwald originally wanted me to do. Set up a press conference. But even if it is off the record, the Navy would figure out it was me in an instant. Or you. I mean who else could it be?'

'I see what you mean. But talking to the Russians? That sounds bad. Like spying-against-your-country bad.'

'Maybe. But, in a weird way talking to the Russians through someone like Pat might be the best thing to do. The Navy wouldn't find out. And it's the Russians who are the people I want most to hear about it. They are the ones who have to show restraint if something like this occurs again.'

Lars seemed unconvinced.

'I wouldn't tell them anything that would endanger an American submarine.'

Lars blew through his cheeks.

'Well?' I said.

'I don't know.'

We sat in silence. I felt I had almost convinced him. I had almost convinced myself.

But. I would be spying against my country, at least according to the Navy.

'Remember that conversation we had with the XO in the wardroom?' Lars said. 'The one where he said the Russians should know what happened?'

'Yeah. I think that's what got me worrying about all this in the first place.'

'He's a smart guy. Maybe you should speak with him?'

42

February 1984, Groton

I decided to meet Lieutenant Commander Robinson outside, at the ruins of the fort which crowned a hill above the oldest part of Groton a few miles downriver from the sub base.

Nobody missed me when I snuck away from my linen closet to drive south into town. I parked outside the library, and gave myself a half hour to wander around to make sure I wasn't being followed. It was a clear, cold, still day, and there were few people on foot. None of them was following me, and the cars parked within sight of the fort were all empty.

The fort itself was nothing more than a quadrangle of grassy earthworks overlooking the broad Thames River and the industrial port of New London on its far bank, where a couple of large freighters were unloading. I had visited it only once: with my parents soon after I had been posted to Groton. It was the site of a battle during the revolution. In 1781 the British, led by the turncoat general Benedict Arnold, had besieged the fort, breached its defences and massacred its defenders. A monument to the battle rose solemnly on the other side of the road.

Now it was quiet. It was also cold.

I stood on top of one of the ramparts waiting, the Thames glittering in the winter sunshine. A muffled crash drifted up from the General Dynamics shipyard a mile or so downstream – the sound of a new nuclear submarine being put together. At twelve-thirty precisely, the XO parked his car on the street a hundred yards away, spotted me and walked along the path from the road into the grassy square, surrounded by the remains of the walls. Down there, no one could see us.

We were both in uniform in our all-weather coats. I considered saluting, but decided not to.

'Thank you for coming,' I said.

'It's an interesting place to meet, Guth,' he said. I could see he was curious. 'A bit cold.'

'I want to continue the conversation we had in the wardroom,' I said. 'And I don't want to be overheard.'

The more I had thought about it, the more I realized that the XO was exactly the right person to talk to. I didn't know him well – we had only served on one patrol together – but I respected his professionalism. He was a conscientious, diligent, talented officer with direct experience with planning for a nuclear war. And that conversation had shown that he was also a thinking human being.

If he agreed with Lars that what Pat Greenwald had suggested was treason, then I would have nothing more to do with her. But if he agreed with Donna . . . I wasn't sure what I would do. But I would respect his judgement.

Approaching him was risky, but he had opened up to Lars and me first, and I hoped that by reminding him of this, I would discourage him from turning around and reporting me.

Robinson frowned, pulling his dark eyebrows together. 'Is this something I should hear?'

'I think so,' I said.

I could see Robinson hesitate. But curiosity overcame caution. And I also felt trust and respect for me.

'I have a philosophical question for you,' I said.

'I have come all this way to discuss philosophy with you?'

'Yes.'

'Go on.'

'I love my country. That's why I joined the Navy. But it's also why I did what I did on the *Hamilton*. I didn't want the country I love to be destroyed. To me, that is straightforward patriotism. Do you agree?'

Robinson nodded slowly. 'I do. And so does Commander Driscoll. That's why we recommended you for an honourable discharge.' He gave me a grudging smile. 'If it were up to me, I'd give you a medal.'

'Thank you, but I'm just glad to avoid a court martial,' I said. 'I was thinking about our conversation. You suggested that it would be good if the Navy was more open with the Soviets?' I waited. I needed his acknowledgement before I went further.

Robinson looked uncomfortable, but then he nodded. 'I remember.'

'It seems to me that it's unlikely that this will be the only time an erroneous order is given to a boomer. Or maybe a missile launch site or a bomber. In fact, I would be surprised if this hasn't happened before. It may even have happened on a Russian submarine.'

'That is certainly possible.'

'In which case it would be good if the Russians knew about it. Because if three missiles are accidentally fired at the Soviet Union one day, they might consider the possibility it was an accident. They might not retaliate. Do you think that's right?'

'I do,' said Robinson, carefully.

'So, philosophically speaking, would it be a good thing if the Soviets knew what we almost did in November?'

Robinson turned away from me and took a few paces, staring at the grassy hump of the old fortification.

My heart was thumping as I let him think. I hoped I hadn't said enough for Robinson to have me arrested. The XO was a diligent officer; maybe that's what a diligent officer should do.

We stood there, apart, for two full minutes. Then Robinson turned and faced me.

'I have two things to say to you, Lieutenant Guth. Firstly, I agree with your philosophical point. A true patriot would not want to see his country devoured by a nuclear holocaust. And if the Russians knew about nuclear near-launches, they would be less likely to retaliate if one were to occur in the future, one where missiles were actually fired.'

I felt a wave of relief.

'I have another point, though, and please listen to it. I am a serving officer in the United States Navy. If I ever learned that you intended to approach the Soviets and tell them anything about what happens or happened on board a nuclear submarine, I would have to report it to the naval authorities. But I believe you were only speaking "philosophically". Is that correct?'

'Aye, sir,' I said.

'So you have no intention of going to the Russians directly, then?'

'Oh no. Of course not, sir.'

'Good,' said Robinson. 'Then I think we understand each other. I doubt we will speak before your discharge comes through. Good luck, Lieutenant Guth. With life after the Navy.'

Robinson held out his hand, and I shook it.

With a shiver, he hunched himself in his coat and turned back to his car.

As I watched him drive off, I knew I had my answer.

April 1984, Paris

They call April in New England 'Mud'. There was no mud in the Jardin du Luxembourg in April, or at least not during the three full days Donna and I spent in Paris.

We stayed in a cheap hotel just beyond the périphérique, and took the Metro into the city every morning. We did all the things young Americans do in Paris. We loitered in cafés, we loitered in museums, we hung around churches, we walked and we talked. Neither of us had ever been to Paris before: in fact the only country I had ever visited in Europe was Scotland. Donna had spent a month in Italy in her junior year at Swarthmore, and her French was pretty good – definitely better than mine.

We fell in love with the city – like so many Americans before us – and we were falling in love with each other.

I had been discharged from the Navy, and spent a couple of weeks at home with my parents before joining Donna in New York. My mother had been happy to accept my explanation that I couldn't divulge why I had left early, and that the discharge was indeed honourable. But my father had not taken my leaving the Navy well, especially when he realized that there was little chance that I would come and work with him on his newspaper. He was a curious newspaperman and he also felt that I should be able to trust my own family; he wanted to know all the details.

I held out.

But now, even more inconsistently, I was about to tell a total stranger everything.

Our three days coincided with the twenty-fourth International Conference on High Energy Physics, which was taking place in Paris that year. The plan, as explained to us by Pat Greenwald, was that we would saunter past a particular bench in the Jardin at 12.40 for each of the three days. If and when Donna saw Irena Boyarova, whom she would recognize, sitting there reading a book in English, we would place ourselves next to her and strike up a conversation, asking her about the book. If she was reading a book in Russian, we would walk on by.

I suggested that we spend the half hour beforehand going back and forth on the Metro to make sure no one was following us. We did this, but we found it impossible to determine whether we were being followed or not in the crowded foreign city.

The bench was just a few yards away from the Medici fountain. There was no sign of the Russian on the first day, but on the second the bench in question was occupied by a small woman with short greying hair wearing a shapeless brown coat. She was reading *The Thornbirds*.

'There she is,' said Donna.

We paused in front of the bench. '*Il y'a quelqu'un ici?*' Donna asked the woman.

The Russian smiled. '*Non,*' she said. '*Asseyez-vous.*' Her face was small and round, as were her blue eyes, which glanced at us quickly, and then went back to her book.

Donna and I unpacked a simple picnic from the bag Donna was carrying – bread, cheese and a couple of oranges – and began to eat. While we had both felt a sense of excitement at these meeting preparations over the previous couple of days, now I wasn't so sure. This was all too much like a John le Carré novel. I didn't like to think of the Russian physicist as a spy, and I certainly didn't like to think of myself as one.

It was cool on the bench; the sunshine that reached us was filtered by the chestnut trees above us. All three of us were hunched in our coats. After we had been sitting for a couple of minutes, Donna turned to her neighbour.

'How do you like that book? It's one of my favourites.'

'Is it? Oh, good,' said the woman in a heavy Russian accent. 'It was recommended to me by a friend. But I have only just started it.'

'Are you Russian?' said Donna. 'You sound Russian.'

Although we were not assuming that anyone would be within listening range, Pat Greenwald had suggested that in the first couple of minutes of conversation we should talk as if we had just met, so that we would be acting that way to distant watchers.

Soon Donna and Irena were chatting happily. Donna had introduced me, and we were sharing our lunch with her.

'So you have something to tell me?' Irena Boyarova asked me with a smile. 'Something about how your nuclear submarine was ordered to fire its missiles and didn't?'

'That's correct,' I said. And I told her in the vaguest terms what had happened.

She was listening closely. But when she started asking more detailed questions about the launch procedure, I demurred. 'I don't want to give away any secrets, here,' I said. 'I just want you to know what happened.'

'And thank you for that,' said Irena. 'We have a friend, Pavel, the brother of one of my colleagues, who is the commander of a Russian nuclear submarine. I have spoken to him and he is very interested in what you have to say. He tells us that in our country the navy believes that it is impossible to launch nuclear missiles without proper authorization, and he says that the Soviet navy believes that is true of your navy as well. Pavel is not so sure. He says we need to be able to convince people that in certain circumstances all the safeguards and checks will not work. But to do that, we need details.'

'I told Pat Greenwald I cannot give away any Classified information.'

'You have done that already,' said Irena. 'And I am not interested in technical details about your submarine or its missiles. But details about weaknesses in the launch procedure are really important. What's the risk? It's not as if the Soviet navy can disrupt the launch orders from outside your submarines?'

I hesitated. Irena was absolutely right; although the launch procedures were top secret, knowledge of them would not put any US submarine at risk. And the whole point of what I was doing, and the thrust of the XO's argument, was that the more the Russians understood about how the US launched nuclear missiles, the less likely they would be to retaliate following an accidental launch.

'Will I ever meet this Pavel?' I said.

Irena smiled. 'Perhaps. I hope so. One day, maybe.'

I liked the idea of this Russian officer who had come to the same conclusion I had, although I doubted Pavel was his real name.

'Are you going to give this information to the KGB? Or the Soviet high command?'

'We will get it to one or two generals who are sympathetic to our cause. Then they can pass it on. In the Soviet Union, the only way to achieve any nuclear disarmament is by persuading those in power that it is in their best interest and the motherland's. And I really believe we can do that. In a few years' time I believe we will see the Soviet Union reducing its nuclear weapons – if the US government changes its tune and is prepared to do the same. Your information will help us get to that point, but only if we have the details.'

I hesitated; I wasn't convinced that the details were relevant, but then I could see that giving them would furnish my story with credibility, and ultimately that was what was important. They would be of no help to a Soviet fast-attack sub creeping up on my shipmates in the *Alexander Hamilton*, of that I was certain.

So I told her the whole story.

She was impressed. When I was done, she smiled and touched my arm. 'Thank you. For what you did. I thank you on behalf of the Soviet population. If you had not had the courage to kill your friend, my country would have been destroyed.'

This thanks from an enemy affected me unexpectedly. I meant to reply, but found I couldn't. In the end, 'thank you' in turn was all I could manage.

'I must go back to my conference,' said Dr Boyarova. 'There is a chance that one of my compatriots may be watching us. If they are, they won't be able to identify who you are until you get back to your hotel. So take your time and, if you can, give them the slip.' Irena smiled. 'I think I irritate them: I make it a habit to speak to random strangers wherever I go – they can't follow all of them!'

'We'll do that,' I said.

'Until we meet again, which I hope we do.'

'Goodbye,' I said, unsure we *would* ever see each other again.

'Do you think she's a spy?' Donna asked, as we wended our way through the little streets around the church of Saint-Sulpice.

'No,' I said. 'She seemed genuine to me.'

'She was very nice.' Donna threaded her hand in mine. 'I hope I haven't gotten you into trouble.'

'Don't worry about it. I've thought this through. Even if the KGB do hear about the near-launch, that's a good thing, isn't it? If anything, they will be more able to pass it on to the Soviet high command than Irena would be.'

'That's true, I guess. As long as you don't get caught.'

'I won't get caught. I expect this will be the last time either of us sees Irena Boyarova.'

The spring sunshine warmed up the afternoon, and we ended up at a cafe on the banks of the Seine opposite the Île Saint-Louis. We ate a cheap meal with a cheap bottle of wine, and then worked our way down to the quai a couple of feet above the river.

'Let's sit down and watch for our tail.'

There was no tail. But we sat on the bench, looking up at the eastern end of Notre-Dame. Donna leaned in to me, nestling into my shoulder.

Neither of us spoke.

After the excitement of the afternoon, I found myself enveloped by a warm embrace of deep happiness. Love does that to you. Paris does that to you. While I had enjoyed the Navy and been good at my job, I had always had doubts about a life spent under the ocean. It was unhealthy. It made having a wife and children extremely difficult. And while I had genuinely believed that the threat of launching our missiles had kept the world safe for democracy, the knowledge that I might be involved in firing them had always made that a heavy burden.

Now we had come so close, the burden had become intolerable.

So I had no regrets about leaving the Navy. I had no idea where my business degree would lead me, but it sounded like a challenge, and one I was eager to meet. It would give me a chance to make something of myself in the world. The outside world: the real world.

And I wouldn't be doing it alone. I would be doing it with someone I loved. The woman resting her fair hair on my shoulder. The future belonged to us both.

Staring at the black water shot through with the shaky yellow reflections of the Paris streetlights and the illumination of the cathedral above us, I was sure the future belonged to us both.

I needed to make that happen.

'Donna?'

'Yes?'

'Will you marry me?'

44

Sunday 1 December 2019, Norfolk

Toby opened his eyes. His wife was staring at him. Her eyes and then her lips smiled when she saw he was awake, and she leaned forward to kiss his nose.

'Good morning.'

'Good morning,' he mumbled in reply. He had woken up confused by a vivid dream involving running around Barnholt beach naked in the rain, and then trying to climb into a locked car that was parked on the sand. At least it hadn't involved Lars's death in front of him – or not directly.

'What is it?' she said.

'What?'

'You winced.'

'I was thinking about Lars.'

'Oh.' She shuffled closer to him under the covers, and kissed his lips. 'Would you like breakfast? Sausages?'

'You don't have to get breakfast,' Toby said. 'We can fend for ourselves.'

Alice's brows knitted in a mock frown. 'Did I hear you just turn down sausages?'

Toby smiled. 'No, you didn't. And yes, I would love some sausages.'

'And baked beans?' Initially, Alice had disapproved of Toby's fondness for baked beans as part of a morning fry-up, considering it weird, but in time he had persuaded her that it was, in fact, perfectly natural.

'Yes please.'

Alice swung her legs out of bed and looked for her dressing gown, which was draped over a chair.

'Alice?'

'Yeah?'

'There was quite a lot of discussion after you were arrested yesterday, about Craig's death. Justin got upset; he didn't believe it was an accident.'

'Uh-huh.' Alice was feigning indifference, but I could tell she was listening closely.

'Lars claimed he had killed Craig.'

'Really?' A little more interest.

'And then later your father told us about Craig's death. And that it was him, not Lars who had killed Craig.'

Alice froze, her back to Toby. 'He *told* you that?'

'He did.'

Alice turned to Toby, her voice cold. 'And by "us" you mean . . .'

'Me and Megan. And then he told Brooke later on. After Lars was shot.'

'I'm surprised.'

'And then he told us about Pat Greenwald.'

'What!'

'About your mother's peace activist friend. And the FBI's suspicion that she had been in touch with the KGB. And Commander Driscoll had been in touch with her.'

'Jesus! Why did Dad do that?'

'We asked him to. We demanded that he tell us. You knew about it?'

'Yeah. Mom told me. But she told me not to tell anyone else and definitely not let Dad know I knew.'

'But why all these secrets?' Toby said, letting his frustration show. 'Wouldn't it have been better all along if you or your father had told your sisters? And me?'

'Toby! These are real, honest-to-goodness-secrets involving my parents and the KGB.'

'Yes. And two people are dead.'

'Because this stuff leaked out.'

'Is that why?' said Toby. 'Do you *know* why Sam Bowen died? Why Lars was shot?'

'No, Toby, I have no idea. Hey, I'm the one who has been locked up for two days.'

Toby paused. He didn't want to start a shouting match with his wife. 'I know,' he said.

'You haven't told the police any of this, have you?' Alice asked.

'No. I can't. Some guy was here from MI5 yesterday morning, with Admiral Robinson who was on the submarine with Bill. He made me sign the Official Secrets Act.'

'Good.'

'But after Lars was shot yesterday, I told the police I wanted to speak to MI5. Tell them what I know, and then they can tell the police.'

'Why would you do that?'

'Because you are a suspect, Alice. I want to get you off.'

Alice snorted in frustration. 'My lawyer has a strategy for that! None of us says anything. Not me, not Dad, and certainly not you. That way the police have to prove I killed Sam Bowen. Talking to them will just help them find that proof.'

'You see, that's what I don't get,' said Toby. 'If you didn't kill Sam Bowen, why wouldn't you or your hotshot lawyer want the police to know the truth?'

Alice glared at him. Frustration had turned to anger. 'If?'

Toby stared back.

'You said "if", Toby. Why did you say "if"?'

'I . . . I didn't mean "if". I meant . . . "since". I meant "since".'

'Well, you didn't say "since", did you?'

Toby hadn't.

'You think I killed Sam Bowen, don't you, Toby?'

'Of course I don't,' said Toby. 'I would never think that.'

'All right. If you genuinely don't think I killed that poor guy, trust me. Do as I ask. You can tell MI5 about Dad killing Craig on the submarine – Admiral Robinson will know that anyway. But don't tell them anything about Pat Greenwald. *Anything*. Do you understand?'

'Won't Admiral Robinson know about that too?'

'He may or may not, I don't know. That's up to him to tell the police about if he does know. It's not up to you. Now, will you promise me?'

Would he promise her? Didn't he have a duty to tell the authorities what he knew? Maybe. But his wife was in big trouble. She was asking him for proof that he trusted her.

He had to trust her.

'OK,' he said. 'I promise.'

Alice went downstairs to make breakfast, and Toby followed her ten minutes later. As he reached the top of the stairs he heard an urgent whisper.

'Toby!'

It was Megan, dressed in checked pyjama bottoms and a light grey T-shirt, beckoning him to her room.

He hesitated.

Her beckoning became more urgent. 'I've got something to tell you. It's to do with Pat Greenwald.' She mouthed the last two words.

Toby joined her in her room. Which was tiny, and most of the floor space was covered in clothes from an open suitcase.

She flopped on to her unmade bed. He remained standing.

'Pat Greenwald is dead.' Megan quickly described what she had discovered from her Internet searches of the previous evening.

'So you think Henry Greenwald might know something about his mother's activities?'

'Maybe. She might have left him papers. Or he might have seen something as a child.'

'It's worth a shot, I suppose. How are we going to contact him?'

'Not we. Maya. I messaged her last night in New York, and she agreed to go and see him. Maya can be persuasive if she wants to be. Especially with men.'

'Bill won't like it if he finds out. And neither will Alice.'

'*If* they find out,' said Megan, with a mischievous smile.

After a satisfying plate of sausages, fried egg and baked beans for breakfast, Toby's presence was requested at the police station in King's Lynn to meet the MI5 officer, Prestwitch.

Having dutifully guarded Pear Tree Cottage overnight, the police had accepted breakfast from Alice and then left. Toby was on his own. He still had no idea how badly the man who had shot Lars wanted to kill him too, and it disturbed him, as it disturbed Alice.

He appreciated the drive alone in his car on the empty Sunday morning roads. It gave him time to think. He checked his mirror regularly, and was relieved that there was no would-be assassin following him.

His initial reaction to Lars's death was to repeat to MI5 all he had been told by Bill, in the hope that they would pass the information on to the police who would use it to solve the two killings, and throw whoever was responsible behind bars before he could murder anyone else. Like Toby. Or Bill, or any of the Guth sisters.

But now things were not so simple.

Firstly, most of what Bill had told him would be known by Admiral Robinson. He was there in the control room on the submarine when Lars had attacked Commander Driscoll. He had arrested Bill for assaulting Craig. And he would almost certainly have been informed about the leak to the KGB, if only to answer questions from the FBI about it in 1996.

Had Robinson told MI5 any of this? And had Prestwitch told the police? These were questions Toby was curious to know the answers to.

That left the obvious point that very little of the information Toby could give Prestwitch was new, or at least new to Robinson.

And then of course there was Alice's demand that he trust her. In particular that he not tell them about Pat Greenwald. He wasn't sure what to do about that.

As soon as he arrived at the station, he was met by Prestwitch, who ushered him into an interview room where Admiral Robinson was waiting for him. Prestwitch seemed a little more agitated than he had been the previous morning: the tip of one of his prominent teeth peeked out beneath his pursed lips. Robinson looked much cooler.

'Thank you for coming in, Toby,' said Prestwitch. 'And thank you also for not talking to the police yesterday. You did the right thing by asking to speak to us.'

'I hope so,' Toby said. He glanced up at a camera pointed right at him.

'The recording equipment is off,' said Prestwitch. 'No one else will hear whatever you say to us.'

'I'm not sure I am concerned about that,' I said.

'We are,' said the admiral.

I bet they are, Toby thought.

'OK,' Toby said. 'There had been some discussion over Thanksgiving about the death of Lieutenant Craig Naylor, who, it turns out, is Justin Opizzi's natural father.'

'Tell us about it,' Prestwitch said.

So he told them about Lars claiming he had killed Craig on the submarine, and about how Bill had subsequently told him and Megan that he had been the one to incapacitate the weapons officer. He tried to gauge their reaction as he did so, especially Prestwitch's. Was this new information to him? Prestwitch showed no surprise, but he was listening carefully.

Admiral Robinson was just watching him.

'Was there anything else?' Prestwitch asked when Toby had finished.

Was there? Should Toby mention Pat Greenwald? He wasn't yet sure.

'No,' he said. 'Now, can I tell the police this? Or have you already told them?'

Prestwitch glanced at Robinson. 'We haven't, but we will. With two murders, there is no doubt that it is relevant, especially since Justin was Craig's son.'

'Didn't you think it relevant yesterday?'

'That's a good question. You now know what happened on board the *Alexander Hamilton* in 1983, and I am sure you appreciate why we need to keep that secret, even now. But we should tell the police that Craig Naylor was killed on the submarine, and you should tell them about Justin Opizzi believing Lars da Silva killed his biological father. But on no account describe the circumstances of Lieutenant Naylor's death. That is and will remain Classified.'

'All right,' Toby said. 'But won't the police need to know why Craig died?'

'I don't think so,' said Prestwitch. 'MI5 will keep a close watch on this investigation, and we will advise the police as necessary.'

That didn't sound ideal to Toby, and he was willing to bet it didn't sound ideal to the police either.

He turned to the admiral. 'Have you told Mr Prestwitch everything that went on on board that submarine?'

Robinson's face remained impassive. 'Everything that could conceivably be of use to the investigation.'

'Not everything, then,' Toby said, looking at Prestwitch.

But Prestwitch didn't seem bothered by Admiral Robinson's answer. 'I only know in broad terms what happened on the *Hamilton*. I don't know the details, and I don't need to. That's why we are fortunate the admiral has flown here to help us.'

'To keep things covered up?' Toby said.

'Absolutely,' said the admiral. 'That's a lot of what intelligence services do. Preserve national secrets.'

Things became just a little bit clearer to Toby. He believed MI5 wanted to find out who had killed Sam Bowen and Lars da Silva, but they wanted to keep the near-launch quiet even more.

There was even a chance that they had been involved in the murders, although Toby couldn't really believe that.

But repeating what Bill had told him about Pat Greenwald would serve no purpose. They almost certainly knew about it already – or at least Robinson did. Plus Alice had made him promise not to. Toby decided it was better to trust his wife than MI5.

Prestwitch asked Toby to wait while he and the admiral briefed the police. Toby fled the station to a small park nearby, and sat on a bench staring at the town's war memorial, still adorned with the armistice wreaths from a couple of weeks before, and the old medieval tower of a long dismantled friary. He tried to make sense of what he knew and what he didn't know, and to decide how much of that to tell the police.

After half an hour, he returned to the station, where DC Atkinson met him and led him back to a different interview room. Inspector Creswell showed up and the recording equipment was switched on.

'Thank you for coming in, Toby,' the inspector began. 'It's a shame you couldn't talk to us yesterday, but I do understand why. We've just spoken to MI5, who have briefed us on what happened on the submarine back in 1983, but I would be grateful if you could tell us all you know in your own words.'

'I'm sorry,' Toby said. 'I can't tell you everything. Only what Mr Prestwitch has cleared me to say.'

Creswell pursed her lips. 'All right. I understand that too. Tell me what you know about Craig Naylor's death.'

Toby told them as much as he thought he could, and probably a bit more. He also told them about Justin's anger at Craig's death, and Lars's false admission that he was responsible. He felt guilty when he recounted Brooke's visit the evening before – he was quite sure Brooke would not have expected what she said to her family to be repeated to the police.

But whoever had shot at Lars had tried to kill Toby too, and if that was Justin then the police needed to find the proof and lock him up.

It was clear from Creswell's questions that Justin was already partially in the frame and Toby had just nudged him further in. Creswell asked detailed questions about Justin, and about his whereabouts over the previous three days, questions that Toby answered truthfully but unhelpfully. He couldn't add much that they didn't know already.

But their next question surprised him. 'Can you tell us something about the relationship between Justin and your wife?'

'What relationship?' he blurted out.

Creswell raised her eyebrows. 'What relationship do you think we are asking about?'

'I don't know.'

'Was there an intimate relationship between Justin and your wife?'

Toby thought the inspector was just guessing. For a moment, his mind followed hers. Was there? Then he told himself to get a grip.

'No,' he said. He didn't say 'not that I'm aware of'. He said 'No'.

'No?'

'No. Justin is Alice's brother-in-law. I believe that Justin used to stay with the Guth family when they were all kids, but then they lost touch until Brooke met him in Chicago.'

'I see. So has Alice seen him much since then?'

'No. Just family get-togethers, when we are all there. Like this Thanksgiving. Christmas, although last year Justin and Brooke went to his mother's place.'

'So your wife and Justin never met alone, as far as you are aware?'

Toby didn't like that last bit. 'No.' Then he thought of something.

'Toby?'

Toby decided he should never take up poker. 'A couple of months ago it turned out they were both scheduled to go to San Francisco on business at the same time. They went out to dinner together; Alice told me all about it.'

'And that's it?'

'That's it. Look, I trust Alice. I know she wouldn't cheat on me, just like I wouldn't cheat on her.'

'Of course,' said Creswell, with a seen-it-all-before smile.

Toby was angry and she could see it. He *did* trust Alice and he was glad he hadn't told her or Prestwitch about Pat Greenwald, just as Alice had asked him.

'How is the investigation going?' Toby asked.

'A man was seen walking rapidly through the pine woods right after the shooting. Similarly vague description to the one you gave: above-average height, woolly hat, rucksack, which was probably carrying the weapon. We think he may have been driving the silver car you saw in the car park. Otherwise, nothing.'

She paused. 'Nothing beyond the Guth family, that is.' She leaned forward. 'I know that you were the one who was shot at. We don't know who did this, but there has to be a chance it was one of the family.'

'Justin?'

'Too early to say. But yes, maybe. Keep your eyes and ears open, and let us know if you learn anything else that might be helpful.'

'You know Alice isn't responsible for Sam Bowen's death now, right?'

DI Creswell just shrugged.

46

Alice set to work on the kitchen. With so many people in the house, it needed cleaning. And rearranging.

Megan was helping. Megan rarely helped, which irritated Alice minorly, but it turned out that it was much worse when Megan helped properly. She wasn't great at the cleaning, but that didn't matter too much – Tara from the village would go over everything again when she came for her regular visit.

The real problem was that Megan didn't understand how important it was that everything be put back in *exactly* its proper place. Seven years on, and the kitchen, Mom's kitchen, was still exactly as she had left it. Soon after her mother's death Alice had noticed how her father, who previously couldn't care where anything was kept, now quietly ensured everything was where it should be. They had never discussed it, but Alice had been happy to go along with it, and in a ridiculous way she was proud that between the two of them they had managed to preserve her mother's order for so many years.

Of course Megan knew nothing of this, and Alice wasn't about to tell her. Megan's view on cupboards was: if it fits, shove it in.

'So who do you think killed Sam?' said Megan as she pushed the flour jar back on the wrong side of the toaster. She tried to make it sound casual, but Alice recognized the tension in her sister's voice.

'I have no idea,' said Alice, as she sorted the spice jars.

'Do you think it's connected to Lars's death?'

'I said, I have no idea.'

'But you must have been thinking about it,' Megan protested. 'In jail.'

Alice wanted to scream at her sister. But she didn't. She turned to face her. 'Megan. Can you leave the rest to me? Please.'

Alice was ready for a barbed comment, or even a hurled insult. But Megan just looked hurt.

'OK,' she said, and she was gone.

As Alice rearranged the flour jar and the toaster, she felt guilty. She knew she was being unfair: for once, Megan was genuinely trying to help her. She was pulling her weight, and Alice knew she should appreciate it.

But it worried her. Megan was smart. The brain that had been able to untangle fiendishly complicated math problems may well be capable of figuring out what was happening at Barnholt.

Toby was smart too, and, unlike Megan, he understood people. He understood *her*. The two of them made a dangerous combination.

Alice stood by the sink staring out at the naked pear tree and the brown and orange saltmarsh beyond. She could feel the pressure building up on her shoulders to the point where it was almost more than she could bear.

She buckled. She lowered her head and sobbed, tears dropping into the kitchen sink.

But then she straightened up. Wiped her eyes. Sniffed. Tried and succeeded to pull herself together.

With her slippery solicitor's help she had handled the police. She had handled her father. She had done her best, her very best, to hold her family together.

And now her sister and her husband were threatening to undermine it all.

Maybe she should trust them. She could sense the change in Megan, habitually her most untrustworthy sister. And Toby?

She had always relied on Toby. She had begged him not to ask her questions and, by and large, he had obliged. But she knew he was asking other people.

Toby was trustworthy. He was absolutely honest. He could always be relied on to do the right thing.

But could he be relied on to do the wrong thing?

It was lunchtime when Toby returned to Barnholt.

Alice was waiting for him in the hall. 'Well?'

'I didn't say anything about Pat Greenwald.'

'Good. Thank you.'

'But now they seem to think you are having an affair with Justin.'

'Justin?' Her shoulders slumped. 'Oh, great.'

'Yep. I think they still think you killed Sam Bowen, and Justin killed Lars.'

Alice shook her head. 'Wonderful.'

Toby put his arm round her. 'We'll figure it out.'

Alice made everyone a lunch of cold turkey sandwiches, everyone being Toby, Bill and Megan.

The Guth family's response to the pressure of the weekend's events was to revert to type. Despite his suspicion of his daughter, Bill was perfectly polite to her, solicitous even. He offered to help with the sandwiches, and Alice let him. But she was in charge.

Megan was surly. And Toby? He had no idea how to behave. He was on Alice's side, that was all he knew. He retreated to politeness.

They all sat down. In that stilted, artificial atmosphere, it was Megan's role to ask the direct questions.

'So who do the police think killed Lars?'

'Hard to say,' said Toby. 'But I know Justin is on their list.'

'That's good for Alice, right?' said Megan.

Alice sighed. 'Not necessarily. The police think Justin and I are having an affair.'

'That's nonsense!' spluttered Bill, flinging down his sandwich in contempt.

'Is it?' said Megan.

Toby glared at her.

'Of course it is,' said Alice. 'He and I had dinner together in San Francisco in September. Otherwise, I've scarcely seen him.'

'And, you may have noticed, Alice is married,' Toby said. 'To me.' He was keen to dismiss Megan's suggestion without fuss. He didn't want to think about it; he didn't want to doubt his wife. Because he knew he could if he let himself.

Megan looked at the two of them. 'Hey, I'm sorry, Alice. And Toby.'

'OK,' Alice said. There were a number of different ways Alice could say 'OK'. The three others around the kitchen table knew that she meant to forgive Megan.

'Did Justin mention Sam Bowen at all when you saw him in San Francisco?' Toby asked.

'No,' Alice replied. 'It was a few months ago. October, I think. I guess it may have been before Sam had started asking questions.'

'We don't know when that was,' said Megan, glancing at her father. 'Sam must have been researching the book for several months at least.'

Bill shrugged.

Alice hesitated. 'But he did start talking about Craig – you know how Justin has always been obsessed with him. He asked me whether I knew what had really happened on the submarine, how Craig had died. He couldn't believe it was just an accident, and he said Brooke had told him I knew more than she did. Which was true.'

'Did you tell him?' said Bill.

'No,' said Alice. She hesitated. 'Although I kind of implied that Craig had been in favour of launching the missiles. I didn't really mean to – what I said was that Dad and Lars were the only officers on the sub who didn't want to launch. Justin got upset at that and asked me for details. I backtracked and said I didn't really know what happened, it was just an impression. But it was clear he took it badly.'

'Do you think he guessed what really happened?' Toby asked.

'I don't think so,' said Alice. 'I suppose he might have figured it out afterward, but I don't see how.'

'It looked to me like he was genuinely surprised when Lars claimed he had killed Craig by accident,' said Megan.

Toby pondered what Alice had told them. 'If Justin thought that the father he admired so much had actually been in favour of starting a nuclear war, he would be upset. He would be even more upset if Sam was going to tell the whole world about it.'

'I wondered about that,' said Megan. 'Upset enough to kill him?'

Toby shrugged. 'Maybe.'

'Maybe not,' said Alice.

They munched their sandwiches in silence.

'I wish we knew what the police knew,' Toby said.

'What do you mean?' said Megan.

'I mean they will have done a load of forensic analysis. They will have interviewed dozens of witnesses. They'll have checked alibis. They'll have searched Sam Bowen's stuff, and his phone records. And they won't tell us any of it.'

'Why should they?' said Alice. 'Especially if they still think I'm guilty.'

'Did you talk to MI5 about Pat Greenwald?' Megan asked Toby.

Bill flinched.

'No,' Toby said, glancing at his wife. 'I decided not to.'

309

'Good,' said Bill.

'Did you know she's dead?' said Megan to her father.

He raised his eyebrows. 'No. No, I didn't. How come *you* know?'

'Googled her last night,' said Megan. 'She was murdered. In New York.'

'How awful,' said Bill. He was clearly trying to give his words the correct weighting of concern: enough to register that that was an awful way for anyone to die, not enough to suggest he was especially concerned.

'Yeah. It is awful. And it was in 1996. The same year the FBI came looking for you.'

Bill chewed his sandwich, trying – and succeeding – to control his annoyance with his daughter.

'Did they find who killed her?' said Alice.

'No. The newspaper report said it was a mugging gone wrong.'

Bill's shoulders seemed to relax slightly.

'There's more to Pat Greenwald than you have told us, isn't there, Dad?' said Megan.

'I've told you what I can,' said Bill.

'Oh, yes?' said Megan. 'And was that the truth?'

'Of course it was the truth!' snapped Bill.

'But not the whole truth?' Megan glanced at Toby. 'The reason Sam Bowen and Uncle Lars were killed has something to do with that woman. It must have!'

'I don't know,' said Bill.

Megan turned to Alice. 'Come on, Alice? You must agree with me?'

Alice didn't answer. But she was glaring at her father.

Toby spoke. 'Don't lie to us, Bill.' He hadn't thought before he spoke those words: they were more direct than would be expected from a recent son-in-law hiding behind politeness. But he said them quietly and sincerely, and that gave them power. He wanted to trust his father-in-law. He wanted Megan and Alice – and Brooke and Maya – to trust him.

He could see that was something Bill wanted also.

'All right,' Bill said. 'There are some things to do with Pat I left out when I told you about her before. And some things that were not strictly accurate.'

Megan, Toby and Alice listened in suspicious silence as Bill explained a bit more about what had happened after he had quit the Navy: about seeing Pat Greenwald in Central Park in 1984, and the trip he and Donna took to Paris to talk to a Russian physicist.

And then he told them about another meeting one evening later on that year.

June 1984 New York

I got a job in a bar on the Upper East Side after I was discharged, while I waited for the business school semester to start. I was staying with Donna in her tiny studio apartment. This was fine for me – her studio was many times the size of the JO Jungle – and she coped pretty well. I was tidy, I was considerate. It was great to be together.

I found adjusting to civilian life a bit of a shock. I had been in the arms of the Navy since the age of eighteen and I had gotten used to the structure. It wasn't so much my own liberty to do what I liked that bothered me, as much as everyone else's. It kind of bugged me if people didn't do what they were supposed to. The manager who ran the bar was a nice guy, as were the other staff, who were mostly students or actors, but the operation was slapdash. Glasses unwashed, drinks unpoured, counter unwiped.

I would just have to get used to it. I was going to have to adjust to the civilian world, rather than the civilian world adjusting to me.

From what the others told me, the bar used to be a thriving pick-up joint, but the AIDS scare was taking its toll. Weekends could get busy, but it was quiet early in the week. One Monday evening a morose-looking guy of about forty in a crumpled suit drank his way through a few whiskies, chatting to me disjointedly as I kept him topped up. He was foreign, probably an expat banker.

After we had closed up for the night, I was surprised when he emerged from the shadows outside the bar.

'Can I have a quiet word?' he said.

I tensed. The man didn't look like a mugger, or a guy trying to pick me up – not that there was much of that any more with the fear of AIDS.

A con man, probably.

I turned to face him. 'No,' I said, firmly.

'My name is Vassily Sapalyov,' he said. 'I am a colleague of Irena Boyarova. I believe you know her?'

'I see.'

'Let me buy you a drink? There is a hotel a couple of blocks away. Their bar will still be open.'

'Haven't you had enough to drink?'

The man laughed. 'I'm Russian. I have not had nearly enough to drink.'

The hotel bar was indeed open, although empty, and Sapalyov bought us both single-malt whiskies. Glenfiddich.

'I love this stuff,' said Sapalyov with a grin. 'I think it is the one thing I enjoy most about trips outside Russia.'

The melancholy seemed to have left him. It was if he was a different person. As if he had been acting before.

'Are you a physicist too?' I asked.

'Yes. Yes, just like Irena.'

I doubted that, somehow. The guy just didn't look like a physicist. 'What is your field?' I asked. I was a nuclear engineer and I had majored in Physics at the Naval Academy: I was planning to ask questions.

'I'd rather not say,' said the Russian.

'You work for the KGB, don't you?' I said.

'Of course not,' said Sapalyov. 'Why do you Americans think all Russians work for the KGB?'

'All Russians outside the Soviet Union.'

'That's ridiculous.'

I didn't care about this joker. But something else caused me much more concern. 'Is Irena in the KGB?'

Sapalyov had intelligent eyes. Not the kind of intelligence that can immediately grasp negative probabilities in Quantum Mechanics. They were shrewd. They could read people. No way was this guy a nuclear physicist.

'Irena is not in the KGB,' Sapalyov said. 'She is a devoted worker for peace and a good friend of mine. The information you gave her has made its way to people who can influence our nuclear policy.'

'I'm glad.'

'We would like to introduce you to Pavel. You may have heard of him?'

'Yes, Irena mentioned him. He is an officer in your navy.'

'That's correct. Like you he is concerned about nuclear accidents. He knows of a similar event on one of our submarines that happened two years ago in the Pacific.'

Despite myself, I was intrigued.

'How do I get to meet this Pavel? He's a serving officer, right?'

'A neutral country. You would have to fly there, but that shouldn't be a problem for you now you have left the Navy.'

'I don't know,' I said.

'What have you got to lose? Just talk to him.'

'To a serving officer in the enemy's navy?'

'But that's the point, isn't it, Bill? He has the same doubts you do.'

I drained my whisky. 'No, Mr Sapalyov. I have done all I'm going to do. I'm not a spy, or at least I don't consider myself a spy, and I won't become one. I won't have any more contact with you in the future, or Irena Boyarova.'

'But there is so much more you can do for the cause of peace,' said the Russian.

'No. That's it.' I stood up.

'You have already betrayed your country,' said Sapalyov. His voice was low, a growl.

I sat down again and leaned over towards the Russian. 'Don't try to threaten me.'

'Why not?'

'Because I don't care. I don't care if you expose me. I don't care if you assault me. I don't even care if you kill me. You don't know what it's like to stare the end of the world in the face, like I've done. I don't care what the consequences are: I will not betray my country. Is that clear?'

And at that moment, I truly didn't care.

'If you can use the information I gave you to make a nuclear war less likely, all well and good. If you want anything else from me, you won't get it.'

Sapalyov's shrewd eyes assessed me. He decided I wasn't bluffing.

'I have no intention of making you do something you don't want to,' he said. 'If you don't want to meet Pavel, that's fine. I – we – are grateful for what you have already told us.'

'And by "we", who do you mean?'

'The Gorky Trust Group. The Soviet peace movement, such as it is.' The Russian reached out his hand and touched my sleeve. 'I just have one last question for you.'

'Yes?'

'Would any of the other officers on the *Alexander Hamilton* be willing to speak to us? After all, they saw the world come to the brink of destruction just like you.'

I thought of Lars. Of the XO. Of Commander Driscoll. Then I thought of the KGB.

'No.'

The Russian let his disappointment show, but after a moment's reflection seemed to accept my refusal. 'I understand. Goodbye,

Lieutenant Guth. And if you change your mind, just tell Dr Greenwald.'

As I walked downtown towards the subway, I was worried. I knew nothing about spies, but there had to be a good chance that Vassily Sapalyov was one. Which meant that Irena Boyarova was probably a spy also. Maybe even Pat Greenwald.

I was still happy with what I had told Irena. Part of the reason for doing it was that the Soviet leadership would know the US had nearly launched nuclear missiles at them accidentally. That had been the XO's rationale, and I thought he was right. But no more. They would not get anything more from me.

I supposed I had laid myself open to blackmail. But I didn't think it would be in the Russians' interest to expose me and what I had done. They wanted me a willing cooperator. And they had nearly persuaded me.

Of course, it wasn't just me, it was Donna. They could try to claim she was a spy as well. I would have to tell her about the evening.

I was willing to risk exposure to draw a line. The best way to extricate myself from this little mess was firmness and courage. I could do it.

And I suspected Donna could too.

49

'Hey, Bill! How are you doin', man?'

I turned to see the familiar figure of Lars fighting his way through the crowd to the bar where I had nabbed a seat for him. We were in an Irish pub in the East Village, and I hadn't seen Lars since he had left Groton for Wisconsin three months before.

'Good, Lars, good. Can I get you a Rolling Rock?'

'You want me to drink that Pennsylvanian shit?'

'It's good beer. You *know* that. I've seen you drink enough of it.'

Lars perched himself on the bar stool. 'Hey. We're in an Irish bar. Get me a Guinness.'

So I got him a Guinness. 'What's the beer like in Brazil?' I asked him.

'Nothing special. They have this stuff they call "beach beer". Tastes like piss, it's very weak, but you can drink a lot of it, especially when it's hot. Which it is. A lot.'

Lars was on his way to Brazil. He had decided to travel via New York, so he could see me. And I had been looking forward to seeing him.

'What are you going to do when you get there?'

'I'll crash with my grandparents in Rio to start with. Then I'm going to get a job on the water. Sailing if I can. I should've done that in the first place rather than join the Navy. It's got to be possible: there's a lot of water around Rio.'

'Do you speak much Portuguese?'

'A bit. I'll learn. It'll be fun.'

'What's cheers in Portuguese?'

'Damned if I know. Wait. *Felicidades*?'

'*Felicity Tarts*!' I raised my glass and drank my beer. Deeply.

It was good to see Lars. It was *really* good to see Lars. Although I was enjoying living in New York, and I loved living with Donna, I missed male friendship. I missed Lars. I missed living cheek-by-jowl with a hundred and forty men in the *Hamilton*. How sad was that? Pretty sad.

One day I would get to the point where I had gotten the Navy out of my system, where I had my own friends, male and female, and my own career that had nothing to do with blowing the world to smithereens. I was looking forward to that point, but I wasn't there yet.

We drank a lot of beer. We talked about our folks. Lars's father had been quietly pleased that he was going to Brazil, his mother less so. I told him about Donna and our plans to go to graduate school. We were on our six or seventh beer, when the rush of words paused for a moment.

'We did the right thing, didn't we?' said Lars in a low voice.

I nodded. 'Yeah. We did the right thing.'

Lars looked me in the eye and raised his glass. 'To Craig.'

I smiled. Lars understood. Understood that although I had killed Craig, he had been my friend. He was still my friend. 'To Craig.'

'You know, a weird thing happened last week,' Lars said. 'Back in Wisconsin. A woman showed up at our house asking for me. She came from New York. Said she knew Donna. And you.'

'Pat Greenwald?' I blurted in surprise.

'So you do know her?'

'Yeah. Kind of. Donna knows her really. They're involved in the peace movement together. She came all the way to Wisconsin to see you? What did she want?'

But actually I could guess what she wanted.

'She wanted me to talk about the near-launch. I remember you asking me back at the base whether you should tell the peace movement about that. I guess you decided you should.'

I hesitated. Looked around the bar, which had emptied a little, but there was no one listening. 'Donna told her about it. Then I spoke with her.'

'Did you tell her much?' Lars asked.

I felt uncomfortable. 'A bit. What about you?'

Lars sipped his beer. 'A bit. Did you speak with the Russians? You asked me whether you should speak with the Russian peaceniks?'

'And you said you didn't know.'

'I did.'

I sighed. 'Yeah, I did. Spoke to a physicist. In Paris. I didn't give her any real secrets.' I glanced at Lars, to see how he took this information.

He breathed in. We were both quite drunk at this point, and struggling to focus on something we knew was really important.

'You know,' he said. 'When some other dumb boomer launches a couple of birds by mistake at somewhere in Russia and the Russians decide not to blow up the world, we'll know you did the right thing.'

'That's why I wanted out of the Navy, Lars. I don't want to have to think about this shit anymore.'

'That's for sure,' said Lars, raising his glass. 'Here's to freedom. And Copacabana Beach.'

I got a phone call a month later in Donna's apartment. I had the night off from the bar, and we had just finished a lasagne she had cooked.

'It's for you.' She passed me the phone.

'Hello?'

'Bill, it's Glenn Robinson.'

'Oh, hello, XO,' I said. It seemed weird to call him by his first name.

'I've got some bad news.'

Something had happened to Lars, I thought right away. Although if it had, I wasn't sure how the XO would have found out about it.

'Yes?' I said neutrally.

'Commander Driscoll died suddenly two days ago.'

'The captain? That's terrible! What happened?'

'He took his own life,' said Robinson. 'Blew his brains out.'

'Oh my God.' The news sank into my consciousness slowly. 'That's awful.' He had a wife, or an ex-wife. And children. 'Does anyone know why?'

'There's an investigation, of course,' said Robinson. 'And they haven't come up with anything yet. He didn't leave a note. It may have been his marriage. Or . . .'

'The near-launch,' I said.

'He didn't take it well,' said the XO. 'He found it difficult to accept what he had done. Ordering a nuclear launch. What both of us had done.' The XO's voice was flat. 'I've found it difficult too, to tell you the truth.'

'But it wasn't his fault!' I protested. 'Or yours. He listened to Lars's objections. He did things by the book.'

'Da Silva didn't do things by the book,' said Robinson. 'And neither did you. Which is why we are all alive today.'

'I'm sorry,' I said. 'He was a good man. I respected him. I admired him.'

'He was,' said Robinson. 'I only served with him on that one patrol, but I could feel how much the crew respected him. It's such a shame.'

We were silent on the phone together. Sharing regrets at the loss of a life.

'Well, thanks for telling me, XO.'

'Do you know how to get in contact with da Silva?' Robinson said. 'I'd like to call him.'

'Yeah. Wait a second, he gave me his grandparents' number in Brazil.' I found it in my address book and read it out to Robinson.

'XO? One thing before you go. Has a woman called Pat Greenwald been in touch?'

'Pat Greenwald? Who is she?'

'Oh, no one. A friend of Donna's,' I said.

'I hope this doesn't have anything to do with what we discussed at the fort?' Robinson said.

'Oh, no. No, not at all. Thanks, XO.'

I put down the phone.

I felt Donna come up behind me and wrap her arms around my chest.

50

Sunday 1 December 2019, Norfolk

Toby listened as his father-in-law subtly changed his story. Again.

Megan was right, he hadn't outright lied to them before. But he had withheld information. Important information.

With each iteration something new had been revealed: Bill killing Craig to stop the missiles being launched, and now talking to the Russians about the near-launch. How much of this could Toby believe now? He had no idea.

It was likely what Bill was telling them was the truth. But what was he missing out?

If Lars were still alive, there would have been someone else to check Bill's story with. Admiral Robinson would be able to confirm some of it. But not the really important stuff. And having a frank conversation with Admiral Robinson would be difficult.

'So, it wasn't Commander Driscoll who gave secrets to the Russians?' Toby asked.

'No,' said Bill. 'Donna just made that up on the spot. To deflect the FBI's attention from me.'

'But you only told them about the near-launch? Nothing else?'
'Correct.'

'So someone else told the Russians more? Gave them the real secrets about the submarine command and the missiles that the FBI mentioned?'

'I guess so,' said Bill.

'Well, who was that?' Toby asked.

Bill shrugged.

'Could it have been Lars?' Megan said. 'He told you he spoke to Pat Greenwald.'

'Yes. But he didn't say he gave her real secrets.'

'He wouldn't, would he?' said Megan. 'But that's really why he came to England. To see what Sam Bowen had to say.'

Toby remembered Lars telling him as much on the beach.

'That's right,' said Bill. 'He asked me all about our conversation with Sam.'

'Including what Sam had to say about Pat Greenwald?'

Bill nodded.

'So maybe it *was* Lars,' Megan said.

Bill looked uncomfortable. 'Lars was more than a friend to me. He and I shared something extraordinary. I'm not going to call him a traitor unless I am absolutely sure. And I'm not; I'm not at all.'

'Even though he's dead now?'

Bill bit his lower lip. 'Yes. Even though he is dead now,' he said sombrely.

'I don't know,' said Toby. 'Brooke was pretty firm that Lars never left the Cottage. They even heard him go to the bathroom about midnight.'

'OK,' said Megan. 'What about Justin? Maybe *he* left the Cottage and killed Sam? To stop Sam writing about how his father wanted to blow up the world.'

'So you are saying Brooke's lying about Justin being there with her that evening?' said Alice.

'No. Yeah. I don't know,' said Megan.

'Brooke wouldn't lie,' said Alice.

Actually, Toby wasn't sure about that. He would lie for Alice.

'Whatever,' said Megan, stepping back from her accusation. 'But,

Dad. You *have* to tell the police all this. Otherwise they'll lock Alice up again!'

Bill swallowed, and looked at his eldest daughter. He appeared to be on the edge of tears. 'I can't,' he said to her. 'You must understand that.'

Alice's face hardened. She got to her feet and left the kitchen table. A moment later they heard the front door bang. They could see her through the kitchen window leaning on the flint garden wall next to the pear tree, staring out over the marsh.

Toby joined her. He put his arm around her and squeezed.

Time to dispel one of the many Guth secrets. 'You know why your father doesn't want to tell the police all this?' he said.

Alice didn't answer.

'Because he thinks you killed Sam Bowen.'

'He told you that, did he?' Alice said, turning towards him. There were tears in her eyes, but also contempt.

'Yes,' said Toby. 'I don't believe him, obviously.'

Alice turned away from him towards the marsh, brooding under a low grey sky. A couple with a dog strode in single file along the top of the dyke down towards the dunes, which were slumbering under their thin, worn blanket of grey-green grass. To the west, an early brushstroke of pink was already tickling the underside of the clouds.

Toby tried to put his arm around her again, but she shook him off. 'You don't believe I think you killed him, do you?' he repeated.

No answer.

The door to the house opened behind them and Megan appeared in the front garden, clutching her phone. 'Nothing from Maya yet, but I got an answer from Vicky,' she said to Toby. 'She doesn't want to talk to me about Craig. If she talks to anyone it has to be Justin – according to her, he's the only one who still cares about her brother.

I guess that's not surprising. And, anyway, it looks like Craig's death isn't that important after all.'

Alice spun round. 'Will you just butt out, Megan? This has nothing to do with you! It's got to do with me and Dad. Can't you just leave us to it?'

'I'm only trying to help,' said Megan.

'But you're not!' said Alice. 'You're only making things worse.'

Megan glanced at Toby. 'Go back inside, Megan,' he said.

'No,' said Megan. 'Anything that has to do with my dad and my sister – and with my mother, for that matter – has to do with me. It's my family. *Our* family. That's important.'

Alice turned back towards the marsh and snorted. 'It's ridiculous to hear *you* say that.'

But Megan wasn't giving up. 'Alice? Why didn't you do more to get yourself off the hook with the police?'

Alice didn't reply.

'Toby and me are doing what we can, which isn't much. But we're trying. But you and Dad. You do nothing. You don't give them anything. Mom told you a lot about all this stuff, didn't she? Well, why didn't you tell the police? Why didn't Dad?'

'Why didn't you tell me?' said Toby.

Alice turned to face her husband and her sister. Her cheeks were wet with tears.

'Isn't it obvious? You're so damned clever, Megan, can't you see it? Can't you, Toby?'

'No,' said Toby.

Alice sobbed.

'I didn't tell you because Dad killed Sam Bowen.'

'What?' said Megan.

Toby was shocked. Someone must have killed the historian, and he had supposed there was a chance it could have been Bill, but he was surprised the thought had occurred to Alice. And if it had occurred to her, that she hadn't dismissed it immediately.

But if she did believe her father was a murderer, it would explain a lot of her own behaviour.

'How can you be sure?' Toby asked.

Alice sniffed and wiped the tears from her cheeks. 'You are right, Megan. Mom did tell me more than you and the others. She thought I should know, so that if necessary I could help Dad after she was gone.'

'Know what?'

'That Dad had killed Craig on the submarine. That she had introduced Dad to a peace activist who had put him in touch with Russian contacts in the peace movement. That he had told the Russians about the near-launch. That subsequently it had turned out that they were KGB.'

'Dad just admitted all that himself,' said Megan. 'That doesn't mean he killed Sam Bowen.'

'No, but it does mean he had a reason to. That's why I went to see Sam Thanksgiving evening. Toby said Sam had mentioned Pat Greenwald in passing, so I skirted around the subject with Sam at dinner.' Toby remembered Alice's earnest conversation with Sam at the table. 'It was clear he suspected something, but I realized

I needed to find out exactly what. So on the way back from the grocery store – in Hunstanton, not King's Lynn – I dropped into the King Willie to talk to him. We had a drink in the bar, but it was closing time, so we went up to his room. I told him I had missed his conversation with my father because I was cooking the turkey, but that in the past my mother had told me things that might be helpful. I discovered he knew quite a lot about Pat Greenwald, and that he was planning to fly to New York this week to speak to her son. Apparently the son remembered seeing his mother with a naval officer when he was a kid.'

'Wow,' said Megan.

Alice sighed. 'Then, after I came back here and put the groceries away, I went to see Dad in his study. I told him what Sam had said. And that night, Sam was killed.'

'Bill never said you spoke to him,' said Toby.

'He told the police,' said Alice. 'He just didn't tell them what we spoke about. And neither did I.'

'So he was lying to us?'

'He wasn't telling you the whole truth,' said Alice.

What a surprise, thought Toby. Bill would probably claim he was trying to protect Alice by keeping quiet.

'And then you think Dad killed Sam?' Megan said.

'That was my first thought,' said Alice. 'As soon as I left Dad in his study, he went over to the pub and knocked on Sam's door.' Alice hesitated. 'And then he stabbed him. To stop him from telling everyone how Dad and Mom had been spying for the Russians. I tried to tell myself it couldn't possibly be true—'

'Quite right,' Megan interrupted.

'But it must be. I'm sorry, Megan, it must be.'

'So that's why you kept so quiet with the police? To stop them from suspecting him?'

Alice nodded.

'But what about you?' Toby protested. 'Are you willing to go to jail for him?'

'I don't know. Maybe. But I don't think it will come to that. If in reality I haven't killed anyone, it will be difficult for the police to prove I have. My solicitor seems to agree that's the best strategy.'

Toby knew Alice would do anything for her father. But even if she thought he had murdered someone? Two people?

'Did you tell your lawyer you thought your father had murdered Sam?'

'No. But I think she knows there are things I'm not divulging. My guess is she assumes they are things that would incriminate me, so she would rather not hear them.'

'But Dad was watching TV with us when Sam was killed,' said Megan.

'No he wasn't,' said Alice. 'The game was over by the time I got back. I unpacked the groceries and then I went to speak with him in his study. If he had gone straight to the pub after that, he would have had time to kill Sam Bowen. Sam would have let him into his room, and if Sam hadn't gone to bed right away, he would still be dressed. Believe me, I've had plenty of time to think this through.'

'Couldn't Lars have done that?' said Megan. 'He would have been just as worried as Dad about the mention of Pat Greenwald. He could have been worried about Sam claiming *he* was a Russian spy.'

'Brooke said that Lars didn't leave the Cottage,' said Alice. 'And until just now I didn't know that Lars spoke to Pat Greenwald about the near-launch as well as Dad.'

'Well, then?' said Megan. 'Maybe Lars jumped out the back window?'

'Or maybe he didn't speak to Pat Greenwald at all back in 1984,' Toby said. 'We only have your dad's word for that.'

'That's true,' said Alice. 'Maybe Dad lied. And we know Lars didn't shoot himself.'

'Oh, you think Dad shot Lars?' said Megan, with scorn.

Alice nodded. 'To keep him quiet. Maybe Lars had figured out what Dad had done. Maybe he was going to tell the police. Or Admiral Robinson.'

'I got the impression Lars knew who killed Sam Bowen,' Toby said. 'I think he was about to tell me just before he was shot.'

'Dad knows how to use a rifle,' said Alice.

'But we don't have one in the house,' said Megan.

'And if we did, he wouldn't have used it,' said Alice. 'He's too smart for that. He would have gotten one from somewhere else.'

'But he was at home when Toby and Lars went for their walk,' said Megan.

'Was he?' said Alice.

'No, he wasn't,' said Toby. 'He left the house about the same time as Lars and me. Went out to get plumbing supplies. The police could check on that.'

'If we let them,' said Alice.

The three of them stood shivering under the bare branches of the pear tree, thinking about the man inside the house.

Was he really a murderer?

'No,' said Megan. 'I refuse to believe any of this.'

'I'm sorry,' said Alice, for once showing some sympathy for her younger sister. 'It's dreadful to think about, but our father did kill someone. Two people. And that's not counting Craig all those years ago.'

Toby's brain was racing through the possibilities. He didn't want to believe Bill had killed anyone. Nor did he want to believe that Bill had shot at him. But Alice was right: it did make sense.

'He told me that he believed *you* had killed Sam,' Toby said. 'To protect him. You're saying he never thought that.'

'Of course he didn't,' said Alice. 'He *knew* who had killed Sam. The whole time. He knew.'

'Did you tell him you suspected him?'

'No. He and I have this tacit thing going on. He doesn't ask questions about me, and I don't ask questions about him. The lawyer's happy with that. It's just you and Megan who are screwing everything up.'

'Sorry,' said Toby.

No apology came from Megan. She was frowning.

'So what do we do now?' said Toby.

'We stay quiet,' said Alice.

'And let the police arrest you again?'

Alice shrugged. 'It's my choice. All I want you to do is to respect that.'

Toby looked up as a flight of geese flew low over the house, and veered left over the marsh towards the Wash, honking.

Then he faced his wife.

'I'll respect your choice as far as your own freedom is concerned. But if Bill really did kill people, the police need to know. He needs to be brought to justice.'

'Toby!' Alice glared at her husband. Then her gaze softened. 'OK. This is difficult for all of us, you too, Megan. I hate the idea that my father killed anybody. He was wrong. But you heard him, and you heard Sam Bowen. The only reason we are alive today is because of what he did on the *Alexander Hamilton* all those years ago. And everything he did after that was a result of that day. He made some bad decisions, but they were difficult decisions. He was trying to stop humanity from destroying itself.'

'I agree he did what he did from the best of motives,' Toby said. 'At least as far as speaking to the Russians is concerned. But he shouldn't have killed an innocent man like Sam Bowen. Or Lars. Or tried to kill me. I'm sorry, Alice: we have got to speak to the police about this, or MI5 or someone.'

'He's my father, Toby. I won't do it.'

Toby swallowed. 'Then I will.'

'Shouldn't we talk to Dad first?' said Megan.

'No,' said Toby. 'That will just warn him we are on to him.' He took a deep breath. 'And he might become dangerous when he's cornered, right, Alice?'

Alice nodded, reluctantly.

Toby's phone rang. He didn't recognize the number, but he did see it was a US international code. He answered.

'Toby? This is Glenn Robinson.'

'Oh, hello, Admiral,' Toby said, with a meaningful glance at Alice. He wanted her to know to whom he was speaking. Alice shot him a look: *don't you dare tell him about my father.*

'I'd like to have a little chat with you, and with your wife and her sisters,' the admiral said. 'Informal. I've got something I want to share with you.'

'OK,' said Toby. 'When do you want to meet?'

'Is this afternoon OK?'

'All right. I'll try to round up the girls. Where?'

'There's a pub called The Pheasant in Thurstead. Do you know it?'

'I know the village.' Thurstead was a few miles inland from Barnholt.

'Good. Say three-thirty?'

'OK. We'll be there.'

'And, Toby? Please don't let Bill know you are coming to see me.'

Toby hung up.

'What was all that about?' said Alice

Toby explained.

'Are you coming?' he asked the sisters.

'I will,' said Megan.

'You won't say I think Dad killed Sam Bowen, will you, Toby?' said Alice.

'I might,' said Toby.

Alice shook her head. Fury burned in her eyes. 'I can't believe you would do that.'

'Toby?' said Megan.

'Yes?'

'I know Alice is pretty certain about Dad's guilt, but I'm not. Let's just leave it a day or so, eh? Listen to what the admiral has to say. See what turns up. Think about it some more.'

Toby knew that if Bill really had murdered the young historian, he couldn't let him get away with it. He also knew that if he defied his wife on this, his marriage would be over. The Guth family would be destroyed. He knew Alice, she would never forgive him. And although the logical conclusion was that if Alice was willing to lie to protect her murdering father Toby was better off without her, Toby couldn't accept that. Part of him admired her loyalty and her bravery. Just as part of him admired Bill.

But she was wrong, and so was her father.

Megan offered a fudge. An excuse to delay a difficult decision.

In theory Toby believed that difficult decisions were best taken sooner rather than later.

He looked at his wife. The anger in her eyes pointed directly at him, hurt. He loved her. Could he really take a decision to lose her that quickly?

'OK,' he said. 'I'll just listen. So will you come?'

'I will,' said Alice. 'And you had better keep your mouth shut.'

52

The Pheasant was a large white-painted pub at the far end of Thurstead's small high street. The village was a cluster of farms, a few houses, a shop, the church and the pub, most of which straggled along a single road in a shallow valley.

The pub was clearly very old, but it had been tarted up in a disconcerting melange of fashionable grey paint and modern fonts. Mid-afternoon in November it was almost empty: a lone walker with his map sat at one table in front of the fire, and at another in the corner sat the admiral, drinking a Coke.

'Sorry we're late,' said Toby, shaking his hand. 'It took me a while to round everyone up.'

By 'everyone' he had meant Brooke, who had taken some persuading to leave the hotel and her husband in Hunstanton and drive over to Thurstead in their hired car. But Alice had eventually coaxed her.

'I thought there were four of you?' the admiral said to Alice.

'Maya's not here,' Alice replied. 'She had to go back to work. She's a flight attendant.'

'She's in New York,' Megan said. 'But you've got the rest of us.'

Toby fetched drinks: white wine for Megan, tomato juice for Brooke and Alice and a half pint of bitter for him. When he returned to the table, the admiral was conducting a stilted conversation with Alice about how pretty Norfolk was. But as soon as Toby set the drinks down, the admiral got down to business.

'Thanks for coming, and for not telling your father.' Alice had told Bill they were driving to Hunstanton to see Brooke and Justin. Not a bad little lie since it plausibly explained why Bill was left out of it. There was even a chance that Bill had believed it.

'I shouldn't be here,' the admiral went on. 'I'm speaking to you informally, as a private citizen. And mostly as your father's friend.'

'OK,' said Alice.

'You know I was the executive officer on the *Alexander Hamilton*'s last patrol, and you may know that after that I spent many years in naval intelligence, which is how I have contacts with the British security services. I may have retired, but I still take very seriously my obligation to keep what happened on that last patrol secret.'

'We understand,' said Alice, slipping into her natural role as speaker for the sisters.

'I believe all of you know what that was. Your mother told you before she died, and then Sam Bowen confirmed it, right?'

'That's right,' said Alice. The others around the table all nodded.

'OK. That should never have gotten out, but it's too late now, and at least it makes it easier for you to understand what's going on.'

'Which is what, exactly?' Toby asked.

'Is the name Pat Greenwald familiar to you?'

Toby glanced at Alice before replying. 'Yes.'

The admiral raised his eyebrows. Megan nodded. Alice stared at Toby.

And Brooke shook her head. 'Who's she?'

'Bill told us a little bit about her,' said Toby to the admiral. 'All of us but Brooke.'

'OK. And how much do you know about her?'

Toby turned to Alice with his eyebrows raised. He had promised not to pass on her suspicions to the admiral, but this was just confirming what the admiral already knew.

She gave Toby a tiny nod.

'We know she was a peace activist,' Toby replied. 'We know the FBI thought she was a KGB agent. And we know Bill and Lars spoke to her. About the near-launch.'

'OK.' The admiral leaned forward, pulling his thick dark eyebrows together. 'What I am going to say now is off the record. I shouldn't be telling you this, but I kind of feel I owe it to you. And to Bill.'

He sipped his Coke. 'What Bill did on the submarine was very brave. At the time, I was all for locking him up and launching the missiles, as was the captain. Fortunately, we were unable to do that, which is why we are all alive today. You guys wouldn't even have been born.

'I owe Bill everything. We all do. You should be proud of your father.'

'We are,' said Alice, flatly.

'The problem is . . .' The admiral hesitated, looking around the table. He took the plunge. 'The problem is that I am pretty sure that your father killed Sam Bowen. And I think he may well have shot Lars da Silva as well.'

Alice and Megan said nothing. Brooke recoiled and checked her sisters' reaction, waiting for a protest that never came. 'That's crazy,' she said at last.

'I'm sorry. I don't think it is.'

'Alice, tell him that's crazy.'

Alice sighed. 'I think he's right, Brooke. I think Dad did kill Sam Bowen.'

'No!' Brooke exclaimed.

'I'm not so sure,' said Megan.

'We were discussing it this afternoon when you called,' said Toby. 'But why do you think he did it?'

'Because he gave secrets to the Russians thirty-five years ago. And because Sam Bowen was on the brink of discovering it.'

'You knew he spoke to the Russians all along?' said Toby, remembering Bill's description of his conversation with the XO, as he then was, at the fort in Groton.

'I had a pretty good guess that he had. I chose to ignore it.'

'Do the police know?'

'No. And neither do MI5, or the FBI. Yet. Just me. And you.'

They sat in silence for a few moments, letting this thought sink in. 'OK,' said Toby. 'Are you going to tell them?'

'That's why I wanted to speak with you.' The admiral's dark eyes bored into each of them. 'I don't intend to tell them. And I suggest that you don't either.' He raised his eyebrows in a question.

'OK,' said Alice.

Megan nodded.

Brooke looked at her two sisters and then nodded also. 'As long as someone tells me what the hell Dad has done.'

'I will,' said Alice.

'Toby?'

Toby didn't know what to do. He was being asked to join a conspiracy to protect a traitor and a murderer. But he was being asked by his wife and by a retired admiral. Was it really up to him to spoil everything?

What were the consequences? Bill would go to jail, probably for the rest of his life. That would be . . . unfortunate, after what he had done to keep the human race alive, but it was justice.

He would lose the Guth family. Somehow, the stress of the previous few days had made him feel closer to them. Toby needed to be part of a family, a proper family. Losing them would hurt.

And his wife would never speak to him again. That would more than hurt; that would be unbearable.

'Don't you think we should speak to Bill about it?' said Toby.

'We discussed this,' said Alice. 'You said we shouldn't. And you were right.'

'But maybe Admiral Robinson could?'

The admiral nodded. 'I've been thinking that. I'll try to persuade him to give himself up. Who knows? He may convince me that he didn't kill the historian, but I think that's unlikely. In the meantime, I want you to keep quiet about the near-launch and Pat Greenwald and any suspicions you may have that Bill killed anyone. That's important if it is the police who are asking, or MI5, or even if it's me in my official capacity. Will you agree to that?'

The three women nodded.

And so, in the end, did Toby.

It was dark by the time they drove back to Barnholt. Alice went in Brooke's car to explain to her what she could about their father, and Toby drove Megan.

'Having fun, Toby?' Megan said, as they pulled out of the pub car park.

'No.'

'Me neither.'

Toby didn't say anything.

'I guess my father really is a murderer after all,' Megan said.

Toby glanced at her. He could barely make out her face, but she seemed close to tears. And who could blame her?

'I guess so.'

'But I thought he was a good man. A great man.'

'He was,' said Toby. 'He is. Whatever he has done can't take away from what he did on that submarine thirty-five years ago.'

'Can't it? I get that he's in trouble, but killing people is not the answer. And only yesterday he tried to shoot you!'

'Yes.' Toby shuddered. 'Yes, he did.'

'And now we are happily driving back to the house. With a murderer inside it. Do you think he'll try and kill one of us?'

'No,' said Toby, trying to sound as confident as he could. 'No. As long as we all keep quiet and don't let on we suspect him.'

'You're not going to tell the police, are you, Toby?'

'I'll leave that up to the admiral. For now.'

'And then?'

'I don't know,' said Toby. 'I really don't know.'

'A cup of tea, anyone?' said Toby when they were in the kitchen.

Brooke was still sobbing from the short car journey. She hadn't taken what Alice had told her well. Which was unsurprising, really.

'Tea?' said Megan. 'What is it with you English people? I was thinking more of a glass of wine.'

'I'll have one,' said Alice. Her face was pale, but her jaw thrust out in a determined way which was familiar to Toby.

'OK,' said Brooke.

'All right. Me too,' said Megan.

Toby boiled the kettle, and got out some mugs and tea bags. Then Bill appeared.

The three sisters and Toby froze. Brooke stopped mid-sob.

Bill couldn't help but notice. 'You're back,' he said.

'We are,' said Alice, coldly.

'Hi, Brooke,' said Bill. He walked over to the kitchen table to try to kiss her. She sniffed and turned away from him.

Bill straightened. 'Toby. I'd like to have a chat with you about something. Can you come up to my study?'

Toby forced himself to smile. 'Shall I bring you up a cup of tea?'

'Sure,' said Bill, clearly thankful for a glimpse of friendliness.

Toby poured five mugs, and followed Bill up the stairs carrying two of them.

Bill's study was tiny, and extremely tidy. A sign of someone who had spent several years living and working in cramped enclosed spaces. A desk bearing a computer screen was wedged under a window looking out at the blackness of the marsh and night sky. A bookshelf took up one wall, and two wooden filing cabinets another. There were at least four photographs of Donna at various stages of her life: one their wedding photograph, and one with the four grown sisters by the pear tree outside the Barnholt house. Five good-looking women.

A kind of wooden trolley contained yarn and tapestry designs, and a half-completed piece of needlepoint lay neatly folded on top of one of the cabinets. Toby could see it was the view of Barnholt, and Bill had made quite a lot of progress on it since Thanksgiving.

He sat down and faced his father-in-law, sipping his cup of tea. He felt he should be scared of him, but he couldn't quite accept that this man had tried to shoot him only twenty-four hours before.

'How's Beachwallet going, Toby?'

'So far so good,' said Toby, surprised at the question. 'The VC is lined up to give us two million. They seem happy with the due diligence.'

'Because if you need any help from me?'

Toby summoned a smile. 'Thanks, Bill. We're going to be fine. We did appreciate your advice at the start.' There was no way in hell Bill was coming anywhere near Toby's company now.

Bill smiled weakly. 'Good. Give my regards to Piet, won't you?'

'I will.'

Toby was pretty sure this conversation about Beachwallet was just a ploy to get Toby into Bill's study.

He was right.

'Toby?'

'Yes.'

'What's going on down there?'

'They're upset.'

'I can see that,' said Bill. 'And I can see they are upset with me. Why?'

'It's been a lot to take in,' said Toby. He was determined not to give Bill reason to think they were suspicious of him.

'Do they think I'm a traitor?'

'No,' said Toby. 'No, they don't. We don't. They know why you spoke to the Russians. And they are proud of what you did on the submarine.'

'Because *I* think I'm a traitor.' Bill sighed. 'Sure I spoke to Pat and Irena from the best of intentions. But I was naïve and so was Donna. We didn't believe they were KGB and they obviously were. I betrayed my country, and I feel guilty about that. I always will.'

'No harm came of it,' said Toby.

Bill grunted. 'I wish Donna was still around. She had a lot of common sense, that woman. I could use her with me now.'

'I wish I had known her,' said Toby. It was true, but Toby was mostly thinking that maybe Donna would have stopped Bill from murdering people.

'So if that's not what's upsetting them, did you tell Alice that I thought she killed Sam?'

Toby hesitated. As he thought it through, it seemed the perfect explanation for the hostility downstairs.

'Yes,' he said. 'I'm sorry.'

Bill seemed to accept it. 'It's OK. I can't expect you to keep something from your wife.' He ran a hand through his thick grey hair in frustration. 'No wonder she's upset. Brooke is no doubt still cross about Craig. And it's no surprise Megan is grumpy.'

'Yup,' said Toby. That was pretty well explained then.

'Does Alice know I won't tell the cops my suspicions?'

'I think so,' said Toby.

'What about you, Toby?'

'Me?'

'Do you think she killed Sam Bowen?'

'No,' said Toby.

'Did you ask her?'

'No. No, I trust her.'

Bill paused. 'All right. I get that you trust your wife. I'd really like to trust her too. I guess what I'm asking is, can you give me a reason to?'

'What do you mean?'

'Do you have proof she didn't do it?'

Did he? Not really.

'No,' Toby said. 'But we do know she didn't kill Lars, obviously.'

'All right,' said Bill. 'But if it wasn't her, who the hell was it?'

Bill's brown eyes were brimming with distress. Or they seemed to be.

'I don't know, Bill. I just don't know.'

Bill's mobile phone rang. 'Hello?' he said.

Toby was close enough to identify the voice, if not the words. Admiral Robinson.

Bill glanced at Toby. 'Yeah, hi. I can't talk right now . . . OK, I'll meet you. Do you want to come here? . . . I know the place. Just above Old Hunstanton . . . OK, I'll see you at nine.'

He disconnected. 'That was Admiral Robinson,' he said. 'He wants to see me this evening. I don't know what he wants to say.'

Toby did.

54

Bill shut himself in his study, only coming down to the kitchen to wolf down the fish and chips Toby brought from a shop in the next village. To say the silence around the kitchen table was awkward would be an understatement.

Toby had told the three sisters about Bill's arrangement with the admiral to meet him above Old Hunstanton later that evening. Brooke decided to stay at Barnholt to see what, if anything, happened.

Megan had suggested that they all watch a repeat or two of *Friends* in the living room. It was a good call, bringing back memories of the girls crowded around the TV when they were children, and distracting them from the destruction of their family in front of them.

Bill put his head around the door at about twenty to nine, announcing he had to go out. Only Toby acknowledged him.

'You know, despite what the admiral says, I still can't believe Dad killed anyone,' said Megan, as they heard him drive off in his Range Rover.

'I'm sorry, Megan,' said Alice. 'I know it's unbelievable, but it happened.'

'Maybe he'll be able to prove to the admiral that he's innocent?'

'Perhaps someone at the plumbing place will remember him,' said Toby. 'Did anyone see the tap he was talking about buying?'

No one had.

'His best theory is that I did it,' said Alice with contempt. 'And I know I didn't.'

'What do we do?' said Brooke. 'When Dad comes back?'

'Depends what he does,' said Alice. 'He may want to talk to us. Confess. Or he may have confessed to Admiral Robinson. Maybe he'll hand himself in to the police.'

'But what if Dad just comes back and says nothing?' said Brooke. 'Goes to bed?'

'Then we go to bed,' said Alice.

'But we can't just pretend none of this happened!'

'We'll have to,' said Alice.

Toby was with Brooke on this. Alice glanced quickly at him. A warning shot.

Bill being a murderer was bad enough. So was Lars being killed. And Sam Bowen. But Toby could see the decision he had put off re-emerging. Whether to tell the cops about Bill, and lose his wife. Or keep quiet. And what? Live for ever with a father-in-law who he knew was a murderer.

It wouldn't work.

Toby would need courage to do what he had to do; he wasn't sure he had it. There had to be some way of avoiding the decision, of finessing it somehow.

Pray for a miracle. Maybe Megan was right; maybe Bill would be able to convince the admiral of his innocence.

He was finding the waiting difficult, and *Friends* was irritating the hell out of him.

Brooke's phone rang. 'It's Justin,' she explained. She withdrew to the kitchen, and reappeared a minute or so later. 'I'm just going to pick him up from the hotel. I told him about Bill. He wants to be here, and I've got the car.'

'I'll go and get him, if you like,' said Toby. He wanted to be doing something. And he wanted to talk to Justin alone. Reluctantly, he could see that Bill must have killed Sam. But it was harder to believe he had shot his old friend Lars. Whereas Justin?

Brooke glanced at her sisters. It was clear she wanted to stay with them. 'Thanks, Toby. I'll give you the address of the hotel.'

Alice heard her husband drive off. She would have preferred Justin not to be around when Bill returned; his presence would make things even more awkward. But she hadn't been able to think of a way of discouraging Brooke from asking him to come over, especially when she herself badly wanted Toby to be there. She should just have come right out and said it wasn't a good idea.

Too late now.

The episode of *Friends* came to an end.

'Another?' said Megan.

'Let's have one from the first series,' said Brooke.

'You find one, Brooke,' said Megan.

While Brooke fiddled with one of the three remotes, Megan's phone rang.

'It's Maya,' Megan said to the others. 'Hi, Maya. I'll put you on speaker. Alice and Brooke are here.'

She tapped her phone and placed it face up on the coffee table.

Maya's voice crackled through the room. 'Hi! Is Daddy there?'

'No. He's off meeting Admiral Robinson.'

'Good.'

The three sisters exchanged glances at this, wondering why that was 'good'.

'I'm in Brooklyn,' said Maya. 'I've just seen Henry Greenwald, like you asked me to. He had some very interesting things to say.'

'Like what?'

'He was reluctant to talk at first, but I persuaded him. I told him two people had been killed, one of whom was Sam Bowen. He said Sam had approached him on Facebook and they arranged to meet up in Brooklyn next Friday. I asked him whether he remembered his mother meeting any Russians or any submarine officers.'

'And did he?'

'Not the Russians. But he said when he was about six he saw his mother talking to a man in their kitchen. The man was wearing a blue uniform. His mother was really angry with Henry, and told him never to breathe a word to anyone about it, which is why he remembers it so well. As he got older, he assumed that his mother was having an affair with the man, and that really upset him. But in 1996, just after his mother was murdered, the FBI came to talk to him about his mother's contact with the KGB, and asked him and his father the same question I did.'

'And did he tell them?'

'No, he didn't,' said Maya. 'He was sixteen. He was angry with the FBI for trying to ruin his mother's reputation so soon after she had died. Plus he didn't want his father to find out. But he was relieved at least to know that the naval officer was a spy rather than a lover.'

'But he told you just now?'

'I said I was persuasive. And his father died a few years ago.'

'That all figures,' said Megan, glancing at Alice. 'It must have been Dad she met.'

Alice nodded.

'That's what I thought,' said Maya. 'That's not good, is it? It means he was spying for the KGB.'

Alice took a deep breath. 'Hi, Maya, this is Alice. There is something you should know. We think that Dad *was* spying for the KGB and he probably killed Sam Bowen and Uncle Lars too. Admiral Robinson told us as much this afternoon.'

'My God!' said Maya. 'That can't be true! Is the admiral going to arrest him?'

'Not necessarily,' said Alice. 'He's talking to him now.'

'I don't believe it.' There was the sound of a muffled sob down the phone line. 'I'd better go,' said Maya. 'Tell me as soon as you have news.'

Megan picked up her phone and disconnected. 'It all hangs together,' she said.

'It does,' said Alice.

The phone beeped in Megan's hand, and she checked the screen. She read for a few seconds.

'Oh my God!' she said. 'No! No, this cannot be what I think it is.'

Her face creased in anguish: a mixture of horror and fear.

'What?' said Alice.

'It's an email from Dad. To all of us.'

'What does it say?'

'Take a look.'

'No – read it out, Megan!'

'OK.' Megan bit her lip, and then began to read from her phone, haltingly:

'Dear Alice, Brooke, Megan, and Maya,

I've just spoken to Glenn. He told me that you know everything.

I'm truly sorry.

I love you all so much.

Goodbye.

Dad

'Oh God!' said Brooke. 'Does that mean?'

'He's killed himself,' said Alice.

'Are you sure?' said Brooke, scrabbling frantically for her own phone. 'Can't it mean something else? I don't know, perhaps he's running away?'

They all looked at each other.

'Perhaps,' said Alice.

'Perhaps not,' said Megan.

'Let me see,' said Alice, grabbing Megan's phone. 'Yeah. I think it does mean he's planning to kill himself.'

'If he hasn't already,' said Megan.

'Oh God,' said Brooke.

'We've got to focus,' said Alice. 'He may not have done it yet.'

'How do you know?' said Brooke.

'I don't, but we have to assume he's still alive until we are sure we are too late. Now, where is he? Toby said he was meeting the admiral at Old Hunstanton.'

'That's right.'

'Are there any pubs there?' said Megan. 'Perhaps they're meeting at a pub.'

'Bound to be,' said Alice.

'Wait!' said Brooke. 'Didn't Toby say *above* Old Hunstanton?'

'Yeah,' said Megan. 'I think he did.'

'I've been driving on that road the last couple of days,' said Brooke. 'There are cliffs above Old Hunstanton. Between the village and Hunstanton itself.'

'That's right,' said Alice. 'There's a lighthouse there and a cliff path to the town.'

'Maybe he's going to jump?' said Brooke.

'Sounds like it,' said Alice.

'He could take pills,' said Megan. 'Or shoot himself.'

'He doesn't own a gun,' said Alice.

'That we know of,' said Megan. 'He shot Lars, remember?'

'There are cliffs. He's suicidal. They're right there; all he has to do is jump.'

'You're right,' said Megan. 'Let's go! I'll drive Brooke's car.'

'I'll call Toby,' said Alice. 'He's going to be a lot closer than we are.'

56

Toby pulled over and checked the address of Justin and Brooke's hotel on his phone. He was on the outskirts of Hunstanton, a Victorian seaside resort. Toby didn't know the town at all – he had only driven through it with Alice once – but according to his phone he wasn't far from the hotel. He had kept an eye out for Bill's red Range Rover as he had driven through the village of Old Hunstanton, but he hadn't spotted it. Easy to miss in the dark.

On the drive he had been figuring out how to raise Lars's death indirectly with Justin. Find some way of ascertaining whether Justin had still been at the police station the previous afternoon when Lars had been shot.

The phone buzzed. It was Alice.

'Toby! We think Dad's going to kill himself! On the cliffs. We think he's going to jump. Can you get there?'

'What! How do you know? Did he call you?'

'He sent an email to all of us.'

Toby turned the car around and headed back the way he had come, as Alice swiftly explained what had happened. It made sense to him. For someone as proud as Bill, the humiliation of exposure would be extreme. Humiliation in front of his family as much as anyone else.

He had noticed a road called Cliff Parade on his way into town, a clue that the cliffs were nearby.

He was there in a minute, and turned left on to the road. Straight ahead stood a squat white lighthouse. The parade curved left between

359

a row of stiff suburban houses on one side and a stretch of green on the other. The street was well lit, which made it harder to see beyond the pools of light on the grass to what were presumably cliffs and beyond that the sea.

He decided it would be easiest to look for Bill's red Range Rover first, then look for Bill.

The lighthouse seemed a natural place for Bill and the admiral to meet. Toby turned off the parade into a short road which passed the lighthouse towards a car park. At nine-thirty on a dark November night it was empty, save for two cars, one of which was the Range Rover.

Toby stopped next to it and jumped out. The Range Rover was only yards from the cliff edge. It was a dark night; the sky was black in all directions, the sea a barely perceptible different shade of ink. A stiff, cold breeze was blowing in from the north. Toby couldn't make out any beach, and in fact he could hear waves breaking against rocks below and out of sight. It must be high tide.

Where to try first? He jogged back to the lighthouse, which was shut up tight.

'Bill!' he shouted. He checked all around the building: no sign of anyone.

What if he didn't get to Bill in time? What if Bill had already jumped? Would that be such a bad thing? If Bill really had killed Sam Bowen and Lars, shouldn't he be allowed to judge himself? To choose his own punishment?

Toby wasn't sure. Despite what his father-in-law had done, Toby didn't want him to die. More importantly, Toby's wife and her sisters didn't want him to die.

Toby had to find him.

He trotted over to the fence that lined the swathe of grass, and that stopped walkers from getting too close to the cliff edge. He hopped over it, and fought his way through bushes until the sea opened up before him.

It was a long way down, and the waves were indeed beating against the rocks at the bottom. He couldn't see a body, but it was too dark to be sure.

If Bill had already jumped, Toby was too late anyway. He was looking for an upright figure above the cliffs, not a floating body below.

Which way?

To the west, Cliff Parade ran towards the town, to the east lay the car park and a path along the cliffs heading back towards the village.

The admiral had specified Old Hunstanton rather than Hunstanton. Toby took the path eastwards.

He jogged along the edge of the car park. Away from the street lighting, it was very dark.

No one.

A sandy path branched off to the left, steeply downhill, and he carefully scrambled down it towards the beach, which was almost entirely covered by angry sea.

He looked back up, along the cliffs.

For a moment he thought he caught a silhouette moving against the black sky, just beneath the cliff edge.

'Bill!' he shouted, but the wind took his cry and dashed it against the waves.

57

Megan drove through the potholes on the lane at forty miles an hour, crunching the underside of Brooke's hired car and jolting its occupants. Alice was in the front seat next to her, and Brooke was in the back.

They sped past the green and the pub and swerved on to the main road.

'Megan!' cried Alice, and she reached across to yank the steering wheel to the left. For a second she was blinded by a pair of headlights coming straight towards her, and a horn blared. The car lurched to the left and straightened up.

'You were on the wrong side of the road, Megan!' Too late, Alice wondered whether Megan had ever driven in the UK.

'Only briefly,' said Megan, as she took a tight curve too fast, the car clipping the verge.

'Jesus!' said Brooke from the back.

'Do you know where we are going?' said Megan.

'Yeah,' said Alice. 'Just stick on this road. We go through Old Hunstanton and then we'll get to the cliffs.'

'We should reply to Dad,' said Megan.

'I'll do it,' said Alice. She stared at her own phone screen. How do you plead with your father not to kill himself? There wasn't time to fashion a well-crafted appeal. Keep it straightforward and quick.

Don't do it Dad! We all love you. Stay alive for us. Please! Alice Brooke Megan and Maya.

She read it out.

'That's good,' said Megan.

Alice hit *Send*.

'Do you think Toby will get there in time to stop him?' said Brooke.

'I hope so,' said Megan. But that's all it was. A hope.

'Dad might hesitate,' said Brooke. 'You know. He talks to the admiral. Realizes he's been found out. Decides to kill himself. Sends a message to us. Then . . . Perhaps he walks around a bit. Can't make up his mind? Suicidal people do that. Maybe your reply will make him pause.'

But Alice was thinking about something else. 'You know,' she said. 'There's something not quite right about Henry Greenwald's story.'

'What's that?' said Megan.

'Henry said he saw his mother with a naval officer. We assumed that was Dad, right?'

'Right.'

'It can't have been.'

'Why not?' said Brooke.

'Because Henry said he was six. If he was sixteen in 1996, that means he was six in 1986.'

'And Dad had left the Navy!' said Megan.

'Correct. Pat Greenwald was speaking to someone else in a navy uniform.'

'Lars?' said Brooke.

'Lars left the Navy in 1984 too,' said Megan.

Megan's phone rang and she passed it to Alice to answer, swerving as she did so.

'Hi, Maya, it's Alice.'

'Alice! Did you see that email from Daddy? What's going on?'

The fear in Maya's voice reached out over the Atlantic to her older sister.

'Oh, Maya, yes, we did get it. And we think it must be a suicide note.'

'Oh God! Where is he?'

'We think he's on the cliffs by Hunstanton. Toby's looking for him now, and we're on our way.'

'Has he jumped? Oh my God, Alice, has he jumped?'

'We don't know. We hope not, but we don't know. Look, Maya. Can you quickly get in touch with Henry Greenwald and ask him if he can remember whether the officer his mother was with in the kitchen was bald?'

'But Dad isn't bald?'

'Precisely.'

Maya was no dummy. 'I'll do it. Wait there.'

The car sped through the darkness.

'So what does that mean?' said Brooke. 'I'm way behind, here.'

'I get it,' said Megan. 'Admiral Robinson is bald. It could have been him in the kitchen with Pat Greenwald. Which would mean it was Admiral Robinson, not Dad, who gave the secrets to the Russians.'

'Dad may have told them about the near-launch,' said Alice. 'But Robinson gave them more secrets. The secrets the FBI were asking about in 1996. And he did that over a period of years.'

Within two minutes Maya's phone beeped. It was a simple text.

Henry says officer was bald. Call me with news.

'I thought so!' said Alice. 'It *was* Admiral Robinson!'

'The admiral has managed to keep what he did quiet for all these years,' said Megan. 'But he would have gotten worried when Sam

Bowen started asking questions. Especially when Sam mentioned Pat Greenwald to us at Thanksgiving.'

As Megan was talking, the pieces were slipping into place in Alice's mind.

'So he had to shut Sam Bowen up. He must have killed him! It wasn't Dad.'

'But the admiral wasn't in England then,' said Megan. 'Dad said he flew over here as soon as he heard about Sam Bowen's death.'

'That's true,' said Alice.

'We don't really *know* that he wasn't in England,' said Brooke from the back seat.

'What do you mean?'

'He could have been here all the time. Then when Dad got in touch with him, he pretended to fly straight to London.'

'Yeah,' said Alice. 'But how did he know Sam had mentioned Pat Greenwald?'

'Perhaps Dad told him?'

'Dad said he told Lars,' said Alice. 'Maybe Lars told the admiral?'

'In which case, Lars would have been suspicious when Sam Bowen was killed.'

'And the admiral would need to shut him up too.'

'If that's all true, why would Dad want to kill himself?' said Brooke.

'A good question,' said Alice.

But the pieces were tumbling into place in Megan's mind as well. 'The admiral needs someone else to be the fall guy, and Dad is the natural person for that. Better than you, Alice. But he can't risk Dad being arrested. There would be a big trial and an investigation, and his own role might come out.'

'OK.'

'And he can't just kill him, like he killed Lars. He'd be the last man standing – a more obvious suspect.'

'So he wants to get Dad to kill himself?'

'He wants Dad to be seen as the murderer. And then push him off the cliff and make it look like suicide, like Dad was overwhelmed with guilt. Everything will be tidied up. With a suicide rather than a murder, the authorities won't ask difficult questions and the admiral will go free. That's why he took Dad to the top of a cliff. I mean, why else choose that place to talk? At night, when no one will see them?'

'And we would back up his story; we'd say we all thought Dad had killed Sam Bowen.'

'But what about that email to all of us?' said Megan. 'Why would Dad send that email?'

Silence for a few seconds as they scrambled for an answer, Megan successfully splitting her concentration between the problem and the dark road ahead.

'Dad didn't send it. It was a hack,' said Alice. 'Must have been. The admiral made it look like it came from Dad.'

'The admiral doesn't look like a hacker to me,' said Brooke.

'No,' said Alice. 'But he was in intelligence for many years. He'll know how to find himself a hacker for hire. One who will keep quiet.' She paused. 'Wait a moment. When I was in custody, the police accused me of hacking Sam Bowen's Cloud account, or finding his password and deleting his notes. I didn't, I wouldn't know how. But someone did.'

'It adds up,' said Brooke.

'It does,' said Alice.

'So what's happened to Dad on the cliffs?' said Brooke.

'The admiral is planning to push him off,' said Megan. 'Fake his suicide. And then say he spoke to Dad and told him he had been found out, and Dad took it very badly.'

'So we're too late?' said Brooke.

'Maybe Toby will stop him,' said Megan.

'But Toby doesn't know what the admiral is up to,' said Alice. 'And the admiral would have no qualms about killing Toby if he thought Toby saw him push Dad off a cliff.'

'Call him,' said Megan.

58

Toby ran back up the path and along the cliff, to where he thought he had seen the figure, but it was difficult to pinpoint the spot exactly. Once again, he slid over the fence and pushed his way through the bushes towards the cliff edge.

Carefully. He didn't want to step into nothingness.

He reached the edge and looked down. A ledge a few yards wide jutted out into the air ten feet below the rim. Gingerly he eased himself down.

He slid the last couple of feet, until he reached firm rock and pulled himself to his feet.

He was correct; he had seen a figure up there. In fact there were two, standing just a few feet apart from each other.

'Bill?' said Toby.

But it wasn't Bill who answered. 'Stay exactly where you are, Toby.'

It was the admiral. And in his hand was a gun. And the gun was pointed straight at Toby.

Toby didn't understand. So the admiral had got to Bill before he had jumped? That was good. And now he was stopping Bill from jumping.

By pointing a gun at him.

That didn't make sense. Shooting someone was not a great suicide-prevention method.

Toby took a step forward.

'Stop! Or I'll shoot you.'

'OK, OK,' said Toby, opening his hands to show he wasn't carrying anything. 'What's going on here?'

'I don't know,' said Bill. 'But it doesn't look good. For either of us.'

The admiral stepped back against the rock so that he could cover both Toby and Bill. 'Come and stand over here, next to Bill,' he said.

For a moment Toby wondered whether to obey. It occurred to him that if Bill and he were going to jump the admiral, now would be the best time to do it, while they were sufficiently apart from each other that the admiral could only cover one of them at a time.

Except that the admiral was pointing his pistol straight at Toby's chest. And he had spent his life in the military; he probably knew how to use it.

Toby moved over to Bill. 'So why did you send us that message, Bill?' he said.

'What message?'

'The goodbye message. Like you were going to kill yourself.'

Bill glanced at Toby. 'He just told me to jump. My guess is Admiral Robinson sent you that message.'

'He's trying to fake your suicide,' said Toby, beginning to understand. It was impossible to see the admiral's eyes in the darkness, but the barrel of his pistol glimmered a lighter shade of grey.

'You gave those secrets to the Russians, didn't you, Glenn?' said Bill. 'You are the spy the FBI asked me about?'

'I was never a spy,' said the admiral. 'I never betrayed my country.'

'Then why did you give them those secrets?'

'Why should I tell you?'

'Because I'm the only man in the world who might understand you,' said Bill. 'I gave them secrets too, remember?'

There was silence for a second or two. For a moment, Toby's body was overwhelmed with a wave of fear, fear which rooted him to the spot and threatened to paralyse his brain.

He fought it.

Stay calm. Stay focused. Just like Bill. Watch out for an opportunity.

They were both only a foot from the cliff edge. The wind roared in his ears and the waves crashed sixty feet below. If they both jumped the admiral, one of them just might overpower him. But the other would be shot, and would probably fall backwards into the sea.

But if they both did nothing, they would both die.

Unless Bill could talk their way out of it.

Wait. Listen. Watch for an opportunity. Conquer the fear.

'I'd like to hear why you did it, Glenn,' Bill said, his voice calm and encouraging. 'There must have been a good reason.'

The admiral spoke. 'OK, I'll tell you.' He paused to marshal his thoughts. 'What I learned in the Pentagon when I was working on Able Archer 83 exercise really shook me up. And then what happened on the *Hamilton* made it all clearer. By the 1980s the Russians were never about to grab Europe and roll their tanks into West Germany. At that stage, they were way more scared of us than we were of them. We had a stronger economy and we were building a much bigger and better nuclear arsenal. And Reagan was making our nuclear policy much more aggressive.'

'I remember,' said Bill. 'He was talking about winning the Cold War.'

'Star Wars. Cruise missiles in Europe. All that talk of the Soviet Union being an "evil empire". It scared them, almost to the point where they were about to strike us first. And I found out later I was right. I worked with the CIA group that investigated the Soviet reaction to the Able Archer 83 exercise. The Russians really did think we were about to launch a decapitation first strike.'

'I can believe it,' said Bill.

'I was really impressed by what you and Lars did on the *Hamilton*. So when Pat Greenwald approached me after she had spoken with you, I thought maybe I could do my bit to stop a war starting. I couldn't change US nuclear policy, but I could help the Russians understand what we were really doing. That we were not really planning a pre-emptive strike. And that if we ever did launch missiles it would be by accident rather than design.'

'It was worth a shot,' said Bill. 'That's exactly what I was thinking. That's what we discussed at the fort in Groton.'

'Yes, it was. I spoke with a Russian physicist who claimed she was a peace activist. Irena. Did you ever talk to her?'

'Yes,' said Bill. 'In Paris.'

'I was pretty sure she was KGB, but I didn't care. That was better, really. More certainty that my message would get through to the Russian top brass.'

'I hadn't thought of that,' said Bill. 'I was worried she was KGB.' Toby was impressed by the way Bill was placing himself on the admiral's side. In fact, he was doing such a good job of it that Toby wondered whether he really meant it. Which was of course what Bill was trying to achieve.

Toby's phone buzzed in his pocket. He ignored it.

'I went further than you. Told them more over a period of years until the wall came down. I wanted them to know what our nuclear strategy really was; that despite what Reagan was saying, we were never about to launch an unprovoked attack.

'Lars knew what I was doing,' the admiral went on. 'He had spoken with Pat Greenwald and then put her on to me. We talked about it over the years, especially after he got out of jail in the Caribbean.'

Toby joined the dots. Bill had told Lars that Sam Bowen was on to Pat Greenwald. Sam Bowen had died. Lars guessed it was Admiral Robinson who killed Sam. So Lars had died.

Toby didn't know whether Bill was figuring that out. Probably best not to mention it if he was.

'I think you did the right thing,' Bill said. 'I'll tell you what. If you leave Toby and me alive, I won't mention any of this. I respect what you did. I respect why you did it. I'll keep quiet. Like I have for the last twenty-six years. I took a risk back then to preserve peace. I killed my best friend. I understand.'

Bill's voice was calm and persuasive. It almost persuaded Toby.

'I didn't mean to kill the historian,' said the admiral. 'I brought a knife with me in case I had to. I would have preferred not to use it, but when I spoke to Sam at the pub, he had so nearly put everything together I had to stop him. Like I had to stop Pat Greenwald before the FBI got to her.'

So it had been the admiral who had murdered Pat Greenwald in 1996, not some random mugger.

'I get that,' said Bill. 'This stuff is bigger than individual lives.'

'What about him?' said the admiral.

'Toby understands too. You'll keep quiet, won't you, Toby?'

That was Bill's mistake. He might have got away with it if he had ditched Toby, said something like: 'you can't trust him but you can trust me'.

'I understand,' said Toby.

'No,' said the admiral. 'I'm sorry, Bill. I admire what you did all those years ago. And I admired what Lars did. But he had to die. And so do you.'

59

Alice's fingers reached up to a handle just above the passenger door, giving her something to cling on to.

With her other hand she pulled out her phone and called Toby. Voicemail.

'Toby, it's me. For God's sake stay clear of the admiral. We think he killed Sam and Lars and he is probably about to kill Bill. Toby, be careful! Please be careful!'

'Shouldn't we call the police?' said Brooke.

'Yeah, you're right,' said Alice. 'I'll do it.' She dialled 999 and told the operator that she was a suspect in the Sam Bowen murder investigation and that she believed a murder was about to be committed on the cliffs above Old Hunstanton by a man who may be armed. The operator sounded sceptical but promised to send officers to the cliffs.

Megan was driving too fast for safety. Part of Alice wanted her to slow down, but part of her wanted to speed up. Of course, they might be too late. The admiral might have already killed their father. But if there was a chance – the slightest chance – that they might get there in time to warn Toby or their father, they should try to take it, even if they risked their own lives.

Alice had lost her mother. Now she was in danger of losing her father *and* her husband. That couldn't happen. She couldn't let that happen. They *had* to stop it. Somehow.

Realistically they were going to be too late. Alice felt the panic rise in her chest, but just managed to prevent it erupting in a scream or a sob.

'Maybe we should wait for the police?' said Brooke. 'I mean, the admiral will probably have a gun. Armed police can handle the situation better than us.'

'No!' snapped Alice and Megan in unison. What Brooke was suggesting might be the sensible thing, but neither woman was in the mood to do something sensible.

They were on a long stretch of dark road, rapidly approaching a bend. Alice could see the headlights of another car approaching.

Megan was driving too fast.

They reached the bend, and their car drifted a few inches over to the other side of the road. That was enough. They hit the oncoming car a glancing blow, their own vehicle spun three hundred and sixty degrees, and hit a tree.

The hood crumpled. The engine cut out. The airbags didn't deploy, but Brooke, who wasn't wearing her seatbelt, catapulted forward into the headrest behind Alice's head.

Alice glanced across at Megan who seemed to be OK. She was staring groggily at the dashboard. Alice looked over her shoulder and saw the headlights of the other car pointing cockeyed at a hedge. It was in a ditch.

Brooke was slumped back in the seat, her face was covered in something dark. Blood.

'Brooke! Are you OK?'

She raised a sleeve to her nose and wiped it. 'I'm OK. It's my nose. It hurts but I'm OK.'

'What do we do now?' Alice said to Megan.

In response, she turned the ignition, which fired, slammed the car into reverse and her thrust her foot down on to the accelerator. There was a painful grinding noise, and then the vehicle pulled back into the road. Megan put the gear in drive. The car crunched forward slowly, and then there was a clatter as something fell off the front, and the car drove free along the road. Only one headlight beam was working.

That didn't bother Megan.

In a few minutes they were climbing the hill above Old Hunstanton and they came to the turn off to Cliff Parade.

Alice called out, 'Turn right here!'

60

'Glenn?' Bill was trying to keep his voice steady.

'No, Bill. No more talking.' The admiral raised his pistol and pointed it at Bill's forehead. 'Take two steps back.'

'No,' said Bill. He stood up straighter.

'Take two steps back, or I will shoot you.'

'No you won't,' said Bill. 'They'll find my body. They'll find the bullet hole. They will know I didn't jump. They will know you shot me.'

The admiral didn't seem put off by this. 'I'll count to five. You jump before I get to five or I will shoot you.'

'No,' said Bill.

'One . . . two . . . three . . . four.'

Bill was still standing upright on the cliff, calmly facing the admiral's pistol.

The admiral swung his weapon towards Toby.

'OK, Toby. Push him backward. Now. Or I'll fire.'

Toby almost did what he was told. Part of his brain told him the admiral's command was illogical. If he pushed Bill off the ledge, he would then be killed himself. And if Bill could call the admiral's bluff, so could he.

On the other hand, part of his brain, the cowardly part, urged him to grab at any straw that might allow him to survive, even for a couple of minutes. Push Bill off the cliff and negotiate.

No.

Toby swallowed. 'No,' he said, drawing himself upright in an imitation of Bill.

The admiral didn't bother starting to count this time. He paused to think.

Toby thought also. The admiral was running out of options. The only one left to him that Toby could see was to shoot both him and Bill then and there, and make a run for it.

In which case, their best chance was to jump him. One of them might live. Maybe both of them; bullet wounds from handguns were not always lethal.

The problem with that idea was that at that moment the admiral was pointing his gun straight at Toby's eyes.

'OK. This is what we are going to do,' said the admiral. 'We're going to go back to Bill's car. Then you are going to drive, Bill. If you don't do exactly as I say, then I *will* shoot you and take my chances. Do you understand?'

'Yes,' said Toby.

Bill said nothing.

'Bill?'

'OK.'

'All right. Bill, you go first.'

Bill hesitated, then squeezed past Toby and began to climb the narrow path upwards.

'You next,' said the admiral.

Toby followed. He could hear the admiral a couple of steps behind him. He was sure that the gun was pointed right at his back.

What was the admiral's plan? Take Bill and him away from the cliffs, drive somewhere deep in the Norfolk countryside – a ditch in the fens maybe – and kill them. Hide their bodies somehow. And then brazen it out.

That seemed the most likely.

Which would mean Toby had a few more minutes to live. Maybe an hour, max.

His chances of getting out of this alive were very low. If any opportunity to jump the admiral appeared, they should grab it.

Toby looked up. Bill had reached the top of the short path up the cliff; if he kept going, he would be out of the admiral's line of sight for a few moments and he could run off into the night.

This was it. A couple of seconds when one of them could get away. Problem was, the one of them wasn't Toby.

Oh well.

'Run, Bill!' Toby shouted.

'Run, and I'll blow Toby's brains out!' The admiral yelled from right behind him.

'Ignore him!' Toby shouted. 'Run!' He waited for the gunshot behind him. Then he realized he would be dead before he heard it.

But Bill paused and stood upright on the cliff top. 'Come on, you two!' he shouted.

Toby scrambled up to join him, his heart pounding. He had really thought he was going to die.

He probably still was.

'That was dumb, Toby,' said the admiral. 'All right. Both of you, walk toward Bill's car side-by-side. I'll be right behind you.'

Toby and Bill did as they were told.

'You should have run then, Bill,' Toby said. 'You'd have got a good start before he was on cliff top.'

'Nah.' Bill grinned.

'Quiet!' came the rebuke behind them.

They could see the odd car driving along the parade, which was only a couple of hundred yards away. They could see houses with lights on and televisions flickering. But the illumination of the street lights formed a barrier as effective as any screen; no one could see through it into the darkness in which they were walking.

A car turned off Cliff Parade, driving fast past the lighthouse towards the car park.

'Stand still,' said the admiral. He was only a couple of yards behind them.

Bill and Toby halted.

The car's single headlight lurched into the car park, the beam swinging through them as the car turned.

Then the beam veered back towards them. The engine roared and Toby was dazzled.

He broke left and ran. Bill broke right.

Toby had no idea what the admiral did. But the car swished past them, then there was a thump and a cry, which was immediately cut off. Toby spun around to see a car skidding into a fence post by the cliff path with a crash.

A body lay a few feet away. Dark matter oozed out of a bald head.

'Toby!' It was Alice's voice. She was running towards him.

'Dad!' Brooke and Megan: Brooke was limping, and her face was covered with blood.

Toby glanced across to Bill, who was bent double, breathing heavily. Then Alice was in Toby's arms. 'Thank God you're all right!'

Bill approached the body, a daughter on either side.

Admiral Robinson's head was a mess. He was definitely dead.

'Who was driving?' said Bill.

'Megan,' said Brooke.

'Figures.'

61

Wednesday 3 December 2019, Norfolk

'Some coffee, Inspector?'

'Yes, please.'

Alice poured some into a mug for DI Creswell, and for DC Atkinson and Mr Prestwitch. They were gathered around the kitchen table at Pear Tree Cottage with Bill, Megan, Brooke, Justin, Toby and Maya, who had just arrived from Heathrow. Justin and Brooke were flying back to Chicago the following day, Maya was going back to the Gulf, and Bill, Alice, Toby and Megan were heading down to London. Megan had decided to stay in London with Bill and look for a job there. She said she wanted to remain close to her family for a little bit.

'I'd like to start by apologizing,' the inspector began. 'In any murder investigation, we have to ask difficult questions. And sometimes we arrest suspects and subsequently release them.'

'That's all right, Inspector,' said Alice. 'I was not exactly helpful. I apologize for that.'

Creswell gave her a quick smile. The inspector looked tired. Toby suspected murder investigations did that to you.

'Thanks to all of you for your cooperation, especially over the last couple of days. There are some things we will never know for sure, but we have pieced together enough to have a pretty good idea of what happened, and we want to share that with you. Obviously, Admiral Robinson's death means he can't fill in the gaps for us, but it also means there will be inquests into the deaths of Sam Bowen, Lars da Silva and Robinson, rather than a criminal trial. That will make things easier.'

'Much easier,' said Prestwitch.

'I expect you will all be called as witnesses. I can confirm, Megan, that the Crown Prosecution Service will not be taking any action against you.'

'That's a relief,' said Megan.

It was hard to be sure what effect running down the admiral had had on her. At first she had just been overjoyed that her father and Toby were alive. Then she had stared at the admiral's mangled body, before being pulled away by Alice. She knew that what she had done had unquestionably saved her father's and Toby's lives, but she had killed someone, and that fact wasn't going to go away.

'On that subject,' Prestwitch interrupted. 'The events on the USS *Alexander Hamilton* remain secret, and you should not divulge them at the inquest, or to the police, or even me. Is that understood?'

Creswell frowned, and pursed her lips in something very close to a grimace. MI5 had not made her murder investigation any easier.

Everyone around the table nodded. Apart from Bill, who looked straight at Prestwitch with something close to disdain.

'My understanding is that the FBI will want to debrief you thoroughly when you get back to London, Mr Guth,' Prestwitch said.

'I have an appointment with them tomorrow morning,' said Bill.

'So what happened?' asked Toby. It would be good to finally hear what the police had discovered in their investigation.

The detective inspector answered him. 'Sam Bowen had been rooting around for months asking a number of officers and crew of the *Alexander Hamilton* what happened in November 1983 on the submarine, and also what happened afterwards. I'm not aware of the specifics of this; I could guess, but I won't.' Here she glanced at the MI5 officer sitting next to her. 'But it was enough to worry Lars da Silva, and Robinson.

'So they both flew to England. Da Silva stayed with you, and Robinson stayed in a hotel in Ely, which, as you know, is about an hour from here. We think Lars told Robinson that Sam Bowen had discovered something important that would incriminate both of them – whatever that was you will know better than me – and told him where Sam was staying. Robinson then went to the King William. We have a witness who saw a man waiting in a car outside that evening; we think that was probably Robinson. We think he saw Alice enter the pub and then leave about half an hour later. Soon afterwards he went up to Sam Bowen's room, knocked on the door, Sam let him in and Robinson stabbed him. He stole Sam's computer and his notes, and arranged for his back-ups in the Cloud to be deleted.'

'How did he do that?' Toby asked.

'We have discovered he had a bitcoin account,' DC Atkinson said. 'That's unusual. He could have been speculating; more likely he was paying someone on the dark web to do his hacking for him.

'When Mr Guth called the admiral after Sam Bowen's death, Robinson was actually already in England. He pretended to fly to the UK right away, then got in touch with MI5.'

Prestwitch interrupted. 'As the senior surviving officer on the *Alexander Hamilton*, he had been in regular contact with the FBI and the Office of Naval Intelligence to ensure that secrecy was maintained. He had told them he was coming and they told me. He didn't tell anyone he was already in the country.'

'At some point Lars must have realized what had happened,' Creswell went on. 'We know he and the admiral met at The Pheasant in Thurstead at lunch time on Saturday, just before Lars was shot. We don't know exactly what Lars said – whether he threatened the admiral, or just wanted to talk to us – but the admiral decided he had to be killed, and quickly. We found the rifle the admiral used. It was a SIG Sauer, once again bought off the dark web.

'Now, Robinson must have realized that sooner or later he would be suspected. So he decided to shift suspicion on to Mr Guth, and then fake his suicide to seem like an admission of guilt. Given the British and American security services' obsession with keeping whatever happened on that submarine secret, he thought difficult questions wouldn't be asked.' Another glance at Prestwitch. 'He was probably right.'

'We will be raising this with the Americans,' Prestwitch said. 'Security breaches like this over such a long period of time are totally unacceptable.'

That was the sound of a buck being flung far over the Atlantic.

'Totally,' said Bill, drily.

'Toby?' Bill said after the police officers and the MI5 man had left. 'Before we leave, do you want to take Rickover for a walk with me?'

'Sure,' said Toby.

They set off, with Rickover at their heels. The marsh was twittering, rustling and gurgling. The big bull and the black-and-white cow stared at them.

'This reminds me of walking down to the beach with Lars,' said Toby.

'I'm sorry,' said Bill. 'Are you OK with this? Going back to where he was shot?'

'No, it's good,' said Toby. 'I love this walk. I refuse to let it become a place I can't go.'

Bill smiled. 'I like it too. I'll miss Lars.'

'He always said he was grateful to you.'

'We shared something, him and me.'

'Whatever else he did, he did do his bit to stop us all getting blown up.'

They reached the dunes and threaded their way through them to the beach. Bill stopped and surveyed the sand and the shifting sea beyond it. All signs of a crime scene had been removed, including the little green boat.

Empty.

Bill bent down to pat his dog, who seemed uncharacteristically worried, circling their legs. Toby hoped the walk wouldn't be ruined for Rickover either.

He drew the clear Norfolk air into his lungs. By mid afternoon he would be back in London with its small sky, its channels of metal and fumes and its walls of concrete and brick.

'Toby?'

'Yes?'

'What do you think of them keeping the near-launch quiet all these years?'

Toby answered immediately. 'I think it's wrong.'

'You know what? So do I. They are just trying to hide a screw up. If our enemies, whoever they may be, knew about it, it wouldn't help them at all. How could it help them? That's a question I have been asking myself all these years. How could it help them? I'm just covering other people's asses.'

'I agree.'

Toby waited. This was what Bill wanted to talk to him about.

'I have a suggestion for you, Toby. When you get back to London.'

Wednesday 11 December 2019, London

Toby emerged from Baker Street tube station and made his way north to Regent's Park. The good thing about Regent's Park in December was that there were loads of empty benches. The bad thing was they were all very cold.

It was three o'clock, morning in Washington and well after lunch in London. He had had to fib to his co-workers at Beachwallet about where he was, co-workers who now included Megan. She was on her third day at the company as a temporary employee. The firm was desperate for warm bodies to do administrative and data-related crap, and Megan was proving surprisingly effective. She was smart, she was enthusiastic and she could figure out unfamiliar systems almost instantaneously. Piet thought she was great.

And Toby thought it was good to have her around.

Alice had been pleased too. For a moment it had looked as if the Guth family would shatter, but it had held together, thanks in great part to Megan. And Toby.

Also, her client had postponed its stock-exchange announcement, so her deal was still live. There were plenty of legal documents to get stuck into, which meant she was happy.

Toby found a bench opposite the little Japanese garden island near the dormant rose beds, and took out his ancient long-retired Nokia phone and his brand new pay-as-you-go SIM card. The website had suggested it was best to use a payphone, but there were scarcely any of those in London anymore, so his plan was to use an old mobile, and only switch it on when he was well away from where he lived or worked. That way it shouldn't be possible to trace it to him.

With cold fingers, he slid the card into the phone and turned it on. He had charged it the day before, and it seemed to work.

He pulled out the Washington phone number he had printed off from the website and stared at it.

He gave himself a moment. Was he sure he should do this?

He would probably be charged with breaking the Official Secrets Act if he was caught, although he had no intention of being caught. And the fact he wasn't a US citizen might help if the worst came to the worst.

He had discussed it with Alice, who had been worried about the risks. But she was also proud that he wanted to do it.

Toby could still pull out. Bill had never put any pressure on him to follow the suggestion he had made on the beach at Barnholt. But Toby felt an obligation to the man who had decided to risk his life by staying with him on the cliffs at Hunstanton.

He also felt a sense of obligation to Lars. Both Lars and Bill were brave men, and their bravery deserved to be remembered.

He took a breath and dialled the number.

'Hello?'

'Hi. Is this Charles Laverick at the Investigative Journalists' Cooperative?'

'Yes, it is.' The accent was American. 'With whom am I speaking?'

'My name is Ed,' Toby said. 'I'm speaking on behalf of a former US Navy Lieutenant named Lars da Silva. I have some information you may find interesting. It's about what happened on board the nuclear submarine USS *Alexander Hamilton* in November 1983. About how the world nearly came to an end.'

AUTHOR'S NOTE

The launch procedures for nuclear missiles on US Navy submarines in the 1980s were, understandably, top secret.

While there are no detailed descriptions of launch and other operational procedures in the 1980s publicly available, there are a small number before and after, and I have relied heavily on these. These are: *Three Knots to Nowhere*, a memoir by Ted Dubay (1960s); the film *Crimson Tide* and the novel by Richard Henrick (1990s); *Big Red: three months on board a Trident nuclear submarine* by Douglas Waller (early 2000s) and the excellent novel *The Trident Deception* by Rick Campbell, a former ballistic missile submarine commander (2010s).

The procedures in force in the 1980s were in some important respects different from those described later once the Cold War had ended, and I have tried to infer these differences as best I can. If I have made mistakes, I apologize, especially to those who actually served on nuclear submarines at that time.

There are elaborate procedures set up in all nuclear nations' armed forces to prevent an accidental nuclear war, and by and large these have worked. But the last line of defence when the machines and the procedures screw up is human common sense. I came across nine near accidental launches during the Cold War relating to humans overriding messages from the system to launch a nuclear war. All of these were covered up initially. There must have been more that have remained secret.

All of these instances took the form of cock-up followed by cover-up, rather than conspiracy. This seems to me far more credible and indeed inevitable than a rogue actor or state causing a nuclear war. It's a little scary.

I should like to thank the following people for their help: Wing Commander Brian Pratt, Ann Estin, Commander John F. Howard US Navy retired, Eric C. Baatz US Navy Retired, US Navy veteran Richard Alan Dow, Caroline Driggs, Peggy Roberts, Andres Kabel, Donna Cansdale, Wayne Leiniger, Nicky Lovick, Liz Hatherell, my agents Oli Munson and Florence Rees and my editor Susannah Hamilton at Atlantic Books. And, as always, Barbara.

A Message from Michael Ridpath

Get a FREE 60-page story

I hope you enjoyed reading this book as much as I enjoyed writing it. Thank you for buying it.

To write a book is to communicate directly with the person who reads it. I like to build as direct a relationship as I can with my readers and so I send occasional newsletters with information about my books and any special offers.

If you sign up to my mailing list I will send you a free ebook of a 60 page story set in North East Iceland featuring my Icelandic detective, Magnus, called *The Polar Bear Killing:*

A starving polar bear swims ashore in a remote Icelandic village and is shot by the local policeman. Two days later, the policeman is found dead on a hill above the village. A polar bear justice novella with an Icelandic twist.

To sign up to the mailing list and get your free ebook of *The Polar Bear Killing*, please visit my website www.michaelridpath.com, where you will also find information about my other books.